AMERIKA

Pocket Books are available at special quantity discounts for bulk purchases for sales promotions, premiums, or fund raising. Special books or book excerpts can also be created to fit specific needs.

For details write the office of the Vice President of Special Markets, Pocket Books, 1230 Avenue of the Americas, New York, New York 10020.

AMERIKA

A novel by
Brauna E. Pouns

Based on a screenplay by
Donald Wrye

PUBLISHED BY POCKET BOOKS NEW YORK

This novel is a work of fiction. Names, characters, places and incidents are either the product of the author's imagination or are used fictitiously. Any resemblance to actual events or locales or persons, living or dead, is entirely coincidental.

Another *Original* publication of POCKET BOOKS

POCKET BOOKS, a division of Simon & Schuster, Inc.
1230 Avenue of the Americas, New York, N.Y. 10020

Copyright © 1987 by ABC Entertainment
Cover photographs © 1986 Capital Cities/ABC, Inc.

ISBN: 0-671-63345-7

First Pocket Books printing February 1987

10 9 8 7 6 5 4 3

POCKET and colophon are registered trademarks
of Simon & Schuster, Inc.

Printed in the U.S.A.

Prologue

IN THE HISTORY of human folly, arrogant fantasies of military supremacy and pathetic illusions of national safety have played a crucial role. The Great Wall of China, the Spanish Armada, the Maginot Line—all were thought to be impregnable. All fell. And with them fell not only governments, but ideals, not only nations, but those unique aspects of the human spirit that were embodied in each conquered civilization.

Through most of the 1980s, the United States of America had regarded itself—and was regarded by the rest of the world—as the mightiest and therefore most secure nation the world had ever seen; it seemed to dawn on no one that those two notions did not necessarily go hand in hand. The American defense system represented the perfect combination of American skill and American will, of vast wealth and limitless ingenuity applied to the problems of survival for this hardiest of peoples. In fact, the U.S. military had evolved the

1

most sophisticated weaponry and communications networks ever known to man.

With that sophistication, however, came a vast complexity, and with that complexity came danger. The taller a building gets, the more it sways in the wind; the longer a bridge, the less it takes to send the whole span crashing. So it was with the American system of defense. Paradoxically, as the system grew more powerful, it grew more fragile; as it took on more and more weight and bulk, it came ever closer to teetering. Some few men and women, both inside the government and out, were aware of this. As in ages past, their voices were not heard.

As these voices of caution were ignored in Washington, however, voices of opportunity were listened to closely in Moscow. In the waning days of the 1980s, the leaders of the Soviet Union, beset by paralyzing economic woes and growing domestic unrest, had less to lose than to gain by gambling on a massive rearrangement of the balance of power in the world. Without warning, on a quiet Tuesday morning, the Russians took the headiest gamble in the history of warfare by launching a nuclear attack against America.

But this attack was no storybook Armageddon of mushroom clouds bursting over cities, of scalded millions murdered in their homes. This was a new sort of war, conceived in shocking simplicity by Soviet scientists. The premise: don't attack targets. Attacking targets, after all, even with nuclear missiles, was essentially as primitive as throwing stones. What mattered was not the individual bases and silos, but rather the electronic network that linked them as an effective whole. The key, then, was to attack and disable the communication systems *among* the targets, thereby crippling the entire system.

High in the stratosphere above America, four enormous nuclear devices were detonated. On earth, the explosions were heard only as a low rumble. No one was hurt by the blasts, nor did they generate a dangerous amount of fallout; no one even felt the concussive power of the bombs. But the explosions were "felt" by every computer circuit, every telephone line, every banking system, and every electrical plant from Maine to San Diego. The detonations created a vast electromagnetic pulse (EMP) that was like a hundred thousand bursts of lightning focused insidiously on America's nervous system. Vast stores of computer memory were instantly erased. The coils of electric generators sizzled and seized. Telephones went dead. The Age of Communications ended in a millisecond, and with it ended America's military, political, and economic hegemony.

The conquest of America, incredibly, had been effected without taking a single life. American missiles stood unharmed in their silos, but could not be activated. Around the world, American forces, their ranks undiminished, were at the ready, but could not be issued orders. In Washington, the American president was given an agonizing and humiliating choice: surrender and agree to unilateral disarmament, the virtual destruction of the dollar, and the essential end of national sovereignty; or resist, fight back with whatever sundered forces could be mustered, and face certain annihilation.

This choice was not a choice at all for a leader who valued human life. With dizzying, incomprehensible suddenness, the United States of America was under the thrall of the Russians.

With Soviet rule came a dizzying torrent of euphemisms and double-speak. The conquest—by far the most cataclysmic and humiliating event in all of American history—was tamely dubbed "the Transition"—as if the shift from capitalism and freedom to communism and subjugation was indeed an inevitable progression. Thousands of loyal citizens were redefined as "subversives" and forced to leave the cities, where, in concentration, they could be troublesome to the new authorities. They were called Exiles—and it was true that their homeland had abandoned them. The most committed of the Exiles became Resisters—guerrilla fighters who endured the most crushing hardships and dangers in the name of those values that, only yesterday, had been the norm. Under the system of the conquerors, logic was stood on its head and language itself was recruited into the service of erasing history.

But who were these Soviets who were now America's administrators, overseers, bosses? Oddly, they did not conform at all closely to our hysterical, Cold War images of them. They were not beetle-browed commissars, nor were they blustering boors who swilled vodka and spouted rigid ideological platitudes. They were modern men and women—cultured, pragmatic, efficient, very often charming, and generally humane. They had humor, they had desires, and they had a vision. Their vision was of a world united and running as a single mechanism according to the precepts of Marx and Lenin. *To each according to his need; from each according to his ability.*

On its face, the prescription was benign enough. Could any thinking person claim that the rhetoric was less dignified or lofty—or even essentially *different*—than the thrilling pronouncements of Jefferson and Lincoln on which the American republic had been based? The Soviets came not to conquer by force, but to win a more total victory by imposing an alternate mythology.

They were offering peace. It was a sort of peace that the great majority of Americans—all those who wanted nothing more from their time on earth than to preserve some fraction of the security and comfort they'd known before—accepted with appalling ease.

It was a sort of peace against which some few Americans—keeping alive the spark of freedom in its armor of defiance—vowed to wage the most intimate and sacred form of battle.

This is the story of three men, each of whom fought for his vision of what the New America might become. Devin Milford—once a candidate for president, now stigmatized as a criminal—was the defiant one, a man who insisted that the real world of politics and power conform to his ideal of a united America.

Peter Bradford was the pragmatic one, an honest man committed to the principle of compromise and to practical approaches to problems that could not really be solved.

Andrei Denisov was the complex one, the enemy and not the enemy, the KGB colonel who harbored a love for America that the Americans themselves had lost.

Most important, this is the story of a people searching for their noblest selves under circumstances that had long been feared, but never truly imagined.

Chapter 1

DEVIN MILFORD STOOD in semidarkness. A single, glaring light caught his eyes—haunted eyes that lay deep in their sockets. He walked to the window. It was barred. Outside, the first light of dawn washed over the bleak west Texas desert, with its bleached sand and gray scrub stretching off to the horizon. He looked past the well-worn wooden barracks, beyond the electrified fences and watchtowers, and scanned the distance. Far off, a hawk circled, gracing the early-morning light with its fringed wings and noble head. Devin ached for the freedom he had lost, the freedom he still dreamed of recapturing.

A metal door clanged behind him and his body automatically tensed. Roll call was early and he knew, as all prisoners know, that any break with routine could mean trouble. He faced the door of the cell and promised himself that he must resist. Resist what? He couldn't have said. But the impulse itself held the last glowing ember of his self-respect.

The cell banged open and daggers of light pierced the dimness.

"83915," the guard said gruffly.

"83915, sir." It came automatically.

"Collect your possessions."

Devin began to gather his belongings. He took a change of clothes—a shirt and pants of scratchy denim, which now hung loose on his tall and wiry frame—and a comb that he could drag only with difficulty through his heavy beard, which had now become flecked with gray. By reflex, he packed a thick book entitled *The New Understanding and the New America,* whose turgid prose all prisoners could recite by heart but none believed. Last, and with special care, he placed in the duffel bag a Polaroid snapshot of two small boys.

"Let's go—chop-chop!"

Devin, in reply, walked to the cell door, duffel in tow, and faced the guard. The guard was short and sullen, and he stared intimidatingly at Devin for a moment, then stood aside. Devin marched out of his cell and into the dank corridor that smelled of stale cigarettes and urine. He did not know where he was being taken, but he knew that he was not afraid. What might come next could not be worse than what had gone before.

Andrei Denisov's penthouse floated high above Chicago, a haven of pleasure and power amid the drab remains of a once-great metropolis. In his entryway alcove, a spray of fresh flowers glowed in the soft light, casting their lavender perfume. Against the huge windows with their commanding view of the oddly quiet city, leather settees suggested indolence and sociability.

Kimberly Ballard, slipping out of her coat in the dimness of the hallway, felt the same mix of emotions she had experienced the very first time she had visited Andrei here. A dizzying sense of privilege mingled with unease; qualms of conscience coexisted with the unquestioning sensuality of luxury. As though brushing those qualms away, she ran a hand through her streaky blond hair, and though she thought she was alone, she instinctively smoothed the silk dress that she was both embarrassed and delighted to own.

She entered the living room and reached for the dimmer that controlled the lights. Midway through the gesture, her arm was grabbed roughly. In that first instant of baffled surprise, Kimberly felt neither fear nor anger, but only sadness that even here, in the apartment of her powerful protector, there seemed to be no safety. She could barely muster the will to resist the grasp that held her.

It was Andrei.

Kimberly smiled. She could not find it within herself to resent his frightening her. She was used to feeling frightened.

Andrei refused to smile back. "God, you're stupid," he snapped.

Kimberly tried to step away, startled by this unexpected welcome, but he tightened his grip on her arm.

"What's wrong?"

"I worked all night, but I took a break at midnight." He paused, awaiting a response. "I went to the little church where you and your friends put on your little play. Your banned, illegal, outlaw play."

A small smile played upon her mouth. She was an American beauty attracted to power but filled with impetuous moods and spontaneous reactions.

Kimberly leaned into him, pleased in spite of herself that he had watched her perform. She playfully tugged at his loosened tie. "Did you hear me sing?"

Andrei released his grip and stepped back, gesturing in frustration. "Do you have any idea what a difficult position you put me in? Any idea at all?"

She brushed past him toward the bedroom. "I can do anything I want," she said petulantly, without a backward glance.

He shook his head as he wearily followed her into the bedroom. "No, you can't. You can't, I can't, nobody can."

"You don't own me," she said, sitting on the edge of the enormous bed and kicking off her shoes.

"No, I don't." She rose and started for the closet. He grabbed her by both shoulders and pulled her toward him. "But that doesn't mean you can do anything you want." He kissed her roughly. She kissed back, laughing a little. He raised his eyebrows, his face softening. "What?"

"You haven't answered my question."

His expression was blank.

"Did you hear me sing?"

He nodded. "Some."

"How was I?"

He laughed, shaking his head in disbelief. "You absolutely amaze me."

"Did you cry?"

He looked at her defensively. "Don't be silly."

"You did, you did!" She kissed him joyfully. "You see, it's so sweet, so innocent. Why would you ban a play like *The Fantasticks?*"

He began to undo his tie and sat on the edge of the bed. His cologne carried with it a whiff of clove that always made Kimberly want to inhale deeply against his neck. She sat next to him, tracing his thigh with her fingertips.

"I will grant you that censorship is an imperfect science, but it is our policy to discourage art that agitates the human spirit." A small smile began to play on his lips. "And *The Fantasticks* is art, however minor."

She slipped out of her dress—the surest way she knew to prevent Andrei from holding forth too long on politics and theory. "It's so dumb," she said, standing rather incongruously, in her slip, in front of a row of formal portraits of Andrei with various world leaders: the aged Castro of Greater Cuba, Mbele of the Socialist Republic of Southern Africa, Barghout of Iraquistan. "You know people will go to plays," Kimberly went on, "whether or not you ban them. And they'll continue to listen to good music and to read good books."

"Yes, my dear, but it is demoralizing to have your pleasures made illegal, to have good taste be a crime," he said, unbuttoning his shirt. "Also it makes it easy for us, when we wish to discipline someone. Every person of taste is by definition a criminal."

She stepped in front of him and took over the task of removing his clothing. She loved the first touch of his skin after his crisp shirt slid from his chest. "I hate politics," she said.

"It is vastly hatable. But necessary." His shirt now discarded, he hooked one finger underneath the thin strap of her slip, pulling it off her shoulder.

She pushed him back onto the bed, playfully tumbling on top of him. "Andrei," she teased, "tonight, when you came to the church and saw us, if you hadn't been my lover, would you have had us arrested?"

He rolled on top of her, gently grabbing a handful of

her hair. "Yes. The others would have been jailed. You, however, would have been brought here for special treatment."

Peter Bradford was awakened at dawn by his inner alarm clock. He lay on his back staring at the ceiling, thinking. His sense of duty allowed no transition period between his dreams and the reality of the day, and his mind was at once active. Active and angular—the words described Bradford's face as well as his personality. He had a square, set jaw, and a determined and almost severe tautness in his smile. Only the eyes suggested humor and softness—and perhaps, as some people saw it, a certain lack of resolve. Peter's thoughts were accompanied by the steady breathing of his wife and partner of the past twenty years.

He got out of bed carefully so as not to disturb Amanda. There had been a time, before the takeover, when no matter how rough his exit, Amanda slept on. She'd been serene, and she'd looked it, with smooth skin, a ready smile, and eyes full of mischief and affection. Since the takeover, her sleep had become more fractured—riddled with uneasy dreams and fears that had left their tracks across her cheeks and brow.

"What time is it?" she mumbled.

"Six. Go back to sleep."

She nodded, knowing she would not return to sleep but to that middle ground between dreams and wakefulness that was so loathsome to her husband. Peter watched as she repositioned her body, smiled at her, and padded quietly into the bathroom.

Downstairs, in the kitchen, Jacqueline Bradford poured herself a cup of ersatz coffee and diluted it with powdered milk and molasses. The brew had a grayish color and smelled like resinous sawdust, but Jacqueline, a pretty seventeen-year-old, had no way of knowing that real coffee tasted different. At first glance, Jackie appeared rather delicate, but this impression of vulnerability belied her physical strength as well as her independence and daring. She looked up from the open textbooks she'd strewn over the table as Peter entered.

"Morning, Daddy."

"What got you up at the crack of dawn?"

She sat back in her chair for a moment and sighed. "I've got a monster day. Can you believe a quarter test, and as if that weren't enough, today's the tryouts for the Area Dance Company."

Peter smiled at his daughter's histrionics and moved to the cupboard for a cup. "What about sleep?"

Without missing a beat she answered, "Plenty of time for that after I'm dead."

He poured himself a cup of mock coffee and faced her, leaning against the counter. "What's the exam?"

"Western civilization."

"Which one? Our version or theirs?"

"How can the famous Milford County administrator be so cynical?"

"Hey," said Bradford, "I'm allowed to be a little cynical. I'm only a hired hand. It's not like the county's named after me."

"No," said Jackie, trying to maintain the grown-up level of banter and, in her enthusiasm, taking it just a shade too far. "It's named for Devin Milford's family— and a lot of good it's done him or any of them."

"Jackie . . ." Peter Bradford began rather sharply, then broke off. The reference had stung him, but it wasn't Jackie's fault. She had no way of knowing of her father's boyhood friendship with Devin Milford, nor of their rivalry in everything from baseball to girls, nor of her father's dim and secret feeling that he was in some way falling short of Milford's ferociously high standards of behavior. "Never mind."

"Well," said Jackie, "I'm glad I'm a dancer. No cynicism in that. No politics either."

Peter shifted his weight to reposition himself. He considered getting into the naiveté of her outlook, but decided it was best not to. "How's your program?"

"Fabulous. I've been working on this one move where I come off a leap and use my momentum to come up in a handstand. I had trouble with that move for a long time. I couldn't develop enough momentum." She smiled proudly. "But I got it."

"Great. I'd like to see it."

"Come to tryouts this afternoon."

Peter looked uncomfortable. "I'll try, honey. But if it's a tryout, I don't want it to look like I'm trying to use my influence for my daughter."

"Sure, I understand." She sighed, looking into her coffee mug as if to be certain he knew she didn't.

He walked over to her. "Jackie, I'm not sure you do. I've got to be fair, and being fair isn't just what I may intend something to be—it's got to *look* fair as well."

He raised her chin and smiled into what could have been her mother's eyes. "I love you—you know that. I'm proud of you and your dancing."

She nodded. "I know. It's just not always easy being the great man's daughter."

He smiled and gave her a quick kiss as he headed for the door. "I'll tell you a secret. It's not always easy being the great man." He buttoned up his heavy winter coat. "Got to go, sweetheart," he said, laughing, and shut the door behind him.

Devin felt rejuvenated by the brisk chill of the morning air. He walked, eyes front, alongside the guard, suddenly aware of the barracks coming to life. Upon reaching the administration building, they entered a small barren hall in which four other prisoners sat waiting, each accompanied, as he was, by his own guard. As Devin sat down away from the others, a woman prisoner entered from another door. No one spoke; all looked directly ahead: five men, one woman, and six guards. A moment later, a man in American army fatigues entered. The American army, Devin reflected bitterly. In essence there was no such thing anymore. The great old cotton uniforms were about all that remained. But then, the same could be said for what used to be civilian America. The guts, the spirit of it were gone. All that was left were some scattered artifacts with brand names on them: shredded Levi's that people still wore, cans of Miller High Life at the side of busted-up highways, rusted-out Plymouths that might last one more winter.

At once the guards commanded, "'Tenshun!"

The six came sharply to attention. The officer gave a small nod and commanded the prisoners to sit.

The officer looked at the six prisoners unwaveringly for what seemed like several minutes. "In a few hours you will have your names returned to you. I am here to remind you why you came to be numbers deserving no more respect than a cipher. You disgraced your country and brought shame and hardship on your families.

"At Fort Davis we have tried to demonstrate the value of having a name that is used in the service of your society, not your own self-indulgence. Now you will always have your number. It will follow you wherever you go. It is waiting to be used again, should you fail to apply the lessons learned here. For those who have any doubt about your rehabilitation, I owe it to you to tell you that if you thought this stay was unpleasant, the next will be worse. You will all rise and take the oath of allegiance. Anyone not comfortable pledging that allegiance is free not to do so."

At once, the six prisoners stood. The officer studied them a moment longer, then turned toward another officer. "Sergeant?"

At his command, the sergeant walked to the head of the room behind the officer and pulled a cord. A large flag dropped from the ceiling—a new and strange flag, frightening by its very benignity. Against a blue background were crossed Soviet and American flags. Suspended in the crux were the white globe and olive branch symbol of the United Nations.

"You lead, 83915," the officer commanded.

Devin hesitated for a brief second, took two steps forward, and faced the flag, as did the other prisoners. They began to recite the pledge of allegiance: "I pledge my allegiance to the flag of the community of American, Soviet, and United Nations of the World, and to the principle for which it stands—a nation, indivisible with others of the earth, joined in peace, and justice for all."

The words came out devoid of meaning or emotion or inflection, as if the voices from which they issued were barely human. But then, emotion was not demanded or even desired. Rote recitation was good enough; the object was compliance, not belief. The goal was to breed the habit of not caring. Insincerity was expected and not punished. The game was far subtler than that.

Peter Bradford lifted the garage door and looked across the bare fields that began at the edge of his property. A light powdering of snow had dusted the dark land; the air smelled electric. He climbed into a twelve-year-old Wagoneer, which was as new a vehicle as anyone in Milford owned. The great U.S. auto-making plants had been idle ever since the so-called New Understanding had gone into effect. Peter turned out of the drive onto the tree-lined street heading toward town. He kept twisting the radio dial as he drove, but all he could find was the double-talk that passed for news: talk about increased production and U.S.–Soviet trade and friendship. He changed the station and got John Philip Sousa. Flicking the dial once again, he was party to a Spanish language lesson.

Switching off the radio, he circled the main square of Milford. In the center of the square was the county courthouse, a relic of the early part of the twentieth century. It was a massive red-brick building adorned with pillars and a dome. Even though he saw it almost every day, for some reason this morning it evoked in him the sort of thought he barely allowed himself anymore: the realization that America had once been a nation of high strivings and of grandeur.

On the courthouse lawn stood the proud statue of a World War I soldier, and also the spacious gazebo that for years had served as the focal point for local ceremonies.

Milford had been a bustling market town when the courthouse was built, a center of commerce for farmers. Soon thereafter, however, the community began a long, slow decline. First, in the 1920s, the new railroad line bypassed Milford. Later, during the 1960s, the new interstate highway also went elsewhere, taking with it the potential business and industry that might have spared Milford its economic malaise.

However, if the town of Milford was considered an economic failure, it was a success in other ways. Its wide tree-lined streets were as uncrowded and inviting as they had been in the twenties, and its gracious old homes were as comfortable as they had ever been. The town had little crime, little poverty, and a genuine sense of community spirit.

Peter passed several battered pickups, an ancient John Deere tractor, and a horse and wagon, as well as a couple of vintage cars. The primary mode of transportation in Milford, however, seemed to be bicycles, which far outnumbered all other vehicles combined. Self-consciously, Bradford nestled his jeep between the rows of bikes in front of the only lighted sign in the square:

HERB 'N BETTY'S CAFE
GOOD EATS

The neon had long since given up trying to hit all the letters, and it wavered gamely in the gray morning light. Peter entered Herb 'n Betty's, nodding to the assortment of farmers, truckers, and loafers who gathered there to play cards, gossip, and drink what passed for coffee. The walls were decorated with an elk head, stuffed ducks, and old basketball trophies; the tables were covered with stained, red-and-white-checked tablecloths. As Peter headed for his regular booth in the corner of the cafe, a farmer stopped him to complain about a long-delayed replacement part for his tractor. Another grizzled old-timer seized his arm, leaning into him conspiratorially to ask about the latest talk of guerrilla forces.

"My wife's sister told me her husband ran off and joined. He was one of them survivalist types. She said there was hundreds of 'em, living in caves in the Rockies."

"Can't believe every rumor comes along—"

17

"Yeah, but what if it's true?"

Peter shrugged. "Not a lot to do with us, I guess."

The farmer shook his head, reluctantly agreeing. Peter moved toward his booth. Before he had time to take off his coat and sit down, Betty, the timeless owner of the cafe, walked over with a cup of coffee. Betty was a local institution—ageless, shapeless, but seldom speechless. She wore a net over her graying mop of reddish-brown hair, and a sleeveless brown sweater over her white uniform.

"What'll it be, Peter?"

"Aunt Jemima pancakes with Log Cabin maple syrup, maybe some little pork link sausages, two eggs over easy, and a glass of fresh squeezed orange juice."

"Yeah, me too." She smiled at Peter, licking her lips as though she could taste the remembered favorites of the past. "Would you settle for soy cakes with some fresh molasses?"

"Don't I always?" Peter smiled.

"If you want better, you'll have to go out to the SSU barracks. I saw a load of stuff go out there yesterday— eggs, pork chops, steaks. Maybe they got your Aunt Jemima. Just tell 'em you're the county administrator and they're in the county."

"Sounds like a plan."

"'Course, you'd have to eat with 'em."

Being reminded that he did, in fact, have options, made him uncomfortable and dimly ashamed. Before she could go on, he hastened to make it clear that what everyone else ate was plenty good for him by cutting in with "I'll take the soy cakes, thanks."

At that moment, Ward Milford walked in. He was wearing his deputy sheriff uniform, clean Levi's, a faded flannel shirt, and a fur-lined parka that had seen him through many a cold winter. His wind-stung face set off the whiteness of his unruly shock of hair. Betty automatically poured him a cup of coffee, grunted a good morning, and shuffled away.

"She's not real chipper this morning," Ward said.

"She's having supply problems."

Ward tasted the coffee and grimaced. "It's tough, living in the middle of the most productive farmland on the planet, and all you can get is soyburgers."

"So what kind of night did we have?"

"Not so hot. A drunk, just passing through, been drinking lighter fluid. Died. Emergency wouldn't pump his stomach."

"Why the hell not?"

"Some new regulation. Triage, they call it. You know what that means?"

"Yeah, doctors decide who to treat and who not to treat. In essence, it means doctors play God."

Ward shrugged. "Anyway, the poor bastard died."

"I'll talk to Alan Drummond about it. I don't like seeing people die like that, even some wino drifter."

"Besides the wino," Ward continued, "we had some runners passing through, probably on some sort of errands for the Resisters further west. We looked the other way. And some kids stole an SSU jeep and took it for a joyride."

"Any idea who?"

Ward's face broke into a sheepish grin. "Probably my son or one of his friends."

"Pass the word, we don't need that kind of problem. Why rattle the cage? And listen, no matter what Dr. Drummond says about his new regulations, I want an honest record of what happens if someone dies, be it a wino, a drifter, whatever."

"You think it matters?"

"It does to me. Dammit," said Peter Bradford, as if

struggling desperately to hold on to his own sense of decency. "It's got to matter."

Ward stared at him, his face suddenly intense. "What matters to me is that my great-grandfather helped build this goddamned country—cut down the trees with his own hands—built his spread into ten thousand acres. The damn county is named after us, and whatta we got now? Fifty damned acres and I'm a deputy sheriff under a system that decided there shouldn't be a sheriff. I worked my whole life, and this is where it goes. Sometimes I feel like we're the only ones who think it does matter. Country's dead anyway."

"Speaking of death," said Betty, who had sidled toward them balancing a couple of plates, "here's your soy cakes."

She clattered the plates down rudely on the table, and the two men, more from habit than appetite, dug in.

After one bite, Peter Bradford laid his fork aside. "This is really awful," he said, his eyes fixed on the colorless lumps on his plate.

Ward's face relaxed into a small but mirthless smile. "That's what really makes you want to give up. You can't even get a good breakfast."

=====Chapter 2=====

A FEW MILES outside Milford, a long, poplar-lined driveway branched off the main road and led to a once-proud Victorian farmhouse. Now, though, the house was in sorry need of repair. Its dilapidated state suggested more than the usual shortages of paint, tools, and building supplies. Those shortages were almost universal during the so-called Transition—that vague and pretty-sounding term for the limbo America had fallen into. But the sad state of the old Victorian farmhouse bespoke another sort of lack—an absence of spirit, a vacuum of hope.

Alethea Milford, standing in front of her bathroom mirror and gazing at her own red-rimmed eyes, saw that same vacuum of hope reflected in her weary face. Alethea was a big woman—nearly six feet tall—and in her soul she knew that frame had been intended to house an outsized destiny. Once, perhaps, her spirit had been generous and expansive; now it was shriveled and pinched.

She took things far too personally, and she knew it. Her brothers Ward and Devin—they could externalize their rage, could make accommodations. She could do nothing but seethe inside—and drink. And in the throes of that drinking, cast herself into more dubious forms of self-abandonment than she cared to think about at seven o'clock in the morning.

It would have all been different, she ruefully considered, if only the whole world hadn't gone crazy around her. She'd been one of those young women whose life was all in place, who had a plan. At the time of the Soviet attack, Alethea Milford had been an honor student at the University of Nebraska. She was studying journalism, and by God she could write the stuff. She saw her future clearly: the trench coat, the note pads, the bylines, the sense of doing something.

And what was she doing now? Ruining herself with alcohol, wallowing in the knowledge of her reputation, and utterly unable to come to terms with the aching love and desperate anger she felt toward her brothers and her father—toward everyone, in fact, who'd shared in her disgraced and disappointed life. "Such a waste," she whispered aloud to her own reflection. "Such a sinful waste."

She stepped into the kitchen and hesitated. William Milford, the patriarch of the family and a strong, unyielding man of the land, sat alone with a mug of black coffee. She looked at this man—her father—who had spent most of his seventy years being successful and respected, and who now looked broken and hollow. He looked up at her, his face set in cold contempt.

Alethea forced a smile. "'Morning, Dad."

He didn't reply. She shrugged.

Outside, Ward Milford climbed out of his patrol car and entered the kitchen. "Hello, Alethea. How's it going, Dad?"

"Damn squatters tore some siding right off the back of the milk barn."

"How much they get?"

"Why?" asked Will Milford, with a sarcasm he found harder and harder to keep out of his voice, even when talking to his own children. "You gonna do something about it?"

Ward hesitated. He knew only too well his father's now-archaic feelings about the rights of property owners; he understood the old man's rage at being so helpless in the end. He sympathized, as well, with the squatters, internal exiles kept in constant motion by the harassment of the authorities. "What can I do, Dad? Want me to go around checking who's got pieces of our barn sticking out of their campfires?"

"You think it's okay for the government to steal the land," William Milford grumbled. "You probably think it's okay for the squatters to rip the damn house down for firewood."

"You know I don't. I'll look into it." He stared at his father, waiting for a response. There was none.

The old man stared stubbornly out the window at the battered barns, rusty silos, and barren winter fields.

Alethea slipped past her father into the hallway, and Ward, sensing a moment when brother and sister might comfort each other, followed her.

"You been cryin' or drinkin'?" he said, instantly sympathetic.

"Cryin' while drinkin'." Her face was flushed, her eyes red. "You have to be real coordinated to be able to do it. Kinda like chewing gum and kissing."

* * *

Amanda Bradford, fully awake at last, joined her children in the kitchen. Dressed in jeans and a sweatshirt, her lithe and almost girlish body stood in painful contrast to her taut and careworn face. Amanda had once had a classic cheerleader sort of prettiness; with age had come a more substantial beauty tempered by sorrow and perhaps too much awareness.

As Amanda entered the kitchen, Jackie was stuffing her books into her backpack. Scott, her "little" brother by a year, was wolfing down a double-decker sandwich of toast, fried eggs, and ham. Scott was dark-haired and handsome like his father. At six-four, he was a budding basketball star in the orange and black Milford High letter jacket.

"Where'd the ham come from?" Amanda asked.

"I swiped it from the training table," Scott said.

"They've got to keep the jocks healthy," Jackie said disdainfully.

Amanda no longer minded the eternal bickering between her two children; at its best, she thought, it was a minor art form.

"You shouldn't steal," she said, helping herself to a bite of ham. "Boy, that's good." She sighed. "Jackie, want some moral support at your tryouts this afternoon?"

"Okay, if you don't say anything."

Amanda walked her daughter to the door. "You're a strange kid—you don't want to be criticized by your own mother." Jackie pulled on her parka. "Be good," Amanda said, straightening her daughter's collar.

"Yeah, give 'em hell, Jack," Scott called. "Just don't get pregnant."

"Jerk," Jackie called, and ran to her bike.

Scott left a moment later, still munching on his sandwich. Amanda trailed after him, waving his parka.

"Take this!" she called.

"Don't need it."

"Take it anyway."

She smiled, watching as her two children pedaled out of sight. Childhood slipped by so quickly, she reflected; happiness, sometimes, vanished even faster. She wondered idly if she and Peter would have had more children if the Transition hadn't come. They hadn't even thought of it then; everything seemed so hard, so different, that along with everyone else they had concentrated on protecting what they had, not reaching out for more.

As she turned to go back into the house, a darting motion at the outer edge of her field of vision caused her to stop abruptly. There was something animallike and fugitive in what she'd glimpsed, as though a fox or a raccoon had found itself cornered by daylight. But in fact the skittish movement wasn't made by an animal. The creature was a human child. As the child tried to sneak around the corner of the garage, Amanda realized that it must have been foraging in the garbage cans that were kept there.

The child wore patched and thrown-together castoffs to fight the sharp cold. The first thing Amanda thought of was Scott's unwanted parka, but she did not take her eyes off the child, who, she could now see, was a girl. The little girl froze under Amanda's gaze like a rabbit caught in headlights. Amanda approached slowly and carefully. She thought she might scare the girl further if she tried to make eye contact—the girl's wide-eyed stare was pure fear—so she let her gaze range over the tatterdemalion outfit: a grown-up-sized plaid shirt whose frayed tails dangled below the waistband of a patched green woolen jacket, oversized boots stuffed with rags. Amanda knew, with a mother's instinct, that

25

this child was loved: the boots had been carefully packed to keep out the cold, and although none of the patches on the jacket matched, they'd been securely sewn.

Amanda stopped a few feet from the little girl and extended her hand in a universal gesture of friendship. "Hi, honey. What's your name?"

The child did not speak. As Amanda knelt in front of her, the girl regarded her with solemn suspicion.

"Where are you from?" she asked, although she knew the answer. The Exile child remained silent.

"Did your friends run away and leave you?" The child nodded. "Would you like to come inside a minute? It's warm and I could fix you a cup of hot milk."

The temptation was too great to resist. Slowly the child nodded. Amanda reached for her hand and the child cautiously accepted. At that very moment, a woman shot out from behind the trees and seized the child's arm.

"No," she cried, pulling the girl toward her. She too was dressed in a makeshift costume. "I'm sorry, we're lost. Come on, Dierdre."

"It's all right," protested Amanda, but the child's mother was already vanishing, dragging the weeping girl toward the open road. She was too far gone in her mistrust to accept the kindness of this stranger; kindness carried danger with it.

Amanda stood perfectly still as the pair of squatters retreated. Her eyes filled with tears, and she wondered for a moment what sort of life the Exile mother had had before the troubles, the Transition. Perhaps she'd been a doctor, a professor, a patriot of some sort who had come to be thought dangerous. The Transition turned everyone's fortunes upside down, and Amanda flushed at the realization that her own position was one of the few that had actually improved. Before the takeover, Peter Bradford had been . . . what? A minor official among dozens of others, living, as did almost everyone in Milford County, in the shadow of the Milford clan. Life was so easy then—a new car every third year, meat on the table, and, with prudent saving, college for the children. An easy life—but where was the distinction? No, the distinction did not lie with men like Peter Bradford, but with those like Devin Milford, the risk takers, the windmill jousters, the dreamers.

Once, Amanda Bradford told herself, Devin Milford had actually dreamed of her. It was back in high school, when Devin and Peter Bradford were close if somewhat unlikely friends, and Amanda Taylor had been pursued by both of them. Even then, with unfailing intuition, she understood somehow that Devin offered excitement, grandeur, and the sort of insecurity that thrilled her but that she could not finally accept. Peter Bradford offered safety, calm, and, yes, love; he was a steady man, a good man. Why then did Amanda sometimes catch herself wondering if she had somehow failed her deeper self in picking him?

Jackie Bradford rode her bike slowly and carefully along the neglected, potholed road, her thoughts on the dance tryouts that afternoon.

So deep was her concentration that she was unaware of the hum of a motorcycle coming up behind her. The hum had mounted to a roar before she noticed.

Justin Milford, nineteen, gunned the engine of his Harley-Davidson, a lovingly tended machine that was older than he was. That motorcycle, the leather jacket and goggles that went with it—and Jackie Bradford— were about the only things in Milford County that Justin liked.

"Hi." Justin was one of those people who could make that single syllable sound intriguing, sexy, and even vaguely threatening.

Jackie was delighted to see him but maintained her cool. "What are you doing here?"

"I woke up this morning and was dying for a kiss. Thought I'd come in to town to see if I could find anybody who looked halfway decent."

"Maybe you better keep looking." She held back her smile.

"I'm always looking," said Justin as they approached the beginning of a long, gradual rise. "Let me give you a tow—you'll want to save your energy for tryouts."

She was flattered that he remembered and stopped her bike. Justin brought the Harley to a halt beside her and handed her a rope that was attached to the rack in back of the motorcycle seat. "Ready?"

He gunned his engine and the rope snapped taut, dragging Jackie Bradford's bike at a giddy pace. The maneuver was gutsy, perilous, intoxicating—the perfect distillation of the effect Justin Milford had on her. At the top of the hillock, Justin stopped short, and Jackie's momentum carried her right into his arms.

He slipped off his goggles, and leaned over confidently for his reward. They straddled their respective bikes and kissed: a flurry of awkward but enthusiastic pecks and smiles.

"I'm only doing this because you remembered my tryout," she whispered.

"It's the right way to start the day," he said with all the confidence of one much more experienced than she. "Gets the juices flowing."

"I'm late for school. Gotta go. I love you."

"What about tonight? The Cavern?"

"My father won't let me go all the way to Omaha."

"Don't ask your father. Just go."

"Let me think. Come by after school. After tryouts. Okay?"

"I might," Justin said, and pulled his goggles down.

Jackie stomped down hard on the pedals and raced, late now, to the safety of school. She heard the roar of Justin's bike as he sped off in the opposite direction.

Kimberly sleepily watched Andrei come out of the bathroom, dressed in slacks and a sport coat; he was one of the most powerful men in the New America, yet he looked less like a politician than like a cross between a successful executive and a professor. He walked to the bed, unaware that Kimberly was awake. He bent down to her and kissed her, surprised to find her arms tightly around his neck, pulling him down onto the bed.

"Get back in here." She smiled lazily, her morning breath milky and warm.

"No time now, but come along. We could make love in the car."

"Pervert."

"There are many women who would love such an offer."

"Maybe you can find one on the way to the office."

He kissed her. Her brown eyes clouded over. He watched her in fascination. This was not an act; frequently she experienced these sudden, agonizing swings of emotion.

"Are you all right? You seemed very sad this morning."

She nodded, as though dismissing it. "I'm fine."

Andrei knew that was not true, but he had learned from public life that it was much easier to let it pass. He went to the closet, picked up an overnight bag, and came back to the bed.

"I need you today," she said.

"You have your play to rehearse. You'll probably not even notice I'm gone."

He kissed her again and she responded slightly. "Remember about tonight," he said.

"Do we have to go? I mean—to Omaha?"

"Yes we do, my dear. The nomination of a governor-general is an epoch-making moment in the political life of your country—of our country. Besides, you'll get to perform." He got up and walked to the door, opening it.

"Andrei—"

"Yes?" He turned back to face Kimberly again.

"I love you."

Andrei nodded. "Be ready at six."

Mikel was waiting when Andrei reached his big, bright corner office high above Lake Michigan. The room was furnished with white rugs and sofas, abstract paintings that had been officially labeled decadent, and sleek silver stereo and video equipment. Atop a large, neat desk stood a framed photograph of Kimberly alongside a small statue of an American Indian. It amused Andrei to surround himself with bits of Americana.

But Mikel was not amused. He was efficient, humorless, and ambitious—the sort of man, Andrei knew, that one must use wisely and watch carefully. Andrei thought it possible that Mikel spied on him for his enemies in the KGB. The possibility neither surprised nor offended him. It was part of the challenge of staying in the game.

"Good morning, Colonel." Mikel rose swiftly from the conference table, his close-cropped hair precisely parted and flawlessly slicked down.

"Good morning, Mikel. You are aware of my trip to Washington?"

"Yes. Your plane is waiting."

"You canceled my day's appointments?"

"Yes. With one difficulty. Magistrate Marion Andrews considers her business urgent. I told her you would see her this evening, upon your return from Washington."

"She is an important woman, Mikel. Invite her to fly with me to Omaha tonight. Did she explain the nature of her business?"

Mikel cleared his throat and grimaced slightly, as if he found the whole business thoroughly distasteful. "It is slightly awkward, Colonel, relating as it does to a time when her political views were less enlightened than they have since become." He paused and looked to Andrei, as if to be sure he should go on. When Andrei nodded impatiently, he continued, "It seems that her former husband, Devin Milford, a political dissident, has been released from custody. Although he is being confined to his home county in Nebraska, she fears he may harm her. She seeks the colonel's reassurance, or perhaps protection."

Andrei nodded, resigned. Protection. That's what everyone seemed to want from him. But protection from what? From a man as principled and direct as Devin Milford? Andrei was well acquainted with Milford's character and ruined career. Years ago, in fact, he'd read transcripts of his speeches, circulated underground in crude and illegal mimeographs. He had been struck by the power of Milford's words, and the name had remained in his memory ever since. "Today, while I am gone, assemble an extensive file on Devin Milford."

They took the elevator down and walked through the

lobby to the waiting limousine. The lobby entrance was discreetly covered by security guards. Two of them escorted Andrei to his limousine. The others climbed into an unmarked vehicle parked behind and followed Andrei's car as it sped away.

Behind the protective glass in his limousine, indifferent to the security guards, Andrei began studying a pile of photographs. "Is everything in order for the Omaha event?"

"Four of the candidates for area governor-general have been notified," replied Mikel.

Andrei signed. "Governor-general. A rather stuffy title, don't you think? Like a Gilbert and Sullivan character."

"It is a position of authority," Mikel said.

Andrei thumbed through the pictures again. "You said four have been notified. Why hasn't the fifth? And which one is it?"

Mikel looked a little uncomfortable. "I have not spoken with the man from Nebraska, Peter Bradford."

Andrei picked out Peter's photo from the others in the file. He thought about the sarcastic gibes aimed at earlier American presidents: "Would you buy a used car from this man?" And he thought, Yes, he would buy a used car from Bradford. And the rest of America would too.

Andrei turned to face his assistant's earnest profile. "Your reason, Mikel?"

"The committee noted Mr. Bradford's lack of experience. There is a feeling that Governor Smith of Missouri would be the nominee of choice."

"But we must wonder why, Mikel?" Andrei said. "Do you know how Mr. Bradford came to my attention? His county is the most trouble free in the Central

Administrative Area. The Heartland, as it is known. His production is far above quota. There is no significant resistance, although they are only sixty miles from the Omaha Urban Zone. He is a family man, much respected."

"He is not a party member. The party leader from Milford, a Mr. Herbert Lister, said he was resistant to the revised school curriculum."

"Are you accusing him of having a backbone, Mikel?"

"I accuse him of nothing."

══════ *Chapter 3* ══════

THE TRUCK LURCHED past the iron gates and picked up
speed. The rutted road ahead pointed straight across
the desert to the east. There were six of them in the
back of the truck, blankly looking back as Fort Davis,
their only reality for years, receded into the desert.
Devin wondered why each of them felt compelled to
look back—he knew that he desperately wanted to look
forward, to see something bright, something substantial, in the future. But ahead of them was just desert
and miles to travel; the only buildings anywhere in this
area were the jumble of jerry-rigged structures they'd
come from.

Devin tried to keep his emotions in check. Part of
him still feared that his release was a trick. There had
been so many at Fort Davis. For him, ambiguity was
the secret of survival: to hate and not to hate, to fear
and not to fear, to resist and not to resist, to dream and

not to dream. And yet with every passing moment, he felt assured that he had truly survived.

It would take time to learn to smile again. He reached into the pocket of the denim shirt they had given him as part of his exit uniform and drew out the creased and faded snapshot he had hidden and treasured all those years. The two boys were younger then, of course, and he wondered what they looked like now, at fourteen and nine. Fourteen and nine! The numbers confounded him, confused a memory of tiny little people just beginning to form personalities, likes, and dislikes of their own.

Devin studied the snapshot closely, as though reexamining an icon. Caleb was four, sandy-blond hair, blue eyes, all seriousness. Billy was nine, an older version of Caleb physically but with more of Devin's free spirit. As he stared at the picture he felt as if he was being watched. He was about to look up to seek out the intruder when the prisoner next to him spoke.

"Yours?"

Devin pulled the snapshot to his chest protectively. He stared at the man intently, finally deciding he could be trusted. He nodded and returned his gaze to the pictures.

"I had a couple of my own," said the prisoner, a heavyset man with a face that looked as if it had at one time belonged to a jovial man.

"Had?"

The man shrugged. "That was four years ago."

"You gonna find them?"

The man watched the desert. "You know it."

Devin looked back at his picture and said softly, "Yeah, I do."

* * *

That morning, at an exclusive private school in Chicago, nine-year-old Caleb M. Andrews, formerly Caleb Milford, was participating in a social-studies class. His school occupied a full block in a comfortable old residential neighborhood, fronting on a gracious street of swaying elms that shaded stately brick houses. Once the domain of industrialists and professionals, the neighborhood was now an enclave of party officials, government lawyers, and scientists. There was a fenced-in playground where carefree children frolicked, but inside the school, much had changed. Teachers were certified by the PPP—the People's Progressive party, the political juggernaut that had swept into power in the midst of the Transition—and their curriculum was written in Washington and approved in Moscow.

Caleb was answering his teacher's question about his nation's past.

"Our ancestors were very rough," he said. "When Americans conquered the country, they killed Indians who had been living on the land peacefully for thousands of years."

"Thank you, Caleb," the teacher, Clara Chavez, said. "Can anyone tell us what the cause of their violence was?"

The boy wrinkled his brow, trying to remember. "It was like . . . survival of the fittest," he said. "The rich people controlled everything and ordinary people, even kids, had to work in factories or coal mines for almost nothing. Wars were fought to make rich people richer."

As Caleb spoke, an elegant woman with commanding eyes, thick wavy coal-black hair, and a sensual, feline smile slipped quietly into the classroom. She had an intense, polished, and somehow serpentlike beauty.

"Good, Caleb," the teacher said. "Can anyone else tell me the name of this violent philosophy they followed?"

The children could not answer; their indoctrination had not reached that point. The woman raised a braceleted hand. The teacher beamed at the opportunity to show her admiration and respect for the woman once known as Marion Milford. "Yes, please do tell the class, Ms. Andrews."

"It's called Social Darwinism. But now we believe in Social Humanism, which means everyone helps everyone else, and we trust our new leaders to help us do that." Marion's voice was gentle, even comforting, but she spoke with absolute conviction.

The teacher smiled. "Boys and girls, let me introduce Caleb's mother, Ms. Marion Andrews, who is a magistrate here in Chicago and also a member of the National Advisory Committee that helps our president and Congress make important decisions."

Even without the glowing introduction, the children would have known that this was someone special by her elegant bearing and clothing. She didn't dress like any of their mothers. Her black silk suit had been made especially for her in Paris, where most of the great fashion designers still flourished. Now, though, their chief customers were the wives of Communist party officials around the world, instead of the wives of corporate moguls and oil princes.

"Thank you, Miss Chavez," Marion said. "But most important, I'm Caleb's mom," she said, smiling. "May I steal him for a moment?"

She led the boy out to the corridor and knelt to his height to face him. Caleb wore dark pants, a white shirt, and the red armband of the Young Lincoln Brigade. He was a blond, blue-eyed child, seemingly intelligent, and eager to please. In the wholesome, open face he presented to his mother was mingled a child's quiet concern and ultimate trust in his mother's power to make whatever it was that had made her pull him out of class all right again.

"Darling, there's nothing wrong," Marion began. "But you know how we've talked about your father maybe someday trying to see you?"

"But he's in the hospital," Caleb said, his face now clouded with apprehension.

"Well, honey, he's out now, but he's not supposed to come anywhere near us. But just in case, I wanted to warn you and your brother not to speak to any strangers, whether you think you recognize them or not, okay?" Caleb nodded silently. "There'll be a policeman to pick you up after school today and take you home, because I won't be here."

"Where are you going?" the boy demanded.

"To an important dinner in Omaha with Colonel Denisov. I'll be back late tonight and I'll come in and check on you then. Mrs. Marin will get your dinner and stay until I get back. Just remember what I said about strangers, okay?"

"Sure," he said uneasily.

"Okay, back to class." Caleb started back into the classroom, but then he hesitated and abruptly turned around and rushed into his mother's arms. "Love you, babe," Marion assured him.

"Me too, Mom."

A short limousine ride later, Marion Andrews delivered the same warning to her firstborn, Billy, a freshman at Chicago's most prestigious private high school. But the older boy's reaction to the news was dramatically different. Caleb, the baby, barely remembered his father; Billy remembered him vividly as a gentle and affectionate man who had played catch with him, carried him on his shoulders, and spoken to him with a seriousness and respect that adults too seldom show to children. A fiercely independent boy, Billy had remained stubbornly loyal to his banished and disgraced father. He'd refused to adopt his mother's maiden name of Andrews, used as a smoke screen for the family's shame. Billy was proud to be a Milford and it was the only name he answered to.

"Where is he?" Billy demanded.

"I don't know. It's hard to get reliable information from that far."

"You're a big shot. You should be able to find out."

Marion sighed. "I'm not going to argue what I should or should not be able to do. I'm telling you that an officer will pick you up after school and be at the apartment."

"I don't want some prole hanging around, watching me."

"I told you not to use that word. It may be in among ninth-graders, but you don't even know what it means."

Billy stared at the ground. "Whatever . . ."

Marion straightened Billy's sweater. "The officer will pick up your brother first, then come and get you. I'll be back late—so don't wait up." She leaned forward and kissed him and started to walk away.

"Mom?"

She turned around, her designer cape moving elegantly around her. "Yes?"

"Do you think he's all right? I mean, in those hospitals they do stuff like shock treatments and lobotomies."

She studied him a moment, not quite sure of what

she should say. "I'm sure he's fine. Otherwise they wouldn't let him out."

"He was real smart, wasn't he?"

"Yes. Yes he was. Okay, honey, I've got to go."

"I want to see him. They have to let us see him, don't they?"

"I don't think that's a good idea. He could be"—she hesitated for a moment—"it could be bad for us."

"I want to see my dad."

"We're not going to discuss it right now. We'll discuss it when I get back. Okay?"

The truck rattled to a halt at the Odessa Relocation Center. Devin and the others from Fort Davis were put into a huge cinderblock compound surrounded by an electrified fence, to await processing. There were perhaps two hundred prisoners waiting there. Outside the fence scores of men and women were calling out names, searching for loved ones or just reasons to keep going.

"My husband," a woman called, "Clarence Babcock . . . disappeared three years ago . . . has anyone seen . . .?"

A dozen voices called, scores of hands waved photographs of loved ones. They had traveled from the east, or from cities like Atlanta, New Orleans, and Houston, where pockets of political rebellion still existed. Many of them had seen a loved one simply vanish, and now, when they could, they traveled to remote relocation centers like this one, seeking some shred of hope. They set out in ancient Chevrolets and Mustangs, and sometimes they abandoned the cars en route because they were unable to get fuel. Weeds grew crazily along the little-traveled roads, burying the vehicles under vines and rushes. The seekers continued on foot, wearing through the soles of torn-up running shoes or old loafers meant for short strolls on urban sidewalks, not for five-hundred-mile treks through landscapes grown threatening and inhospitable.

There were thousands missing, tens of thousands. Devin half listened for the occasional instructions over the PA system. *Stay with your own group. You'll be processed by camp. No talking . . . move along.*

He did not mind the waiting. Prison had taught him to take the long view. This was a bureaucracy and bureaucracies were not evil, only slow and inane. Evil took other forms. Sometimes it was guards who came in the night to take you to small rooms where they attached electrical devices sometimes to your temples, sometimes to your private parts; sometimes, it was doctors who watched without expression until it was time for them to give you the drugs that were worse than the shocks. *That* was evil; compared to it, waiting in line was a taste of paradise.

Devin walked toward the edge of the fence and looked out toward the town, which from his vantage point looked almost deserted. His eyes scanned the dusty town square and the drab, unpainted buildings. The air smelled of concrete dust. As lifeless as it all appeared to him, it seemed a glorious glimpse of freedom.

A man's voice jarred him from his reverie.

"First time I was in Midland-Odessa I was eighteen years old—stopover from Phoenix to Houston. You flew over oil fields for twenty minutes. Lot of money here."

Devin turned around. The man was fiftyish and overweight. He continued to talk.

"Kind of like going home—sure looks like it's changed."

Devin nodded, not wanting to carry this any further. "Just get in with that Fort Davis group?"

Devin nodded again.

"You hear anything? About the country, I mean, like what's happening?"

Devin shook his head.

"We can talk. They don't care."

"Guess I'm out of practice."

"Where I was they let you talk. Musta hatched about twenty escape plots a day—formed a hundred resistance groups for when we got out. You do stuff like that? You know, to pass the time?"

Devin studied the man a moment, then turned and walked away. He approached his group and a prisoner eased past him.

"That guy—he's a plant," the prisoner whispered.

"Thanks."

The newcomer looked at Devin with beseeching eyes. "I heard they nuked Seattle—you hear that?"

Devin shrugged. He didn't trust this man, either. Soon the line was moving faster.

The dirt road twisted through the hills north of Milford, the forbidden area out by the Special Services Unit camp. The SSU was one of those paramilitary, quasi-police organizations that created terror by its very vagueness. Among the citizenry, no one quite knew what the SSU did or even who its members were. It was a hodge-podge—so rumor had it—of Russians, for whom life in the military itself held more appeal than any true patriotism or ideal. In some tellings, the SSU was terribly brutal; in other versions of the story, it was simply ineffectual if not benign, a sort of hidden national guard that was at the ready but almost never called to action. In reality, the SSU operated like the organization in Poland that it was based upon—an overseer group, assigned to the countryside, which never intermingled with the local population.

Either way, the SSU turf was off limits to civilians—which was exactly why Justin Milford, in his leather and his goggles, could not resist going there. He rode his Harley down the middle of the road until he reached the best vantage point he could find. Then he swerved his motorcycle into the woods, glided past the trees, and came to a stop alongside another cycle parked by an old shed.

His friend Puncher, a big, tough farm boy with red hair, a square jaw, and a sweet lopsided grin, was inside the shed, using a pair of binoculars to study the snow-covered fields in front of them. Justin knelt beside him and heard the rumble of engines in the distance.

"How long they been out?" Justin asked.

"Ten minutes," Puncher said. "It's a tactical unit."

"Company strength?"

"Platoon."

"Lemme see," Justin said, seizing the field glasses.

He observed two black attack helicopters, hovering like giant malignant insects, fire rockets at some distant target. A moment later five black tanks lumbered into view and they too opened fire. A burst of flame shot fifty feet into the air.

"The same drill as last time," Puncher said.

"The bastards are efficient," Justin muttered.

More helicopters shot into view, firing their rockets; a line of personnel carriers came down the road by the river, and soldiers leaped out of them, firing automatic weapons and flinging grenades.

"Hey, look at that!" Puncher cried. "What the hell are they doing?"

Justin took the binoculars. Off in the distance a fire had started, a long, thin line of flame and crackling debris, as if a huge string of firecrackers had gone off. The acrid smell of phosphorus stung their nostrils.

"A Viper," Justin declared. "The sons of bitches are testing a Viper."

"A what?" Puncher asked.

"It's called a Super Viper—you know, as in snake. It's a hose, packed with explosives, two hundred meters long. It clears a mine field. A rocket shoots the hose across the field, they set it off, and it clears a path twenty feet wide, for two hundred meters."

"Jesus, who's got mines?" Puncher asked.

Justin shrugged. "Maybe some of our people. Or maybe they're testing it for somewhere else in the world."

Before the flames from the Viper had died down, the exercise abruptly ended. The soldiers returned to their vehicles and within minutes the fields were empty and silent again, with only a fast-rising plume of thick black smoke to testify to the SSU's violent assault.

"Time?" Justin asked.

"Twenty-eight minutes, from barracks to withdrawal."

Justin shook his head in wonder.

"Of course, nobody was shooting back."

"Someday," Justin said.

Puncher stood up. "Jesus, I wonder. I mean, are we just playing games?"

"Hell no," Justin said. "We know things they don't know we know. Someday we'll hit the bastards."

"You goin' to the Cavern tonight?"

"Maybe," Justin said. "Don't know if Jackie can get away."

"She's a princess. Pick up somebody there."

"You're really primitive, Puncher. Maybe you'd feel more at home on the other side."

Peter cornered Dr. Alan Drummond on the courthouse square, before the city council meeting. The chief of staff at Milford County Hospital was fiftyish, a husky black man with graying hair and a kind of delicate and battered humanity about him. Although an exile, he was a necessary commodity—a doctor—to the Milford community.

"Got a moment, doctor?"

"Always, Peter, for you."

"Ward told me about the man who died at your hospital last night. It sounded like those new Triage guidelines killed him."

"Drinking lighter fluid killed him. But the guidelines didn't help any. The rule was clear. I wasn't supposed to do a thing for him. A matter of priorities."

"What about your Hippocratic Oath?"

"You want me to disobey the guidelines? That's essentially the same as disobeying the National Advisory Committee."

"If a life is hanging in the balance, I want you to ignore them if you have to."

"Will you put that in writing, Peter?"

"No."

A wry smile crossed Alan Drummond's face.

"That's smart of you. Back in Philadelphia, I put something in writing once. Cost me a two-hundred-thousand-a-year practice. I wasn't political—just doing the decent thing. Some other people didn't quite see it that way, and now I'm in Nebraska. Nothing against your home state, Peter, but if we're talking about circles of hell, I've fallen far enough, thank you very much. Far enough so that I'm keenly aware of how much farther they might have pulled me down—if the idea of minority doctors didn't fit in quite so neatly with their propaganda. So now I think about politics and guidelines, jump when the advisory committees say jump, and worry about informers on my staff. And yet, dammit, I hate for people to die in my county if there's a chance of saving them."

"My advice is pick your shots, Peter. You can't save everybody."

The two men went into the council chambers. The city council met weekly in a large conference room that featured portraits of Lincoln and Lenin on the far wall. Their session did nothing to lighten Peter's spirits. Someone reported that the local VFW chapter was refusing to march in the Lincoln Day parade if the SSU troops participated. There was a lot of talk about black-market skimming of already scarce consumer goods and about whether the county could meet its production quota. Some people wanted to blame everything on the Exiles, wanted to turn the SSU loose on them. Before long, Alan Drummond was embroiled in an impassioned defense of those who had fallen much farther than himself.

"You don't understand the first thing about it," he raged. "They didn't ask to be sent here. Some of them have been here for years—three years now. They aren't farmers but they're trying to make a living on those pathetic little plots of land they gave them. But when they come into town, they're treated like outcasts, like dirt. Dammit, they're Americans!"

"Don't get riled up, Alan," said one of the council members, a red-faced hardware merchant. "I just wish all the exiles were people who wanted to work and make a place for themselves."

"That sounds too damn much like what bigots used to say about blacks," Alan Drummond said bitterly. "You don't understand what these people are up against."

"The White House sent them here," another council member declared. "Let the White House feed them."

"Wait a minute," Peter said at last. "That's easy to say. But it's us who have to deal with them. I don't know if you heard, but the exiles rioted in Missouri last week. I don't want that here."

"Let 'em riot. The Special Service Units can handle 'em."

"Not in my county," Peter said firmly.

And so it went. Peter thought that whoever said "divide and conquer" damn sure knew what he was talking about.

As the meeting broke up, the men headed for the doorway amid a humming chorus of gripes, groans, and unresolved complaints. Peter Bradford, having heard enough of his neighbors' sorrows for one morning, hoped to slip away without being buttonholed. But as he was halfway down the corridor, Ward Milford motioned him over. The deputy sheriff looked dramatically pale and tenser than he had seemed at breakfast that same morning.

"What is it, Ward?" asked Peter, with ill-concealed impatience.

"New Exile list just came in."

"Can't it wait? I really need to get out of here."

"No, Peter. It can't wait. Read it." He thrust the computer printout into Peter's hands and scrutinized his expression as the county administrator scanned the list of unfamiliar names. For a moment he had the distracted look of a busy man whose time is being wasted. Then he winced.

"Devin."

"Yes. My brother Devin's coming home."

Peter paused and his gaze seemed to look back twenty, thirty years. "Your brother; my friend. You'd think we'd be a little glad. Know what I mean?"

"You get used to things the way they are," said Ward. Not too many bumps. "Everything in its place."

"And some people's place is to be gone."

"We'll get used to him not gone just like we got used to him gone."

"Maybe not so easily," said Peter. "I love your brother, and he's trouble."

"I love my brother, too. And I hate myself for half wishing that he wasn't coming back."

Peter Bradford walked out into the daylight alone. His mind reeled and the sudden glare stung his eyes. He wrestled with his conflicting emotions about Devin Milford's imminent return. He'd worked so hard to establish order, to keep the peace, to maintain some semblance of normalcy among his neighbors. Yet he knew all that he'd achieved was fragile. He knew the unrest and the anger that remained, just waiting to be set off. He trembled to acknowledge that maybe he himself yearned secretly for the explosion. It was the kind of daydream he could not allow himself.

Suddenly, Peter was seized by an urgent longing to talk to and be comforted by his wife. Walking quickly across the town square, seeing nothing along the way, he hurried to the state-owned grocery store where he knew Amanda would be shopping. Amanda, as the wife of the county administrator, didn't need to stand in line with the others as they waited for their scanty rations of flour, vegetables, and sometimes meat. She chose to. The thought of special treatment was repellent to her.

"Peter," she said cheerfully as he moved toward her, "what brings you—"

"I need to talk to you," he said. "Come across to the park with me."

Startled by his urgency, Amanda Bradford hesitated. She glanced over her shoulder and thought of asking the woman in back of her to hold her place in line. But no, even that might be perceived as special privilege, might create resentment. She silently abandoned the queue and followed her husband.

Peter Bradford sat down on the edge of a battered bench, oblivious to the cold. His wife sat beside him. She reached for both his hands and tried to read his agitated face. "It's Devin . . ."

Amanda's first thought was that Devin Milford was dead. Her breath caught.

"He's coming home."

"Thank God." Amanda caught the fleeting wounded look on her husband's face, but it was already too late to explain. "When did he get out of the hospital?"

"He wasn't in the hospital, Amanda. He was in a prison camp."

"All this time?"

Peter nodded.

"Those bastards."

Peter moved toward her, then thought better of it, staying where he was, a little hurt, perhaps half angry.

"Yeah. Well, I thought you'd like to know."

"Oh, Peter," she said. "Don't. I hate what happened to Devin, and I'm glad he's going to be all right—whatever that means—but we've been married twenty years, for God's sake."

She took his arm, and he looked down at her sadly. "That's the way it is when you're second choice to a hero."

"He wasn't a hero when I married you—I'm not sure he's a hero now." She smiled. "I think you're a hero. You've held your family together and this county too. I don't love Devin Milford. I don't even know who he is anymore. I love you." Her eyes glistened. "For such a smart man, you can really be dumb sometimes."

She kissed him and he smiled almost bashfully. "And to think I risked my place in line for this," she kidded, feeling anew about Peter the way she always wanted to feel about him.

Chapter 4

FOR TWO HOURS they were shown "indoctrination" films: crude, committee-approved rhetoric about the administrative areas and the PPP and all the other glories of the Transition. Finally there was a lecture, warning the almost-ex-prisoners to be Good Citizens, to be Positive and Patriotic, lest they once again be declared "antisocial" and in need of "reeducation." Devin nearly shuddered at the prospect.

After the films, Devin and forty or fifty others were herded into a converted barracks that now contained a dozen green metal desks and twenty or so file cabinets left over from World War II. Each desk had a clerk behind it, checking records. In time, Devin was called before a thin and severe young woman who studied his file with a glazed expression.

"Your records were left in the truck from Fort Davis. That's why you had to wait so long." She spoke with a slow Texas drawl, her large brown eyes focusing on his file. "Are you somebody important?"

"No."

"Well, you got a red tag on your file and that usually means something important." She looked at the file again. "Huh. It says here you ran for president in 1992." She scrutinized Devin's face. "Is that a joke?"

"Yes."

She looked at him suspiciously. "You must've really screwed up. Were you a fascist?"

"No."

"It says here you were in a mental hospital too."

"No. They sent me to Fort Davis."

"Well, the file's probably screwed up. Most of them are. But if it's peachy with you, it's peachy with me." She regarded him again and smiled. "The prison record's what counts anyway and yours looks real good. You have to go through orientation and delousing and then the magistrate'll see you."

"What? We were cleaned at the camp."

The interview had ended. The young clerk closed Devin's file. "Next."

When Andrei's jet landed at Dulles Airport, west of Washington, a military helicopter was waiting to whisk him westward to the command headquarters of General Petya Samanov, an "adviser" to the American government. In fact, Samanov was the single most powerful man in the country.

His estate, Birdsong, was built in the 1790s by one of Virginia's first governors. The red-brick mansion sat atop a low hill, circled by oaks and lush farmland composed of gently rolling fields where generations of Virginia's finest, fleetest horses had grazed. A bronze plaque by the front door boasted that Washington,

Jefferson, Madison, and Monroe had all visited here, and Petya Samanov gloried in this connection.

Until the Transition, Birdsong had been a historic landmark, open to tourists, but it had fallen into disrepair until Petya chose it for his home and head-quarters. He kept an office in the White House, but it was here that he preferred to spend his time, amid the magnolias and the sweet-gum trees.

As his helicopter alighted in the field beside the mansion, Andrei admired its clever defense network. The casual visitor saw only the house and outbuildings, the barns, ponds, jumps, white fences, and tall trees; no one would discern the regiment of KGB border troops that was on duty in the bunker beneath the largest barn, or the squadron of attack helicopters less than a mile away, screened by century-old oaks. Petya could hardly have been safer in the Kremlin itself.

The hand-carved door of the graceful mansion flew open and Petya himself burst out of the vestibule, his arms outstretched. He was a tall, robust man of sixty, deeply tanned, with shrewd brown eyes, graying hair that was thinning on top, and long bushy sideburns. His quick and easy smile illuminated his face with friendly charm. He wore gray flannel trousers and a tweed jacket, as befit his role as country squire. Andrei took the steps two at a time and embraced his friend and mentor.

"My general," he said in Russian, truly moved.

"Andrei, my dear boy," Samanov said, in English. "It is such a delight to see you, even under these dubious circumstances. Come in, come in."

He led the way into a huge drawing room with fires roaring at either end, where two dozen men and a few beautiful young women were drinking and talking. The men, most of them old friends from university days, gathered around Andrei. They shook his hand, embraced him, and made jokes; soon Andrei was grinning like a schoolboy, relaxing as he never could in Chicago.

The men, primarily KGB officers, were dressed in business suits and looked quite American. Andrei took the women to be callgirls—they were Russian, for security's sake—invited by Petya for whatever moments of relaxation might occur.

"We are all here," Petya said. "All the area advisers, and the advisers to the South Florida Space Zone and the three International Cities."

"I hope I have not delayed you," Andrei said.

"We would wait for you forever, Andrei," Petya said with a wink. "Or at least another ten minutes. Come, we must begin."

He led the way into the dining room, where his guests left drinks and women behind and took their places around a long mahogany table whose surface was so exquisitely polished that it glinted. Elaborate silver sconces adorned one wall and on the opposite wall was an electronic overlay of the U.S. Petya Samanov stood before the map, his face somber now.

"Gentlemen," he began, speaking in Russian. "Comrades. We can all be proud. The men in this room have accomplished a peaceful occupation of a magnitude unprecedented in the history of the world. But for our efforts, what might have happened? Nuclear holocaust? Internal rebellion? We have bought time."

His guests glanced around uncertainly, sure he had not summoned them so urgently because he wanted to praise them.

As if reading their thoughts, Petya frowned and continued. "However, much remains to be done. There is continued unrest in the Soviet Union. Moreover, there are problems here in America. Alaska has never been pacified and it is costing us ten divisions, plus an unacceptable amount of air power, just to control it. There are lesser pockets of resistance in the Rockies and West Virginia.

"You know the details; I will not belabor them. The central committee met yesterday in Moscow. There was, I am told, much anger and impatience. The committee demands that America be neutralized immediately."

The men around the table were confused; America *was* neutralized, was it not? It was Andrei, whose intimacy with Samanov was well known, who dared speak.

"Sir. America is a country without arms or an army. There is little or no communication between areas. The people are self-occupied and dispirited. What more is wanted?"

A smile played on Petya's lips. "Our brothers in the Kremlin fear ghosts—the ghosts of American power and independence. At yesterday's meeting a most serious antighost measure was discussed. A certain faction proposes to explode low-yield nuclear devices upon one or more American cities, as a demonstration of our resolve."

"Which cities, Comrade General?" one KGB officer asked.

"None in Virginia, I trust," Samanov said dryly. "Gentlemen, the point is that we are under great pressure. Our timetables must be accelerated. The Kremlin fears that Americans may realize they have options. Not military options, of course, but they could organize and refuse to cooperate. They could unite in spirit. They could provoke us to take actions none of us wants. We must move quickly. I have a plan, the only one I believe will avert disaster. The United States of

America must cease to exist. It must be reformed, broken up into separate countries, based upon the administrative areas you now direct. Only such a demonstration of American helplessness, I am convinced, will prevent the extreme elements in the Kremlin from proceeding with their nuclear demonstration."

There was a long, startled silence. The KGB officers, men not easily shocked, exchanged astonished glances. Again, it was Andrei who spoke. "General, we here today seem to be in a most difficult position. We must negotiate some sort of balance between those in the Kremlin who want this nation utterly prostrate, and the Americans themselves, who wish to cling to some semblance of dignity and independence."

"Well put, Andrei," Samanov said.

"Thank you, General, but it is only a pretty phrase. To reconcile those objectives, we need a plan that all concerned can live with."

"And that," said Samanov, without missing a beat, "is precisely what we have. The specific mechanism for dismantling the United States will be what we are calling the Third Continental Congress. The whole idea will be to *persuade* Americans that they are participating in the process, not that they are being forced. This will require tact and subtlety. We must do in a few months what took the Romans generations—we must develop an indigenous ruling class, Americans who look to us for leadership yet have the trust of their fellow citizens."

Petya lowered his head and spoke now in a different tone. "Too often, the world has viewed us Russians as a rude, uncultured people. It is a lie! We are the nation of Tolstoi, of Chekhov, of Pushkin, of Tchaikovsky. We are a great and sensitive people. The eyes of the world are upon us, and it is our great and historic responsibility to make this occupation a humane one."

Andrei Denisov had heard this speech, or others like it, often enough to follow along by rote. But he wasn't listening. He was already thinking how Petya's plan might be implemented in his home territory.

Amanda took a seat at the back of the darkened, nearly empty auditorium just as her daughter began to dance.

Jackie seemed buoyed up by the recorded music as she gyrated masterfully across the stage alone. She'd chosen a piece by Aaron Copland for this audition— "Fanfare for the Common Man," a raucous tone poem that was kinetic, vibrant, redolent of American myth. It called for movements that were expansive, loose-limbed, muscular, for strutting postures that might be feminine but could never be finicky. In her stark white leotard and with a single red ribbon holding back her hair, Jackie mimed a physical wisdom beyond her years. She was part dervish, part temptress. She was riveting.

When Jackie had stepped onto the stage, Amanda's face had been unconsciously composed into the mixture of interest and support that mothers have always worn when their children performed, recited, or played a sport. But by the time Jackie turned and flipped into the handstand she'd worked so long to perfect, Amanda's mouth had dropped slightly open, her eyes just a bit wider with the awe that anyone, parent or not, feels at a great performance. She had almost forgotten that Jackie was her daughter in those last uplifting moments of movement; she was transfixed simply by the technical expertise and deep emotion that a performer was conveying to an audience.

The music stopped, and as the other contestants broke into unrestrained, even enthusiastic applause, Jackie was abruptly an anxious teenager again—thrilled with her dance, yet eager for approval. Soon all eyes were on the judges, three women with clipboards, staff members of the all-powerful Area Cultural Committee in Chicago. They conferred, huddled over their note pads, until finally one of them rose, a thin, plain, intense woman in a dark suit.

"The committee would like to thank all of you. Dance is such a joyous expression, with a long tradition. As we have traveled the last three weeks to these area tryouts throughout the Central Administrative Area, it has been very gratifying to see so much interest in the return to traditional dance, with its grace and discipline, after the undisciplined and unseemly contortions of recent years. Thank you again. Mrs. Knox will let you know the results."

Amanda saw Jackie's face fall. The woman's words were an unmistakable slap at the modern dance that Jackie loved—and had just performed—and a defense of the classical ballet that was officially favored by the Russians, in America as well as in their own country.

Amanda stood up, crestfallen. The judges stood in front of the stage, saying their goodbyes. Amanda gathered her courage and walked slowly down the aisle. She stood there a moment until one of the judges noticed her and smiled stiffly.

"Yes?"

"I'm Amanda Bradford," she said, holding back her anger. And that was not easily done. Too much had happened that day. The child in her yard, the news about Devin, and now this woman's cruel rejection of Jackie.

"Jacqueline's mother," the teacher, Mrs. Knox, prompted.

"Yes," the judge said. "And you're concerned that my comments were directed at your daughter."

"I'm concerned about the fairness of the judging process," Amanda said tersely.

"There's a lot more to these competitions than being a potentially good dancer, Mrs. Bradford."

"My daughter was wonderful. How can you possibly not give her a chance?"

"We're looking for the kind of dancer who is able to become part of a corps—one of a group expressing the kind of spirit and attitude we'd like to see in our young people." The woman's face was a frozen mask; Amanda realized that she could never penetrate her wall of ideology.

Moments later, in the car, Amanda embraced her weeping daughter. "Oh honey, it makes me so damn mad. I could kill."

Jacqueline stopped crying, gaining control. "Could you really, Mother?" The question hung between them as they drove away.

Finally, in late afternoon, the group of Fort Davis prisoners reached the courtroom. It was a small, drab box with walls painted a hospital green and the sour smell of industrial soap in the air. The chamber was adorned only by the US-UN-USSR flag above the judge's bench. Devin waited his turn before the magistrate, fighting the rising panic in him.

"83915," the judge droned, without looking up.

"83915, sir," Devin parroted back.

"Devin William Milford, you are assigned to live in the town of Milford, Nebraska, and not to travel more than twenty-five miles from there for any reason." The judge paused a moment, as though trying to remember something. "You're Devin Milford?" he asked, for the first time looking directly at the man before him.

"Yes, sir."

The judge seemed undecided, as if he wanted to say something, to establish human contact. The hesitation passed. He met Devin's eyes for a moment, and Devin looked away. At once, the judge resumed his business-like tone. "You will reside at the home of your father, William Bradley Milford. You will report without fail to the designated authorities once each week. If you violate your parole, you will be returned to confinement. Do you understand?"

"Yessir."

"Next case," the judge intoned.

"Sir." Devin felt the bailiff grasp his arm, but he stood firm. "My children, I have to see them. I—"

"You have your instructions," the judge snapped, cutting him off. "Bailiff."

Devin turned and walked to the back of the courtroom. The guard at the door looked at him and smiled. "Well, how's it feel to be a free man?"

Andrei was back in his Chicago office by late afternoon. Still disturbed by the meeting with Petya, he sought diversion by watching the films Mikel had assembled of Devin Milford's doomed campaign for president. Milford, Andrei acknowledged, had been a magnetic figure; there was power and passion in him, a brutal candor, and a tide of restless energy. Yet there was also a quality of injured innocence in Devin that was peculiarly American. Andrei recognized that innocence as both his strength and his weakness.

On the monitor, Devin Milford delivered his campaign speech: "Since the takeover by the Soviet Union and the shift by which the United Nations has become its surrogate, we have remained concerned with our own individual, selfish interests, ignoring that we are one people, interdependent.

"What we thought was impossible has happened," Milford continued on the TV screen. "We have been subjugated by a foreign power. And if we are honest, we cannot blame our defeat on the EMP or the original surrender. We must blame it on the condition of our society before those things happened. On our loss of purpose, our lack of vision, our lack of faith in ourselves and—"

The door opened and a shaft of light cut across the screen. Kimberly was ushered in by Mikel.

"What's this?" she asked.

"Devin Milford. He tried to run for president once."

"He's very attractive."

"He should have been shot," Mikel said.

"He was released today after five years in a prison camp."

Kimberly wrinkled her nose. "I guess he's not so attractive anymore." Andrei looked at her, a twinkle in his eye, and said, "A lesson to us all."

All three of them were drawn back to the image on the screen. After a moment Kimberly said, "I don't remember seeing him before."

"He was denied access to the media. He traveled across the east making this speech and gaining support. When he started to become a threat, we removed him from the race." He switched off the tape.

"Why are you watching this now?" she asked.

"He's the closest thing to a true leader your country

has produced during the Transition. I need to understand, and prevent, such phenomena."

"But you have all the power, all the weapons."

"It is a cliché, Kimberly, but true, that ideas are more powerful than guns. Most people do not understand that, or believe it, but Milford did. A French philosopher once noted that courage is the only emotion that is more contagious than fear. This man has, or had, five years ago, the kind of courage that has toppled more secure empires than ours. So I am interested in the nature of Milford's appeal and whether five years of the reeducation process has had the desired effect upon him."

"I'm surprised you didn't just kill him, if he was such a threat."

Andrei's face clouded and by reflex he cast a hard glance at Mikel. "Killing is rather barbaric and ultimately counterproductive."

"As counterproductive," put in Mikel, "as indulgence sometimes is."

"Mikel," said Andrei, "didn't you have some correspondence to attend to?"

Scowling, the aide left the office, and Kimberly nervously lit a cigarette.

"What is it, darling?" asked Andrei, seeing the trouble in her face. "I thought you had rehearsal this afternoon on your new play."

"I did. It's about Robert Shelter. The man who wrote my play. Someone arrested him. I know you're too busy to check on everything that happens, but—"

Andrei interrupted. "I ordered it."

Kimberly was shocked. "Why? How could you?"

"The outlaw theaters are getting out of hand. I have been entirely too lax. They are proliferating and as they ridicule the government—they are getting dangerous."

Kimberly looked at him, his words sinking in. "I'm going to do Robert's satire."

Andrei shook his head, looking more like a father dealing with a willful teenager than a man speaking to his lover. "You do this, it is at your own risk."

She turned angrily and headed toward the door.

"Kimberly. I am not free to do anything I want, the way I want. I have superiors to whom I must answer. I am surrounded by spies and informers—both American and Soviet. There are old men in the Kremlin who have always been, and still are, suspicious of our entire plan of occupation. They would feel much more comfortable with America crushed by an iron fist. And they may yet do it."

She watched him a moment, then walked out the door. Andrei turned back to his desk.

Peter Bradford sighed as he stopped the Wagoneer in his driveway and saw the Harley. He promised himself he'd be civil to Justin, if only out of respect for the Milfords. But as a father he couldn't be expected to approve of this romance. Justin had no future; it was that simple. Maybe he'd gotten a raw deal because of Devin, but the local PPP would never give him a college recommendation, or a travel permit, or an employment certification. Justin was left with few options: a laborer's job, if he were lucky, jail or exile if he continued his "antisocial" behavior.

Peter got out of his car and headed for the back door just as Jacqueline and Justin came through the front door. "Hi Justin. Where are you guys going?"

"Out for a ride," Justin answered.

"You got gas?"

"Sure, corn gas," Justin replied, smiling. "Borrowed from the tractor."

Peter looked at his daughter, who kept her face slightly averted from him. "Honey, can I speak to you for a minute?"

"What for?" Her eyes were still red from crying after her disappointment that afternoon at the dance tryouts.

"Just come here, please. Excuse us, Justin."

"Sure." He shrugged, watching Jackie. She followed her father back into the house and then stopped at the door, remaining a dozen feet behind him. Peter realized instantly that she would come no closer.

"Where are you going?"

"We told you. Out. For a ride."

"I don't like you going out with him."

"Really? I'd never guess. You're so subtle."

"Look, Jackie. He's a loser. And you're not. It doesn't make sense."

"I like him. His father works for you."

"And I can tell you that boy is no source of pride to the Milfords."

"Well, that's what's important, all right," she snapped, and headed for the door.

He did not want to fight. "Look, your mom and I have to go to Omaha. I don't want you out after curfew."

She turned to look at him, tears in her eyes. "God, Daddy, you don't understand anything." She raced from the house and moments later he heard the roar of the motorcycle. Peter shook his head, wondering what he had done wrong.

An hour later, Peter, in his best suit and tie, and Amanda, dressed in a simple blue evening gown, were speeding along the freeway toward Omaha. They had an armed escort, two UNSSU motorcyclists, their red lights flashing. The lights blotted the stars out of the vast midwestern sky.

"These escorts make me feel like a fool," Peter grumbled.

"Worse yet, they make you look like the enemy."

"Thanks."

"I gather you had words with Jackie and Justin when they left."

"She knows how I feel about that boy."

"Did you ask Jackie how her day went?"

"I didn't have time. Why, something special?"

"Tryouts for the district company."

"Damn, I forgot. How'd it go?"

"She was rejected."

"Somebody beat her out?"

"Yes, the bitches who were doing the judging."

"Why?"

"She was too good. Too original. Too individual." She laughed darkly. "All the things we taught her to be."

"What the hell does that mean?"

"It means the judges denounced modern dance. They want the Bolshoi in Nebraska. Politically acceptable ballet. You know what one of them had the nerve to say to me? 'Sometimes cooperation is more important than talent.'"

"Somebody actually told her that?"

"They told me. But we know all about cooperation, don't we?" she said bitterly.

"That's not fair."

"Jackie losing isn't fair. I watched it. She was amazing."

"Maybe I can look into it."

"You'd better do a damned sight more than just look into it. She's our daughter and she deserves to have a chance."

"Everybody feels that way."

"I don't care. Everybody's not as good as she is."

"Settle down," he said quietly. "I know you're upset . . ."

"Look, Peter. I understand why I have to stand in line for tomatoes, and why Scott has to sneak extra meat from the training table when you could have practically anything you wanted delivered to the back door, but this is different. This is your daughter's life and I don't know whether it'll be worth a damn—but she has a right . . . not to be penalized for being good."

"You don't think I love her as much as you do?"

Amanda looked out into the darkness at the emptiness of the barren fields and deserted highway. "I don't know. Maybe. Sometimes I think what you love most is some idea of what's fair you carry around in your head."

"None of this is fair. We have to hang on to what we believe in."

Amanda realized that she had gone too far. She saw the hurt on Peter's face and regretted having caused it. She took his hand, not wanting the evening to be lost. "I believe in my daughter. I believe in you—maybe sometimes I even believe in myself. That's all I believe in."

Peter squeezed her hand. She took his arm and put it around her shoulders, sliding across the seat next to him like a teenager. She put her head on his shoulder.

The car, with its motorcycle escort, disappeared into the night.

Justin, with Jackie hanging on behind him, piloted the old Harley along a moonlit, tree-flanked country road. He kept his lights off. He knew the way, and at the proper moment he steered across a field to an abandoned barn that loomed dark and ominous against the moon-bright, snowy fields. He turned off the engine and a heavy blast of rock music, forbidden by the authorities, rang out in the sudden quiet.

"You sure you still want to go?" he asked. "Omaha's rough and gettin' there is dangerous."

"Good," she said.

"Jackie, I don't want you to get hurt."

"I won't get hurt."

She wondered if he understood how her life had changed that day, when those judges had rejected her dance, had shattered her dream. She looked at Justin, touched by his concern, and somehow felt older than he, wiser, ready for whatever came.

Justin shrugged and pulled his goggles off. "Okay, then let's party."

They hurried into the barn and were greeted by about a dozen teenagers. Lanterns cast long, eerie shadows across a floor still strewn with hay. Couples danced amid the bales as bottles of homemade wine circulated along with homegrown joints. Jackie took a swig of the wine and, when a joint made its way to her, considered taking a hit.

Justin pulled her close. "Hey, you don't do that stuff, remember?" She looked at him defiantly, then laughed. "Just take it easy," he said. "It'll be a long night."

"Not long enough for me," she said.

Andrei arranged to receive Marion Andrews in his office while Kimberly was still dressing. The three of them would take the flight together, but he knew that Marion would expect time alone with him. He didn't mind; he thought she was one of the most interesting American women he had met. She had become a powerful political figure in the PPP stronghold of Chicago, and she was also Petya Samanov's mistress— an intoxicating combination.

Marion swept in, elegant as always in a blur of French perfume, pale blue silk, and glowing pearls. "Marion, you look stunning," he said, kissing her cheek. "Petya sends his love."

"I'm jealous. You saw him today, and I haven't been with him in two weeks."

"He plans to rectify that situation very soon," Andrei said. "Can I fix you a drink?"

"No, thank you. We have a long night ahead."

"As you wish," said Andrei. "But tell me what is on your mind."

"I hate to trouble you with what may seem a personal matter."

Andrei sat beside her on the sofa. "I understand from Mikel that your former husband has been released and you are concerned for your safety and that of your sons."

Her eyes darted quickly to meet Andrei's stare. "I don't know why they paroled him," she said bitterly.

"I imagine he's rehabilitated," he said. "Otherwise he wouldn't have been released."

"He could be dangerous. He should never have been freed. Maybe there was a bureaucratic error," she continued.

"I understand you have police protection."

"Yes. But that's not enough. I want assurance that he never leaves Milford County."

Andrei nodded. "I've given this some thought, Marion. You know Peter Bradford, the Milford County administrator?"

"Of course I do. He was Devin's best friend—they were in Vietnam together. I haven't seen him in years."

"Is he a man you would trust?"

She gave the question a moment's thought. "Yes. He's an effective administrator." She paused for a moment. "He's not a stooge, if that's what you mean."

"I'm going to meet him tonight at the Omaha dinner. Maybe he would find it in his interest to look after your husband. I'll make it clear that certain bureaucratic plums he wants for this county depend on his satisfying me on this matter."

Marion smiled for the first time that evening. "Thank you, Andrei."

"Tell me more about Peter Bradford," he said.

"He's not particularly imaginative or ambitious politically. People like him. I imagine he is a good county administrator."

"Excellent. He's emerged as a dark-horse candidate for governor-general of the entire five-state Central Administrative Area. The Heartland, as it will soon be called."

"You know the party advisory committee supports Governor Smith of Missouri."

"The wonderful thing about advisory committees is that you can always tell them what to advise."

Marion nodded. "He's not dangerous like Devin, there's nothing visionary about him. But there's this streak of midwestern stubbornness in him. You might regret such an appointment."

"The question is, can a man serve two masters? Could Peter Bradford, a patriotic American, serve our interests and those of his own people too?"

She smiled icily. "That depends on who defines those interests."

Andrei looked at his watch. "Kimberly should be here soon. The plane is waiting."

"Oh, you're still seeing your actress?"

"Yes."

"Appearance and illusion."

"Beauty and soul," he countered.

"Instability."

"Madness."

Marion laughed. "Yes. I forgot. With you that would be a virtue."

Kimberly arrived, and walked into their conversation. She was dressed elegantly in a low-cut, black sequined gown. "I'm not interrupting, am I?" She kissed Andrei. He breathed deeply against her hair, which gave off a scent of hothouse orchids.

"Not at all." Marion rose from the couch. "You look beautiful."

"I'll second that," Andrei said, moving toward the door. "Ladies, shall we?"

The gilt and red plush ballroom of Omaha's Riverfront Hotel was packed with several hundred middle-aged county administrators and their spouses. Streamers and balloons adorned the huge room, and, above the speaker's platform, a giant U.S.-UN-USSR flag hung limp amid blue clouds of cigar smoke.

Kimberly, backed by a twelve-piece band, was singing "Younger Than Springtime." The music, and the women's gowns—carefully preserved, most of them, from pre-Transition days, and vaguely brittle—created a kind of time warp, as if the Forties or Fifties had somehow returned. Peter and Amanda were among the dancers, Amanda humming along with the music, eyes closed.

"Reminds me of the senior prom," Peter said. "Wanna neck?" Peter spun Amanda around expertly. She laughed, her tension melting away. "Glad you came?"

"Sure, but what's it all about?"

"Coordination. Regional unity. All that good stuff."

"What was the call from Chicago about?"

"Nothing, really."

"Chicago calls for nothing?"

"Well, we've had a good production record, and I may get some award or something."

"My hero."

Kimberly concluded her medley with "I'm Gonna Wash That Man Right out of My Hair." "Let's go outside," Amanda said, taking Peter's hand.

He guided her onto a terrace that overlooked the Missouri River; mist rose lazily from the placid water.

"Do you remember," asked Amanda, "when we were first going out, you used to hold your breath during a kiss. I always expected you to suddenly turn blue and keel over."

"That's what you were thinking about when we kissed?"

"After we had been married a few years you learned to breathe."

He laughed and shook his head.

"I remember the first time we made love—I had this terrible thought: what if he has to hold his breath? That'll be ninety seconds maximum."

Peter couldn't believe what he was hearing. "You did not."

"Absolutely. The important thing is *you* did not."

They hugged affectionately, listening to the songs that continued from inside, making the moment seem a suspension of time. Amanda turned in his arms and looked at the river.

"Sometimes—it seems as though nothing has happened."

Peter nodded. "You know what I always wanted to

do? Just get on that river—take it down through Kansas and Missouri, all the way to the Gulf. Devin and I—well, it was Devin's idea. We were reading *Huckleberry Finn*. We must've been nine, or maybe eleven or twelve. Anyway, his old man called the state police. They found us about a half hour after we'd launched our raft—probably about fifteen minutes before we would've sunk."

Amanda smiled. "I'm game."

"We'd better get back in."

"No guts, huh?"

"We'd have to carry too many travel permits," he said, pulling them abruptly back to the present. "No room for your knapsack."

They had just returned to the noisy ballroom when a young man in a dark suit stopped them.

"Mr. Peter Bradford?"

"Yes."

"Colonel Denisov would like a word with you."

"Of course." He shrugged to Amanda. "Save my place."

Ward Milford had feared it might go this way. The old man hadn't had a good word to say about Devin in more than two years. For that matter, he hadn't exactly been jumping up and down about Devin's campaign platform back in 1992, all that fiery rhetoric that sounded to a conservative man-of-the-farm like revolutionary talk. But when Devin had disappeared . . . that was it. Traitor. He might as well have been a terrorist.

"Well, that gives the bastard twenty-four and a half miles to stay away from here," Will spat out when told Devin would be restricted to a twenty-five-mile radius.

Ward argued, standing up for his brother, if only

because there was no one else to do it. Certainly not Alethea, who left the table almost as soon as the subject came up and the volume of conversation, in turn, did likewise. And certainly not Ward's wife Betty, who knew trying to sway Will Milford would be like convincing a river to flow upstream. Nonetheless, she fed Ward an occasionally supportive half smile during the argument and, ultimately, followed him through the swinging door when he opted for the quiet of the kitchen.

He stood at the sink, calming himself, his face a portrait of frustration. Betty leaned against the refrigerator and waited until Ward first shook his head and then grinned, almost sheepishly.

"Guess I should have known better, huh?"

She smiled and moved to him, touching his arm. "He'll have to get used to the idea. Just like with the squatters."

Ward grinned and gave a short, sardonic chuckle. "If he gets used to it that well, we're in for some real good times around here."

"That'd be a switch."

The two stood silently for a long moment. Ward broke it, wrapping his arms around her in a brief bear hug and then heading for the side door. "Gotta make the rounds," he said almost apologetically. He opened the door to leave but paused as he noticed her faraway expression. "What?"

"I wonder if we'll find out what happened?"

He shrugged, feeling a little strange by his own answer. "I don't reckon it makes a lot of difference now."

Betty studied his eyes and expression. "I suppose not. But it sure was strange. He was one of the few people who really tried to do something, and then—

gone. Like he just fell apart or something." She shook her head. "I don't know. When the going got tough . . . and with so many people counting on him."

"Yeah, I guess maybe they were," Ward said, suddenly bitter. "Maybe they shoulda counted on themselves a little." And he closed the door behind him.

Ward wheeled the patrol car down the poplar-lined driveway, swerving to avoid the black UNSSU Rover parked at the intersection with the main road.

"Shit," he muttered, glancing as he drove at the dark, tinted windows of the Rover and the shadowy driver inside. "Alethea's carriage awaits."

Major Helmut Gurtman, the German-born SSU commander for Nebraska, had been Alethea's lover for more than a year. The affair had not gone unnoticed in her little hometown; it had caused many of her friends to scorn her and poisoned Will Milford's love for his only daughter.

After the dinner's angry turn that evening, Alethea was only too glad to make her exit. But as always, her anticipation was double-edged. Pleasure and degradation would be blended in her evening's activity.

The driver of the Rover, a bearded Cuban she had seen before, didn't bother to disguise his admiration for her appearance, and as she watched him watching her in the rearview mirror, she felt an excitement well within her. Helmut looked at her that way, as if he were mentally undressing her. Alethea asked the driver for a cigarillo and he promptly produced one, taking his time to light it, making it clear that Alethea's lips would touch the filter where he'd held his mouth. His gaze lingered as she crossed her legs. She closed her eyes, inhaled deeply, and thought of Helmut. His hair was long and fine and brown, and his eyes so dark they seemed to blot out the light. For Alethea, he held an allure of sexuality and power that was somehow heightened by the guilt she felt every time she wanted him.

"You look quite lovely tonight," Helmut said when she arrived, and handed her a fluted glass brimming with French champagne, splashing a bit on her arm as he did so.

She looked, in fact—in her tight, black satin dress, spiked heels, and garish makeup—like an expensive whore.

"But why so glum?"

"It isn't easy trying to teach that Lincoln and Lenin stood for the same thing," she said, her words laced with bitterness.

"Ah. And I assume this is why I continue to receive the most amazing reports about you, that your history lessons reflect a most, shall we say, pugnacious and retrograde Americanism."

She was silent.

"It is also said that you have visited the exile camps and taught the children there."

"Oh, are they the enemies of the people, too?"

He shrugged. "The sins of the fathers."

"God, that's a laugh, you quoting the Bible."

He grabbed her by the hair suddenly and jerked her head close to his, then, almost in the same motion, caressed the back of her neck.

"That hurt," she said timidly.

He held her face close to his, flaunting the domination that was so much a part of their relationship. His tone was almost taunting, sweet and cruel at once: "What am I to do with you?"

He kissed her, hard, then tightened his grip on the

hair above her neck, pulling her lips a scant three inches from his. The two remained poised in that position, as if awaiting a signal, or an answer.

"You bastard," she said softly, the timidity now replaced by something else. Something sexual.

He kissed her hard again.

She did not resist.

She never did.

The club known as the Cavern sprawled through the basement of an abandoned warehouse on the outskirts of Omaha. The place was dim, noisy, and illegal. It echoed like an airplane hangar and smelled like a brewery. Its only concessions to decor were some ancient cable-spool tables and rickety chairs with generations of initials carved into their backs. Some nights, kids showed up and found the club locked and deserted. Police raids, they said. But it always opened up again.

No one seemed to understand how the Cavern stayed in business. The youths who ran the place didn't answer questions; they took in money and after that the club seemed to run itself. There were rumors of payoffs to the police, or that the authorities viewed the club as an escape valve where kids could blow off steam. Whatever the reason, the Cavern was the only place in the state where teenagers could dance to live rock and meet kids from other towns. It was an outlaw club, with an aura of danger as pungent as the clouds of marijuana smoke that wafted through it, and it was very popular.

A kind of hybrid rock and roll was blasting from a band attempting to recapture a free and abandoned style of music. Very few people in the Cavern that night had ever heard "real" rock before. To them, rock was a kind of forbidden religion—one whose idols they worshiped gladly, yet one that might have come to them from another century.

Jackie, Justin, and their friends arrived, and gathered around a long table. Jackie felt exhilarated to be part of a world where people her age could be what they really were and not what somebody a million years old wanted them to be.

The band plunged into "Johnny B. Goode" and Jackie and Justin got up and started to dance. She made every step look good, her movements rough and sensual. It was as though the music expressed itself perfectly through her, as though its anger and hunger had found a natural outlet.

They sat a few songs out, drank and talked, then danced again. The music had an intensity that could not be ignored.

As if the place needed to cool down, the band went into a medley of dreamy old ballads. Songs like "In the Still of the Night," "Teen Angel," and "It's All in the Game." Jackie melted into Justin's arms. The sound of blaring whistles and wailing sirens shattered her reverie.

"It's a raid!" someone yelled.

Everyone who had been on the dance floor or at a table began to run. People screamed and raced in every direction. Jackie, terrified and immobile, panicked at the thought of being separated from Justin by the bodies plunging all around her. But Justin deftly reached through the churning crowd and grabbed her hand. He squeezed it and said, "Keep cool. I'll try to get us out of here. If they catch us, don't tell them your real name."

He pulled her back to their table. Puncher was

standing on a chair, looking for an escape route. One of the kids from Omaha ran up to them. "Follow me," he shouted above the whistles and yelling.

There was an instant of indecision. The kids from Milford all looked toward Justin. He nodded once, and they all followed the boy from Omaha. He led them behind the bandstand to a trapdoor, then squeezed through it and ran along a dark, narrow passageway. Screams and whistles followed Jackie as she held tight to Justin's hand and sprinted through the darkness toward an open door. They all poured out into an alley.

"Oh God, we made it," one of the girls said, and broke into tears.

"Okay, we've got to split up and find our cars," Justin said. "Keep in the shadows."

Suddenly a powerful searchlight pierced the dark alley, encircling and trapping them all. Jackie was blinded. She heard dogs barking, then a wailing siren and men yelling, "Nobody move!"

"Cops!" Puncher roared. "Run!"

For an instant Jackie froze, her pulse pounding in her temples. Justin seized her arm above the elbow. "Come on," he hissed. They raced down the alley with police and dogs in pursuit.

High atop one of the buildings a block from the alley, a group of men were watching.

The door to Andrei's suite was left ajar. A young man escorted Peter in, then left quickly. It was a comfortable suite, not grand. Peter's eyes moved to the terrace where a figure stood, silhouetted against a dark, wintry evening. The sound of police sirens cut into the night. Peter walked to Andrei, disturbing his reverie. The Russian turned toward the source of the interruption.

"I'd like to show you something," said Andrei.

Peter approached him. In the distance he could see the fracas between the police and kids. The helicopters, searchlights, and popping sounds of tear gas exploding seemed unreal.

"What's going on?" he asked, without taking his eyes away from the disruptive scene.

"On our reports we call them 'disturbances.' It is young people attacking symbols of power. Those they can see—your president, senators, public buildings, the police, of course. It makes them feel they are accomplishing something. What's your opinion of such disturbances?"

"Pretty stupid. Sad, actually."

Andrei watched him carefully, waiting to see if Peter might retract his candid opinion. "It is controlled provocation. Agents stir up the young people so we can let them feel rebellious at the same time that we can keep track of them—scare them, arrest some, perhaps even move them to other parts of the area."

Peter continued to watch the disturbance, his jaw set tight. He was not in favor of such manipulative tactics; he found them repugnant.

"I can see you do not approve. What would you do?"

"I guess I'd try to find a way to use the energy a little more productively."

"For whom? You or us?"

"Maybe both."

Andrei raised his eyebrows. "Do you think that is possible?"

"It better be."

Graciously, with an old-world ease Americans still found surprising, Andrei motioned Peter back into the warmth of the sitting room. When he spoke again, his tone was thoughtful, speculative. "You know, Bradford, no one in the Kremlin believed America would go down without a fight. They thought it would take a bloodbath—or a nuclear attack."

"I guess it surprised us, too. The country was filled with millions of guns. And we supposedly had a tradition of not letting anyone tell us what to do."

"Maybe it had become just that—a tradition. Perhaps you had just gotten too soft, too selfish, too afraid of losing what you had to protect it."

"We had no plan. At first it was our own troops just keeping order. Then the UNSSU Peacekeeping teams. By the time anyone realized what was going on, the Special Service Units were completely in place and they seemed invulnerable. Not to mention the communication problem. Nobody had any idea what was going on anywhere else."

"I'll let you in on a secret Soviet strategy. We believed that the Electro Magnetic Pulse would disrupt your military communications enough for us to succeed. And your banking system. What we didn't expect was that without communications the United States would revert to a collection of separate peoples— separate regions. We've just restricted communications from area to area—with the intent to diminish the sense of national unity, of common purpose, so to speak. And it worked. People in one area don't care about anything but what happens to them."

"You just got the drop on us," Peter said somewhat defensively.

"You don't believe that. We both know the Soviet plan worked because you lost your country before we ever got here."

Peter stared incredulously at Andrei. "You sound disappointed that you succeeded."

Andrei did not respond. Suddenly he felt as if he had

been a little too open with Mr. Bradford. "Why is it you wish to help us?"

Peter appeared shocked. "I don't wish to help you. I wish to help my country."

"There is no country."

"My people then. My family—my community."

"Why do you think we should accept that your purposes and ours are compatible?"

"I'm not saying that you should accept it. You asked for this meeting."

There was a burst of fire in the street. They both watched the people below scattering like apples from an overturned cart.

"I'm enough of a realist," Peter continued, "to know you're not going to let America become a threat to you." He looked at Andrei. "But maybe there's a way for us to pull together more as an area. Hell, give us an incentive. Give us the incentive of getting rid of the occupation and maybe we'll prove that we can function and not be a threat."

Andrei turned from the disturbance and looked at Peter, somewhat solemn. "It's a tragedy, isn't it? A great country, a great idea. You have no idea how many people looked to the American experiment as the answer—the hope. Now we'll never know."

"What?"

"Whether it would have destroyed itself anyway."

As Justin, Jackie, and their Milford friends moved warily toward their cars, Justin looked down the street back toward the club and saw the Cavern disc jockey casually chatting with a police officer.

"It was a setup," he declared, climbing into the station wagon. "Can you believe this bullshit?"

He whipped the car down a deserted alley, taking

evasive action even though it seemed they were not being followed. But within seconds, the headlights of another vehicle cut into the empty street behind them.

"Jus, there's a police car back there," Puncher said, his voice sticking in his throat.

Justin skidded around the next corner at fifty, and the other car followed close behind. They drove without lights toward the outskirts of the city, the police cruiser always following too close for comfort. After several miles the cars headed down a country road along the river. Justin drove carefully and slowly for a bit, stringing their pursuers along. Then, swiftly, with screaming tires and groaning axles, he cut the car sharply down an overgrown dirt path. After a few moments of inky darkness on all sides, they knew they'd gotten away. Justin drove a bit farther, then stopped the car and, for the first time since fleeing the Cavern, looked over to Jackie. She sat shaking quietly beside him. He moved closer and put his arms around her, holding her tenderly. She reached up and kissed him hungrily, almost desperately, the unaccustomed wine spicing her breath. With nervous laughs born of a close call, the others in the backseat egged Justin on until he turned back angrily and demanded quiet.

They all drove back to Milford in silence, exhausted from the chase. About a half mile from the barn, Justin pulled the wagon to the side of the road and the pickup followed suit. Before Jackie knew what was going on, he'd managed to persuade everyone in the wagon to hitch a ride to the barn in the back of the pickup. Suddenly, after all the bodies, all the noise, all the racing and dancing and running, they were completely alone.

Justin grabbed the handle and ripped the car door open. He pulled Jackie out of the car with him and they stumbled a short ways down a wooded path. He held her to him, listening to the night sounds around them. Over her shoulder, he could see a stream with a mass of ice chunks bobbing by, their whiteness caught by the moonlight.

"Sorry, Jackie," he said, still holding her close. "This was really stupid. We're like a bunch of kids—not Resisters. We don't even know what we're for or what we're against." He held her at arm's length and studied her tear-streaked face. "Let me tell you, if I ever ask you to do anything with me again, I'll make damn sure that I know what I'm doing. Okay?"

It was as if she weren't listening. She leaned into him again, kissing him passionately. He held her, confused by her behavior.

"I want to make love," she said finally.

"Jackie—"

"Maybe we'll never get a chance. Maybe we'll be killed trying to get home. I want—"

"Stop it, Jackie. I love you. I want to make love to you." He paused. "I always want to make love to you, but not like this. I'm standing here listening to you and I feel like—well, like it doesn't matter who you're with tonight, like I don't matter . . ."

He shrugged, unable to complete his thought. She looked away from him and stared into the stream. She said nothing, just stood there sighing and shaking her head. When she finally spoke, her voice sounded melancholy.

"We're never going to have anything, are we, Justin? I love you, but it's like all our life is going to be like . . ." She sighed again as if it were all too much for her to understand. "I don't know. Forget it, it's nothing."

Justin grabbed her, forcing her to look at him. "No,

it isn't. There's going to be something, I promise. It's just not going to be this."

He pulled her into his arms, staring up at the gibbous moon, swearing silently that one day he would give her all the things he could not give her now. "C'mon. I've got to get you home."

After Peter had been led away to meet with Andrei, Amanda found herself alone and uncomfortable, surrounded by strangers she did not care to know. But her loneliness in the glittering ballroom did not last long; she had no sooner reached the sanctuary of her table when Marion Andrews joined her. They had never been friends in the old days, really; at best, they were acquaintances who didn't travel in the same circles. Now, their dissimilarities polarity seemed even more distinct—Marion a political powerhouse and a mannequin for haute couture, Amanda a country wife wanting only her old serenity—and yet here was Marion, magistrate and PPP disciple, talking with Amanda as if they had always been the best of pals. To Amanda, Marion seemed somehow calculating, her sleek charm too practiced, too easy. And so they chatted—a bit awkwardly for Amanda, who asked about the boys but thought it best not to mention Devin.

After a while, Marion excused herself and was replaced soon after by the singer, Kimberly. The difference between the two was, to Amanda, quite remarkable, and she found herself enjoying Kimberly's innocent chatter about songs and plays, and her indifference to the political pomp that surrounded them.

Peter finally arrived at the table with Andrei. Amanda was prepared to dislike Colonel Denisov, and was almost disappointed to find him so charming as he warmly took her hand and praised her husband. Amanda was surprised, and perhaps a little bit ashamed, to find herself actually enjoying the evening.

As the dinner was served—real pork chops edged with fat that had never tasted quite so savory, fresh peas, ice cream with real cream in it, and honest-to-God coffee—Amanda wondered when these political types would get around to speech making. She knew many of the faces from functions she had attended with Peter and from news pieces on Natnet, the national government television network. She dreaded the thought of listening to harangues on the quality and honesty of life under the New Understanding.

She found herself thinking about Devin. He had been a wonderful speaker, with his unsettling habit of telling the truth making him all but unique among politicians. When he was in Congress, he'd begun one memorable speech, "You people make me sick." The speech had stretched his fame far beyond the borders of Nebraska. Now all that was changed. Amanda wondered what five years in Russian prisons had done to him—and guessed she'd find out soon enough.

She looked at Andrei Denisov, so sophisticated, so urbane. So "American." And yet he was one of the people responsible for putting Devin in prison. For what? For being an American? For loving his country? She wanted to hate Denisov, but somehow that emotion was forced, not natural. It was all so damn confusing.

Andrei arose suddenly and clinked his spoon against a wineglass. The buzz of the crowd at the tables slowly died down until the room was almost silent. Andrei cleared his throat before speaking; he had their undivided attention.

"Ladies and gentlemen, I have a very special announcement to make."

Amanda glanced at Peter, who seemed to be watching Andrei intently.

"Since Congress established the administrative areas in 1993, there has been little change," Andrei went on. "The UN Advisory Office has been very successful working with the five state governors and enlightened members of the state legislatures. Studies by our own Area Advisory Group and the National Advisory Group have determined that a central coordinator for each area needs to be established. There is still unrest in the areas, as most of you know, and our efforts to restore the kind of national communications network which existed prior to 1993 have met with less success than we had hoped. Sabotage and, frankly, the increasingly diverse nature of the areas have forced us to come together more as a region, with more area-wide planning for the future. We would all like to speed the day when foreign advisers of every kind will be able to leave your soil."

Peter and a few others spontaneously applauded, and Amanda joined in, though she was a little hesitant, unsure of whether enthusiasm over such a prospect would be deemed appropriate by Denisov and his ilk. After several seconds of applause, Andrei signaled subtly for quiet and received it almost instantly.

"I'd like to take this opportunity," Andrei said, "to introduce the nominees for the new post of governor-general of the Central Administrative Area: the area you have come recently to know as Heartland."

Amanda was mildly curious. She wondered if Peter would know any of the candidates, and hoped he didn't get caught up in any of the political wrangling that would no doubt follow the "coming together" of this "Heartland" thing. He had worked hard as county administrator, and had managed to do it all without selling his soul to the PPP or compromising his belief in what used to be called the American Way. Amanda hoped whatever this new alignment called for, it wouldn't take that away.

"I would like to have the nominees stand as they are announced," Andrei went on. "Please hold your response until they all have been named. Oh—and I should also tell you these candidates have been approved by the National Advisory Committee, the office of the national adviser, and your own area senators and representatives to the National Congress."

When he read the first four names, the only one Amanda recognized was William Smith, the governor of Missouri and a none-too-popular one at that. The others must have been local PPP types in their own regions, Amanda thought. None of them got a particularly noteworthy introduction, until Andrei got around to the final nominee.

"Now, last but not least," Andrei was saying, "I give you a brilliant local leader, one of the rising stars of the Heartland . . ."

He paused for dramatic effect. The crowd's interest was piqued, because Andrei had already lavished more praise and enthusiasm in that simple preface than he had on all of the others combined.

". . . my good friend, the county administrator of Milford County, Nebraska, Mr. Peter Bradford."

Amanda spun around, shocked. Peter avoided her eyes as he stood and turned to Andrei, who timed his own applause with Peter's rising. Marion Andrews, seated at the next table, stood and applauded, and within seconds the entire room was standing, applauding. Amanda watched in disbelief as her husband, stiff and uncertain at first, began to warm to the ovation, beginning to grin and to wave back at the crowd as if the applause were intended solely for him—and indeed it seemed as if it were. Peter held out his hand to Amanda and she realized to her horror that she was expected to join him. Dazed, she stood up and forced a smile as the cheers washed over them.

She looked up at Peter in profile, an arm's length from him but feeling a million miles away. To Amanda, he had never looked more handsome or self-confident. Looking around at the faces in the warmly applauding crowd, she knew in one awful instant that her honest, decent husband had never been more fulfilled in his life.

He looked like a politician.

Amanda wanted to cry.

Chapter 5

AMANDA AWOKE EARLY from a brief and troubled sleep. She looked over at Peter sleeping peacefully, his tranquil face illuminated by the light of their digital clock on the nightstand.

The ride back from Omaha had been a nightmare. Her mind returned to the conversation they had in the car. Peter had started out incredibly happy, intoxicated by the ovation and all the attention, seemingly unaware of her concerns. Halfway back to Milford she found that she could contain her anger no longer.

"You knew," she said evenly.

"Not really. I'd been told there was a possibility. I didn't want to raise false hopes."

"You didn't trust me. The rest of us are involved, you know." Her anger bit into the tension between them. "What if we don't want to move to Chicago—or Kansas City—or wherever it would be? What if we don't like the idea of collaborating with the Soviets?"

Peter didn't answer. She watched him stiffen, seething silently for a moment, before he could trust himself to answer. Finally he said, "You think I'm a collaborator."

"I—no—I don't know. I know I don't want you to be. It just gets confusing. Trying to hold on to values you believe in—not being sure what the difference is. Am I collaborating just because I go along with things and try to survive?"

"There's no choice," he said coldly.

"Isn't there? Maybe there are little things. You know the other morning, a child was in the yard—foraging, like an animal. Cold and hungry. Her mother grabbed her away when I offered her something; she grabbed her away because of who I was. She realized I was the wife of the county administrator, and that made me a threat—an enemy."

Peter sighed. "That's nonsense. They just know there's a regulation against loitering in town." He looked at Amanda. "They get government relief."

Amanda wasn't listening. "Do you know, I have never even been out there. I don't even know what it's like out there."

"There's a limit to what anyone can do. They're a mixture of people—some college professors, some criminals. It's hard to deal with them as a group. That's why there's the blanket policy of as little fraternization as possible. They have their own council to solve their own problems internally."

"You make it sound so neat, so logical."

"It is logical," he said, watching Amanda's face tighten. "That doesn't mean it's ideal." He reached out to her, resting his right hand on her knee. "Am, I think there are a lot of things I can do something about as governor-general. There's no place to hide. Things change; whether you want them to or not. All you can do is to see if you can influence the change, make it something better. I think I have a better chance of doing that if I'm in a position of power." He smiled, a kind of sad, small smile. "Somebody has to be governor-general. Maybe if that somebody is me, I can figure out a way to keep our little town pretty."

Now, lying in bed next to the man she had built a life with, she thought of Devin and what would have been if, so many years ago, she had felt and known all that was pressing on her heart tonight.

She'd known Devin Milford all her life. He and Peter had been inseparable from the first grade on. Although they'd always been friendly to her, there came a time, when she was fourteen or so—a gangly tomboy with budding breasts that she tried to ignore—when they admitted her to their world. When kids started dating, she quite naturally paired off with Peter. He was popular, a star athlete, a leader. Devin, even then, was different. He and Peter had been co-captains of the Milford Wildcats football team their senior year. But Devin kept to himself much more than Peter did. Even though others looked to him for leadership, he remained somehow aloof. He read a lot more than anyone else and had ideas that seemed strange to seniors in high school. Amanda was drawn to Devin, but there was something unsettling about him. He was always finding something wrong, something to attack. Amanda had never been critical; she liked things the way they were. She never felt uneasy at the thought of living in Milford, where she'd been born and had grown up, for the rest of her life.

Devin had been attractive, of course, lean and hard, with those dark, watchful eyes and that wide, sexy mouth. A lot of the girls were afraid of him. He had a worldly swagger to him, as though he'd formed opinions of things no one else even knew about, and that was unsettling to "nice" girls like Amanda, still a virgin when she started college after two years of going steady with Peter.

They'd all gone to the University of Nebraska. Amanda pledged Chi Omega and proudly wore Peter's Kappa Sig pin; Devin, typically, rejected the fraternity system and took an apartment off campus. Amanda and Peter went to one party there but left early when some of Devin's long-haired and bell-bottomed friends started smoking marijuana. Even then, Amanda realized that Devin represented a world not beyond her ken, but beyond her nerve—a world of Charlie Parker albums, vodka punch, rude but vivid talk. She was attracted by Devin's moody isolation, his vast self-sufficiency, but they'd drifted apart in college, with different interests and different circles.

Then, the summer after her freshman year, Peter had gone off to work in the oil fields. Boys who worked double shifts were saving as much as four hundred dollars a week. Amanda had been home that summer, working in her father's hardware store, and Devin had been home, too, shingling the barns at his father's farm.

They talked at the Fourth of July parade and she invited him to drop by her house. He did, and the next Saturday he asked if she wanted to go fishing. There was a little lake about two miles west of the Milford farm where nobody went much, and they walked there and fished, not too seriously, and talked and joked. He told her he was thinking about enlisting in the marines, which made no sense to her at all, with so many people being killed in Vietnam. Devin said he was sick of all the controversy, from people who'd never even been there, and he thought he'd go see for himself.

They sat on the end of the little dock, watching the sunset, darkness settling around them. Neither of them said anything about leaving. They just kept talking and she began to feel like she'd never felt before. She was spellbound. He was so beautiful, serious one minute, funny the next, and she just wanted to go on looking at him and listening to him forever.

They sat until the moon shimmered over the calm lake. Finally he said, "I better get you back."

She answered, "No—not yet, please."

That night she gave him gladly what Peter had never asked for, but always thought would be his.

It went on like that for a week. They spent each night at the lake or in a barn near his house, making love and talking about everything but the future. She knew from the first that she and Devin had no future, that he was quicksilver, soon to dart away.

Then she got a letter from Peter saying he was coming home. She told Devin and he just nodded. That was their last night together.

Several things happened then, in quick succession. First, she told Peter that she'd "seen Devin" a few times. Bronzed and hardened by his months in the oil fields, Peter cursed and leaped into his car, roaring off in the direction of the Milford farm. She never knew what happened there; neither man ever talked about it. Within a week Devin made good on his plan to join up with the marines. At the end of the summer, Peter did the same thing.

Amanda was devastated. She imagined them both being killed. But they both came back safely and everything was as it had been before. Devin and Peter were friends again. Amanda resumed her relationship with Peter and her episode with Devin faded into unreality.

They didn't see much of Devin, except at Christmas, and when he came back to be best man in their wedding. After that, Amanda was busy raising a family and she hardly thought of Devin at all.

But now, after the fight with Peter, the memories of Devin, and the news of his return, were almost more than Amanda could bear.

By midmorning Amanda had the house to herself; the kids off to school, Peter to work. She sat in her kitchen, a cup of untouched coffee before her, staring out of the frost-tinted kitchen window. The walls were closing in on her, the silence of the house suffocating. She grabbed her winter coat and walked out the door, a blast of winter chill hitting her immediately. She got into the station wagon and started to drive, with no particular destination in mind. She passed the Milford farm and, at a small rise, pulled to the side of the road, got out, and walked to the front of her car.

She looked down upon a sight that defied all memory and logic.

The exile camp had sprouted along a muddy creek, sprawling up the hillside. It resembled a shantytown, the likes of which had not been seen in America since the depths of the Great Depression—Hoovervilles, they called them then, but now there was no one so handy as a president to blame. Some two hundred men, women, and children lived in fifty-odd shacks, tents, lean-tos, and rusted-out vans and hatchbacks. The dwellings were crudely constructed from scraps of lumber, tarpaper, tin, canvas, even from huge cardboard boxes that still said Frigidaire or Kelvinator. Fires blazed in barrels, and the soggy ground was littered with old tires, rusty bedsprings, discarded furniture, and farm implements. Every imaginable variety of junk lay scattered about.

Amanda got back into her car and drove a quarter of a mile to a soggy, rutted road that led into the camp. She got out and looked around, not quite knowing how to proceed.

Children in ill-fitting, cast-off garments passed by as they played some sort of game, barely acknowledging the woman in clean, pretty clothes. From the adults, however, she received suspicious looks as she made her way toward a modern farmhouse, the only permanent structure amid the makeshift dwellings.

She made her way to the front door of the house, where she was met by a large, crude-featured woman.

"It's a little early for the tourist season."

"Hello. I'm Amanda Bradford."

"I know who you are. Can I help you?"

"I don't know, really. I just—"

The woman interrupted. "Never been out here and thought you'd like to see the way the scum—no, what is it you call us? . . . squatters—live."

Amanda felt herself flush.

"What happened? Junior League run out of projects?" the woman snapped.

"To be perfectly honest, I don't know why I'm here. Maybe I should have come sooner, but I didn't, and I'm here now, so maybe you should take advantage of that instead of trying to make me feel miserable—which, incidentally, you are doing one helluva job at."

The woman stared at her a moment, then smiled tightly. "Fair enough. I'm Esther. Welcome to America's Russian-inspired real-life animal park." She turned aside and, with a sweeping gesture, invited Amanda to follow.

For the next hour they hiked from tent to shanty to rusty school bus, as Amanda met the people of the exile camp. They seemed cold and hungry and unquestionably frightened. And yet, because Esther was her guide, they greeted her with civility. Some of them, clearly, had been well-to-do; she spotted a few tattered L. L. Bean sweaters and Brooks Brothers shirts amid the layers of rags and cast-off clothes.

In time, Esther took Amanda and several of the camp's leaders to a nearby barn for a talk. Amanda recognized it—at one time the barn had been part of the old Milford farm. Now it was used as a meeting hall. The exile leaders were thoughtful, wary people who retained their dignity even in their distress. They sat in a circle, on milk cartons or stumps of wood, Esther skillfully taking charge of the conversation.

"I'd like to introduce Amanda Bradford. She wants to help but isn't sure how. Right, Amanda?"

She nodded.

"Does anyone have any suggestions?"

"We need food," a woman said.

"And clothing, particularly for the children."

"And material to build decent houses with."

"And help in building them," another man said.

"Wait a minute," said Esther, "we're getting ahead of ourselves. We sound like a bunch of beggers. What we need first, most of all, is respect. We need for the people in Milford to treat us as human beings, Americans, not trash." Esther turned and stared straight at Amanda. "So, what do you suggest?"

Justin slipped through the crowded high-school corridors during the class change. He watched the sea of passing faces, aware that many seemed uncomfortable with this sullen rebel prowling their closely watched corridors. Justin ignored them, scanning the faces until he found Jackie.

"Justin. What are you doing here?" She wore a plaid shirt and a crewneck sweater. In school, she looked like what she was: a sheltered teenage girl.

"Got to talk to you. C'mon."

"I've got a class."

"Come on." He took her by the arm and led her into a quiet spot partially hidden under a stairwell.

"Jus? What's going on?"

"I . . . I had to see you."

"You're not in trouble, are you?"

"No, nothing like that."

"I'm late for class. Besides, if the monitor catches us, I could be in real trouble."

"I'm splitting," he blurted out, and she knew at once that he meant from Milford, not just from the school.

Jackie tried to mask her alarm, yet somehow she was not at all surprised. "Why? Where?"

"My old man talks about these runners—guys working with the resistance. Most of them head west. There's a big movement out there."

"That's really stupid, Justin," she said angrily. But not for nothing was she Amanda Bradford's daughter; she too felt the nobility and appeal of his quixotic decision.

"Well, that just about answers my next question."

Even unasked, the question was terrifying. Jackie studied Justin's face a moment, trying to gain some control over her rising anger. "You want me to come with you? You're crazy. I can't just leave. What about my family—my dancing?"

If Justin had expected any other answer, he didn't let

it show. He was one of those who would rather bear a thousand wounds than admit that he was wounded. He shrugged and turned to go.

She reached out to stop him. "Jus, wait. Look, I don't know—it's scary. Let me think about it. I gotta go. Will you wait?"

"Awhile."

She kissed him and started to leave, stopping dead in her tracks. "Damn!"

Justin followed Jackie's gaze and saw a kid of thirteen coming down the hall. He was wearing blue pants, white shirt, and red tie as well as the red armband of the Young Lincoln Brigade.

Justin pulled her to him. "If we just pretend we're makin' out . . ." He kissed her, and when she struggled free, the monitor was upon them.

"What are you doing?" he demanded, with an exaggerated air of self-importance.

"I wanted to ask her something."

"Everybody's supposed to be in class."

"It was important," Jackie said. "I'm going right now."

"I have to report it. What's your name?"

Justin showed his teeth. "Max Smith. And this is my sister, Abigail."

"Those aren't your names. I'm calling the principal."

Justin grabbed the boy by his collar. "Listen, you little red-tied pimple, you're not going to call the principal. You're going to walk quietly down that hall or I'm going to tear your stupid head off. Understand?"

"It's okay," Jackie said evenly. "I'll go to the principal's office." She looked at Justin. "You're making it worse."

The boy started to yell. Justin clapped one hand over

his mouth and wrestled him to the floor. "Don't, Justin, please!" Jackie grabbed Justin, and the boy broke loose, jabbing his whistle into his mouth and blowing with all his might.

Doors flew open, teachers and students poured out. Several of the teachers seized Justin. One of them who appeared was Justin's aunt Alethea. She started toward Justin but stopped, realizing that by this time there was nothing she could do.

Minutes later, Justin and Jackie were escorted into the office of the principal, Mr. Purvis, a plump, nervous man. Purvis had learned to defer to the real power in the school, Vice-Principal Herb Lister, the top PPP official in Milford County. Lister, a small, balding man with a pinched face, was clearly delighted by the scene before him.

"Jacqueline, do you know that an unauthorized meeting is grounds for expulsion?" he demanded.

Alethea, who had joined the group, said, "Okay, Herb. So they're guilty of a capital offense, why not take 'em out and shoot 'em in the quad during lunch!"

"You're here to help, Alethea," the principal said softly.

"You people think you can get away with anything," Lister said. "The Milfords of this world are no longer better than the rest of us. I'm bringing this issue before the advisory committee—since it involves the county administrator's daughter and a well-known hooligan and malcontent from a former elitist family. And we'll see—we shall see a lot of things. Like how it's possible for people of questionable loyalty and character to continue to teach."

"Just a moment, please," the principal pleaded. "I have a responsibility here."

"No you don't," Lister declared. "This is a political matter and that is my area of responsibility."

With a final leer at Jackie, he stalked down the hall.

Peter Bradford was on an emotional roller coaster. He was angry with Jackie, determined to get Justin Milford out of her life. And yet, when he walked into Herb 'n Betty's that morning he was overwhelmed by the townspeople's heartfelt congratulations on his nomination. "Hey, I'm just one candidate out of five," he protested, but as far as his friends were concerned, his selection was already official.

Peter was still beaming from the warm feeling of the morning when Alethea and Jackie unexpectedly entered his office. He was sitting at his desk, surrounded by a mountain of paperwork.

"Safety in numbers, huh?"

Alethea smiled. "I'm a witness. Parents sometimes categorically disbelieve their own kids."

Peter looked to Jackie. "We've never had that problem." He noticed that she held back a little. "Well, at least until now. Well, kid, all I can tell you is that your timing is lousy."

"It was no big deal, really."

He got up from his desk and walked to her. "Not according to Mr. Lister." He kissed her. "You know, one of the interesting things about life today is you never know what's a big deal and what isn't. I'll have to think of a way to handle this."

"I think you should just fire Mr. Lister. He's so dumb he's dangerous," Jackie said.

"Well, you're right about one thing. He's dangerous."

"Peter, it wasn't her fault," Alethea said.

"I could have guessed that, with Justin involved."

"He's really not so bad; he's sort of like Devin—got good stuff in him, but it bursts out in funny places. Honestly, this was all pretty innocent," she continued.

"Alethea, he attacked an eighth-grader."

Alethea smiled. "You have to know the eighth-grader."

Peter walked back to his desk, but did not sit down. "I know it's all very funny, and it's only us folks who are in a place of authority who can't take a joke. I, as you may or may not know, come to this not a big fan of your favorite nephew, despite your assurances, Alethea. And I'm particularly not ecstatic about Jacqueline's hanging around with him." He turned and looked directly at Jackie. "Which I must tell you, young lady, is at an end."

Jackie was growing increasingly frustrated. "You never even asked me why it happened—why Jus wanted to see me."

"You're right, I didn't. Sometimes it doesn't matter so much why something happens as what it causes."

Jackie had had enough. She walked to the door and turned to her father. They stood a moment, unable to bridge an emotional gap each was only beginning to be aware of. "He needed me," she said softly, and left.

The train ride up from Texas was a slow, dirty purgatory, lurching between the horrors of the past and the uncertainties of the future. Amtrak's service had not improved under the new regime. The passengers in the car were scattered, as though avoiding contact with one another. It wasn't crowded and no one sat next to anyone else.

Devin spent most of the trip sitting alone by a dirty

window, crouched in the manner of those long confined, as if there were always a barrier, always a cage, around them. On the last night of his journey, a few hours out of Omaha, he was stirred out of his restless sleep. A car's headlights raked across the windows of the train. Suddenly, with a jolt, the train came to a halt. The passengers peered out the windows. Cracks and pops of gunfire cut into the night. A man dressed in black threw open the door to Devin's compartment. An M-16 preceded him, held out in front of his body. Over his face the man wore a black stocking cap with the eyes cut out.

"Everybody up and face the windows," he commanded harshly. "Put your travel visas and valuables on the seat behind you." He watched each of the passengers closely, his gun now held at gut level. He reached out for a man's visa. "You're from Houston." He laughed, a short and cynical cackle. "You an oilman? All of you are collaborators. You wouldn't be riding around on this train if you weren't. I'm going to give you a choice: either get off this train right now and join the Texas Guards, or give up your cash and valuables to support the resistance."

Nobody moved. In the silence, guns exploding a short distance away could be heard. The man started to move down the line, picking up the wallets and personal belongings. He walked to Devin.

"Where's your visa, man? And your stuff?"

"I don't have any," Devin answered slowly, reaching into his pocket as if to prove his point.

"Watch it dude," the man threatened.

Devin cautiously pulled out his papers. The man looked at them.

"Devin Milford. I be damned." His face broke into a

grin. "I heard you speak. I'm a 'Nam vet too." He shrugged. "Hell, I would have voted for you. Get your stuff, the commander'll get his rocks off seeing you."

"I'll stay," Devin said quietly.

"What the hell for?"

"Just my preference."

"They get your balls?"

Devin remained silent.

"Shit. You sure turned gutless. Things got a little rough in ninety-two and you folded. The hell with it. You're not worth the trouble. Maybe I should cut you off right here—save you the trouble of livin' the rest of your life."

Devin just looked evenly at him. The man stood firm, then finally moved away to fill his bag from the rest of the car. Outside, a car honked—the signal to withdraw. As the man came back down the car, he stopped beside Devin, who was again facing the window.

"You're nothin'," he grunted. He started to leave, then suddenly reached out and gave Devin a vicious chop to the back with the butt of the gun. Devin pitched forward. The Resister thought briefly about shooting the man he had once admired, but the insistent horns outside changed his mind. He walked out the door of the train, his black figure blending into the darkness of night.

It was still dark when the tarnished Amtrak train pulled into the terminal. Built in 1890, the station had retained an atmosphere of grandeur with its vast vaulted ceilings made of stone from nearby quarries. At this time of night, it was virtually deserted.

Devin got off the train alone and walked slowly down

the platform toward the main waiting room. Once inside, he stood perfectly still for a moment, trying to get his bearings. He spotted two soldiers along the far wall—one national guardsman, one SSU. The American soldier wore an olive-drab helmet liner, the other a white liner with wraparound blue stripes: the mark of a UN peacekeeper. Instinctively, Devin moved away from them, circling around the perimeter of the cavernous room, as might a fugitive.

Ward was standing against the far wall, studying this newcomer. When he finally recognized him, he was shocked at how Devin had aged, at how thin and gaunt he was. Devin's beard was new, and Ward was startled by the fact that it was almost entirely gray, a sharp contrast to the chestnut brown of Devin's hair and mustache. Ward pushed his felt hat back from his forehead, sighed, and walked slowly toward his younger brother.

When Ward was still some thirty feet away, Devin looked up, instinctively aware that he was being approached. His look caused Ward to hesitate for a moment.

"God, Dev—" He stopped abruptly, his sadness at what Devin had become spilling into his voice.

Devin tried a smile and a shrug. Tears filled his eyes. Slowly, he extended his hand. "Hello, Ward."

Ward ignored the hand and gave his brother a bear hug. Carefully, Devin put his arms up to Ward's waist. They held each other, as Ward grimaced to hold back his tears. "It's the shits, man. God damn if it ain't."

And then he attempted a joke. "What a pair we are," he said. "Me fatter'n ever and you about to dry up and blow away." Ward reached down and grabbed Devin's duffel bag. They walked toward the exit side by side—they didn't exactly feel like strangers, just not like the brothers they'd once been.

They drove most of the way in silence, the faint light from the dashboard illuminating their faces. For most of Ward's life, Devin had outshone him. Ward had dropped out of college after one year, gotten married, and joined the sheriff's office. Unlike Devin, he had been content to live and raise his family in Milford. He knew he was not a glamorous man or as intelligent as Devin. Yet he had never resented his brother's success.

Or had he? In the buried psychological life of families, no emotion is ever quite unalloyed by tinges of its opposite. Had Ward Milford been a more sophisticated or self-aware man, he might have wondered if his curiously dispassionate greeting of his prodigal brother might not have had some deeper cause.

Finally, as they neared town, Ward's voice broke into the silence. "You get much news down there?"

Devin shook his head.

"That's what we figured." Ward sighed. "Never heard from you so we figured you never got anything from us, neither."

"You write?" Devin asked tentatively.

Ward nodded. "To you, care of the state. You?"

Devin shook his head. "It wasn't permitted."

Ward suddenly pulled the truck to the side of the road, leaving the motor running. "Look," he said. "There's some things you oughta know. We took some heat back there. Dad lost most of the farm. They confiscated it, said it was reparations—for you being a people's enemy. They moved a bunch of Exiles on our land. And they bumped me out of being a sheriff. I'm not complaining." He smiled, though he found it difficult to keep an accusing edge out of his voice. "I guess I'm lucky to be around at all. I guess what I'm sayin' is don't expect a hero's welcome or anything like that."

Devin was silent a moment. "If it had been my choice, I wouldn't have come back."

"Yeah. Well, just so you know what you're walkin' into."

Ward pulled back onto the road and the truck was quickly swallowed by the darkness.

The sun rode the horizon as they drove up the poplar-lined driveway to the Milford house. Devin was shocked to see its broken windows and peeling paint. Like all of us, he'd remembered his childhood home as grander than it really was. During the period of his imprisonment, the once-stately Milford homestead had grown in his imagination to plantation-home proportions, with columns, porticoes, deep and richly shadowed porches. What he saw instead was a modest farmhouse giving off a whiff of rotted beams and no longer quite straight on its foundation. He said nothing.

"I'll just drop you," Ward said. "I've got to make a run into town. The deputy gets the dawn patrol."

"No problem," Devin said.

Devin stood before the old Victorian farmhouse but did not enter. Instead, he walked across a stream, which ran, uneven and lovely, through the field. He scooped his hand into a small eddy around a large cluster of rocks and, with the first simple pleasure he had known for years, brought the frigid liquid to his lips. He took in the precious landscape, the farmland lying in winter calm. He turned from the bank and crossed the field to a small cemetery, standing alone in the middle of the field, silhouetted against the gold-red sky. Rows of simple markers stood erect, sheltered beneath an ancient oak where four generations of

Milfords lay. This spot had always seemed sacred to Devin. He wondered if he still had the moral fiber to think of it, or of anything, as holy.

He walked. His steps were guided not by conscious thought, but by a bone-deep recollection of the contours of the land, the textures of fields and stream banks underfoot. The sun rose and grew warm even through the winter chill. The light changed from lavender to rose to gold to white, and still Devin found himself wandering. If not content, then at least he was free of the constraint that had barred his movements for so long.

He stopped abruptly on the crest of an elm-graced hill, thunderstruck by the sight of the exile camp scattered above the creek bed. In front of some of the tents, small fires burned in oil drums and smoke curled from little stacks protruding, crooked, from the lean-tos. The sounds of people awakening drifted across the field to him: a child's cry, someone's hacking cough. Not quite ready to face this new reality, he turned and walked back toward the house.

There was a light in the kitchen now. Devin found Alethea, wearing an old brown robe and lacing her coffee with Scotch. He could not repress a wince at the sight of her—his little sister, whom he still remembered as a pink-cheeked, bubbly girl, sitting there now with the sallow complexion and sunken eyes of an alcoholic, defeated by life.

Alethea was the first to speak. "Devin?"

"Such as he is," he said. "Morning, Ali."

She ran to him. Hesitating for a moment, she stood in front of him. "Devin, Devo . . . oh." She threw her arms around him, then backed away, suddenly aware of how much she had aged. Her hands darted to her face in a shy gesture of protectiveness. "My God, I'm a mess. You shouldn't see me before I'm quite ready for the world."

He gazed at her wordlessly, feeling both love and confusion.

"Well, you don't look so great either, now that I mention it," she said. "Where ya been? A prison camp or something?"

"Or something." He smiled. "You look good, Ali."

"I look like hell. Too much booze and sleeping around." She tried to laugh. "You know me . . ."

He didn't know her, not anymore, but he was starting to guess, and his face mirrored his concern.

"Hey, lighten up, it's just a little homecoming joke. I'm still a simple schoolmarm. I teach the kiddies how Marx became the father of our country. Revisionist History 101, we call it." She moved toward the stove. "How 'bout some coffee?"

"Sure. Please."

She filled his cup. "It's not real coffee, you know. But you must be used to it too." He took the coffee and sat at the once-familiar big, old table. "Can you talk about it, Devin? Marion said it was a hospital, but after they took the farm we figured it must be jail."

Devin nodded. "Southwest Texas. Fort Davis. I'm sorry about the farm."

His voice broke, and she sat next to him.

"Ali, what are all those places down by the creek? The tents and trailers—"

"New owners," she answered. "Reverse homesteading. Instead of taking unused land and making it productive, you take productive land and make it useless. I shouldn't say that, some of the people are quite nice. They're Exiles; internal exiles. Kind of the great leap backward. The advisory committees figure the country life and hard work down on the farm is good for the soul. Trouble is, they don't know what they're doing and the government made some mistakes in deciding what kind of troublemakers to send. You'll get the rundown from Dad." She started out the door, but popped back in, thinking better about her last comment. "Don't expect much from him."

"I know. Ward told me."

She nodded. "If you want to go into town with me . . . Ward usually runs us in—gas for the cops, you know."

Devin smiled and nodded.

She stared at him, then rushed back to the table to embrace him. "I'm glad you're back, Dev. I didn't know if I'd ever see you again." She let go of him and rushed from the room. Devin took a sip of coffee and looked around, suddenly feeling caged. As if he had nowhere to go, he walked through the door Alethea had just gone through, into the dining room, and started for the stairs. Hearing a footstep, he stepped back into the shadows of the hall and watched as his father came down, one slow step at a time. The old man was still ramrod-straight, but he had aged; his face was more lined, his shoulders stooped, and he moved tentatively, one hand clutching the banister. Devin stayed in the shadows, a grown-up child hiding from his father. As Will shuffled into the kitchen, Devin stole the opportunity and climbed quickly up the stairs. He rushed down the hall and into his old room. It was nearly bare now, with only a bed and desk. He sat on the bed, staring at the faded flowers of the wallpaper. The tiny bedroom, he realized, was almost exactly the size of the cell where he'd spent the past five years.

Chapter 6

DEVIN'S SON BILLY was home in Chicago on the morning his father arrived in Milford. As if telepathically connected, his thoughts were of Devin, as they had been ever since his mother told him of Dad's release. Billy guessed that the only reason she told him was to explain why a cop was guarding their apartment. Otherwise he might never have known.

Billy knew no matter how mean or unfair, his mother loved him. She just didn't understand him. She thought that because she didn't love his father anymore, her sons shouldn't either. His mother felt strongly that because she had changed her name back to Andrews, her sons should too. And she had sold all that to Caleb. He thought his father was a criminal, some kind of wild man who would come and carry him away.

Billy knew better. Caleb was only nine; he barely remembered their father. But Billy, at fourteen, had many memories of a tall, strong man who loved to laugh and romp with his sons, whose voice was low and gentle, but could bring a crowd to wild cheering. Billy remembered riding horses with his father at his grandfather's farm in Nebraska, and playing in the surf at Cape Cod.

Most of all, he remembered when his father ran for president. Billy had gone to some of the rallies and his father would introduce him and say he wanted his sons to inherit a better America. People would shout and wave flags and sometimes even cry.

Billy didn't know much about politics, but he knew that what his father stood for had been right, and that his father was a good, brave man. No matter what his mother said, no matter what they taught him in school, he knew that was the truth. He knew something more, and it was the most important thing he could know: he was like his father.

Early that morning, Billy had dug deep into his closet and brought out a long-hidden envelope full of pictures. Stilted poses of his father in battle fatigues in Vietnam. Shots of Devin being sworn in to the House of Representatives by a huge, white-haired man. A wedding picture, his mother looking beautiful in white lace. And pictures with the boys: father and sons at the beach, sailing, playing baseball, posing beside a Christmas tree. And finally, a folded newspaper clipping that showed his father struggling against the four policemen who were arresting him. After that, there had been nothing, nothing at all for five years, until this week when his mother said his father was free.

All at once, his door flew open and Billy jumped up, startled. His mother filled the doorway. "What are you doing?" she demanded.

"How about knocking?" He started stuffing the pictures back into their envelope.

"What *are* those?" She ran toward him and began to grab for the pictures. He turned away, protecting his treasures as she tugged at his arms. It was as though she were obsessed. He was barely stronger than she, but just as determined. After a moment, Marion gained control of herself. Billy retreated to a corner, clutching his memories.

"How long have you had those? And where did you get them?" Although she no longer grabbed for them, her voice was insistent.

"They're mine. You don't have any right to touch my stuff. He's *my* father."

"He's destroyed his own life. Almost ruined ours. Now do you want him to finish the job?"

"I don't even know what you're talking about. All he did was fight against the Russians. *Your* damn Russian friends."

"Don't say that! You don't understand . . ." As she trailed off, Billy suddenly saw Marion not as his mother, but as others, grown-ups, must see her.

But he pressed on. "I understand plenty. You're not the boss of everything. I want to see my dad."

"That's out of the question."

"You can't stop me," he said defiantly.

"Billy, you must understand. Your father committed crimes and was sent to prison. He has been released, but he's an exile in another state. If he tries to come here, he'll be arrested and sent back to jail."

"Then I'll go where he is. I want to live with him."

"That would be absurd. You'd have no privileges. No education. You'd be an Exile, like he is."

"I don't care."

"We have a wonderful life now, Billy, which I have been able to create for us in spite of your father."

"That's a laugh," Billy said bitterly. "All you did was

screw some Russian general in Washington. You think I'm stupid. Everybody at school knows that."

She shot forward, quick as a cat, and slapped him hard. Still clinging to his pictures, he ducked, trying to avoid another blow.

Suddenly a third voice at the doorway shouted out, "Stop it, stop it!"

They turned and saw nine-year-old Caleb, tears rolling down his cheek.

"Caleb . . ." Marion said, simply stating the fact of him there in the door.

"Hi, Cay," said Billy with a casual wave, an almost silly gesture of denial.

For a moment after that, nobody knew what to do. Then Marion straightened, and brushed away the tears of frustration and rage. Nothing was going the way she wanted it to.

Billy rushed past his brother. He still clung to the pictures. He stopped only to grab his coat; then he raced from the house.

Marion moved toward Caleb, knelt down, and held him in her arms.

"It's all right, darling. Billy's just upset. He doesn't understand how wonderful our life is now. How bad it was before. You understand, don't you, darling?" She let go of him, and Caleb nodded dutifully.

"You're a good soldier." She stood up, Caleb clutching her hand. "We're going to be fine," she said.

In the Bradford kitchen, standing in front of an open door, Peter tried to remain calm. His eyes flashed with anger as he stared out onto the driveway. Shining indirectly through a misty-clouded evening sky, the crescent moon cast just enough light for him to make out Justin.

"I told you you were not to see Jackie. After that business at school the other day—"

"I have to tell her something," Justin interrupted urgently.

"I think you've told her enough already," Peter said, adamant, and shut the door.

Peter walked to the dining-room table where Amanda sat watching him in silence. Jacqueline stood back from the table, furious. No one spoke. Their silence was interrupted by a knock on the door. Jackie started across the room.

"Jackie."

She turned and glared at her father.

"If you're going to make the Area Dance Company, you're not going to have time for him."

"You got me in if I promised not to see Justin? What was it, Daddy? A deal? Did you do it for me or to make sure you got what you wanted?"

From outside, the knocking started again. "Just a minute, Justin," she shouted.

"I got you in because you deserved it. And I didn't think you should be penalized for being my daughter."

Peter and Jackie were at a standoff. Amanda walked over to her husband and touched his arm gently. "What if they just sit in here and talk?" she said softly. "We can't stop them from seeing each other."

Peter looked from his wife to his daughter, furious but trapped. The logic of Amanda's words was inescapable. He opened the door and stared coldly at Justin. "This is my home and Jacqueline is my daughter. You've got fifteen minutes," he declared, and stormed out of the room.

Justin stood in the doorway, confused by the sudden burst of anger. "Hi, Justin," Amanda said. "You're letting the cold in. There's some soda in the icebox."

She walked out of the room, closing the hall door behind her.

Jackie walked over to him and kissed him. "You're cold," she said, leading him into the kitchen.

He stood stiffly. "What the hell is this? Your parents tell you everything you've got to do?"

"They're my parents, Jus. Daddy's just being a father."

Jackie led him to the table, trying for levity. "C'mon. Take off your coat and stay awhile. We've got fifteen minutes. Whattaya say we make love?"

Justin didn't smile. He remained standing. "My uncle came home."

"That's great."

"He's wasted. They blew him out. Maybe they even did a lobotomy or something. I don't know."

She walked over to him, feeling his pain. "Oh, Jus."

"I can't hack this anymore," he said. "This system. The way they twist people's lives. I've got to fight back. Look, we can go to the Rockies, or even Alaska. If I stay around here, the best I can hope for is some job as a laborer. The same for you—you said so yourself. This is our chance. If we wait, we'll get sucked in, like everybody else."

"I can't go, Jus. Not now. They've reinstated me for the Area Dance Company."

Justin stiffened, as if he'd been struck. "Screw the dance company! Your old man fixed it."

"You said yourself I deserved it."

"And you're buyin' it? They reject you and you're sad, they tell you you're good and you're ready to buy into the whole goddamn scam?"

"I am good, Justin."

"It isn't about being good. It's about being one of them."

"I'll spend my life being me, Justin. I can have a good life."

"I thought you wanted me in your life. That's what you said. Or have you forgotten so fast?"

She lowered her eyes. "I haven't forgotten. How could I? I want you both. You and my dancing."

"But you can't have us both," he said. "It's two different lives. You have to choose."

"Oh God, Justin. That's what my father said."

"Well, for once he was right. Choose, Jackie. Me or them."

The question, the ultimatum, put her in an emotional vise. But it was unfair to expect her to come with him.

"Justin, I love my dancing." She could barely hear her own words.

"More than you love me?"

"No. But . . . I just can't run off to Alaska. Maybe later. Maybe . . ."

"Okay," he said slowly. Then, his words coming faster and louder, "Good luck, Jackie. I hope you're happy."

He was out the door in an instant. Jackie froze, too proud to call after him, but when she heard the sputter of his motorcycle, she rushed out with an agonized cry.

Justin sat astride the bike, ramrod-stiff with awareness that the door had opened behind him. He turned and glared at her. She'd never seen that look, which she knew well, directed at her. It stung deeper than she thought anything could. "Justin," she said softly.

They maintained their positions, waiting for each other to make another move. Finally, Justin jerked down his goggles and gunned the engine.

"I love you," she cried, forgetting everything except the fact that he was going. But her words were drowned out by the thunder of his bike's motor, and suddenly he really was gone.

The welcome-home dinner was Alethea's idea, though she herself could not have said whether she conceived it on a generous, loving impulse, or as a cruelly ironic comment on the hostile band of strangers that the Milford family had become. She recruited Betty, Ward's plump, good-natured wife, and the two of them spent the afternoon scrounging around for the ingredients for some of Devin's favorite dishes: Irish stew, sweet potatoes, cornbread, and chocolate cake.

Alethea decorated the dining room. It was a formidable task, because even in better times, it had been a dark, gloomy room, with heavy Victorian furniture, thick drapes that swallowed the light, and portraits of grim ancestors. Alethea had always thought, with those eyes on you, who could enjoy a meal. She put up red, white, and blue ribbons, and again she was scarcely aware whether her true intention was to honor her brother or in some sense make a mockery of the patriotic colors that had brought so much misfortune to them all. Above the sideboard, she hung a hand-lettered placard that said WELCOME HOME, DEV, but even the printing, scrawled in her shaky hand, seemed ambivalent.

In all, the ambience fell far short of festive.

Will Milford, stern and silent at the head of the table, cast a pall over the evening. Ward gamely tried to keep conversation going, mostly with Alethea, whose spirits were kept afloat by a large glass of Scotch. She gulped from it frequently, knowing that each sip was a rebuke. Betty sat silent, worrying about Justin, who had not been seen all day, although she hardly expected him to show up for a family dinner. And Devin, the guest of honor, sat on the edge of his chair at the foot of the table, picking at his food. He had no appetite for food—it had taken him a few minutes to realize that they'd fixed the dishes he'd liked best—and not for conversation either. He was almost as silent as his father.

"First they took the farm and put the Exiles on it," Ward was explaining to Devin, "then they took our house, then Alethea's. We wound up with just this house and the fifty acres around it."

"Isn't it wonderful, to all live together under one roof the way our ancestors did," Alethea quipped. "Talk about your nuclear family!"

"The Exiles are mostly helpless out here," Ward continued. "Don't know the first thing about taking care of themselves. Can't dig a cesspool or a leach line. Damn near had to keep them from pissing in the streams."

"They're city people, but most of them are good folks," Betty protested.

"If they're so good, what'd they do to get themselves sent here?" Ward demanded.

"The same thing Devin did to get sent to prison," Alethea retorted. "Standing up to the government."

"We'd do a hell of a lot better in this county without them," Ward insisted. "Some of them steal grain from the elevators—that's one reason we might not reach our quota this year."

"Is it better to ship it to Russia? What do we get for it there?" Alethea demanded. "I'm sick of blaming the Exiles for every damn thing."

The room became suddenly quiet. Finally, Betty said with forced cheerfulness, "I think it's time for a surprise." She disappeared into the kitchen, and in a moment returned carrying a cake.

Devin grinned, boyish again, in spite of everything, at the prospect of the sweet spongy dough and the chocolate icing that had been coaxed into delicate elf-curl points. Betty led the off-key singing. *Welcome ho-ome to you, Welcome ho-ome to you, Welcome ho-ome Dear Devin, Welcome ho-ome to you.*

The song broke off when Will lurched to his feet, banged the table, and stamped out of the room. In the hush that followed, Alethea went to Devin and kissed him. "Well, almost everybody's glad you're home," she said gently.

A hint of amusement danced in his eyes. "Three out of four ain't bad," he said. "Better than my last vote count."

They all laughed a little too much, grateful for the break in tension.

"You gotta understand him," Ward said. "All his life—ten thousand acres. Milfords worked hard for this land. Hell, we used to produce six hundred thousand bushels of corn, and a hundred fifty thousand of wheat."

"What about milk for half of Omaha," Alethea said sarcastically.

"Damn you, Ali," Ward grumbled. "Why do you do this?"

"We're not those Milfords anymore. If we've lost, then think of all the people in the country who've lost even more. How about their lives? How about Devin? He's been in a prison camp for five years and we're sitting around mourning our past. We've lost what our forefathers built, not what we created." Alethea looked around the dining-room table. "Look at us, we sit around clinging to our last fifty acres. We're not doing anything, we've given up. All we do is peek through the windows at the awful squatters, thinking, Well, there goes the neighborhood."

"What are you doing, Ali?" Ward asked. "What are you doing to make it better? You call getting drunk and sleeping with that—"

"Stop it, Ward," Betty demanded. "Don't you say anything else."

Alethea pushed back her tousled hair and tried to regain her dignity. "We all have our weaknesses. I try not to hate the Russians, the Exiles, or even myself." She stood up. "I'm sorry, Dev," she said. "This is one hell of a homecoming party." She stumbled into the kitchen and out the back door.

Devin got to his feet and followed her.

He started out to find Alethea, but when he saw the light in the barn he was drawn to it. Devin crossed the yard, beneath a broad and starry sky, and stopped at the barn door. His father was spreading hay into the troughs of his dairy herd, using this most basic labor to exorcise his anger. Four cows chewed silently in their stalls.

"Dad."

The old man looked at his son, then turned away and continued to work. Devin found a second pitchfork and wordlessly began to help him spread the feed. For five minutes they worked side by side, until Devin said, "We've got to talk sometime."

The old man kept on working. His face was sweaty and red, his hair hung down over his eyes.

"Like it or not, I'm your son," Devin said.

"There ain't nothing about you that's mine," Will said evenly. "And there ain't nothing about me that's yours. Let's leave it that way."

"I want to try to explain . . ."

"You've been a part of something else for twenty years, something that hasn't done us any good, hasn't done anybody any good."

"I understand how you must feel," Devin said. "I respect how you've lived your life."

Will lowered his fork and stared coldly at his son. "Do you? You've lived your life like it didn't mean a damn what I did—or my father or his either. Three generations of Milfords have worked this land, carving it outta nothing: all good, loyal Americans. Building up this country. Then you come back from Vietnam tearing it down. Then you go off on some showoff thing against this new bunch. The only good it did was call attention to yourself."

"I was trying to do the right thing. To help save America."

"You lost the land!" his father shouted. Fighting for control, he plunged his fork into another pile of hay. Devin watched him, anguished, silently pleading for acceptance.

As if Will heard his thought, he stopped pitching and glared at Devin. "They say I got to live with you. Eat with you. But that don't mean I've got to talk to you."

He spread the hay furiously. Devin laid his pitchfork against the barn wall and walked slowly back to the house.

At dawn the next morning he moved out.

Andrei and Kimberly were watching home videos of Devin Milford. Images of Devin's face illuminated the huge screen. He was laughing, younger then, lifting a small child into the air. It was Billy, age three. Devin brought the child back into his arms kissing him, and reached around to bring Marion into the frame. Random shots of Devin's family on the Milford farm. Alethea, Ward, Betty; young children running amuck across the fields.

Kimberly watched the videos silently. Something about this man moved her. She stared at a shot of Devin alone. He stood a little away from the Milford clan, looking over the land, then back to his family. Kimberly recognized the look of great sadness on his face. A second later he waved to the camera and smiled.

"He knows," she said, speaking quietly into the darkness of Andrei's apartment.

The tape stopped. Andrei started to rewind it. "What does he know?"

"That something is going to happen."

He looked over to her and saw that she had tears in her eyes. "What is it? Why are you crying?"

"I don't know. It just seemed so sad. It was as if he was having a good time with his family, but he's still alone. Except maybe with the boy."

Andrei walked over to the machine and took the tape out. "It was interesting how happy he and Marion seemed. A few years later, she betrayed him." He walked over to his desk and rummaged through a pile of tapes and files. "Here's a tape of him announcing his candidacy for president." He started to put the tape in. "Do you remember him much?"

Kimberly repositioned herself in the chair. "I've never been particularly interested in politics."

Andrei turned the machine on. Devin stood before a podium in Washington at the Vietnam Memorial. He had an undeniable charisma, Kimberly thought. She found herself listening intently to his speech—about the sense of greatness Americans had always assumed to be an integral part of their heritage but which was destroyed with Vietnam. He spoke of the dangers of the New Society which the Kremlin had designed for America, supposedly to give Americans the opportunity to be "truly equal."

"We are now equally enslaved," she heard Devin say. Those words echoed inside her, touching her core. "Americans have allowed themselves to be immobilized by their own fears. Immobilized by their own selfish concerns. Immobilized by a lack of understanding of the freedom secured by our forefathers, into which most of us were born—and now have lost. I have come to ask you for your support in an effort to regain our freedom. The battle will be long and hard. But freedom is not free. And ultimately we must choose what we believe in: the high demands and risks of freedom, or the security of the slave and the tranquillity of the grave."

Andrei moved to the VCR and turned it off. He watched Kimberly, who had been deeply moved. "Look at yourself. He's touched you."

A tear rolled down her cheek. "I don't know. He's—"

"American?"

"I don't know. While he was talking I started to think about 'being an American.' I never thought of myself as patriotic or anything, I just always thought of myself as me. Of course, I was an American, but it was just there. There wasn't anything I had to *do* about it."

"Would you follow him?"

Kimberly looked at Andrei quizzically.

"As a leader," he continued. "Would you follow him as a leader?"

"Yes."

"Why?"

"I'm not sure. He knows things I don't. He understands things I'd like somebody to understand. Like you, but you're Russian."

"What about Peter Bradford, the man we met in Omaha? Would you follow him?"

She was quiet a moment, trying to recreate the evening. "He was a nice man. He makes me feel safe. Devin Milford doesn't make me feel safe. He talks about choices and sacrifices. I don't think I'm willing to make either one. Andrei, I don't want to play this game anymore."

"It isn't a game. This man spent five years in prison because we were afraid of how he'd make people feel. I wish I could understand what it is about him."

"Why? What difference does it make? You're in control."

He laughed and walked over to where she sat. He touched her cheek gently, tracing the path the tear had fallen down minutes before. "You Americans. You're such a mystery to everyone except yourselves." He became serious. "If I could somehow understand this man, I think I would understand America."

Kimberly looked at him playfully. "If you could understand me"—she laughed—"you'd understand—"

"America?"

"Me," she said smugly.

They kissed, playfully at first, then deeply. He led her into the bedroom, stopping only to turn on the living-room lamp. Shafts of light spilled into his bedroom, caressing Kimberly's beauty. It accented her porcelain skin, and her eyes shone.

She pulled back the bedspread and pulled Andrei to her. Embracing and kissing, they fell onto the bed. He began to undress her, unbuttoning her dress, sliding it off of her milk-white shoulders. He kissed her neck, then pulled off her satin teddy, exposing her beautiful breasts. She slipped out of her panties as Andrei took off his clothing and lay down beside her, running his hand up the smooth skin of her thigh. He began to kiss her breasts but she gently pulled his mouth to hers. She wanted him inside her. Now.

They began to make love. Kimberly's hands moved up and down Andrei's back, slowly at first, in rhythm to their lovemaking. She felt herself take flight, riding a wave of ecstasy. She was aware of his rapidly approaching orgasm and dug her nails into his back, grinding herself into him, taking him further, deeper. At that same instant, she started to climax. She put her arms around his neck, holding on to him firmly, urging him softly.

"Yes, Andrei. Yes, yes."

They were two people meshed, body and soul.

Andrei lay atop Kimberly for a moment, his sweat mingling with her own sweet scent. All of his life, he had played games with women in bed, using sex as a battleground to act out unresolved conflicts or achieve control. But there was something else with Kimberly. When he made love to her, his heart opened a bit, and an aching need washed over him.

After a moment he fell onto his back, his breath becoming more even, synchronized with Kimberly's. She propped herself on her elbow, tracing his nose and then his lips.

"Welcome to America." She smiled, kissing him again.

Devin pitched a tent beside a stream about a mile from the farmhouse. Since boyhood this had been a special, private place for solitude and introspection.

But now the solitude was shattered by shouts from over the hill, reminding him that the exile camp was only a few hundred yards away. More than anything, Devin wanted some time alone, to settle back on this land that had been his home, to try and recapture some of the serenity he felt was at last his due. But the noise from camp drew him like a siren song; a sense of solidarity with these outcasts simmered in his blood and would not be denied.

At midmorning, he topped the hill and looked down on the camp, slowly accepting its abrasive reality. Finally, he drew near. He passed damp clothing, hanging on a line, a cluster of children playing on a heap of old tires, and an old woman in a black shawl, carrying a load of sticks. No one paid attention to him; with his lean and hungry look, dark pants, and black corduroy coat, he might have been an Exile himself. Devin heard music, a stringed instrument, and followed the haunting sadness of the melody to a small trailer.

He stopped outside and listened. The woman who had passed him carrying an armload of sticks approached him. She dropped the sticks beside the door, staring at him suspiciously.

"You a music lover?"

"No," he answered, feeling at once like an intruder. "I'm sorry."

From inside the trailer, the music stopped. A white-haired, serene-looking gentleman appeared at the door and spoke. "Gert. You back?"

"Of course I'm back, Dieter, that's why you can hear my voice."

The couple stared at Devin as he started to move away. A worried look passed between them.

"Sorry to have disturbed you," Devin apologized.

"Wait a minute." Dieter scrutinized Devin closely. "Come in here a moment."

After a brief hesitation, Devin followed Gert and Dieter into their trailer. Its cramped interior was jammed with the sort of gewgaws that once abounded in middle-class American living rooms but which had now become exotica: Dresden figurines of vacant-eyed shepherds and lissome ballerinas caught forever in the middle of a pirouette; Hummel statuettes of perfect children who would never know hunger, fear, or bafflement. Gerta started to make tea at once, as the two men sat down on a leather sofa whose torn cushions leaked horsehair stuffing.

"I was going to vote for you, in spite of the way you messed up. It's amazing, really. The history of communism is filled with good men and their good intentions—men who couldn't survive the struggles for power."

Devin raised his eyebrows. "The history of communism?"

"Yes. America is now part of the history of communism," the old man said, and smiled. "Interesting way to think of it, wouldn't you say?"

Gerta brought over a tray full of tea cups. "We would've been better off in the GDR."

Dieter smiled up at his wife. "One of life's little jokes. We escaped from East Germany to come to the promised land; now the promised land has become worse than what we left."

Gerta reached across piles of papers, figurines and mementos, distributing the cups. "At least we lived with it—learned how to manipulate it."

Her husband sipped his tea. He put the cup down. "But we didn't stay. Maybe we are destined to be outsiders, like you, Mr. Milford." He winked, conspiratorially. "I used to follow your ideas. I even read your speeches. Interesting premise, but forgive me for saying so, a little overstated, perhaps simplistic." He shrugged. "But that's the difference between the American experience and the experience of Europeans."

Devin shifted his weight on the love seat. He sipped the weak tea. "You're a musician?"

Dieter smiled at the obviousness to that question. "I was first chair with the New York Philharmonic. We were exposed by a friend—"

"Who wanted to be first chair," Gerta added.

"So, we were betrayed—not unlike you, Mr. Milford. A fact of life; even in America."

Devin's eyes clouded. "Betrayed? Just by the people, I guess."

"No one specific?" Dieter asked. "Perhaps someone closer to home?"

"What? The KGB?"

"Yes, most likely, but usually there is someone you trust—"

The path this conversation was about to take was proving too much for Devin. He found himself growing agitated, feeling confined. He stood up quickly. "I must go. Excuse me."

Dieter rose apologetically. "Forgive me. I had no intention to be rude—"

"It's—it's all this is—" He looked to Gerta. "Thank you for the tea; I'm sorry." And he left.

The two looked after him, then at each other.

"You had expected something else?" she asked.

Dieter stared at her a moment, then turned away abruptly. He felt very irritated with himself, the conversation, perhaps with life in general.

* * *

Down by the creek, two boys were playing catch with an old tennis ball. Devin knelt and watched them, until the ball bounced his way and he tossed it back, glad to become part of the game. One of the boys was shy and awkward, but the other tossed the ball with natural grace.

Devin was swept away by thoughts of his own sons, with whom he had not shared such simple pleasures for so many years.

He did not at first notice the slender woman in boots and a parka, holding the hand of a little girl.

Amanda had come to the camp several times now. Peter neither approved nor forbade her visits. So she came, and did what she could, trying to accept how very little she could truly change.

She walked with Dierdre, the child she had discovered in her yard a few mornings before. She had brought the girl some of Jackie's old clothes and had gotten to know her mother, Carla Tankinoff. They were Exiles, Carla explained, because she had protested when Dierdre's father, a physicist, was arrested for political activism.

In the cruelest blow, they were sent to this camp in Nebraska, hundreds of miles from him. Amanda was touched by Carla's courage. "We'll survive," she had said. "We have to, because our family will be reunited."

As Amanda approached, Devin was attracted, not immediately by her familiarity, but by the contrast between her clothing and that of the Exiles. Even "dressed down," her clothes looked newer and nicer. As they passed, the recognition hit him like a thunderbolt. She became aware of his stare, and returned it. She smiled, matter-of-factly, somewhat politely, and walked on.

Devin was paralyzed. One part of him would like to have run from this encounter, another part could not. "Amanda . . ."

She stood still in her tracks. The voice ran through her body to the pit of her stomach. She turned slowly and gazed mutely at the damaged image before her. Little Dierdre felt herself caught in Amanda's tightened grip and wriggled to escape. Amanda realized this, and let go, the child skipping away toward her tent.

At that moment, Devin wished he had not spoken. He felt naked and inadequate. When he could bear the silence no longer, he said, "It's Devin—Milford."

"Yes, I know. Devin. Of course I know." She walked to him slowly, kissing him on the cheek, then pulled back, aware of how inappropriately she had acted. "God, what a fool I am. I almost said how are you?"

He gazed at her and smiled. She had aged; there were lines in her face he had not known before, yet she was still the same Amanda: the same kindness and honesty she had possessed as a child and which would still be a part of her at eighty.

"I recognized your hair," he said. "The way you tilt your head I'd know you anywhere."

Amanda started to laugh off the remark in a polite counter to flattery, but his words were so direct and honest that tears welled in her eyes and an unexpected sob escaped her throat. She stood in front of him, shaking her head. "Oh no—" She rushed into his arms, holding him tightly, as though some long-ago locked-up feeling had suddenly broken free.

"Can we talk?" he said, gently stroking her hair.

"Yes. Please."

"I have a little place," he said. "Right over the hill." She laughed, and wiped away her tears, and they walked back to his campsite. He had a fire, within a circle of stones, with a grill atop it. He made coffee and they sat on a log, drinking and talking intimately. She didn't ask about him at first. She told him about Peter and her children and old high-school friends. They had talked an hour before he told her that he had received no word from Marion and his sons for five years.

"You never heard from them at all?" she asked in amazement.

"Only the divorce papers. They . . . the prison authorities . . . didn't allow any communication, in or out."

She saw that he still wore his wedding ring. She was shocked to realize that he didn't know that Marion and his sons were in Chicago. She had no idea whether she should tell him. This cautious, hesitant, passive man was not the Devin she had known all her life. Her instinct was to wait.

"Does it matter to you? About them?" she asked.

He looked at her sharply, as if the question were absurd. "My sons are all I have left," he said. "They're all that matters."

"Then why are you here?" she asked. The words, spoken, sounded cruel.

"I had no choice. They sent me here. I need time. I don't want my boys to . . . to see me like this."

"They'd love you, Devin. It wouldn't matter to the kids—"

He stared into the fire. "I'm—I don't know who I am anymore. Or what I think. Five years in that hole. Every minute of every day. You try to hang on but pretty soon you don't even know what's them and what's you."

She touched his hand. "Let people help you." He looked at her. "I want to—"

"I don't know if it will matter."

"It will. I believe in you."

He looked back at the campfire. "Don't make me a hero, Amanda."

She suddenly felt angry—perhaps betrayed. She could not believe that Devin would give up. She spoke quickly. "You remember in college, when both you and Peter had gotten back from Vietnam? You were filled with such rage—it scared me. For a while I thought you were the man I would spend my life with. But you were too scary. I remember, you said, 'If you can't take the edge, forget me.' I married Peter because I didn't want to live on the edge. I wanted safety. But now things are changed and we all live on the edge. Even in Nebraska. Now I don't have a choice. And you, after all you've been through, you don't either."

Her words spilled out, surprising her. She felt she had gone too far, said too much. She stood up. Devin did not speak and would not meet her eyes.

"It's funny," she said. "I've told myself a hundred times how disruptive you were. Always stirring things up. Never satisfied. And that there must be something wrong with you. And I was glad I didn't love you."

Amanda turned and walked rapidly away.

Chapter 7

BILLY PICKED HIS way through a vacant lot, dotted with small fires and indigents. It was a lawless free zone. The boy watched with amazement as people squabbled over territory and fought bitterly for no apparent reason at all. Quickly, a patrol wagon slid into the street. The policemen rounded up several of the indigents and threw them into the back of the van. Then it disappeared quickly into the night.

As Billy wandered toward a quiet alley, he found himself confronted by a small gang of youths.

"Lost little boy," said the leader, not much older than Billy.

"Look, I don't have anything. I'm looking for—"

"Bet ass you got nothin'."

"Smack? You wanna start easy. Speed up, slow down. Sugar—little Domino?" The young tough leered.

"I want to . . . I need to find the resistance."

133

"You're looking at it."

"I need . . ." Billy stammered.

"You need too much." The leader lashed out suddenly and smashed Billy in between the eyes. The rest of the gang then jumped in to finish him off. A little way down the alley, an older man watched with satisfaction.

"That's enough. Beat it out of here." The youths slapped each other a few high fives, then ran off down the alley. The man bent over Billy, who lay motionless, bruises all over his face. But he was less interested in the boy's condition than in the envelope full of pictures that lay in the jacket pocket. The man removed the package, crossed the street and made a mental note to get to a phone for the short call he had to place. Several minutes later, a small Toyota ambulance pulled up. The man nodded to the driver, then walked quickly down the street, pausing only to toss the empty envelope into a barrel of trash.

Andrei had been summoned to Washington by Petya Samanov. Just as he was to leave for the airport, he received a call from Samanov's office informing him that Marion Andrews would accompany him on the flight. Knowing the involvement between Samanov and Marion, Andrei was hardly surprised.

Once airborne, they found themselves talking politics.

Marion spoke firmly. "It's going to be hard to sell Peter Bradford to the advisory committee."

Andrei gave a wan smile and stretched. "The wonderful thing about the advisory committees is you can always tell them what to do."

"Maybe in the Soviet Union," she said, deadly serious. "But not here."

"Oh? How do you explain, then, the success of our occupation?"

"You see the Transition purely as your victory, Andrei. What you don't consider is that many of us, politically active Americans, were determined to make the best of the Transition. We took the opportunity to create an America we believed in. There were millions of people who never participated in the so-called American Dream—feminists, blacks, all the have-nots had goals not unlike your own. My God, we had an underclass—ten to fifteen percent of the population was perpetually illiterate, on welfare, or in prison. Now finally, that situation is improving."

He laughed softly. He was amused by her zeal and her naiveté. "Ten to fifteen percent? In Russia, Marion, less than five percent of the people benefit from our society. We who are clever or lucky—party members, scientists, athletes, the military elite, a certain type of artist—we reap the rewards while the other ninety-five percent make all the sacrifices. Of course, all this inequity is in the name of the perfect Communist Man, who I'm told will arrive any day."

"You're very cynical to be in the KGB," she said coldly.

"You don't understand the KGB, Marion. You say you want a new society, but what you really want is power. Don't confuse love and lust."

"And the KGB doesn't believe in power?"

"We believe in survival. Survival is power without dogma. Our goal is success, not ideology or meaning."

"That's disgusting," she snapped. Studying him for a few moments, she said, "You're very frustrating. That's a Soviet characteristic, isn't it?"

He smiled, his eyes closed. "Not Soviet. Russian."

A limousine met them on the Dulles Airport runway

and whisked them into Washington. The city was a pale parody of its former self, a collection of grand buildings whose architecture bespoke a sovereign power that no longer existed. The streets were all but deserted.

The White House itself was unchanged, except that the Transition flag flew out front, side by side with the U.S. flag. Marine and army guards stood every ten yards. An East German UNSSU captain saluted as Andrei's car glided through the gates. A U.S. Marine sergeant met the visitors beside the west wing and held the door.

General Samanov had left his Virginia mansion reluctantly. Now, at the White House, he occupied a huge corner office that had traditionally been used by each president's top adviser. He greeted Andrei with a hug and Marion with a kiss, inviting both of them to relax. A bottle of vodka, three crystal glasses, and a tin of caviar were set up on an elegant antique table. Samanov put on a tape of Russian music, then poured each person a drink. He raised his glass. "To the Third Continental Congress." The trio drank in unison and sat in comfortable chairs set up around the table.

"Ever get tired of the balalaika, Petya?" Andrei asked.

"Getting tired of the balalaika is treason. Punishable by the firing squad."

"Maybe a firing squad is the best way out." Andrei grinned. "A lifetime of balalaika?"

They all laughed. The general leaned across the table and poured more vodka for Andrei. "Our superiors see our hold on the world cracking. Did you know there was a rebellion in Manchuria? Our own Manchuria! There are factions in the Kremlin that want the final solution to the American problem, and quickly. Otherwise they might just selectively attack four or five

American cities. A couple of million dead would placate them. They'd see it as an example to the entire world."

Andrei was shocked. "Why?" he said.

Samanov poured himself another drink. "When you lose and fail it is understandable. When you win and fail, that brings madness." He looked at Marion and returned her smile. Andrei watched their exchange and decided that Petya had already discussed the Kremlin's threat with her. Andrei wondered at the breach of security: could an American be trusted with information like that?

"The Third Continental Congress will divide America into six or more separate states," Marion said. "It's a call for a constitutional convention to amend Article IV, establishing the right to enter into regional associations."

"Precisely, my dear, precisely," Petya said. "And that is what we are here to discuss. Leadership. And the Heartland, as it shall soon be called, must lead the way. So the question we face is who is to be the first governor-general of the Heartland. We have two candidates, actually. The front-runner, Governor Smith of Missouri, a man who has served us faithfully for eight years now."

"A known quantity," Marion added.

Petya smiled at her with pride. She could be consumed with such ruthlessness and power, and like a chameleon could change within a matter of seconds into a pliant lover. He was not quite sure which excited him more. "Exactly, Marion. And our second candidate is our Nebraska dark horse, Peter Bradford."

"He is a good man," Marion said. "But unpredictable."

"You should both know that the Kremlin prefers Smith," Petya said, looking directly at Andrei.

"The Kremlin is ten thousand miles away," Andrei said angrily. "If Smith is the governor-general, we will have riots. We've already had them in his own state. The people loathe him. They perceive him as our stooge. We must play a more subtle game if we want to pacify this country. Why can't the Kremlin understand that?"

Petya smiled. "Andrei, it has been the same with all colonial powers, from the Romans to the English to us. Those at home look at us in the field and think we have gotten soft, gone native, so to speak. We deal with people, they deal with theories. They have not absolutely mandated Governor Smith, only expressed a strong preference."

"Smith would be a disaster," Andrei said. "We must have someone credible, someone the people will trust, yet who is willing to listen to reason. And that is Bradford. I truly believe I can work with, and through, this man."

"You know, Andrei, that if he turns on you, and the Heartland falls apart, the whole decentralization plan crumbles. Your career would suffer. As, of course, would all America. Most severely."

"I understand the risks," Andrei said staunchly. "Bradford has the personal qualities. What remains is to package and sell him. And we can sell him—for God's sake, that's why we control the media!"

"We can sell him, but can we control him?" Marion said.

"Well put, my dear," Petya said, enjoying playing off his two confidants against one another. "And that is why I have developed a plan that I think will guarantee the success of Peter Bradford."

Andrei relaxed, realizing that at last Petya had come to his senses.

"I believe Mr. Bradford will make an excellent public symbol, a spokesman, a salesman for what we wish to achieve," Petya said. "But he has no experience in high-level political maneuvering. Certainly you, Andrei, will advise him. But I think it is imperative that he have day-to-day guidance from his deputy governor-general."

Andrei was engrossed in Petya's strategy.

"Therefore," Petya continued, "I'd like to introduce the ideal person to be Bradford's deputy and political adviser." He turned to face Marion. "Marion Andrews."

Marion smiled warmly. "Thank you, Petya."

Andrei felt as if his king had been put in check. Marion had sold Petya on this, of that he was sure. Now, not only did she stand to gain regardless of whether Bradford succeeded or failed, she was also in a position to oversee—or check up on—Andrei's activities.

He felt sick.

"No one is better qualified," Petya said. "Don't you agree, Andrei?"

Andrei was silent for a moment, waiting for the news to settle in. "Absolutely."

"Well, we will discuss the details later. Right now, the president is expecting us."

"I need a minute to freshen up," Marion said. "If you don't mind keeping him waiting."

"He can wait," Petya said. The two men rose and remained standing. Marion walked over to the general's private bathroom.

Petya smiled indulgently. "A remarkable woman," he said.

Andrei smiled in grudging agreement. Petya watched him a moment. His fondness for Andrei grew each time they were together; he often felt like a father watching his son emerge from an awkward adolescence to the confidence of maturity.

"Andrei, are you ever sorry you took the Central Administrative Area?"

"Rather than—"

"The overview with me. Or the planning staff in the Kremlin."

A thin smile played on Andrei's mouth. "Sometimes, Petya, there is more to be done at the end of the tentacle."

Petya laughed, walking to him. He reached out and embraced him. "So you say."

Finally Andrei stepped back. "Is there any point to this meeting with the president?"

"Not really," Petya said. "It's more of a courtesy call. It is not of a personal interest that we meet with him, but of a historical interest."

Andrei raised his eyebrows, his face uncomprehending. "He will be the last president of the United States."

Devin paused so that the sound of his own footsteps crunching over crusted snow would not distract him from what he thought he was hearing. Music? Could it be that the sounds of strings and brass were issuing from the barn where he had kept his first pony so many years ago? He approached. The music grew louder. He poked his head in the half-opened door and saw a ragtag orchestra rehearsing, twenty or so musicians watched by twice that number of Exiles of all ages. He noticed Dieter Heinlander playing the cello. Some of the Exiles were pressed against the walls; others watched from the hayloft that served as a balcony.

The orchestra was wrestling its way through Mozart's Haffner Symphony. The strings traced out elegant figurations that suggested an orderliness that Devin feared had vanished from the earth forever.

He slipped in a side door and took a place along the wall, wanting only to be an anonymous listener. The orchestra, although clearly a mixture of amateurs and professionals, played with great feeling. When they finished, the people watching roared with their approval. The conductor, clad in an ancient and frayed pair of ill-fitting tails, was amused by the applause for a rehearsal. He grinned and waved, half jokingly accepting the response.

"More! Encore!" someone cried.

Then a husky black man in a tan overcoat stepped forward from the violin section and raised his hand for silence. "Thank you. Maybe we're getting better," Alan Drummond said with a smile. "Recently, a new Exile joined us. Unlike most of us who have been uprooted and sent hundreds, even thousands of miles from our homes—for this man it is a homecoming."

Devin didn't know how this man had recognized him, but he saw where his words were leading. He wanted to flee, but remained.

"He means a lot to me," Drummond continued. "Actually, I have never met the man. What I mean is that it was through his actions that I first became an active Resister of the policies of the New America. He awakened in me a sense and feeling which had lain dormant most of my life. The feeling of being American—not just someone who does the best he can for himself and his family, but also for his country. I would love to impose upon him and introduce the former representative from Massachusetts to the Congress of the United States, and the only real candidate for president in the 1992 election, Devin Milford."

There was a smattering of applause as people began turning their heads, straining to see him. Alan pointed at Devin, who was still standing against the wall. Dieter stood up and walked to him, roughly putting his arms around Devin's shoulders, bringing him forward. The applause increased, and a few people began to cheer. Devin wasn't sure how to respond. At first, he felt frightened and intimidated, not knowing how the Exiles would receive him, but as the applause built, he began to warm to the passion of the ovation. When the chant of "Mil-ford, Mil-ford" began, he raised his hand for silence.

"I—" Devin's eyes were tearing. "I—thank you."

There was scattered applause, followed by an awkward moment. Devin sensed that they wanted comforting words but tonight he had none to offer them. He turned to the conductor. "Maestro . . ."

The orchestra played, Brahms this time, and when they had finished, people crowded around to shake Devin's hands. Then they drifted out of the barn slowly.

With the last handshake, Devin looked around to find all the Exiles gone except for Alan Drummond and five others. "Devin, let me introduce you to the Exile Council," Alan said. "You can trust all these people. We believe the camps are infiltrated but everyone here has been checked way, way back." He grinned. "We're genuine antisocial, reactionary enemies of people."

Devin grinned.

"We want to do anything we can," Alan said. "But

we're scattered. There must be hundreds of groups like us across the country, maybe thousands trying to find some way—something to do."

Dieter broke in, "Resistance is not enough. Even courage is not enough. It must be sensible. There must be a plan. We need serious political leadership. That's why it's so exciting to have you here."

Devin was seated on an old metal chair and they pressed around, surrounding him. "What the hell do you want from me?" he demanded. "I'm one man. I failed. I tried and I failed. I was beaten. No one stood up in ninety-two."

"They did stand up!" Alan exclaimed. "All over the country."

"I didn't see them," Devin said, and he knew at once that the words were not true, that they embodied five years of pent-up bitterness. "It doesn't matter," Devin said.

"You can't just sit here and do nothing," a woman cried. "You have a responsibility. You . . ." She was too angry to finish.

The others looked at him waiting.

Devin looked back at them in anguish. "I'm sorry," he said, with genuine grief, and walked out into the darkness.

Justin did not leave Milford County immediately after he roared away from Jackie's home on his motorcycle. His plans were unformed and unsettled.

He called on Puncher and some of his other friends to say a proper goodbye and go out in a blaze of glory. They were gathered in the darkness beside a remote stretch of highway in the southern part of the county. Several of the boys carried rifles and one had a pair of

Molotov cocktails. Justin was at the wheel of a pickup truck that had four spotlights rigged across the top of its cab. Far to the south, a pair of headlights glittered on the highway.

"Okay, get ready," Justin commanded. He pulled a bandanna over his face and the others did the same.

Moments later, a big semi roared into view. Justine drove the pickup straight at the truck, his searchlights beaming directly into the driver's face. Blinded, the driver wrenched the wheel. The semi twisted and skidded crazily out of control. It jackknifed, sending the trailer portion into the ditch. When the driver climbed out, he raised his hands in the air automatically. Justin greeted him with a shotgun.

"Get down," Justin ordered.

"Sure, buddy, you got no trouble from me, okay? Just watch that a little, all right?"

"Is the back door boobied?" Justin said impatiently.

The driver was a small, paunchy man. "Yeah," he said. "I got to release the circuit."

"Do it," Justin said. "And do it right, because you're the one opening the door."

The driver climbed back into the cab and flipped a switch under the dash. "What are you, amateurs?" he grumbled. "No driver's dumb enough to fool around. You think I care if the gooks don't eat?"

"Open it!" Justin commanded. The driver unlocked the back of the truck and swung the door wide.

Puncher shone a flashlight inside. "Son of a bitch, would you look at that!"

Inside the truck was a cornucopia the likes of which none of the boys had ever laid eyes upon: hams, sides of beef, crates of fruit and vegetables, spices, boxes of pastry, cases of wine. A king's banquet.

"Jesus, let's split it up," a boy cried.

"Pull the pickup around," Puncher ordered.

"No," Justin said coldly. "Burn it. All of it."

"Man, are you crazy?" a boy asked.

Justin spoke again. "If we take it we'll be like them. We're better than that."

"What about our people?" a boy protested.

"Burn the damn stuff," Justin said.

Puncher brought up a Molotov cocktail and started to light it. The driver, still covered by shotguns, looked at Justin and grinned. "That's a tough kid," he said. "Maybe dumb, but tough."

"Take off," Justin said. "Down the road."

The driver shrugged and started to run. Puncher tossed one of the firebombs into the truck. Others did the same. They stood and watched as the flames began to eat away at the meats and crates of fruit and vegetables.

"Barbeque," Puncher said.

"Let those bastards go hungry for a change," Justin said. "Come on, let's go."

Puncher pulled him aside. For a moment, the two friends stood together in the flickering firelight. "You coming back to my place?" Puncher asked.

Justin pulled off the bandanna and shook his long blond hair. "No, man," he said. "This barbeque is my goodbye party. I'm headin' west."

He started for the pickup, then turned back and gazed a moment at the burning truck, the wasted food, the gesture that so few would understand.

This one's for you, Devin, Justin thought, standing alone on the now deserted road. The rig burned fiercely, the fiery flames shooting up wildly, illuminating Justin's eyes. Justin heard a whining sound piercing the night. He looked up and saw two helicopters far off approaching.

He got into his truck and took off down the highway.

Peter was asleep when Ward Milford called about the hijacked truck. He got up quietly, dressed, and drove to the scene at once. There wasn't really anything he could do, but he felt a responsibility; there hadn't been much crime in the county and he thought anything as big as this deserved his personal attention.

When Peter arrived, a small army of police and military officials was clustered around the charred wreckage of the food-supply truck. Ward and another deputy were there, as well as a contingent of UNSSU troops led by Major Helmut Gurtman.

The tall, black-clad commander greeted them with a curt nod. "Have you questioned any of the Exiles?"

"We're covering all the possibilities," Ward said.

"What did the driver say?" the German asked.

"He said they blindfolded him," Ward replied. "He never saw their faces."

"I think we can handle this, Commander," Peter said pleasantly.

"This is not an ordinary hijacking. The contents were burned, not stolen," Helmut said sharply. "That makes this an act of terrorism. Terrorism is our responsibility."

"We'll put an escort on your supply truck," Peter said. "That should solve the problem. I'm sure it was a hit-and-run job from outside the county."

"Such certitude is rare," Helmut said. "I thought it interesting that we have this incident only days after the return of the dissident Devin Milford."

"I guess now there'll be somebody to blame everything on," Ward grumbled.

"I simply point out the coincidence," Helmut said icily. "Perhaps his presence excites the adventurous."

"Look, I think your prison camp took care of Devin," Peter said, his bitterness only slightly concealed.

"Keep me apprised of your progress," Helmut said, and without waiting for a reply marched back to his jeep.

Peter turned back to Ward. "What do you think?"

The big deputy shook his head. "Pretty good job. It could have been outsiders. Maybe somebody followed the truck up from Kansas City."

"Drove all that way to burn twenty thousand dollars' worth of food?" Peter said. "What about Devin? Could he have been involved?"

Ward was surprised—and angry—that Peter could so readily suspect Devin. "Hell, you've seen him. I don't think he could rob a piggy bank right now. And besides, goddammit, my brother was a politician, not a terrorist."

"You're right." Peter was quiet for several seconds. "I'll see you back in town."

"Peter?"

Peter turned back. "Yes?"

"Just for your information, Justin hasn't been home for a couple of days. I think maybe he's left for good. I don't expect that to break your heart, as far as your daughter is concerned, but I thought you ought to know."

Amanda opted to ride her bicycle to Milford High. Riding made her feel somewhat exhilarated, perhaps due to the unencumbered movement, perhaps simply because she felt completely in control. She pulled off the road onto the sidewalk and walked her bike into the faculty parking lot, where there was a combination of bicycles, pickups, and motor scooters. She slid the bike into the rack and started toward her alma mater.

She walked through the empty corridors, then stopped outside a classroom and looked inside. It was empty.

Down the hall she saw Vice-Principal Herb Lister walking through. "Excuse me . . ."

Lister turned around and was instantly officious. "Mrs. Bradford. What an unexpected pleasure." He walked over to where she stood. "Congratulations on Peter's nomination."

She found herself instantly resenting his use of Peter's first name. "Thank you. I was looking for Alethea Milford."

Lister's face darkened a little at the mention of Alethea, but he maintained the facade of courtesy. "I believe she and her class are in the cafeteria. Everyone is working on the banners for the Lincoln Day parade. Here, let me take you; I was just going that way."

He walked her over to a small, nondescript building, then left. The cafeteria had been transformed into a workspace. Tables had been pushed to the edge of the room. Long rolls of cloth and butcher paper were stretched across the floor. Alethea stood against the far wall, supervising a group of students. As Amanda approached her, Alethea looked up quizzically, her guard going up.

"May I talk to you?" Amanda asked.

Alethea cocked an eyebrow. "I suppose if you have the party's permission . . ."

Amanda stiffened at the quip. "Look, I didn't come here to be your friend. I came about Devin."

"Does Peter know you're here?"

"No," Amanda admitted.

Alethea glanced around. "Let's go over here," she said, leading Amanda to the far side of the room.

"I saw Devin yesterday," Amanda explained. "We talked about Marion and his sons. He wanted to see them."

"What good does that do?" Alethea snapped. "He doesn't have the will or the resources."

"There's something you should know about Marion. What happened to her," Amanda said. "She's in Chicago. She's done very well since then. She's a magistrate and a member of the National Advisory Committee."

"Party member and everything," Alethea remarked.

"Party *leader*," Amanda corrected her. Alethea seemed impressed. "We saw her at the reception in Omaha," Amanda continued. "I don't know whether she was just opportunistic or perhaps had something to do with what happened to Devin."

"She had something to do with . . . ?" Alethea wasn't following Amanda very well.

"I don't know. She seems very . . . well connected."

"The bitch," Alethea snapped. "Was it true about her and the Russian general?"

"I don't know. I don't think so. Anyway, she asked Peter to make sure Devin didn't try to see her or the children. She's afraid of him. She's . . . she's changed her name, and the boys' names, back to Andrews."

"I don't understand why you're telling me this," Alethea demanded. "Why don't you tell Devin?"

Amanda lowered her eyes. "Peter made me promise not to tell him."

"Aha, the plot thickens," Alethea said. "So you keep your promise by telling me instead."

"I trust you'll do what's right," Amanda said. "I know you love him."

Alethea stared at her a long moment. "After all these years *you* still love him." Then, with an ironic smile, she said, "That's a long time for a high-school crush."

Amanda did not answer. The silence was finally broken when Alethea's students called to her. Four of them held up a twenty-foot banner they had just painted: WE ARE THE FUTURE, it proclaimed.

"Gives you hope, doesn't it?" Alethea said bitterly.

Peter sat at his desk, thoughts short-circuiting his mind. He tried to calm the nervousness rising in the pit of his stomach, but each time he achieved a modicum of relief, he'd think about just one more issue in his life. He was swimming in enough self-pity to fill the Atlantic. There was the Russian, Denisov, seriously considering him for governor-general, and Amanda, distant lately, putting all of her energy into the Exiles, fearful of his impending appointment. And then, there was Jackie. He had had her reinstated in the dance company but she remained withdrawn, hostile, as if she blamed Peter for Justin's disappearance. Ah yes— Justin. Peter hadn't reported Justin's absence to the SSU, although the law clearly required it. He also knew, intuitively perhaps, that Justin and his friends had hijacked the food truck. Justin the rebel, so much like Devin.

Thoughts of Devin sped through Peter's mind, like a tape recorder on fast forward. When Devin had first appeared at his office, Peter could not contain his shock at the image that stood before him. Devin seemed a fragment of the man he used to be, brittle physically and emotionally, as if at any given moment he would break. Peter had driven Devin to the interrogation office, where all Exiles had to go before they were allowed to be reinstated into their respective county. The conversation consisted of idle chatter, and uncomfortable pauses. Devin wanted to know what had happened with the peacekeeping units—the army, navy, etc. Peter filled him in: "discharged or integrated with the national guard." The ride was short; ten minutes, if that, but long enough for both men.

After arriving at the interrogation center, Peter had followed Helmut Gurtman to a control booth, from which he saw Devin placed on a high stool in the center of the room. What Peter witnessed was perhaps more painful for him than it was for Devin, an inhuman process he could still remember verbatim.

Peter talked to Devin as they drove away from the center, although he wasn't at all sure that his old friend was listening.

"Look, Dev. Let me just say something, okay? Maybe it doesn't make any difference, maybe it does. You know I was never very interested in politics. Even when we got back from 'Nam, it was always you who had the idea things should be different. I guess I'm just not visionary like you are. Now they've picked me to be a candidate for the whole area. God knows how; I'm not in the party or anything, but if I'm elected, I'm going to do it. I think the only way to get rid of them is to get ourselves together. I think we can make it as a people—even if it means giving up some of the idea of what we always thought we were. That's where I am—we all still admire you and love you, man—you know?"

Sitting at his desk thinking about it weeks later, Peter still felt very self-conscious. His stomach squirmed at the memory.

As though materializing out of his dream, Devin Milford threw open the office doors and marched angrily toward Peter's desk.

"My sons are in Chicago," he said, fuming. "You knew it and didn't tell me."

"Who told you that?" Peter demanded. "Was it Amanda?"

"No."

"Nobody else knew," Peter pressed.

"It wasn't Amanda. Dammit, what difference does it make? The point is I know where my sons are."

Peter saw the fires rising in his old friend. He'd seen that passion before. In high-school sports, sometimes. In Vietnam, when he'd thought the war was right, then back home, when he'd decided it was wrong. He knew that once Devin made up his mind about something, there wasn't much anyone could do to stop him.

"I'd like to help you, Devin," he said. "Our friendship means a lot to me. But there's nothing I can do. There's nothing you can do."

"I've got to see my kids."

Peter pushed a piece of paper across his desk. "Dev, have you read the parole stipulation?" he said gently. "One of the conditions is that you not see Marion or the boys. No calls, no letters, no visits, nothing."

Devin glanced at the paper, then crumpled it and threw it aside. "They're my children. I have a right—"

"You have no rights—that's the point. Don't you understand? You're an Exile. What's more, Marion is a powerful woman now and she's determined that the ban will be enforced. If you try to leave here, to go to Chicago, to see those boys, you'll be fighting the SSU, the Chicago police, PPP security, and God knows who else. They'd send you back to prison for good."

Devin was perched on the edge of the wooden chair

across from Peter's desk. As if suddenly realizing the overwhelming odds he faced, he buried his face in his hands. "At least let me write them. Call them. Just so they'll know I'm alive. That I care."

Peter shook his head wearily. "Devin, she won't allow it. All I can tell you is to be patient. Maybe things will change. I'll talk to her, after things settle down. But for now it's impossible."

"Peter, I spent five years in darkness, and all that kept me alive was the memory of those boys."

"I understand. But as a friend, the best advice I can give you is don't get your hopes up. Devin, you may never see them again."

Devin stood up. The fury was back in his eyes. "I'll see my sons," he told Peter calmly.

Chapter 8

MILFORD COUNTY WAS up before dawn making ready
for the Lincoln Day parade—almost everyone participated, one way or another.

For years, it had been the Fourth of July parade, but
in the first years of the Transition that proud tradition
died out, not by official decree but because people were
afraid and dispirited. Then, as the new regime adopted
Abe Lincoln as the spiritual father of the New America, and as the PPP extended its power to towns the size
of Milford, the traditional Fourth of July celebration
was replaced by an officially sponsored Lincoln Day
parade.

At first people had tried to boycott the new event,
but the PPP had ways of encouraging attendance—
school clubs and sports teams, for example, had to
participate or be disbanded—and in time the parade
became popular again. At least parts of it were popular.

A bright late-winter sun was rising over the town as bands and floats began to gather. Officials put flags and banners into place, and workmen made last-minute repairs on the reviewing stand that stood on the courthouse lawn. The day was clear and cold as people streamed into town from miles around.

A few miles west of the bustling courthouse square, Devin Milford was asleep in his tent. Just after dawn, two all-terrain armored vehicles plunged across the creek outside of his camp, stopping a few feet away. Two SSU snowmobiles pulled up behind. Several soldiers jumped out of the carrier and tore open the flap to the tent. Devin was startled awake. The men reached inside and quickly dragged him to his feet. He shivered in the morning cold.

Helmut Gurtman stepped out of his vehicle and stood directly in front of Devin. "Where were you last night?"

Devin looked confused. "Here—what—"

"You're under arrest," Helmut said, and climbed back into his Rover.

The guards threw Devin in the back of the truck. It made a 180-degree turn, and sped away over a ridge, followed by the snowmobiles.

The Bradfords were up early, eating breakfast and trying to avoid the tensions that afflicted everyone except Scott. He was in his basketball warm-up suit, attacking a platter of scrambled eggs and toast. Jackie sat across the table, sipping weak tea, looking very unhappy.

"You guys look nice," Amanda said, and looked at Peter. "You too."

He was wearing dark wool pants, a tweed coat, plaid shirt, and black knit tie. That was about as formal as anyone got in Milford, white shirts being reserved for weddings and funerals.

"If we're going to Omaha, we should have gone before this dorky parade," Scott declared.

"Own up, you love it," Jackie said. "All you jocks love it."

Scott ignored her. "There's this great coach there, used to play for the Bulls, Leon Henderson—he could really help me."

"A little more work on the math could help you," Amanda said.

"I think you should finish school and—"

"Mom, I want to play. Now's the time; they're giving white players a break. Sort of a quota system. We didn't used to have a chance. But nobody wants to watch the game if it's all black guys."

"How can you possibly say that?" Amanda stared incredulously at her son, as if he were a total stranger. "You'll just become part of that whole sports thing. Making people feel—I don't know . . ."

"Proud?" Peter said loudly.

She stared at her husband. "That's not what happens. They use it like a pacifier—the 'circus' part of 'bread and circuses.'"

Scott laughed and shook his head. "God, Mom, you're weird, you know? Bread and circuses. What's that? Geez."

"That's when you give people what makes them feel good and distracts them from what's really happening," Jackie declared. "The Romans did it."

Peter feigned surprise. "Who could've believed it? A kid actually learned something in school."

Jacqueline made a face at him. He grinned, looking at Amanda, who was still quite upset. The phone rang.

"It's the red phone," Amanda said matter-of-factly.

Peter nodded and walked into the other room.

"Hey, Mom, lighten up," Scott said. "You take things too seriously, know what I mean? Look, I'll be a big star and say, 'Hi, Mom!' when they show me on the Natnet."

Amanda frowned. "I'll look forward to that."

A few minutes later, Peter walked back into the kitchen, a strange look on his face. They all looked at him.

"That was Andrei Denisov. He called from Washington. Something's up. I'm supposed to meet him in Chicago tomorrow."

The tension of Peter's words settled into the kitchen, bringing back a strained feeling to the Bradford clan.

Devin sat wearily on a high stool, an intense white light blazing into his eyes. He knew the technique all too well. The blinding light forced him to shut his eyes as a voice from the darkness demanded, "Eyes open."

He struggled to do so, remembering the agonizing pain of the jab to the kidneys that came to those who disobeyed.

"You say you were with the Exiles, listening to music, talking, past eleven. And you have witnesses," Helmut Gurtman said, his voice filled with contempt. "Your witnesses may have lied, of course. Even if they have not, it is illegal for you to fraternize with the Exiles. You are aware that I could send you back to Fort Davis at a moment's notice for violation of parole, are you not?"

Devin blinked into the light and said nothing. He was blind now; his world was white pain.

"Oh, does the light bother you? Remove it, Sergeant."

The light snapped off. Devin continued to look forward.

"Actually, I bear you no ill will. In fact, there is a certain sympathy I feel with the Milfords, and you. Through your sister."

Devin's sight returned. He looked at Helmut, who met his look, expressionless.

"I know your sister quite well," the German added.

It slowly dawned on Devin what Helmut meant. His face reddened.

"Perhaps you did not hijack the truck," Helmut said. "But you may excite others. There may be those who wish to use you for a symbol. It is therefore necessary for you to make a symbolic gesture. A public confession. An appeal, perhaps, for what you have come to understand about the New America. Its advantages—the disadvantages of clinging to old ideas. Do you understand?"

Devin stared, eyes front, and said nothing.

The music was leaden and pompous, and to sensitive ears it might have seemed better suited to Red Square than to the main street of Milford, Nebraska. Trombones razzed out martial bursts of sound, drums hammered out rhythms that suggested the relentless tramp of goosestepping boots. The Lincoln Day parade was under way.

Local policemen on motorcycles led the way, followed by a high-school honor guard wearing the blue uniforms, red hats, and armbands of the Abraham Lincoln Brigade. They carried flags—the flag of Nebraska, the U.S.-UN-USSR flag, the new Heartland flag, the old U.S. flag with the stars removed.

This riotous confusion of banners mirrored the confusion of loyalties the townspeople felt, and were meant to feel. Amid so many emblems could any one insignia have meaning? And could any one patriarch be taken as the symbolic soul of the nation when enormous portraits of Lincoln and Lenin were carried side by side?

LONG LIVE PEACE AND BROTHERHOOD

LINCOLN, FATHER OF SOCIAL DEMOCRACY
LENIN, FOUNDER OF OUR WAY

HEARTLAND, OUR HOME

LONG LIVE THE U.S.–SOVIET ALLIANCE

A troop of Little Lincoln Brigadiers, aged six to eight, carried the WE ARE THE FUTURE banner and were cheered by their parents as they marched by, grinning and waving.

The high-school sports teams marched by in uniform, Scott in his basketball outfit, Puncher in his football uniform, and the girls in the Dance Club, including Jackie, who basked in the attention even as she disapproved of the spectacle.

A tractor pulled a float that held the ladies of the Quilting Club, and other floats with winsome teenage beauty queens followed the procession to the end of town. There was another float that boasted a fifteen-foot cow, the proud symbol of a dairy cooperative. Betty Milford marched proudly with other sponsors of the country 4-H Club. Clowns, jugglers, drill teams, equestrian clubs, danced merrily. Ranks of the Kiwanis, Lions, Elks, and B'nai Brith and Demolay marched by proudly.

Peter Bradford winced a little as the first Lincoln-Lenin banners passed by. He had always thought that particular symbol was too unbelievable. Lincoln and

Lenin were about as similar as desert and beach. And yet no one seemed to protest, or even notice, this political odd couple anymore; even the schools taught that they were great soulmates.

Peter stood in the most prominent position on the reviewing stand. Taking its lead from the Kremlin and the great Red Square parades, the PPP was obsessed with every detail of rank and position. Slightly behind Peter and to his right was Helmut Gurtman in full dress uniform, his medals gleaming atop his black overcoat. On his left, a half step behind, was Herb Lister. A full step behind them, all in a row, were the members of the county council, with Alan Drummond, the exile representative, at the far end. Behind them were the rows of wives, including Amanda, who was not amused by the protocol.

Groups of farmers marched by, and leaders of the government-controlled labor unions. More bands followed, trailed by the Milford County Sheriff's Department, with Ward Milford driving the lead car. But this benign and homespun progression of faces was only a prelude for the more ominous spectacle to come. Off in the distance, a mechanical hum was gradually mounting to a roar.

People strained to look down the street as two helicopters shot into view, skimming the treetops. They zipped past the crowd, climbed higher, performed a stunning series of dips and spins, then abruptly vanished. There was a momentary hush, then the SSU convoy raced into view, black vehicles perfectly regimented. The weaponry bristled, and the effect was raw power and intimidation. Accompanying this display was "The Internationale," played by the high-school band. No one seemed aware that this anthem, now the theme song of forced compliance, had once been a paean to brotherhood. The townspeople watched in a kind of deadened awe.

At the sight of the SSU, Peter's face turned cold. He remained standing correctly, but there was no mistaking his attitude toward this display. What he found himself resenting most about this exhibition of raw power was that, in its way, it was thrilling.

Almost as quickly as they appeared, the SSU vehicles were gone, leaving an odd emptiness. Then, from around the corner, marched two dozen old men, old soldiers in full battle dress, members of the local VFW. A couple of them had difficulty marching. One ancient World War I veteran, shrunken now inside his uniform, was being pushed in a wheelchair. The unit's color guard was a single American flag. The only difference was that it was being carried upside down.

At the veterans' head, behind the flag, was the dignified figure of Will Milford, wearing the World War II uniform of a major. He walked stiffly, a little haltingly, eyes front.

As the old soldiers approached the reviewing stand, the image of the upside-down U.S. flag—banned now, never seen in public—sent a bolt of electricity through the crowd. The applause began far up the street and roared like thunder as the old men reached the stand.

Peter heard the roar before he understood it. Then he saw the flag and felt the thrill that all the others felt. He knew there could be trouble, but for that first spine-tingling moment it seemed not to matter.

"What is this?" Gurtman demanded.

Peter did not reply. The people on the reviewing stand, the leaders, the politicians and powerbrokers, were stunned, visibly shaken, as this symbol of rebellion passed. Someone at the back of the stand began to clap. Peter turned to see Amanda, head held high and defiant, her eyes looking past the two men, toward the flag making its way to the stand. Others joined her, until many of those on the reviewing stand were applauding and cheering along with their supposed followers in the street.

"What is happening?" Gurtman cried.

"Sentiment, Major," Peter said. "You must have had some contact with it, even in East Germany."

"The flag is forbidden."

Peter nodded. "Yes, the flag is forbidden."

The veterans executed a creaky right face and stopped at parade rest before the reviewing stand. The ovation continued, and then Peter saw—soon everyone saw—another unscheduled spectacle as a ragtag band of two hundred Exiles marched into view.

They were all there, men, women, children, dressed in their accustomed rags and tatters, and they too carried banners:

DIGNITY

HUMAN RIGHTS

OUR CHILDREN ARE HUNGRY

WE'RE AMERICANS TOO

The townspeople who had given the VFW marchers a mighty ovation just moments before greeted the Exiles with a nervous silence, the kind of silence that might accompany a display of bad manners. There were regulations to keep the Exiles out of town. The Exiles marched in silence, the quiet now gripping the court-house square.

Peter was nonplussed at this intrusion. He glared accusingly at Alan Drummond, but Alan returned his stare without wavering.

Major Gurtman watched the Exiles' march with cold amusement. He was no politician, but he understood the Soviets' strategy was to divide and conquer, and he realized he was seeing that policy brilliantly executed. The townspeople had been genuinely touched by the gesture of the VFW, but were unsympathetic and hostile toward those they considered outsiders.

The Exiles halted at the side of the square, their banners still flapping in the cold wind. Amid the tense silence, Peter Bradford stepped to the microphone. He shared the tension, anger, and uncertainty of the moment, but forced himself to be calm and chose his words carefully.

"Friends and neighbors," he began. "Thank you all for coming to our Lincoln Day celebration. There may be bigger celebrations somewhere, but none better!"

The applause helped ease the tension. He smiled and continued. "We live in unsettling times. I hope we're moving toward a new life where our spirit—your spirit—keeps us together. We can't stop change. What we can do is follow the example of Mr. Lincoln and turn defeat into victory, despair into hope. And we can start that right here in Milford County."

The crowd was a little confused by the message, but applauded enthusiastically. Peter held up his hand for quiet.

"As is customary," Peter continued, "I would like to introduce the Milford party chairman, Herb Lister, and Major Gurtman, of the United Nations Special Service Unit, and invite them to say a few words."

The crowd muttered its displeasure. Herb Lister

waved stiffly but did not try to speak. He had attempted a speech the previous year but had been hooted into silence.

Helmut Gurtman was not so easily intimidated. He stepped forward with the self-assurance of a man who commanded the mightiest military force within five hundred miles. "I too extend my thanks for being able to serve the people of this area," he began. "But I would like to give my opportunity to speak to someone else. Someone well known to you. Someone who now wishes to confess his past errors and present a very personal message of peace and understanding."

The crowd shifted uneasily, fearing the worst from this man. Gurtman turned and nodded to the rear of the reviewing stand and soldiers escorted Devin Milford forward.

Amanda gasped and there were scattered cries. Devin was dressed in simple, loose prison garb, and his face was grim, his emotions hidden. The soldiers guided him with the gentlest touch on his arm; he had learned the routine at Fort Davis. Just before the microphone he paused and glanced out at the crowd.

"My God, Devin," Peter muttered, and then the soldiers pushed him forward.

"I present to you Mr. Devin Milford," Gurtman said contemptuously.

Gurtman and the soldiers stepped back, leaving the captive alone at the microphone.

Devin gazed out over the crowd, at the far horizon. He hesitated and the entire gathering seemed to hold its breath. A full minute passed.

The crowd was still frozen in silence.

The courthouse clock began to peal the hour.

Devin's face seemed carved from stone. Whatever

the German wanted, he would not oblige him, no matter the cost.

Gurtman spoke again to the soldiers. Peter clenched his fist and wondered if he would have the nerve to intercede.

Then there was a stirring. At first the sound was unclear, barely definable. Dieter Heinlander, the cello player, started it. In his gruff voice he began to sing, "Oh say, can you see . . ."

In the silence, the words were an electric current, uniting them all.

Other Exiles took up the anthem. ". . . by the dawn's early light, what so proudly we hailed . . ."

Amanda was the first on the reviewing stand to sing. Tears burned her eyes as she looked out on the ragged band of Exiles, people who were her friends now.

With Amanda, other townspeople joined in the song—the one they had mumbled through at football games for so many years, and thought a nuisance, the one that was banned now. Soon it spread through the entire square, cresting like a wave.

"And the rockets' red glare, the bombs bursting in air . . ."

Helmut Gurtman, for the first time in memory, seemed indecisive, as the national anthem echoed through the town square. "That song is forbidden," he shouted.

"Arrest them all," Peter suggested sardonically.

Gurtman barked a command to his soldiers. They seized Devin's arms and started to lead him away. Peter stepped in front of them, stopping them, and turned to their commander.

"You have a thousand emotionally charged people out there," he said. "I suggest that the less you make of this, the more you gain. Remember, *you* brought him here."

Gurtman flushed, furious but uncertain. He was a soldier and this was politics, unknown terrain. He stiffened, breathed deeply, and looked out over the crowd with impotent loathing.

". . . o'er the land of the free, and the home of the brave." The people finished the anthem and cheered and embraced one another.

"You take him," Gurtman snapped at Peter. "I will deal with him later." He marched away, followed by his men.

Peter stepped to the microphone. "God bless you all," he said. "And God bless America too."

Peter quickly led Devin across to his office in the courthouse. There had been enough crowds and displays of emotion for one day.

"Thanks for your help," Devin muttered.

"Thank the townspeople; they saved your butt," Peter said.

Others soon joined them—Amanda, Alethea, Ward, and Betty. They all embraced Devin, and a few tears were shed. Devin said, "I saw Dad; where is he now?"

"He was tired," Ward said. "Somebody drove him on home, just after your brilliant speech."

Devin grinned. "Damned if he didn't look great in his uniform."

"You looked great too, honey," Alethea said, smiling back at him. Devin had made her feel proud, something she had been sure she would never feel again.

"Let's get out of here," Peter said. "I've got a bottle of whiskey I've been saving for a special occasion, and this is definitely it."

They all started along the courthouse corridor, laughing and talking, but abruptly fell silent when they saw Helmut Gurtman awaiting the approaching group. Tall and sinister, in his black uniform with the glittering gold medals, he blocked the door.

"There is someone I wish to see," he said.

"The man's done nothing," Peter Bradford said. "All he did was stand where your men placed him."

"You anticipate me incorrectly," said Gurtman with a malign, forced smile. "I wish to see another family member, one who will accompany me gladly. Alethea?"

He held out his black-gloved hand and Alethea, shamed but helpless to resist, moved toward him. Gurtman understood that humiliation could be repaid in many ways.

Will Milford sat hunched forward in the shadows of his dining room, at the head of the table, staring at one of the photographs on the sideboard. There was just enough light cast from the kitchen for him to make out the face of Mary, his long-dead wife.

"Damned if I don't wish you'd been here today," he was saying. "Us old farts, we marched in there and gave 'em some hell, and after that Devin, he stood up to 'em too. What more can they do to us? Burn down our house? Kill us?"

He laughed into the darkness. "Hell, that's about all's left now. I've lived too long, Mary. Things don't make sense anymore." He heard a knocking at the door but ignored it. It could have been the Angel of Death, he didn't care. "They won't leave a body alone, Mary," he muttered.

The door opened and closed, and Will heard footsteps. A shadow fell across the table.

"Dad?"

Will looked up uncertainly. Devin stood in the doorway.

"I . . . wondered if Alethea was home yet."

The old man slowly shook his head.

Devin could not guess his father's mood. He knew he had intruded, but something in him had to reach out.

"Dad?"

Will looked up at the tone of the voice. "She was raped, you know. They tell you that?"

Devin's lips moved but he could not speak.

"Right after they took the houses. Alethea's and Ward's too. She got mixed up in some fool thing—trying to blow up something. She always was a spunky kid. Mary and her were like they came from the same seed—even when she was little—more like buddies than mother and daughter."

Devin sank carefully into a chair. He prayed he wouldn't break whatever spell had led his father to confide in him.

"Caught her after curfew, four of 'em. Foreigners." He shook his head. "Don't ask me why she's still going out there. It make sense to you?"

"I don't know," Devin said softly.

Will stood up and Devin did the same. The old man put out his hand. "I respect what you did there today," he said. Devin shook the hard old hand, too moved to speak. Will turned and walked toward the stairs. "I reckon there's no point in you bein' down at the creek like one of them damn squatters."

He started slowly up the stairs. Devin watched him go, then he took his father's place at the head of the table.

* * *

It was far past midnight when the Rover stopped at the end of the long driveway and Alethea climbed out. She didn't shut the door, just walked away. The driver cursed her in Spanish and roared into a U-turn, slamming the open door in the process.

Devin heard the commotion and was waiting in the kitchen when she came in. Seeing him, she leaned back against the wall. She wore a dark blue windbreaker and had a fresh, ugly bruise on her right cheek.

"Waiting for the bad girl to finally get home?" she asked.

At that moment, he felt more compassion for her than he had ever felt for anyone in his life. "Ali . . . I'm sorry . . ." he began.

"I don't want your goddamn sorry," she said wearily, in a flat voice. "I don't want the pity . . . the understanding . . . the forgiveness . . . the—"

"It's my fault," he said.

"Hey, that's good. That'll do it. That'll let me sleep better."

She tried to push past him but he grabbed her and held her tight. When she winced in pain, he released her.

"Fine," she said. "A little sadism from the bad guys, why not a little from the good guys? It must be a trend."

"For God's sake, don't take this alone."

Her face tightened in pain. "What're you gonna do about it? Dammit, what's anybody gonna—"

Choking back a sob, she ran from the house, across the dark lawn. For a moment Devin was frozen, then he raced after her.

She was running fast but he was faster—for an instant he was the fleet athlete of three decades past. When he caught her, she fought him for all she was worth, hitting, kicking, and crying. He held her tight until she went limp, crying in jagged, choking gasps. He continued to hold her, tears streaming down his face as the frustration of a lifetime spilled out in their union of grief. Finally, purged of tears, if not sorrows, he led her back into the kitchen. They sat at the battered old table and after a time she began to talk. She showed little emotion, as though it were something that happened to someone else.

"The patrol caught us," she began. "We scattered. Reinforcements were sent. They found me behind the hardware store. In the trash dumpster, actually. Funny, huh? They took turns with me, four of them."

"Ali, you don't have to . . ."

"Yes, I do have to. I complained—as you might guess—and lodged a protest with the SSU. A few days later a car arrived from the barracks. I was taken to the commander. Helmut had the men beaten in front of me. At least he said they were the ones, I wasn't sure. It made me sick, but I was glad. It felt good to get even. He invited me to dinner in his quarters. He was charming. Told me I was still beautiful, still desirable. He made love to me. I let him. Again and again. Then he tired of me. I felt rejected. Tried to make myself desirable for him. In the end I humiliated myself. Begged him to see me. He did. He turned me over to his second in command. And he watched. I thought, Jesus, where does this end? I told myself when I reach sergeant, I'll kill myself. But I didn't go back. Just drank a lot. Then he called. Said he wanted me. Needed me."

She moved her hand aimlessly across the tabletop; her eyes brimmed with tears. "So now it comes in streaks," she continued. "We're like a bad addiction. You don't really like it, but it's all there is. Every time I go back, I swear I won't do it again. It hasn't been so bad. He never really hurt me—until today. How can I hate him so much and be so afraid he won't want me? Pretty degraded, huh? That's the way people react. If it doesn't happen to you, you have all sorts of ideas about how strong you'll be—how you'll live up to the idea in your head, all those expectations of yourself. But then, you just end up surviving. No heroics—no strength of character. Not even dignity. Just afraid your rapist won't take you to bed."

═══ *Chapter 9* ═══

THE PHONE RANG for a long time before the Major roused himself to pick it up. "Gurtman," he said, his voice suddenly as clipped and icy as though he'd been wide-awake.

"Helmut, it's Mikel."

"What the hell time is it? I was sound asleep."

"In answer to your question," said Andrei's aide, "it's four A.M. But I must say I'm surprised that you'd be able to sleep after the humiliation you suffered today at the parade."

Pricked, Gurtman sat up straight in bed, intent now on defending his version of events. "I suffered no humiliation, Mikel. I performed my function. Crowds are mercurial, irrational—"

"And defiant," Mikel interrupted.

"Occasionally defiant," Gurtman acknowledged.

"And occasionally in need of being reminded that defiance does not come without a cost."

"It's late, Mikel. What are you getting at?"

"Gurtman, with all your posturing and your strutting, does it ever occur to you that you should rattle your saber a little louder? Either that or keep it sheathed."

"It's not my way to keep it sheathed, Mikel. You know that."

"Precisely. Which is why some of us feel a more convincing show of force might be appropriate after the embarrassment you were handed today."

"And just who," Gurtman asked, his ears now burning from this assault on his vanity, "does this 'some of us' include? Does it include Colonel Denisov?"

"This is not an official phone call, Gurtman," said Mikel. "In fact, this conversation has never taken place. Sweet dreams, my gentle major."

Late one night in the Chicago Loop, the police raided an outlaw cabaret and spoiled Kimberly Ballard's greatest role.

She had been playing Miss New America for a week; it was a star turn, a sensation. She'd emerge onto the little stage as a southern belle, in an antebellum gown, twirling a parasol, coy and innocent. But then she'd begin to sing a set of mocking lyrics, and her modesty gave way to an immodest striptease. Her chaste dance gradually changing to a bump and grind, she'd slink out of her petticoats to reveal a bikini fashioned from the U.S.-UN-USSR flag.

Kimberly thought the song she sang was silly. One couplet went, "Tell me the truth, tell me a lie, what matters to me is my piece of the pie."

Cole Porter it was not, Kimberly thought, but she made the lyrics work, with her acting, her singing, the magic of her transformation from debutante to slut, which made it clear that sex and politics were only too closely linked.

She thought the secret of it all was that she didn't really care about politics. Satirize the Soviets, satirize the Americans—it didn't matter to her. What mattered was to touch people, to reach them. Outlaw theater was what touched them now in Chicago—not Shakespeare or Tennessee Williams, but short, barbed little skits that reflected the hypocrisy and frustration of the audiences' lives. The crowded little theater—a converted warehouse—was electric, in large part because what they were doing was illegal. Actors and audience were joined in rebellion and danger, creating a tension that was close to the pitch of battle.

To Kimberly, the theater was home, the only place she could lose herself and become someone else, live another life. For five wonderful nights, two shows a night, she had been Miss New America and it was an answered prayer.

Then the police came.

She had just stripped to her bikini when the whistles began blowing. The music stopped abruptly and she was left standing on the stage, half angry, half frightened, half naked. What was interesting, she thought, was how little panic there was. It was as if everyone had been expecting this all along. It was all so ridiculous. It was just a funny little skit.

A policeman was standing on a chair instructing the audience to march peacefully out the doors. Everyone seemed to be falling into line. Kimberly joined them, head high. A man gave her his coat to wear over her bikini and she marched out past the lines of police toward the waiting black vans. Street people stared at those under arrest.

As she neared a van, a policeman blocked her way. "Not you," he said. "You can go."

"What?"

"Go home, get out of here."

Then she understood. "I demand that you arrest me," she said defiantly. "I'm as guilty as anyone else. You can't—"

Mikel approached Kimberly and the policeman. "Get away with this?" he asked, finishing her sentence. "You are under the protection of the area adviser. You are not under arrest. You are free to go. In fact, I would be happy to escort you home."

Kimberly saw the other actors staring at her from inside the van. "Damn you, arrest me," she cried. "This is an outrage."

The door of the van slammed and moved away. She broke away from Mikel and stormed down the dark street. People on the sidewalk began to taunt her. A black man moved sharply through the crowd and took her by the arm. Her breath caught and she tried to pull away, but the stranger's hand held her fast. His grip was fierce yet somehow gentle, and her fear seemed to flow out of her at the place he touched.

"Give us some room, brothers," he said to the crowd that surrounded them, and yielding to his tone of quiet authority, the people parted to let them pass. "The little sister's lost," he purred. "We gonna help to get her found again."

Confused but grateful, Kimberly let the black man lead her around a corner and into an alley behind a jazz club. Jazz, like rock and roll, was proscribed by the new regime; the authorities had dubbed it—as the Nazis had—a "Judeo-Negroid perversion." And now Kimberly understood: this kind man, who introduced himself as Jeffrey, was regarding her neither as white nor black, rich or poor, but was adopting her as a fellow outlaw.

"You're safe," he assured her, waving his hand toward an archaic Rambler sedan. "This car'll take you home. Trust them."

The car pulled up to them. Kimberly studied his face intently. "I don't know who you are, but you look familiar to me somehow."

Jeffrey opened the car door. "It's not important. Don't forget, no matter what your gig, there are Americans around somewhere."

He did not afford her the time to respond but gently helped her into the car, which took off immediately.

Kimberly gave the driver Andrei's address. She didn't speak—she felt too angry, too distracted—and when the car dropped her off the black man was still as much a mystery as he'd been when he first grabbed her arm.

She hurried into the apartment, propelled by her rage. Unsure of what to do, she went to the phone and dialed the number of the military command post. She identified herself and asked for Andrei. A man's voice announced that he was out of town.

"I know he's out of town. I know he's in Washington. I need to speak with him."

"I'm afraid that's impossible," the voice said.

"It isn't impossible. You've done it before. Why are you doing this to me? Did Mikel tell you to? I must speak with Andrei, do you hear?"

By then she was screaming, but it didn't matter, because the person at the other end of the line had hung up. Kimberly turned and caught a glimpse of herself in the mirrored wall. It was an absurd figure, disheveled, frantic, and still in her bikini. She walked toward the image, reaching up to touch the makeup on her face. It made her look like a whore. Curious and frightened by this perception of herself, she began rubbing furiously at her makeup.

The convoy pulled up to the Bradford house at dawn. The leading cycles pulled fifty yards past the house, flanking the road, ready to cut off any traffic from outside the town. The limo, preceded by a station wagon, pulled into the driveway, while the trailing cycles covered the road in the direction from which they had come. Four men wearing suits got out of the station wagon. One moved to the front of the yard, another to the rear, and two covered each side. All the lights on the vehicles went off, except for the blinking reds on the motorcycles covering the road.

Inside, Amanda's face, partially in shadow, partially illuminated by the light from the bathroom, was tight with passion. Her head rolled to one side as she tried to catch her breath, taking little short gasps. She searched and found Peter's mouth, then threw her head back, her arms clinging tightly to his back, then falling open. She breathed deeply. Peter was sweating, trying to catch his breath.

"Must be getting older," he panted.

"It should happen to everyone. Maybe we should have more parades. When was the last time you woke me up like this?"

"A real workout," he said, glancing at the bedside clock.

"Always the romantic."

He moved to get up. She held him down. "Kiss me."

Peter gave her his light "I'm in a hurry" kiss.

"No, a good one. A sexy one."

He kissed her passionately.

"Mmm . . . now you can get up."

"Thank you very much. I'm only half an hour late."

He rushed into the bathroom and climbed into the shower. Amanda leaned back, closed her eyes, enjoying the after-warmth of the lovemaking. Her reverie was interrupted as Peter returned to the bedroom and began to dress.

"I'm gonna miss you, Peter. I love you, you know."

He heard a car door slam outside. "It's the car they've sent for me." He finished dressing quickly and walked over to the bed. "I love you too, Am. I'll call you this evening."

After he left, Amanda sank back into the pillows, thinking of that old test—when a glass is half filled with water. She was not sure if she felt half empty, or half full.

Devin heard the roar of engines and leaped out of bed, looking for the source.

It was an SSU vehicle but it wasn't coming for him. Devin saw Helmut Gurtman, a quarter mile away, atop the hill, overlooking the exile camp, studying it with cold intensity, like a jackal eyeing a kill.

With the sure survival instincts of the fugitive, Devin studied Gurtman's posture and knew that trouble was coming. Almost without a conscious decision, he packed his few belongings to move on.

When Peter got off his plane in Chicago, he was surprised to find Marion Andrews waiting there. He stammered that it was a wonderful surprise, although in fact her sleek self-assurance made him nervous. "I suppose you're my welcoming committee?" he joked.

"Well, actually not," she said. "I'm going with you."

"I thought I had arrived."

"You have. But Andrei went to Washington last night and would like us to meet him there. Welcome to politics."

In Milford, Ward received a call that morning from Helmut Gurtman. "This is your official notification that the United Nations Special Security Unit will be conducting maneuvers in and around the town of Milford, commencing at 0700 hours tomorrow."

Ward didn't know what the hell he meant. "Is there something you want me to do?" he asked. "You sure don't need my permission."

"You will want to issue an advisory to townspeople to stay indoors and off the streets and roads. Those who violate the order will be subject to arrest and will be in extreme danger."

Gurtman hung up. Ward slowly put the phone down. He went to the window and looked out at the quiet streets of Milford. The town and its people were as placid and defenseless as a pen full of lambs.

Twenty guests, men in tuxedos, women in bright gowns, were gathered around the long mahogany dining-room table in Petya Samanov's Virginia mansion. Twin chandeliers glittered above them, and servants hovered nearby with wine. Petya sat at the head of the table, beaming. Marion was opposite him, wearing the emerald necklace from the czar's collection that he had given her. Every important leader of government was among the privileged guests except the president, and his exclusion was a calculated snub.

After coffee and brandy had been served, Samanov rose to his feet. "In Russia, where as most of you know I come from, we have a saying. Actually we have a great many sayings, most of them untranslatable. But the one I have in mind is something like this. Make your adversary a friend and together you will plant a field. Make him a slave and you cannot bury him enough times."

His guests smiled politely, not quite sure what the point was.

"Unfortunately, we do not always follow our old sayings," Petya quipped, and everyone laughed.

Everyone, that is, but Peter Bradford. He did not understand how a trip to Chicago that morning had somehow led to this lavish dinner in a mansion outside Washington.

"As you all know," Petya continued, "it is our wish to hasten the day when we return to our own homeland and leave the rebuilding of America to our American friends. Tonight we have an honored guest who will help us reach that goal more quickly. Kindly join me in a toast to the first governor-general—the Governor-General of the Central Administrative Area, or Heartland, Mr. Peter Bradford!"

Samanov lifted his glass. Everyone at the table stood and did the same. Peter, unsure what he should do, got to his feet. He saw Andrei and Marion smiling at him. Andrei seemed genuinely pleased; Marion's smile was more calculating. All around him the most important men and women in America were studying him, toasting him, repeating his name. It might have been a politician's dream come true.

But that was not how Peter felt.

He felt trapped.

Halfway across America, Devin was having a very different kind of dinner at a tiny table in a small, cramped kitchen. At this dinner, powdered milk was drunk rather than champagne and hearth-baked yams had to stand in for prime ribs. But the company was good, a jovial young man named Clayton Kullen and a black minister, Reverend James Blackstone and his wife, Melanie.

"So there are five of us, hiding in a cave," Clayton was saying. "And we hear shooting, I peek out and see this fellow here, running like crazy, and the railroad police are after him, guns blazing, and pretty soon I see that he's headed straight for us, bringing the police with him. So I yell, *'Hey you, go find your own cave!'*"

Everyone laughed. "That's not quite true," Devin said quietly. "He hid me in his cave. Or else I'd probably be dead."

"I don't know," Clayton said. "You looked like a pretty fast runner."

Reverend Blackstone had been studying Devin carefully as Devin busied himself with a yam, very much aware of the scrutiny. "You say you're headed for Chicago?" he asked.

Devin nodded.

"Chicago's the wrong way," the minister said. "Most folks through here are headed the other way."

"What's your identification number?" Clayton asked abruptly.

Devin froze; the activity at the table stopped. Clayton smiled gently.

"How long?" he asked.

"Not long," Devin admitted.

"Family in Chicago?"

Devin kept eating. Finally he said, "My children. I'm going to . . ."

He didn't finish the sentence. He didn't know how to.

"To what?" Clayton pressed. "To see them? Join them? Kidnap them?"

"Clay, leave the man alone," Melanie said.

"It matters what kind of help he needs. What he wants to do."

"I'll start with seeing them," Devin said. "Look, I'd appreciate your help. Maybe if you can just point me in the right direction." He stood up, anxious to keep moving, uncomfortable with their curiosity.

"Sit down," the minister said. "Finish your dinner. Some of us get real put off when people don't finish their dinner."

Melanie Blackstone smiled and touched Devin's arm. He sat back down.

"You've climbed aboard the oldest railroad in America, mister," the minister said. "The underground railroad. Used to help slaves, a hundred-odd years ago. Runs in all directions. All hours. More reliable than Amtrak. God works in mysterious ways."

Devin stared at the man uncertainly.

"What he's saying," Clayton added, "is that we can get you to Chicago a lot faster and safer than you could on your own—if you got there at all."

"I appreciate it," Devin said.

"Devin Milford," Melanie said. "It took awhile to make the connection. You're thinner, and you didn't used to have the beard."

Devin shook his head guardedly. "I'm sorry. It's a mistake some people make."

"That's too bad," Reverend Blackstone said. "Because I'd sure like to shake that man's hand someday."

Clayton smiled. "Okay, let me put it this way. I have friends in Chicago who can find out where Devin Milford's children are. Now does that interest you?"

Devin started to smile. They all began to laugh.

* * *

Not long after Petya Samanov's toast to Peter, the guests began to say good night.

Peter and Andrei were Samanov's houseguests, there in the mansion, and they settled before the fire in the downstairs study with a bottle of brandy between them. Peter had taken a sip or two; Andrei was drinking heartily.

"Do you realize this brandy was put down just as Hitler was rising to power in Germany?" he said.

"If it's older than I am, I kind of lose interest," Peter said. He didn't want to talk about brandy; he wanted to talk about his role, this crazy new position he had been thrust into, but Andrei wouldn't give him the chance.

"You're not intrigued by history—the twists and gyrations." Andrei smiled. "A communist and a capitalist drinking spirits from the time of fascism's greatest power. At that very time Stalin, that great fascist, was, under the guise of socialism, murdering millions and imprisoning millions more. I'm partial to this year. It was also the year my grandfather died in the Gulag." He took a quiet sip of brandy, as if drinking a silent toast.

Peter watched, suddenly feeling sympathy for this man. "I'm sorry, I don't know what to say," he said quietly.

Andrei shrugged. "My grandfather is now a hero of the Soviet Union, an honor posthumously bestowed. Stalin is dead and discredited. My grandfather is dead and recredited. And his grandson is one of the few responsible for elevating Mother Russia at last—to its position as the only true power in the world."

He raised his glass and drank. Peter did not.

Andrei smiled at him. "I wouldn't drink to that either, if I were you."

Andrei sighed and poured himself another glass of

brandy. He offered one to Peter, who shook his head. "Never trust a man who won't get drunk with you," Andrei muttered, staring at Peter. "We learn how to survive, even become the power we hated. You will too. We both have our share of problems. Ours is that seventy-five years of communism have produced a people who wish to be led. A people who know in their bones that to make decisions is to court disaster. We control the world and we don't have any competent people to run it."

He stood up and warmed himself before the fire. After a moment he raised his glass again. "To my honored grandfather," he said. "Posthumously rewarded—died—suffering—disgraced—filled with hate and hopelessness—in great pain—alone—just he and the hard frozen ground of Lyubyanka."

Andrei lifted his glass. After a moment, Peter stood and lifted his as well. They drained the glasses, then stood in silence for a while. Peter heard a peal of laughter from upstairs. Marion ought to be laughing, he thought; she's wearing the czarina's emeralds.

"Andrei, I'd like to talk about politics. About me. About this new job. I feel like I'm a pawn on somebody else's chessboard."

Andrei grinned. "Yes, we must talk. You have the job, now what does it mean? First of all, there is one bit of news that must be broken to you."

Peter braced himself for the worst—and got it.

"Marion Andrews is to be your deputy, and intimate adviser on political matters."

"That's a hell of a thing to throw at me. What if I don't want the job on those terms?"

"Don't overreact. She's smart. Obviously she's well connected. Use her."

"Use her? She's got her own agenda, her own ambitions. I don't trust her."

Andrei looked Peter full in the face. "And we don't trust you," he said. "To be precise, senior officials in the foreign ministry in Moscow do not trust you. You are not a party man. Thus you are uncontrollable, untrustworthy. Marion, on the other hand, is committed to ideology and to her own hunger for power. Those are qualities they understand in the Kremlin. They see you as not having enough at stake."

"I have my country at stake," Peter said stiffly.

Andrei shrugged. "I have persuaded General Samanov, and he, somewhat against his better judgment, has persuaded the Kremlin that you are the right man. But he needs a guarantee, security."

"What if I won't do it?"

"Someone else will. Someone less capable. Less humane."

"It would set your timetable back."

"True. And that could be dangerous for your hope for America, as well as mine."

Peter, still angry, still embittered by the games the Russians were playing, asked, "And what is your hope for America?"

Andrei's reply was entirely sincere. "To salvage as much as possible," he said.

Word of the SSU maneuvers had spread fast through the county. At dawn the courthouse square was deserted. Even Herb 'n Betty's Cafe was closed, for the first time in memory.

At precisely 7:00 A.M., the main gate of the SSU barracks swung open and locked in place. Inside the compound, four black attack helicopters rose into the air, then hovered above the road. Then, with a low rumble, the entire battalion came racing out toward the gates—attack vehicles, light tanks, snowmobiles, armored personnel carriers, all directed by Helmut Gurtman in his command vehicle. Just after clearing the gate the column split, the snowmobiles and all-terrain attack vehicles speeding across the fields, heading directly toward the town of Milford.

They raced through the courthouse square at forty miles an hour. Ward Milford, watching from the sheriff's office, felt himself tremble—their speed and sound were menacing, even to him.

The convoy roared past the Bradford house on the edge of town. Scott watched openmouthed. Amanda and Jackie stood in the doorway close together, their faces fearful.

Moments later the speeding vehicles passed the Milford farm. Will ran out into the yard. "Sons of bitches," he yelled, shaking his fist. Alethea, watching from an upstairs window, began to sob.

It was a gray, cloudy morning. The day's first stirrings had begun at the exile camp: two men started the outdoor cook fires; a child entered one of the outdoor privies; a woman hung wash on a line. Suddenly the roar filled the camp. People emerged from their tents and shacks to search the sky. With the stoicism of those who have been through catastrophes before, they reacted not with panic but only with quiet resignation.

Helmut took his place at the crest of the hill, east of the camp. He studied the scene with a kind of pleasure, a smile playing across his gaunt face. He held out his hand and a sergeant gave him a flare. He sent the flare soaring above the exile camp; it cast an eerie red glow, as in medieval paintings of hell.

Responding to the flare, a long line of attack vehicles, each filled with armed troops, shot down the hill from the east and formed a phalanx facing the camp. The troops raced across the creek to the camp, weapons at the ready, awaiting their orders. The people began to back away from them, just as Helmut sent up a second flare.

The flare still hung in the dark sky when the four helicopters came swooping in low from the west. They hovered over the camp, banked, and returned to circle, dip, and perform intricate maneuvers above the terrified Exiles. They dropped ever lower, until people flopped on their bellies for safety. The raging wind from their blades had blown down many of the tents, and wet snow swirled crazily on the agitated ground. Children screamed but their cries could not be heard above the roar of the engines; their openmouthed faces were mute masks of terror.

Finally the helicopters took up positions at the four corners of the camp, hovering there like sentries. There was a moment's respite. Mothers clutched their children as men searched for weapons and routes of escape.

Dieter Heinlander stood outside his trailer with his wife, gazing across the creek at the row of troops. "What are they going to do?" Gerta asked.

"Perhaps that is all," Dieter said. "An exhibition, to scare us, to show their strength."

Gerta asked in despair, "Have we not suffered enough?"

It is the nature of the beast, Dieter thought, and held her closer.

Then Helmut shot off the third flare and a wave of tanks roared over the hill from the west: a dozen great black monsters in a perfectly straight line, picking up speed as they moved down the slope toward camp.

The Exiles began to scream, running everywhere, but there was no escape. The tanks to the west, the line of armed men to the east, the hovering helicopters standing guard—all were ready to crush anyone who fled the camp.

A tank reached a tent high on the hill and demolished it with ease.

A young man ran from one tank into the path of another and was crushed.

A woman, running with a baby in her arms, tripped and fell. A tank ran over her leg and her child was thrown screaming to the ground.

Trailers were tumbled over and shacks crushed. An old man tried to beat on the side of a tank with a hammer and was thrown senseless to the ground. The troops across the creek began to fire into the air. One of the demolished shanties was ablaze and smoke filled the air. The noise was deafening: the wheeling and smashing. But another sound, more fearsome, resounded: the mounting cries of the Exiles.

When the tanks had completed their sweep, a moment's peace settled over the devastated camp. Families found one another, and comfort was given to the wounded. Then the tanks wheeled about and made a second run through the camp. This time some of the Exiles just sank to the ground and did not resist.

To Helmut, watching from the hillside, the attack had a marvelous symmetry. The Exiles saw chaos, but from his vantage point he saw only perfection: two clean, regimented lines that did not waver or break. His forces had not gone there to kill, only to execute this elegant maneuver, and if people died, it was because they had panicked or resisted.

He fired yet another flare, and within minutes his

force had withdrawn, as abruptly as it came, leaving behind the dead and dying of the broken camp. Helmut climbed into his vehicle and, without a glance at the devastation below, drove away across the fields toward the barracks.

Peter was having breakfast on a bright, glassed-in porch that overlooked the rolling hills of northern Virginia. Three horses gracefully grazed in the distance on the emerald carpet of green. As he finished his coffee, an attractive woman in a Soviet army uniform, a member of General Samanov's staff, entered and smiled at him.

"On your call to Milford, sir. There seems to be a problem. We cannot get through."

"What's the matter?"

She shrugged. She spoke with a light accent and was a bit plump but very pretty. "Lines down?" she asked. "It is common."

Peter poured more coffee. He decided he'd try to reach home later. It couldn't be that hard.

As the convoy roared back to the barracks, past the Milford and Bradford homes, through the deserted courthouse square, hundreds of townspeople wondered what it had left in its wake.

Alethea was in her kitchen piling together all the clean sheets she could find; she had heard the cries from over the hill, the gunshots, the raging helicopters, and she had no illusions about the fate of the exile camp.

Will Milford appeared in the doorway. He had his parka on. "I'm going out," he said. "Nobody locks me in my own house all day."

Alethea crossed the room, still clutching the pile of sheets, and kissed him. "They're squatters, Dad," she said.

He scowled at her. "Just 'cause I don't want 'em on my land don't mean I'd let 'em die like dogs. Let's go!"

He grabbed the first-aid box from the table and marched out the door.

Tears welled in Alethea's eyes. She quickly followed.

"The red phone was busy and the other one was just dead," Amanda said.

"Didn't he say he'd call?" Jackie asked.

Amanda went to the kitchen window and looked over the fields in the direction of the exile camp. "He said he'd call when he got the chance."

Scott asked, "What do you think they did?"

"God, I don't know," Amanda cried. "I wish your father was home."

Suddenly she knew she must do something. She walked to the closet and grabbed her parka and boots.

"Mom!" Jackie cried.

Amanda sat down and started tugging at one of the boots. "You two stay here. I'll be back as soon as I can."

"Mom, you can't go out there," Jackie said. "Scott?"

"Come on, Mom. They'll be checking the roads."

"At least wait till you talk to Dad," Jackie urged.

Amanda stood up, zipping her parka. "I trust you to stay here until I get home," she said. "Don't worry about me."

She kissed Jackie and turned to kiss Scott. "I hate to ask a sixteen-year-old kid to kiss his mother . . ."

He walked over to her and gave her a quick kiss.

Then she hurried out the door, before she changed her mind.

At the exile camp, Alan Drummond had set up a field hospital in what remained of the barn that had been used as a community center. Its floor was littered with the dead and dying, and outside the carnage seemed to extend forever.

Several fires still smoldered, sending ghostly wisps of smoke across the ruined landscape. Bodies lay unmoved. Mothers searched the debris for their children as children cried helplessly for lost parents. One man, his head bloody, crawled slowly in an ever-widening circle. An unofficial system of triage had emerged, as the dying were left to die and those with a chance of life were carried to Alan Drummond's hopelessly overworked medical center.

Will Milford was helping some of the survivors search through the wrecked dwellings for bodies or whatever valuables could be salvaged. Alethea was helping Alan, cutting her sheets into bandages and applying them to bleeding men and women. All she knew was what she had learned in a first-aid course, years before, but her efforts were better than nothing. She thought she must be in shock. She could not believe that human beings, even Helmut Gurtman, had caused this senseless slaughter; it was easier to think of it as a natural disaster, like a flood or tornado.

And yet she knew that Helmut had done it, out of hate, out of a need for revenge, out of some reservoir of malice that would never be totally understood.

The others did not see Amanda arrive at the camp. She walked in alone and soon her face mirrored the devastation she saw. She had been here before, and done what good she could, but she was not prepared for this horror, so far beyond her ability to correct. She saw the crushed body of a woman she recognized, recoiled in shock, then began digging through the wreckage of a leveled shack. Tearing at the debris, she uncovered the mangled body of a child. Her face blooded, her features distorted by the final moments of terror, the lifeless girl was not immediately recognizable. But after a moment Amanda realized that it was Dierdre, the girl who had come to her yard that morning.

Amanda held the child close, as if her warmth could give life, and then she began to stagger toward the hospital.

Alethea saw her coming and ran to meet her. She reached for the child, then slowly drew back her hand.

"I've got her," Amanda whispered.

Alethea looked from the child's still face to Amanda's haunted eyes. "I'll . . . I'll get someone," she said.

She returned in a moment with Alan Drummond. His face was weary, his white coat soaked with blood. When he spoke, it was with an odd formality. "Thank you for coming, Amanda."

"The baby . . . she needs . . ."

He shook his head; he too was in shock. It did not keep him from working, but it kept him from thinking of anything but the patient before him. "She needs nothing, Amanda. She's gone." He reached out and touched Amanda's cheek.

Amanda turned and started up the hill, the dead baby clutched in her arms.

"You'd better stop her," Alan said. "She's in shock."

Alethea looked at him. She thought she loved this man, for his goodness, and yet she rejected his advice. "Why?" she said, more to herself than to Alan. "Why the hell not take the corpse to town? Let the townspeople have a dose of reality." She ran into their battered little hospital. "Come on," she cried. "Anybody who can walk. Get up. Help the others. We'll go to town."

She ran through the camp, summoning others. "If you're not hurt, help those who are," she told them. "We've got to go where people can help us. We can't stay here and die."

She came to Dieter, sitting on the ground beside his crushed trailer, the body of his dead wife nearby, covered by a blanket. "Come on," she said. "Please."

He shook his head slowly. "No. I'll stay."

Soon she had most of the survivors, more than a hundred of them, on their feet, starting to move. They stretched out along the road for more than a mile. Amanda still led the way, the small body of Dierdre clutched awkwardly to her. Alethea helped a girl who used a tree limb for a crutch. Will held one end of a makeshift stretcher on which an unconscious woman was sprawled.

The walk seemed endless, surreal. It was dusk when the first marchers reached the town, not sure what might await them there but believing it must be better than the hell they had left behind.

Peter climbed into the back of Samanov's limousine for the ride to the White House. Marion sat between him and the general. As the gentle countryside flashed by, Samanov said, "There is much to do and little time. You must force changes beyond what you feel your countrymen can tolerate."

"You ask a lot," Peter said. "They still love America. You want them to forget it."

"The alternative is worse," Samanov said. "Your

leadership can save your people. Marion will help. You will be a good team. What was it Andrei called you? Ms. Inside and Mr. Outside."

"Is that my job? A front man?"

"Peter, I truly do want to help you," Marion said. "You may not believe it, but I do. Give me a chance."

Peter forced a smile and moved slowly to what really was on his mind. "General, I've been trying all day to reach my wife," he said. "They can't get through. I don't understand."

Petya Samanov smiled. "A minor matter," he said. "Don't worry; I'll take care of it."

The procession of exiles continued; passing houses as dark and silent as death, Alethea began to wonder if the townspeople would have the decency to acknowledge them at all.

"Wait!"

Alethea turned. A woman stood in her doorway. Mrs. Harrison, a seamstress. She rushed down her walk into the street. "Let me help her," Mrs. Harrison said, and put her arm around the woman Alethea had been half carrying. Without saying a word, she gently guided the woman toward her home.

Alethea looked around: she saw the door to another house open and a man and a woman hurry forth. By the time she reached the corner, a half dozen of the worst-injured Exiles had been taken in.

Amanda reached the courthouse steps with the dead baby still in her arms. Ward met her there. Several members of the county council—called to an emergency meeting—stood behind the deputy. Herb Lister, red-faced with anger, glared at her and at the procession of Exiles behind her.

"Amanda, let me take her," Ward said.

But grief-shocked, her eyes glazed and her expression vacant, Amanda would not hand over her ghastly bundle to the deputy. Instead she turned to Lister, who was too appalled to retreat from her slow but relentless advance. She pressed the corpse, already stiffening and misshapen, into his arms and backed away.

Early that evening, three hundred miles west of Milford, Justin reached a sign that said:

CAUTION—BORDER
CENTRAL ADMINISTRATIVE AREA
PREPARE FOR INSPECTION

Justin wheeled off the road and climbed a ridge until, lying flat, he could see the distant checkpoint. Gates blocked the road and a high wire fence stretched off in both directions. He studied the movements of the soldiers and trucks and soon realized they were putting up more fencing, extending it as far as the eye could see—sealing off the border between Nebraska and what had once been Colorado and what was now officially known as the Semi-Autonomous Zone.

Justin waited for darkness and then he began to ride south along the fence. Crickets rasped and the sharp air of the high plains stung his face. The fence went on for mile after mile. He rode with his lights off and followed the fence by moonlight. The terrain was rough and he went slowly. After a while he noticed the plowed earth on the other side of the fence. He passed one sign that said DANGER—LAND MINES but he didn't need the sign to tell him what the troops had done. Anyone who wanted to could cut through a fence in this isolated country but would then have to face the uncertainty of that plowed earth. The sign might even be a bluff—who could say?

By midnight he guessed he'd traveled a hundred miles or more and still the fence stretched on. It was time to make a decision. He couldn't exist in this wilderness forever. He had to get back to the road, get started west again—that, or turn back in defeat. He stopped at a point where the fence dipped down into a gully and where he might not be so visible. He took from his pack a blasting charge he'd stolen before he left Milford. He placed it carefully under the fence, lit the fuse, and raced back behind a rock.

The explosion must have echoed for miles. When the dust settled, he saw the gaping hole in the fence. Grinning, he kicked his Harley into life and hurtled through the opening.

Justin pumped one fist above his head, partly in defiance and partly to prime his nerve as he picked up speed. From a distance, in that cold night, he was a tiny figure, cowboylike, against the vast landscape of the west. He sped on, across the plowed earth, confident now, proud, ready to resume his odyssey, and then there was another blast, and Justin and his Harley were lifted high into the air. When they came back to earth, one of the Harley's wheels kept spinning for a long time, but the boy was silent and still.

For a second day, Peter could not get through to his home. He went to the White House that morning and even the operators there could not reach Milford, Nebraska. Some local disturbance, they explained. Peter choked back a moment's fear.

He had other worries. General Samanov wanted him to address Congress that very afternoon. He had protested, but Samanov had said, "You do not fully appreciate the importance of your role. Right now you are more important than the president, by far." Everything being relative, he might have added.

Peter was baffled by what he should say. Samanov did not much seem to care. The clearer vision seemed to come from Andrei. "Peter, you must stress that decentralization can work, that we are entering a new era with new challenges, and Heartland can lead the way," the younger Russian said. "That, I suggest, is your message."

Peter wasn't sure he believed it. He needed time to think, to focus on this speech they wanted. He borrowed a spiral notebook from a secretary. They offered him an office—"Take the Oval Office if it will inspire you," Andrei said—but he declined and went for a walk instead.

He left the White House and started along Seventeenth Street, toward the Mall. It was a bright, crisp day and he savored the morning air. At first he found himself walking aimlessly, then realized he had a destination all along.

He walked on past the Vietnam Memorial. He had been there before and thought it deeply moving. Its critics were right to hate it, he thought. It was the most eloquent possible indictment of their folly—but he did not want to ponder that great black wall today.

Instead he strode toward the massive temple that was Abraham Lincoln's memorial.

A guard saluted sharply. Peter climbed the stairs and entered the rotunda, read the words inscribed on its walls, then gazed at the man himself.

Peter tried to imagine what Lincoln would have done had he been in Peter Bradford's position. Lincoln, a rough and eloquent idealist: the complete American.

He thought of Amanda. He desperately wanted her advice, because for all her loathing of politics, her thoughts fell naturally into humane and sincere expression.

He took out his notebook and began to write. In his mind he was not writing notes for a speech, but a letter to his wife. Perhaps he would even mail it. He looked again at Lincoln and began to write: "You can't look at those eyes and not think what being an American has meant."

He shook his head, then continued. "Now there's an end to it. Soon there will be no America, at least as we've known it. It will be history, distorted, just as Lincoln has been—the man who kept the Union together, now embraced by those who would tear it apart."

Halfway down the steps, Peter saw the man who'd been following him, some sort of bodyguard; perhaps now he was reporting on this odd behavior. Peter ignored him; this intruder did not matter at all.

"I need to talk to you, Am. Things are moving too fast. Maybe there's still time to stop. It's hard to know what's right. I wonder about myself. The choices I make could affect millions of people; what if they're the wrong ones?"

He looked east on the Mall, to the Capitol, where he was supposed to speak that afternoon. What could he say that would have any meaning to those dispirited politicians, the ones who still dreamed of freedom and the ones who had given up hope? Did he, or Nebraska, really matter to them? Or was it all an elaborate charade?

He began to write again.

"It seems that I'm about to become part of a system that some future generation will rebel against. Will I be hated by people who never knew me, who don't understand why I'm doing what I must do? Old truths, new generations; maybe freedom is something you can't inherit."

Peter sighed, wrote "With Love to Amanda from Peter" at the bottom of the page, and hurried down the steps. His bodyguard silently fell in behind him.

The SSU convoy roared into the Milford courthouse square. Soldiers jumped out and began to set up roadblocks. Snow flurries swirled around them. A dark-haired officer, followed by five heavily armed men, marched to Herb 'n Betty's Cafe and kicked open the door. His men followed him inside, their weapons at the ready.

Betty was pouring a cup of mock coffee for a man in one of the booths. Startled, she dropped the pot. "See what you made me do!" she cried. "Get outta here."

The officer looked at her and laughed.

"Go on," she yelled. "What the hell do you think you're doing, anyway?"

"*Cerrado*," he said, loud enough so everyone in the room turned to watch. "Curfew."

"Listen, don't you tell me . . ." she began. Bill Grey, the man she had been serving coffee, stepped to her side.

"Better do what they say," he warned.

"Out. Everybody out," the officer said. He was handsome, in a sullen way, and there was no hesitation in him. His men lined the room and began to prod people out the door. Only Betty held back.

"You. Outside."

"It's my place," she raged.

He shoved her roughly out the door. Outside, her customers were being loaded in the back of a truck.

The officer was trying to turn off the faded neon

"Herb 'n Betty's Cafe" sign. *"La luz,"* he said. "Off. Out."

"It don't turn off, turkey," Betty said. "It's been on for thirty years and it's gonna stay on."

The officer cursed in his native tongue and gestured toward one of his men. With the butt of the gun, the underling smashed the neon. Gas hissed, the light flickered, then finally went out.

Betty, still in her apron, screamed at the officer, but his soldiers lifted her into the truck. When the Cuban finished battering the neon sign, he gazed angrily at his prisoners.

"Cerrado," he said. "Curfew."

Betty beat on the back of the truck in frustration. Already soldiers were starting to board up her cafe. The truck started to move, carrying the dazed prisoners away; gentle snow surrounded it as it eased down the street.

It was only an hour later that Ward burst into the county council chambers. Helmut Gurtman was there, with Herb Lister and two other council members, Fred Tate, the owner of the hardware store, and Mel Austin, the town's leading lawyer. Ward hadn't taken two steps when two SSU guards grabbed him.

"What the hell's going on?" Ward demanded. "Get off me."

He yanked free. Helmut nodded and the soldiers stepped back. Ward stood there a moment, trying to put it together. He regained a little of his composure and walked toward Helmut.

"Your tanks are blocking traffic," Ward raged. "And what the hell do you mean, arresting people for drinking coffee?"

"Settle down, Ward," advised Mel Austin, the lawyer.

"As of 0800 hours this morning, the town is blockaded," Helmut said. "No one is permitted in or out. An absolute curfew is in effect."

Ward and the German were nose to nose. Ward was almost as tall as Gurtman and twice as broad. "You have no right to do this," he said. "No authority to bring your troops in here."

"The actions are at the request of the Milford County Council," Gurtman declared.

"Bullshit," Ward shot back.

"It's true," Herb Lister said. "There's been a flagrant violation of the law. Exiles are threatening to take over the town. Established authority is either absent or in dereliction of duty."

"What's that supposed to mean?" Ward demanded. "That you acted when Peter Bradford and Alan Drummond weren't here to oppose you?"

"It's all quite legal," Mel Austin said.

"Did you not lead a group of townspeople to the exile camp in violation of the curfew?" Gurtman demanded.

"An illegal act of defiance," Herb Lister said.

"An act of decency," Ward said. He turned to Mel and Fred. "What are you two doing, being part of this?"

"It's legal," Mel said.

"Be realistic," Fred said. "What choice have we got?"

"What choice?" Ward raged. "We can stand up to this Nazi, and show a little guts—"

"You're a deputy," Herb Lister said. "You enforce the law as we define it, or you're out."

Helmut said calmly, "Your choice is simple. Either you and your men enforce the curfew or we will do it alone."

Ward stared at the German in rage and frustration. He was outgunned. It was as simple as that.

"If there's no more business at the moment," Helmut said with taunting sincerity. "I would say this meeting's adjourned."

They drove from the White House to the Capitol in two limousines, the president's and Samanov's. Peter rode with Samanov, and he was not unaware of the symbolism involved, however jovially the general had issued the invitation.

The drive up Pennsylvania Avenue, complete with motorcycle escort, took only a minute or two. Peter was struck by how few people were on the streets, and with what disinterest they regarded the passing of their leaders.

He was speaking to a joint session of Congress—members of both the House and Senate meeting in the vast House chamber, with the president, the vice-president, members of the Supreme Court, and other dignitaries looking on.

The speaker of the house, a bony, crafty old buzzard, shouted out his introduction—"a new leader, a new generation, the first governor-general of the Heartland region, my good friend Mr. Peter Bradford"—and the sergeant at arms escorted Peter to the podium. He noted how the PPP loyalists applauded enthusiastically, while the other members only gently touched their hands together.

Suddenly he was facing them, the six hundred or so men and women who ruled America, or pretended to.

He had thought and thought about the speech. He

realized that he could not express all the fear and uncertainty and suspicion that he truly felt—those must remain hidden, if he was to be a public man. But neither was he willing to deliver the pep talk for Heartland that Andrei wanted; the government's propaganda machine was already boosting Heartland and he didn't intend to be another cog in the machine.

Peter had only one rule of speechmaking—keep it short. He had scribbled a few notes on the back of an envelope as they drove to the Capitol and added to them as he was being introduced. Now, for better or for worse, he began to speak, partly from the notes, more from his heart.

"Mr. Speaker, Mr. President, Mr. Vice-President, members of Congress, ladies and gentlemen . . ."

It was a mouthful, and after he got it out he paused and said, "I never expected to be here."

He spoke with such innocence and candor, no one could doubt his sincerity. His audience chuckled with amusement and sympathy.

"Like most Americans," Peter said, "the course of my life has not been what I expected. I think of the history of our country and wonder at its growth and change. I wonder if Washington or Jefferson could have imagined the shape and condition of the country just two centuries after their lifetimes. I wonder at the amazement and possibly the despair of Abraham Lincoln if he were to have seen the changes since the nineteenth century. Yet somehow, despite all the changes, our country has survived.

"I come from a part of the country where life, in many ways, is simple and predictable.

"Every spring when the ground thaws we plant a seed. In the summer it grows to maturity and is harvested. In the winter the earth rests, waiting for new planting. And when we plant again, it is not the same stalk of corn or grain that we saw standing beautiful in the field the summer before, but the seed is the same and given time, effort, and good fortune, another crop will emerge to feed hungry people.

"The seed is in the ground. It is the history and experience of two hundred years. I promise you I will give it my time and my effort, and with the help of the people of my area—the Heartland—we will see a bountiful harvest.

"Thank you and God bless."

There was a hush as his speech abruptly ended; four-hour-long orations were not unknown in that chamber. People were looking around, not sure what they had heard, or how they should respond.

General Petya Samanov, the most powerful man in the chamber, maintained a poker face, even as Andrei Denisov began to applaud enthusiastically. It had not been what Andrei had asked for, yet his sense was that it had been good, perhaps better than he had expected. The parable of the seed, Andrei thought, all the better for being of uncertain meaning. Had it seemed to hint at American independence, an American rebirth? If so, so much the better.

Andrei leaned close to Samanov. "It is good," he said. "Good."

Samanov slowly nodded and began to applaud. Marion watched him carefully, then she too began to clap vigorously. Soon the listeners rose to their feet and the chamber echoed with applause and cheers.

Peter, still at the podium, was genuinely surprised. His face beamed, masking a thought that had suddenly occurred to him: if these people approve of me, something must be wrong.

* * *

The bus rolled east through the darkness, across southern Illinois, passing Springfield, Abe Lincoln's home, through the heart of America. Devin and Clayton had seats in the back, where they could talk if they kept their voices down.

"How'd you get into the underground railroad business?" Devin asked.

Clay laughed quietly. "Just lucky, I guess. No, I was an Episcopal priest, serving up tea and salvation to nice old ladies. A pleasant life. Useful, in its way. A few good works thrown in—a center for the homeless, that sort of thing. But then the Transition came and I had to choose. It was like slavery, like the Vietnam War, one of those great moral issues that defy fence straddling. So I talked to God and God and I agreed I ought to try to help people who were being oppressed by this regime. Ergo, the underground railroad. Except that, instead of slaves, we're mostly helping political dissidents—hiding people who'd be imprisoned if they were caught, trying to reunite families, that sort of thing."

"How many of you are there?"

"It's hard to say. A lot. Religion in America had never been tested like this before. You could always play at social reform, with no greater penalty than pissing off your congregation, or maybe losing your job, but now we've got people in jail, hundreds of them. You pay the price if you stand up to the New America."

"I was away five years," said Devin. "Before that, it didn't seem that they were going after religion."

"They never did," Clay said. "They were smart. Let's face it, by the 1980s religion was not a major force in American life, so why stomp on it? Scare it, buy it off, co-opt it, the way they did business and politicians and journalism and everyone else. For most churches today, it's business as usual. Ask them about the Russians, and you'll get some mumbo-jumbo about having faith and the Lord working in mysterious ways."

"But some of you resisted?" Devin pressed.

"Oh sure. The Catholic church hasn't been so split since the Reformation. We Episcopalians have a pretty good record, relatively speaking—a lot of our guys act like they're docile, but they're secretly helping us. You know who's really made out like bandits in the Transition?"

"Who?"

"The evangelicals. The TV preachers. They ate it up. Had an answer for everything. God's punishing us because we'd been a nation of adulterers and druggies and homos and abortionists and all that; in other words, the Ruskies got us because we didn't pay attention to Jerry Falwell and Jimmy Swaggart. So what's their answer? Keep the faith, brothers, and keep them cards and letters coming!"

Devin laughed. "And the checks with 'em."

"You got it. The Russians like that message. Down south, they treat the evangelicals real good. They won't let them have their own TV networks again, not yet, but they let them on Natnet once in a while. And those guys would kill to get on the tube."

Clay grinned in the first light of morning. "It's a funny world."

"Yeah," Devin said. "My sense of humor keeps getting challenged."

Jackie was in her room, gazing out at the new morning. Tears rolled down her cheeks.

Her mother came in quietly and put her arms around

her. For a time no words were spoken; icicles caught the sunlight and glinted in the window.

Finally Jackie, still looking out at the empty fields, said, "I have this daydream. That he comes back. He's on his cycle and he says he couldn't live without me. He—"

She broke off, embarrassed. Amanda stroked her hair and Jackie continued. "He says, no matter what, he'll take care of me. We'll be all right." She looked up at Amanda, eyes bright with tears. "I didn't go with him. He asked me to go and I didn't."

Amanda said, "I don't think either of you was ready."

Jackie stiffened a bit. "You don't know. You always had Daddy."

Amanda smiled wistfully. "Once . . . I had a choice, a little like yours. But he was"—she shrugged—"too scary."

Jackie gazed at Amanda with surprise, maybe new respect. She had never imagined there might have been drama or conflict in her mother's early life.

"I thought Daddy was, you know, your childhood sweetheart."

Amanda smiled. "I had a long childhood, dear. There was room for two or three sweethearts." She hugged herself. "Anyway, all that was years ago."

"Mom, do you ever, like, wonder what would have happened?"

"Maybe sometimes. Not often. I'm very glad I married your father. Look at the bonus I got—you and of course your brother the hulk. See what I would have missed."

"You could have skipped that." Jackie smiled a little.

Amanda walked to the door, then turned back. "If

he loves you enough, maybe he'll come back, if he can," she said. "And if he does come back, maybe you'll still have enough love for it to make a difference."

Jackie weighed her mother's words, then shook her head in bemusement. "God, Mother, you're supposed to be trying to cheer me up."

Amanda smiled a bittersweet smile. "Sorry. Best I can do."

The bouncing of the bus awoke him. He looked up and saw an armed national guardsman moving down the aisle. He pulled himself together, trying to show no emotion.

"Relax, it's okay," Clayton said. "A border check. We're about to enter the late great state of Indiana."

The guardsman was lanky and casual. He glanced at their IDs and moved on.

"See, I told you those papers were cool," Clayton said. "You ever been to the Industrial Area?"

"Not lately," Devin said drily.

"It's not a pretty sight. What the Russians wanted mostly from us was agricultural—our farm capacity. If we would produce more and eat less, they could eat more, which is how it's working out. Plus, they wanted to make use of our high-tech capacity, and some of our scientific and medical knowledge. Then there's Hollywood. The Russians love our movies and they knew they could never duplicate Hollywood on the banks of the Volga. Essentially, Hollywood now is doing what it always secretly wanted to do—making trash, pure and simple. No phony-baloney art. Just sex and violence, except the message has changed a little. I mean, Rocky doesn't beat up on commies anymore—he's after neo-fascists now."

Devin was looking down the road at the checkpoint they were approaching. The border guards on the Indiana side wore different uniforms than the Heartland guards. Past the guards, beyond the high, electrified fence, was an open area patrolled by jeeps with mounted machine guns.

"Anyway," Clayton said, "the point is that the Russians didn't have much use for industrial America, the so-called Rust Belt. It was dying anyway, so they speeded the process. Maybe you know some of this, heard it where you were. They stripped most of the new mills—the robotic assembly lines—anything that was better than what they had in the Soviet Union. Then they just let the rest atrophy. No new equipment, no replacement parts. They figured anything we could make here, the Japanese and the Koreans could make better and cheaper. Which maybe made sense on paper, but what they did was leave an entire region—Indiana, Ohio, Michigan, Pennsylvania—with something like fifty percent unemployment."

"My God," Devin said.

"And they won't let them out," Clayton continued. "It's like a disease that they've quarantined."

They cleared the checkpoint and moved into the outskirts of Hammond, Indiana. They passed block after block of shabby motels, fast-food joints, and tent cities that had sprung up in vacant lots. Thousands of men milled about, gazing up anxiously as the bus moved past.

"What're they doing?" Devin asked.

"Trying to get across. Out of this wasteland to someplace where there's work."

"Will they?"

"Not many. They'll hang around here, in these camps, then drift back to wherever they came from."

"American refugees," Devin said. The words, the very idea, chilled him.

"A few will join the so-called Volunteers for America," Clay said.

"The what?"

"I guess they started that while you were away. American workers volunteer to go work in Russian factories for five years. They get subsistence wages. Their families, back here, get a monthly payment."

"What's it like? Does anybody know?"

"Not really. They show movies of the happy American workers and their happy Russian comrades, but nobody really knows. It sounds pretty good—a way for a factory worker to use his skills. Nobody's come back yet. Maybe they shoot them at the end. Time will tell."

Devin stared out at the empty faces of idle men.

"We'll be out of here in a minute," Clayton said. "And they'll still be here."

The dying man had been a professor of philosophy and a Republican political activist; now he was an exile, and the death rattle was already gurgling in his throat.

"Unplug him," Alan Drummond said.

The nurse hesitated. It was an order she had never received before.

"He's gone," Alan said wearily. "We need the machine for others."

The nurse did as she was told, cut off the life-support system, and Alan Drummond took one long last look at the professor. They had been friends. Many nights at the exile camp had been brightened by this man's intellect. But his intellect had not saved him from an SSU tank.

Alan stood in the Milford County Hospital's

intensive-care unit, which was pitifully unprepared to handle the flood of patients who now crowded its wards and corridors. He looked up in surprise as Herb Lister, followed by two SSU soldiers, entered the room.

"May I see you, please?" Lister said.

Alan loathed Lister, but understood his power. He followed him into the corridor, crowded now with wounded Exiles on makeshift cots.

"What do you want?" he demanded.

"This is terrible," Lister said. "This is a small county hospital, never intended to serve so many people."

"What the hell do you expect us to do?" Alan raged. "Put them out in the parking lot?"

"No, doctor, I have a realistic solution. You and your patients are being transferred to the People's Acceptance Hospital in Omaha."

"You're crazy!" Alan shouted. "They'll die on the way."

"They're dying here, doctor. Surely you agree this is a humane move, to help these innocent people."

"Innocent—you bastard. You stood by and let Gurtman and his troops slaughter them and then you talk to me about humanity."

"You medical types don't often understand politics, doctor," Herb Lister said coldly. "You have two hours to move them. Our volunteers will help."

Alan looked out the door and saw the buses, the troops, the teenagers from the Lincoln Brigade. One of the teenagers marched up to them. "Just point the way, doctor," he said brightly. "We're here to serve."

Alethea awoke at dawn, looked at Helmut asleep next to her, and carefully got out of bed. She slipped on a robe and stood at the foot of the bed, studying her lover's face. In sleep, his long, handsome face was relaxed, the cruelty gone. There was an elegance, even a beauty to him.

For a moment his face seduced her. Without its accustomed hate and barbarism there seemed at least the hope that he could be different, could be gentle, loving.

And yet she knew better.

She backed away and her eyes fixed on his revolver, hanging in its holster, on the wall above his head. She looked from the one to the other, from his face to his gun, from the dream to the reality.

She stepped forward quickly, reached out, and touched the butt of the gun. She hesitated, barely breathing, then wrapped her strong fingers around the weapon and slipped it from its pouch. For an instant she froze, fearful of waking him, fearful of his wrath, then clutched it firmly in her hand.

Alethea stepped to the window, breathing deeply, and looked out at the rows of tanks and helicopters crouching under the glare of the mercury-vapor floodlights.

She turned back to her lover. His white shoulder, outside the sheet, looked vulnerable, almost frail. She raised the gun. It wobbled badly. She took a step forward, holding the gun with both hands, trying to steady it, aiming at his head, so dark and quiet against the black pillow.

The gun was still now, aimed; Alethea took a deep breath and held it; her finger started to tighten on the trigger.

His eyes opened. He smiled. It was an open, trusting, wonderful smile, the finest smile he had ever given her.

"Was I such a bad lover?" he asked.

The quip disarmed her; she loosened her grip on the trigger, but kept the weapon pointed at his head.

"Don't move," she said.

"I'm just going to sit up," he said cautiously. He propped himself up against the headboard. "So you're finally going to have your revenge. No doubt I deserve it. But have you ever killed a man? Particularly a naked man?"

He tossed the sheet aside, exposing himself.

"There's something about killing a man with his clothes on that neutralizes the process. Somehow the naked body, unprotected—ceasing to function, turning an odd color—is so much more real. Can you do that? Here I am, helpless. This man who has subjugated you, the monster who has made love to you and made you feel happier, more fulfilled, than ever before in your life."

He reached slowly for a cigarette. He kept his eyes on her as he lit it. Her hands were starting to shake; the gun seemed to weigh a ton.

"Even last night, Alethea, were you thinking about killing me? Was that why it was so exciting? Did you have your revenge planned? Think of it—one squeeze of that trigger and a small piece of metal will cut off that lovemaking forever. Can you actually kill what has given you such pleasure—and pain?"

He smiled as she let the gun drop to her side; it was the old, arrogant smile now.

"I'm not a murderer," she said softly.

Helmut relaxed a little. "No, you're just weak. Pathetic." He sprang out of bed and ripped the gun from her hand. She did not resist, did not even move.

"I'm sorry I couldn't do it," she said.

He pointed the weapon at her. "I lack your scruples."

213

She saw him slowly tightening his grip on the trigger, savoring the process. She did not move; she accepted her fate and thought it somehow just.

She stiffened as she heard the click of the firing pin on the empty chamber. Then her body went limp.

"I was wondering when the gun would tempt you," he said.

He pulled the trigger again. This time the roar of the gun filled the room. The bullet smashed a mirror behind her. Alethea began to tremble as Helmut laughed heartily.

Someone pounded on the door. "Go away, I'm fine," Helmut said. Then, to Alethea: "Would you like to come back to bed?"

Her mouth fell open in disbelief. She thought she would rather die than be touched by him again. Her clothes were in a pile beside the bed, and she began to pull them on.

"I won't be back," she said.

She pulled her sweater over her head. She felt strong, clean. "I'm free of you, Helmut. Just as if you'd killed me—or I'd killed you."

He smiled and tossed the gun aside. "Once you realize you are too weak to do what is necessary, you are a slave."

The People's Acceptance Hospital in Omaha had been a regional Veteran's Administration hospital before the PPP changed its name. It was a huge, red-brick building, erected in the 1920s, surrounded now by a bright new electrified fence. National guardsmen manned the gatehouse and patrolled the lobby. One of the guardsmen stood stiffly beside a door on the west side of the lobby. A sign on the door said KEEP

OUT—NO ADMITTANCE. On the other side was a long corridor that led to the hospital's west wing, the psychiatric unit.

It was through these doors and into this closely guarded wing that the limp, torn body of Justin Milford had been brought several hours after his motorcycle set off a land mine along the Colorado border.

Now he was in a large ward that contained a dozen beds. The patients were mostly young men, each on an intravenous hookup, some asleep and others awake. One morning, several days after Justin's arrival, three doctors entered the ward and walked slowly past the patients. Those who were awake watched the medical team with silent, suspicious eyes—alert eyes, suggesting alert minds, trapped in bodies that were all but lifeless.

Justin had slept, assisted by various medications, for seventy-two hours. Now he was awake, his eyes smoldering with fear and confusion as he looked from one doctor to another.

One of them, a tall, middle-aged woman with bushy eyebrows behind thick glasses, smiled at him. "Well, Mr. Milford, you're finally awake."

The two other doctors were men. One was a slender young man named Jan. He muttered to the other doctors, "He's in an eighty percent physical block—ECy2."

The woman kept on smiling. "My name is Helen, Justin. I'm one of your doctors. You had quite an accident."

It was with great effort that Justin spoke. "Am I . . . is anything . . . ?"

"Everything's intact. You won't be hobbling around on anything artificial."

Justin managed to nod. "When . . . can I leave?"

The older doctor was gaunt and grim. "Not for some time," he said. "How soon you get out depends on how well you respond to treatment."

Justin was confused. He tried to speak, but was too weak.

"You've exhibited some very destructive tendencies," Helen said. "We're going to help you get over some of the bad things that have contributed to your attitude and response so that you have a chance to be a more productive member of society. You'd like to have a good life, wouldn't you?"

Jan stepped closer to the bed. "We have no restraints here," he said, with a chilly smile. "Our rule is, Make it out the door and you're free. Go ahead!"

He pulled back the sheet. Justin gasped for breath. He lifted one hand a few inches off the bed. He tried to raise his head. One leg trembled. But he could do no more. He fell back onto the bed, exhausted.

"We'll come visit you soon, Justin," Helen said, and the doctors started back toward the door. Bright sunlight filled the ward. Spring was on the way.

The first thing Devin saw when he reached Chicago was a huge billboard across the street from the train station. It showed two smiling faces, twenty feet tall, of a man and a woman. They looked wholesome, well fed, prosperous, and their gazes were pointed upward as if they had found the truth. Underneath the faces were the words FOR THE HEARTLAND!

Devin, unnerved, leaned against the side of the terminal.

"What's the matter?" Clay said. "You look like you've seen a ghost."

"Up there," Devin said. "That's my wife. And Peter

Bradford. I knew he was being considered for some kind of big job, but with Marion?"

"Looks like they're destined for great things," Clay said. "Come on, let's keep moving."

Clay led them to a safe house in a north-side ghetto, where a black woman named Emma fed them and gave them a floor to sleep on. The next morning, after breakfast, Clay informed Devin that they were going to a meeting.

"Where? Who with?" Devin asked.

"You'll see."

They walked to the Loop and Clay guided them to what remained of the John Hancock building. The windows at street level were boarded up and winos slept in the lobby. Every knob or fixture of any possible value had been stolen. The elevators no longer worked, of course, and Clay led them up the stairs. They stopped at the tenth floor to catch their breath.

"There're lots of deserted skyscrapers now," Clay explained. "Vertical slums. This was an insurance building, but who needs insurance when Big Brother takes care of us all?"

They started climbing again.

"How much farther?" Devin asked.

"Courage. The higher, the safer. Squatters live in the first ten floors or so. A lot of kids in the next few."

"Kids?"

"Yeah, ten or twelve years old, homeless. They beg, sell drugs, sell themselves, form gangs, and fight wars. The authorities pretty much leave them alone. Too expensive to put them in jail. Anyway, if you can make it to, oh, the twentieth floor, you're home free. The cops are too fat to climb that far. Here we are, ladies and gentlemen, twentieth floor, cosmetics, ladies' lingerie, and on your left, antigovernment plots. Last stop on the underground railroad."

Clayton pushed open the door that led to what once had been a huge office complex.

"Raise your arms and move slowly," he said.

Devin did as he was told. They moved through a maze of what had once been small offices, then encountered a black man leaning against a wall.

"Jeffrey," Clay cried.

"Clayton, my man."

The two embraced.

"Still twisting the news?" Clay quipped.

"Night and day." Jeffrey grinned. "I am the Dan Rather of disinformation." He turned to Devin and extended his hand. "Glad to meet you, man. Been an admirer—you know. Come and meet the group."

Jeffrey led them into what had once been a conference room, where highly paid actuaries had discussed mortality rates and term-insurance options. All that remained now was a magnificent view of the Chicago skyline—no one could steal that. Eight men and women awaited them, and they soon gathered around Devin, greeting him with handshakes and warm words. They greeted Clayton with affection, too, and in time they settled in a circle on the floor.

"Well, this is it, the movement in Chicago," Jeffrey said. "Each of us represents a group, cells you might say; some are a part of the establishment, others underground. We don't interact much, except on very special occasions, like greeting Devin Milford."

"There's no leaders," declared a man named Quinlan, a tough-looking fellow in workclothes. "We do our own stuff. That way we don't get hooked into nothin' that don't measure up. Leaders screw things up."

His outburst was greeted with an awkward silence. Devin guessed he was being reminded that he had been one of those leaders who failed.

"Look, let's get something out in the open," Jeffrey said. "Nobody blames you for what happened when you ran for president. You got our hopes up and then the bubble burst, but that wasn't your fault. Maybe we were all unrealistic. The thing you may not know is that while you were gone you became a hero, kind of a folk hero, to a lot of people. I don't think the Russians understand it or you wouldn't be here now. But whether you like it or not, you've got it."

Devin nodded but didn't reply. He didn't want to be a hero. He wanted their help, but he knew to let things unfold in their own way.

"But listen," Jeffrey continued, "I'm a journalist, and I've got this pesky habit of wanting to know how the pieces of a story fit together. You don't owe us any explanations, and if you want to skip the whole business, that's fine. But I confess to being curious as hell about how you and Marion Andrews ever got together, and about how it happened that the two of you turned out as wildly different as you did."

It was not a question, exactly, but it hung heavy in the silence that followed, and Devin, surrounded by people he instantly trusted, found himself thinking back over long-distant events he hadn't let himself reflect on in years.

He laughed. "Well," he began, talking more to himself than to the others, "we met at Harvard. How's that for an elitist backdrop? I was in law school, Marion was still an undergraduate. We met at a party and . . . well, let me be candid. I wanted to go to bed with her because of the way she could argue politics. She was a fireball—incisive, committed, smart as hell. And beautiful. She moved in with me. We got married. And eventually we both practiced law. Viewed from the outside, we were the perfect young American professional couple.

"The problem," Devin went on, "was competitiveness, and politics turned out to be what the competition focused on. I'd been active for years. I was radicalized by Vietnam, I was disgusted by the Nixon scandals, I was depressed by the apathy and nest-feathering indifference that came after. I made my feelings known, and in 1982 I was drafted to run for the state legislature. This was Cambridge, remember, liberal land, and a guy like me could win without a major party machine behind me." He broke off and gave a rueful laugh. "It never dawned on me that Marion wanted to run herself."

"Well, I ran and I won. In eighty-six, a congressional seat opened up, and I was asked to go for it. By then I'd realized that my marriage was being corroded and that Marion was furious. I would have gladly stepped aside and let her run—she would have made the better politician, as later events have shown. But by then the whole machinery of the system was cranked up: I was the one with two terms' experience, not her; I was the one who could win and get to Washington to represent what I believed in. So what was I to do: make the gallant gesture and let the conservatives win the seat, or win the seat and jeopardize my marriage?

"I went to Congress. Chalk that up as mistake number four-twenty-three. Then in D.C. as a freshman rep, I made errors four-twenty-four through ten thousand. Jesus, I was green! Protocol, lobbies—it was Greek to me, but by God I said what was on my mind, and my constituents sent me back for more in eighty-eight. I went, along with one of the most frustrated political wives in a city full of them.

"Then World War III came and went practically without anybody noticing. Even now, I'm staggered by how it happened. Remember air raids in grade school? The nuke freeze movement? The nightmares of mushroom clouds and radioactive milk? Those unspeakable horrors at least made a certain kind of sense: something cataclysmic would happen, and the whole world would be changed. But now *nothing* had happened—some magnetism in the sky!—and America was gone.

"Congress, like everyone else, was dumbfounded, paralyzed. Resolutions were passed. Speeches were made. No one would face up to what the surrender terms to the Soviets really meant. *I* faced up to it, for better or worse. I knew that America was no more. The United States was occupied territory, as pathetic as any newsreel you ever saw of Czechoslovakia or Poland.

"Marion was smarter than I was—as she'd been all along. She was among the very first to see the writing on the wall and to grasp how to turn it to her advantage. I'd been the star under the old system of American democracy. Okay. *She'd* be the star under the New Understanding. She joined the PPP practically before the PPP was instated. She was on her way.

"That's about the time I decided to run for president," Devin said, shaking his head at what seemed now to have been an act of pure quixotic folly. "I didn't have a chance, you understand. The Democrats and the Republicans had put up party-approved stooges, who were well financed and who had access to the media. Even if by some miracle I could win the balloting, there was nothing to stop the authorities from diddling with the vote count. But I wanted a forum. I wanted to tell my fellow Americans that the country was being raped, that the idea of cooperation was a sham, that the thought that the Soviets would ever leave was a grotesque illusion.

"If no one believed me, everything would have been fine. But of course I was just the mouthpiece for what everyone already knew but lacked the gumption to acknowledge. I spoke people's own thoughts back to them—and that, I guess, is what made them think of me as dangerous. You see, I wasn't brilliant, I wasn't intellectual. And God knows I wasn't subtle.

"Marion used to taunt me about that, in fact." He gave a wistful laugh. "'Be a little subtle,' she used to tell me. 'And watch your blind side.' Well, the blind side is exactly where they hit me. One day I was the dark-horse contender for president; next day, according to the official dispatch, I was a lunatic who had cracked under the pressures of campaigning and needed to be hospitalized. Going by the record, I've spent the last five years recuperating from a nervous breakdown that I never had. And I guess that brings you up to date."

Devin broke off his narration with a self-effacing shrug, as if denying the import of his personal travail. His listeners sighed and rearranged themselves on their aluminum chairs.

"The thing I still don't understand, though," Jeffrey said, "is when the real rift came, when your wife turned against you."

Devin blinked, paused, looked down at his fingernails. Absently, he shook his head no as he spoke. "She didn't turn against me. She wasn't there. I . . . I'm not sure I know what you're talking about."

Jeffrey retreated from his aggressive interviewer stance. He glanced quickly at the others in the room and silenced them with his eyes. Then he forced a smile and threw an arm around Devin Milford's shoulders. "But tell me, brother, what can we do for you while you're here?"

Devin hesitated, as if he needed to rid himself of the taste of something rotten before he could speak again. "I'm here to see my sons," he said. "It's a personal matter. Maybe it doesn't concern you at all."

"No, we'll help you," said one of the policemen. "We owe that much to Devin Milford. It won't be easy, believe me, but we'll give it a shot. Then, maybe once you've got your personal affairs in order, you'll care about politics again."

═══ *Chapter 10* ═══

IT HAD BEEN the worst time of Amanda's life. The carnage at the exile camp, the confrontation with Major Gurtman, the burial of the dead Exiles, the forced evacuation of the survivors to Omaha, the new curfew—to endure all this, and without Peter, was almost more than she could bear.

Yet she had survived. She had made the decisions that otherwise would have been Peter's. She and others had defied the curfew to attend the mass funeral service at the exile camp and the SSU had backed down. She kept trying to reach Peter, kept expecting him to call, but it was as if Milford had been isolated from the rest of the universe.

On the second morning after the funerals, she and the children were in their kitchen when several military vehicles stopped in front of the house.

"What's going on?" Scott demanded.

Amanda hurried to the door, expecting to confront armed soldiers, but instead she found a pert, dark-haired young woman on her front porch.

"Mrs. Bradford, I'm Margaret Sawyer, your new aide."

"Aide?" Amanda said, quite bewildered.

"Actually, I'm on the governor-general's staff, but I've been detailed to help you with the move and all your new responsibilities."

"Move? What move are you talking about?"

"To Omaha. His headquarters are there, and we were sent to help you move."

"I've got to talk to my husband," Amanda said, looking out into the yard, where soldiers were taking up defensive positions. She wondered: against what? "He's been in Washington," she added. "I haven't talked to him in several days."

"But didn't you see his speech to Congress on TV?"

"Yes, we saw him," Amanda said wearily.

"I thought he was wonderful."

"Yes, he was." Amanda sighed. She thought that if her husband was speaking to Congress and yet could not get through to his wife on the phone, then something was very wrong, something that neither of them understood; all she wanted was Peter safe at home with her, and for their lives to return to where they had been before all this political madness began.

"If you're my aide," she said, "please get my husband on the phone."

The rusted step-van said *A&A Plumbing* on its side in faded red letters. It was parked in a deserted warehouse on Chicago's south side just a few blocks from Comiskey Park. Devin and Clayton were standing beside the truck, along with two of their Chicago allies, Quinlan and a man named Miller.

"We followed your boys for two days," Quinlan said. "So the driver knows the routes."

"You've got to decide if you make your move at school or at home," Miller said. "You have to realize they may not recognize you. They may panic at first. But don't wait too long. Once their mother gets back in town, it'll just be harder." He extended his hand. "Good luck."

Devin shook Miller's hand, then Quinlan's. "I appreciate it more than I can say," he told them.

Devin opened the back of the truck and climbed in amid a jumble of pipes and plumbers' tools. He held out his hand to Clayton, who did not take it.

"I think I'll tag along," Clayton said, and jumped into the truck with Devin.

"What about your other work?" Devin asked.

"Close it up and let's go," Clayton yelled to the driver.

Quinlan slammed the door shut and the truck eased out of the warehouse.

As they pulled away, Clayton said, "You asked about my other work. You know what, I don't really know what I've been doing. Since I left the church I've been helping people to escape. To where? It's like shuffling beads. The truth is, we've reached the first time in history where there's no place left to escape to. America, England, Israel, Canada, there was always a beacon of hope somewhere. Now there's just one world and it's all bad. So it's time to build a better one. Maybe helping you is as good a first step as any."

Just enough light filtered into the back of the truck for Clay to see Devin's grin.

"Now I'll shake your hand," Clayton said.

"Now I'm not sure I want to," Devin said.

They laughed, shaking hands warmly. Comrades.

It was Andrei who finally got the call through on the air-to-ground telephone on the flight back from Washington.

"You don't know my wife," Peter had told him. "She won't budge. At least not until she talks to me."

Andrei had shrugged and picked up the telephone. In a moment he was talking to Mikel. "I don't care how complicated it is," Peter heard him say, "do it. Have Major Gurtman send a communications truck to the Bradford home. Patch it through. Just get Mrs. Bradford on the phone. Oh Mikel, also, get me some flowers and champagne, for Kimberly."

He put down the phone and smiled at Peter. "Such is the way of the world," he said. "Flowers and champagne for a mistress—the movers for a wife."

"How long should the call take?" Peter asked.

"Not long. As long as it takes to drive a truck from our barracks to your house at top speed. Mikel can be efficient when you put the fear of God into him. Or should I say the fear of the KGB?"

In truth, it was less than twenty minutes later that Helmut Gurtman's Range Rover and a SSU field communications truck arrived in the Bradford driveway. Amanda hurried out and the radio operator gave her his seat, showing her how to operate the radio. She pressed a button and, to her amazement, heard Peter's voice.

"Amanda, can you hear me?"

"Peter—it's so good to talk to you. Where are you?"

"In a plane, headed for Chicago, with Colonel Denisov."

"We all watched you on TV. You were wonderful."

"Honey, things are moving fast. I want you to meet me in Omaha. There is a house already set—"

"Peter, when are you coming home?" Now there was an edge in her voice. She was relieved to talk to him but she was very much aware of Major Gurtman looming beside her.

"Honey, that's the point. I don't have time to come home. You'll have as much help as you need—"

"Peter, do you have any idea what's been going on here?"

"I heard there was some trouble with the Exiles."

She glanced at Gurtman, his face a cold mask, and she was intimidated, despite herself. "It was more than that," she said softly. "I think you should come home."

Peter, twenty thousand feet above southern Illinois, barely able to hear her, much less understand her concerns, didn't know what to say. "That's impossible, Amanda," he said. "Colonel Denisov will guarantee your safety."

She looked at Helmut again. "It's not my safety I'm worried about. I can't leave Milford. Peter, what we're saying is going over a speaker. Major Gurtman is right here, now."

Peter looked to Andrei for help. "She says she can't talk because Gurtman is there. She seems to be afraid he'll do something, harm the town or the Exiles, if she leaves."

"Let me talk to her," Andrei said. He liked to believe that calming distraught women was an easy task for him.

"Hello, Mrs. Bradford? How are you?"

"I wish I could say I was fine, Colonel."

"Don't worry about a thing. We can resolve whatever is worrying you. I just want to congratulate you on being—what do you say?—the new first lady of the area."

"I . . . thank you . . . but . . ."

"Let me talk to Major Gurtman. And you please listen to what I tell him."

Amanda stiffened as he took the phone. "Major Gurtman, sir."

"What is the situation there?"

Helmut started to speak in Russian, but Andrei ordered him to use English.

"There is a curfew in effect."

"By what authority?"

"My discretionary authority. Also, a request from the county council for our intervention and the restoration of order."

There was a long silence. Peter did not understand what was happening, but he saw Andrei's face and knew he was making some sort of complex political calculation. Peter had never really read Machiavelli but he guessed Andrei was what people meant when they called someone Machiavellian.

Maybe it's time to read him, he thought.

Finally, Andrei said, "Major, you are to rescind the curfew and return to your barracks."

"Sir, I must protest. The community is filled with insubordination. The rebellious behavior of the Exiles —abetted by certain townspeople—"

"The governor-general assures me the local authorities are in a position to maintain order. Those are my orders. That is all."

"Yes, sir!" Helmut said sharply.

"Mrs. Bradford," Andrei continued. "Are you there?"

Helmut got up from his seat. The look he cast at

Amanda frightened her. She was glad that he left the truck. "Yes, Colonel."

"Are you satisfied that you will be able to leave?" Andrei asked.

"I guess so. Thank you."

"You may feel your townspeople need you, but so does your husband. Here he is."

Amanda said, "Peter, if you'd only seen what they did here."

"Whatever it was, we'll fix it," he said. "I need you, honey. You don't know how much."

"Some things can never be fixed," she said. "I'll see you in Omaha."

"Great!" Peter said. "And, sweetheart, don't worry. Everything's going to be fine."

The school building had ivy clinging to its crumbling bricks. The children of Chicago's upper crust had been educated there for more than a century, from the days of the meat-packing barons to the new elite of the Transition. For the past several decades the school's janitor had been a man named Keyes, a wily, wizened old fellow who had watched the elites come and go. He had equal affection and equal contempt for them all.

At precisely two o'clock that afternoon, Keyes went to a second-floor men's room and began stuffing rags down the toilet bowls. As soon as one was well stuffed he flushed the toilet and he adjusted the handle so the toilet would keep on flushing indefinitely. Soon all four toilets were overflowing and Keyes slogged through the mess he had made and headed downstairs to the office.

A secretary, Miss Raleigh, a plain woman with a winsome smile, was on duty in the office.

"Toilet backed up. Better call a plumber," he said.

A knowing look passed between them and Miss

Raleigh reached calmly for the phone, as if toilets backed up every day.

A few blocks away, Devin was in the back of the truck, pulling on his overalls. "It's time," he said.

"The driver told me to wait here," Clayton said. "He thinks two inside is enough. I trust him."

Devin felt himself panic. "I don't know what I'm doing," he said. "What if he doesn't want to see me?"

"Hell, man, you're in the middle of it," Clayton said harshly. "A lot of other people are at risk helping you—"

The truck lurched to a stop. Devin heard the front door slam and looked at Clayton.

Clayton nodded reassuringly. "Let's get your boy."

A man named Barton threw the door open. He was a big, homely man, a plumber and a member of the underground. "Grab a tool kit," he said.

Devin nodded and they climbed the steps to the school. "Just follow my lead," Barton said. "Plumbing's easy. Look like you don't give a damn and you've got all day. We've got a saying; all you've got to remember is, Hot's on the left, cold's on the right, and shit don't flow uphill."

Keyes, the janitor, met them at the door. "It's upstairs, gents," he announced. "A regular Niagara Falls."

He led the way. Water was cascading down the stairs. An assistant principal was standing at the bottom of the stairs looking worried. "Hurry, hurry!" he called.

Barton, shambling along, said, "Don't panic, pal."

"See, here's what'll happen," Keyes said. "There's a class break in a couple of minutes. Your kid, he's got a class right down the hall. They'll all come by, gawking and splashing in the water."

"You mean he'll be part of a crowd?" Devin said.

"We got somebody'll put him in position," Keyes said.

"How can I talk to him? We may not even recognize each other."

"Work it out, pal," Barton said. "We ain't got all day."

They reached the men's-room door just as the bell rang. Devin held back, searching the faces of the children who burst from the classrooms.

"Come on," Barton called. Devin followed him into the bathroom, now an inch deep in water.

"Look busy," Barton said. "Take out the snake and start jammin' it around."

Devin sank to his knees and began trying to unclog one of the toilets. A dozen boys were looking in the door, savoring the disaster. Devin saw a boy he thought was his son, but then a teacher herded him toward a group of boys, moving them all toward their next class.

In the midst of the confusion, Miss Raleigh stood against a wall, helping the teachers and hall monitors keep an eye out. She caught sight of Billy walking with a group of his friends, pushing their way through the crowd to see what was going on.

Billy had reached the door of his class when Miss Raleigh stopped him.

"Billy, could you come with me for a minute?" she said.

"What's up?"

"I have a message for the plumbers." She handed him a folded slip of paper and started to walk with him back to the bathroom. When they reached the door, she guided him inside. "Thanks, Billy. I didn't want to get my shoes wet." She shut the door behind him and quickly walked away.

Billy heard the door close behind him and took a step forward toward the plumbers.

"Hey, there's a note for you guys," he announced.

Devin slowly stood up and faced him. Billy returned his look, suddenly very nervous. There was something about the man . . .

"Billy," Devin said.

"How'd you know my name?" the boy said, but softly, with wonder. "What's going on here?"

Barton said, "The note's for you, son."

Billy unfolded the slip of paper and looked at the three scribbled words: *It's your father.*

He gazed at the tall, thin man in the overalls.

"Hi, William," the man said gently.

"Dad?"

"You're so big, I couldn't believe it."

Billy ran into Devin's arms, five years of pent-up emotions exploding in tears. "I didn't think I'd ever see you again," he sobbed.

"I know, I know."

Barton started grabbing up tools trying to hide his emotions. "We gotta get out of here."

Billy looked up at his father. "You're not leaving again, are you?"

"I want you to come with me."

"Where to? Mom says . . ."

"I don't know. It may not be safe. But I want you with me. That's where you belong."

"I know. That's what I want too."

Barton walked to the door. "Let's go," he said.

Keyes was waiting on the other side of the door. "You guys go out the way you came," he said. "I'll take Billy down the freight elevator."

The boy turned to his father. "Dad?"

"It's okay. We'll meet outside."

They embraced and then Billy and the old man hurried off. Devin and Barton ambled down the stairs at the leisurely pace of their profession.

"Hey, what about the toilets?" the assistant principal called to them.

"All fixed," Barton assured him.

"What about this mess?" the man demanded, pointing to the small lagoon that now spread across the main hallway.

"Not our union, pal," Barton said, and they marched out of the school.

The truck waited at the curb. They tossed their tools inside.

"What happened?" Clayton demanded.

Before Devin could answer, Billy and Keyes came running toward them. Devin embraced the old man. "How can I thank you?"

"Hell, I oughta thank you. I ain't had so much fun in years," the janitor said. "Take care of that boy; he's not like a lot of them around here."

Devin and Billy climbed into the back with Clayton and the truck lurched away. Devin laughed with relief and put his arm around Billy, holding him tight.

"Brother Clayton, I want you to meet my son, Billy."

The SSU troops had worked quickly and efficiently: the Bradford home was now an empty house.

Amanda stood, a little dazed, in the middle of the living room, looking at the empty shell that had been her home for most of her adult life.

She felt like a gypsy, an Exile. She had not seen Peter in almost a week; her belongings were outside, packed in military trucks; and all that lay ahead was an abstraction called Omaha, plus the dubious honor of being first lady of Heartland.

She laughed bitterly. She had been first lady of this wonderful, vibrant, growing house for fifteen years, and nothing that politics or the PPP or the Russians could offer would ever equal that.

Scott came stomping down the stairs, clutching an old hockey stick. "Hey, Mom, let's get crackin'."

She gazed at him not in anger, but in wonder. "Aren't you the least bit sorry to be leaving? Don't you think?"

He shrugged. "Hey, we're moving up to the big time. Can't be too sentimental."

"Your home . . . your friends."

"You and dad are my home. And my friends'll come see me in Omaha. I mean, it isn't the moon."

Amanda sighed. "Sometimes I really wish I had your perspective. Or that you had mine."

"Stay close, Mom. You'll catch on." He grinned and went outside.

Margaret, Amanda's young aide-de-camp, popped in the door. "All set?"

Amanda hesitated. She liked Margaret. She wished she could tell her how it felt to be leaving a home you loved, and never intended to leave, but somehow she didn't think Margaret—with all of her efficiency and decorum—would understand.

"I . . . I have to get Jackie," Amanda said, and started up the stairs.

Her daughter was poised at the landing, in jeans and sweater, holding a cosmetics case.

"Honey, they're waiting."

Jackie didn't even look at her. She seemed frozen.

"What's the matter, baby?"

"I just got my room the way I want it." Her voice was hushed, not far from a sob.

Amanda took her hand. "I know."

"I love my room, I really do."

"I know."

Amanda tugged lightly and Jackie took a step down the stairs. "I don't know anybody in Omaha."

"I don't either."

"You have Daddy."

"I hope I have him. I hope we both have him." Jackie stopped, halfway down the stairs. "What if Justin comes back and I'm not here? He won't know where to find me."

"Your father is the governor-general of the area. I'm sure even Justin will figure it out."

They reached the empty living room. Jackie smiled wanly, taking it all in. "I love this house. I never thought I'd leave it."

Tears burned Amanda's eyes. "What about flying off to dance on the great stages of the world?"

"You know what?" Jackie said. "I don't think I'm ever going to do that."

The limousine was waiting. It was at the head of a small convoy that included two jeeps and the four trucks that were moving their belongings. As they entered the Milford courthouse square, they saw that the town had come alive again, had shaken off its mantle of fear.

"They ended the curfew," Amanda said. "At least Major Gurtman follows orders."

"Is that a plus or a minus?" Jackie said wryly.

"They were all going stir crazy," Scott said.

"I was in town awhile ago," Margaret told them.

"They've been ringing bells and honking horns—quite a celebration."

"Good for them," Amanda said.

As they passed the courthouse Amanda saw the people start to glare at their convoy. She saw their celebration turn to anger as they shook their fists and yelled. Amanda was shocked by the ugly display of hostility. "Why are they doing that?" she cried.

Jackie was openmouthed with dismay. Scott sank down in the seat, hoping not to be recognized.

"They don't know who we are," Margaret said. "The windows are smoked so they can't see in."

"They think we're Russians or something," said Scott.

"Maybe they're not so far off," said Jackie.

They had gone back to the garage where the plumbing truck was kept. Men were working on other cars and trucks. They paid little attention to Devin, Billy, and Clayton. There was a bucket of soft drinks—a local brand, called ChiCola—and Billy prowled around the garage, sipping the soda and watching the mechanics.

Devin, sitting against the wall with Clayton, watched his son with a sense of wonder.

"He's fourteen," he said. "Almost a man. But still a boy. Look how gracefully he moves. I'll bet he's a good athlete. You could see it, even when he was younger. My God, what a beautiful creature."

Clayton laughed. "Just a kid, wandering around a smelly old garage."

"You wouldn't say that if he was yours. Then you'd know what a miracle he is."

"Do you see his mother in him? Or is that an impolite question."

"Sure I see her. In his physical grace. And in the quickness of his mind. I was always a plodder, but Marion is intuitive, her mind's like a computer going a hundred miles a minute." He grinned and added, "But mostly I see me in him."

Billy joined them. "What's up?"

"I was saying I thought you were a lot like your old man."

Billy laughed. "You got that right. Hey, are we really going to be Resisters?"

"You might say that," Devin replied.

"What'll we do? Blow up stuff?"

"There are a lot of ways to resist."

"Well, what's the plan?"

The two men grinned at the boy's bluntness.

"I thought we'd start by getting your brother," Devin said.

Billy thought about that, unsure what he should say. "The thing is," he ventured, "he won't want to come like I did. Mom's got him real scared."

"Of me?"

"Yeah. It's like you're some evil person who'll hurt us."

Devin's face reflected his bewilderment. He'd never imagined that one of his own sons could fear him.

"Plus, he's real gung-ho on the Lincoln Brigade stuff. He heads it up."

Devin was thinking hard, trying to decide. How could he rescue a boy who didn't want to be rescued, who didn't remember his father the way he, Devin, remembered his son? "How does your mom feel about that?"

"You gotta be kidding. She's like the head of the local party and all that. She's really heavy in-to it."

Clayton said, "You'll have to decide soon. If you wait, it'll be too late."

Devin, lost in his own thoughts, stammered, "What?"

"In a little while they'll look for Billy and set off the alarm."

"They can't know it's me," Devin said.

"Doesn't matter," Clayton answered. "They may interpret it as a terrorist act against your wife. Or a kidnapping for ransom. Whatever, they'll take it seriously. It isn't going to be a situation where a kid's a little late after school."

Devin gazed into space. "Maybe I should forget it. I don't want to hurt him."

"Maybe you owe him a chance at least to meet his father," Clayton said. "To see the truth, face-to-face. To make up his own mind."

Devin wrestled with that possibility. It was not the danger he feared, not the police, but the horror of confronting a son who hated him.

He asked Billy, "Will you help me?"

Billy hesitated, then slowly nodded. "I can show you the best way to do it," he said. "When his school lets out, there's a lot of confusion. That's the time."

Devin nodded his agreement. Clayton produced a pencil and paper and Billy drew them a map of the school. He marked the door from which Caleb came out, as well as the place where the police escort waited for him.

It could be done, Devin thought. At least a meeting, a chance to talk. A memory to leave with the boy, for the years ahead.

It was only noon. They had at least two hours to wait. Devin thought the noisy, smelly garage was becoming oppressive.

"I'm going to take Billy out for a walk," he said. "You want to come?"

"I don't think that's a good idea," Clayton replied.

"Oh hell, there's a park out there, beside the river, and a lot of people wandering around. Nobody'll notice us. Dammit, Clay, you can't spend all your life being afraid."

Clayton shrugged. "Okay, just be careful."

They crossed a street and entered a shabby, rundown park. Wrigley Field loomed a few blocks to the south, and across the park Lake Michigan sparkled in the midday sun. They took a bench that faced the lake. At first Devin didn't know what to say. After all these years of dreaming, the reality of the boy left him speechless.

"What do you want to do?" Billy asked. "I mean, when we leave Chicago?"

"I'm not sure," Devin admitted. "I'd like to go back to Nebraska. I guess that's my home now. Your grandfather, your aunt and uncle—things have been hard and they could use my help. But I don't know if the . . . the authorities will let you live with me there. If not, I don't know."

"Could we go to Alaska and join the resistance?"

"That'd be a last resort," Devin said. "I don't see what they're accomplishing. I'd rather just live underground in some city. Change our names; I'd get a job and you could go to school, and try to live a normal life. Maybe, someday, your mother will agree to let you live with me, openly, if we convince her that's what you want. Maybe, someday, you'll want to go back with her . . ."

"No!"

"It's always possible, Billy. It'd be an easier life. The decision is yours."

"What she wants isn't what I want," Billy said.

"The thing is, we don't know what may happen. We don't know how much time we have. You have to learn to look at time differently, to look at the people you love differently. That's what I learned in prison. Some people have a lifetime together and some people only have an hour or a week or a month. But an hour can be more than a year, a week can be more than a lifetime. Time is what you make of it. You can waste a lifetime or you can make a single afternoon precious."

Devin watched the gulls soar over the lake. He wondered if any of this made sense to a boy of fourteen. A few hard-won truths were all he had left to give. He looked at Billy, whose gaze had never left his face.

"It's like when someone is dead or . . . away. The relationship changes, but you don't stop loving them. When I was in prison, I loved you more than ever before. Sometimes I would think of you—of you and Caleb—all night long. It was sort of like praying, I guess, except it was just the three of us. I told you how much I loved you and I told you what kind of boys . . . men . . . I wanted you to be and I told you I'd survive and see you again. Believing that, and believing you still loved me, was what kept me alive. Literally. You kept me alive."

Billy took his father's hand. "I heard you," he said. "I could feel you . . . in the night. Like when you used to come in and kiss me good night and we'd talk until I got sleepy. You weren't really there but I pretended you were and it was just the same. I talked to you and prayed that you heard me."

"I did," Devin said.

They sat in silence for a time. Devin wondered how tragic it was that the message had not gotten through to his other son, that Caleb had been turned against him. Perhaps it was because he was younger, he thought, or perhaps it was simply in the genes. Kids were different —you learned that fast, as a parent—and probably Caleb was a great kid who just happened to be more like his mother. He guessed he could see a little of it now, looking back to when Caleb was just two or three, but it was hard to judge a child at that age.

"Dad, can I ask you a question?"

Devin turned and looked into Billy's somber, open face. "There's nothing you can't ask me," he said.

"Tell me about you and Mom. I mean, what was it like when you were young? Did you love each other? What was she like then? I just . . . sometimes I don't understand what happened."

Devin smiled. Sometimes he didn't understand what had happened either.

"Your mother was a beautiful, wonderful, brilliant woman," he said. "And I loved her very much. Whatever happens, son, remember that."

Billy had attended Caleb's elementary school and he knew it as well as his own. He showed Clayton where to park the step-van and led Devin through the azaleas to a window that looked into the school auditorium.

The auditorium was packed with students and parents. Onstage, a choir was singing a song called "Heartland, Our Heartland."

"It's new," Billy explained. "Part of the big Heartland push they started a couple of weeks ago. It's like we're supposed to forget Nebraska and Illinois and even the U.S.A., and just love dear Heartland. Forget that."

Devin listened for a moment. The song's words were

mundane at best, and offensive if you understood their intent, and yet the sweet young voices gave them an innocence and beauty that was beyond criticism. How very shrewd they are, he thought bitterly.

When the choir finished the song, a slender, intense boy with sandy-blond hair stepped to the microphone. Even before Billy spoke, Devin felt a chill.

"That's Caleb," Billy said.

Devin gazed at his younger son in wonder. The boy was slender and angelic, and yet there was something stiff and mechanical about him.

"I warn you, he believes all their crap," Billy whispered.

"We are the voice of a new generation," Caleb began, in a monotone. "The destructive ways of the past are gone. We will replace them with our vision of the future. The party will lead us to the new age.

"We are grateful to our Soviet brothers for saving the world from destruction," Caleb continued. "And we can now join them in a world of socialist brotherhood."

Devin turned away. Billy squeezed his arm. "It's not really his fault. Between Mom and the teachers, he never knew any different."

Devin nodded. "I know. He's a believer, like I was. We just latched on to different things."

When Caleb finished his speech there was a roar of approval from the audience. A band played "The Internationale," and everyone began to file out of the auditorium.

"This is it," Billy said. "You know where to go?"

"I know," Devin said. "Will you be okay?"

"Sure."

Billy was waiting when Caleb came out of the school. Across the street he could see Sergeant Moran, the officer assigned to bringing Caleb home, with his partner. Caleb emerged with some other boys, but when he saw Billy he broke free and joined him.

"What're you doing here?" he asked nervously. "You get out early?"

"Yeah. How'd the program go?"

"Great. I almost got the whole thing memorized."

"That's swell. C'mere."

He grabbed Caleb's arm and steered him around to the side of the building.

"Where're we going?" the younger boy asked.

"I want to show you something."

"But the officers, they'll—"

"Don't worry. This won't take a minute."

They were around at the side now, with bushes between them and the street.

"Listen, Cay, all that stuff Mom told us about Dad. How crazy and dangerous he is, you know?"

Caleb stiffened. "Yeah . . ."

"Hey, it's not true. Honest."

Caleb backed away. "How do you know?"

"I just know. Look, I don't want you to be scared . . ."

Billy still had Caleb by the arm. But Caleb tried to pull away. In that moment Devin stepped around the corner of the building. He stopped a few feet from the boys and squatted down.

"Caleb," he said softly.

"It's okay, honest," Billy said.

Caleb, clearly terrified, began to struggle. "Dammit, don't be so stupid," Billy said, and held him tight.

Devin was afraid to move. But time was precious. "It's all right, son. No one's going to hurt you," he said. "I just want to talk to you. To say hello."

Caleb quit struggling and stared fearfully at the man before him. "You're really my father?" he said.

"Yes."

"You're old."

Devin had to smile. "I've had a hard life," he said.

"They said you were crazy."

"The Russians say a lot of things. Do I seem crazy?"

"What do you want?"

"Just to see you. Say hello. Talk."

Devin slowly stood and moved a step closer. Caleb seemed frozen. Devin put out his hand, and after a long pause, his son took it. Then, quickly, as if he might be contaminated, Caleb broke off the handshake.

It was Billy, first, who sensed that something was wrong. He turned and saw the two policemen looking for Caleb, walking toward the school. The policemen started up the school's front steps. The father and sons were frozen. Caleb took a deep, sharp breath. Devin's eyes pleaded with him, but the boy's eyes were as cold as his mother's sometimes were.

"Help me!" he cried. "Here, help!"

The policemen raced around the corner of the building and stopped, facing them from fifty feet away. Caleb struggled to break free from Billy.

"It's my father," he screamed. "It's him."

The policemen drew their guns. Devin swept Caleb up into his arms, where the boy kicked and fought furiously.

"Let him go, Milford," Sergeant Moran shouted. "Nobody has to get hurt."

Devin realized that Caleb was a shield, protecting him for an instant from the uncertain policemen.

"Just let him walk over here," Moran said.

Devin ignored them and spoke instead to his son.

"You're going to be all right," he said. "Just calm down. It's okay."

Caleb did calm a little. Billy, standing behind them, said, "Don't give him up. They'll shoot you."

Devin spoke again to his younger son. "I want you to know that I love you. No matter what they tell you. I'll always love you."

Caleb nodded tentatively. Devin lowered him slowly. "No matter what they tell you," he repeated, and let go of his son.

Caleb ran toward the two policemen.

"Shoot him," he cried. "Kill him!"

The officers knelt and aimed, but Caleb, running blindly toward them, was in the line of fire.

"Put your hands on your head and turn around, or we'll fire," Moran called.

"Go to hell," Devin said bitterly.

Moran had raised his gun when Billy stepped in front of his father. He didn't say anything, just stood there, head high, defiant.

"Dammit, Billy, get out of the way," Moran yelled.

"Go to hell," Billy said proudly.

Moran turned to the patrolman who was with him and said, "Take Caleb to the car and get some backup." Then, to Devin, he said, "Don't risk the boy's safety. You don't stand a chance."

Devin stood firm; there was nowhere to go, and that fact was becoming more and more clear to Devin.

"We can't both make it," he whispered to Billy.

"I'm staying with you," Billy whispered, a quaver in his voice.

"Stay with me in spirit, Billy. The only way to do that is to let me divert these guys long enough for you to reach the truck. You can't hesitate. This is our chance to resist."

"What about you?" the boy asked. "They'll put you back in prison . . . I'll never see you again."

Devin hugged his son. Moran was inching forward, but still thirty feet away.

"I can take whatever happens, as long as I know you're okay," Devin said. "Tell Clayton to take you to Milford. They'll hide you there. They're your people."

Billy was sobbing now. Moran slipped forward.

"Give us a minute, Sergeant," Devin said.

Moran stopped, figuring time was on his side.

"Come on, Billy. Be a big guy . . . I need you . . . I need you to know you're strong."

"I know. I'm sorry."

"I love you." Then Devin turned to Moran and said, loudly, "We're coming up to you." He paused. "I'm giving up."

"Put your hands up, Milford," Moran commanded. He was twenty feet away now and sure he could shoot without hitting the boy.

"When the moment comes," Devin whispered to his son, "run for the truck and—no matter what happens —don't look back."

Billy nodded stiffly.

"Hands on top of your head," Moran said. "Turn around. Walk backward slowly."

Devin did as he said. Billy walked beside him. When they were only a few feet from the sergeant, Moran reached for his handcuffs. Devin heard them rattle. "Now," he said.

Billy bolted. Moran turned toward him and in that instant, Devin threw himself against the officer and knocked the gun from his grasp. The two men struggled as the boy ran, their knees and elbows rasping on the sidewalk, each trying to push the other aside and reach the weapon.

Billy was out of sight now.

Moran grunted; Devin hissed. Rolling backward across the policeman's legs, Devin gave a desperate lunge, thinking he could finally reach the revolver. But it was gone.

Devin looked up and found the revolver pointed at his face. It was in the hands of a boy in the white shirt and red tie of the Lincoln Brigade.

Devin froze. The boy's hands trembled and Devin knew that had he charged, the student wouldn't have a chance. He was about Billy's age, Devin guessed. Devin raised his hands slowly above his head.

"Good work, son. I'll take the gun now," said Moran.

The officer, breathing heavily, took out his handcuffs and smacked Devin hard across the face with them.

Kimberly sat on the sofa, her face sallow, her eyes lifeless, oblivious to the incessant ringing of the phone. Finally it stopped and the room once again became deafeningly quiet. She felt enraged by the police raid and further angered by their stubborn refusal to arrest her. After many days and sleepless nights of introspection, Kimberly realized that she had to leave Andrei. Her anger wasn't political, but personal; she felt betrayed. She had wanted desperately to reach Andrei in Washington and tell him just exactly what she thought, but that was not possible. Her calls were still not being put through. She resigned herself to the fact that ultimately it didn't matter—her actions would speak for her.

She got up from the couch, grabbed a coat from the closet, and took a taxi to the south side of Chicago. She knocked on the door of a shabby apartment which she knew belonged to Cliff, a rather limited and introverted gay actor in her troupe. She, as the "star," had done favors for Cliff, and felt he owed her.

He opened the door and stared incredulously at Kimberly, who stood before him with a tentative smile.

"Hi, Cliff."

"What's up, Kim?" he said, making no move to invite her in.

"Can I come in?"

"I don't know," he said timidly. "Look, Kim, I feel really lousy, but you know what the problem is—"

"Sleeping with a Russian isn't contagious," she snapped.

"The hell it isn't. You can catch it by having been in the same play—especially an outlaw play."

Kimberly's eyes softened. "Please, I don't have any place to go."

"Go home, back to your apartment."

"I don't know what I'd do. Do you? If you were desperate—"

"Somehow I've never seen you as helpless. At least compared to the rest of us."

"I've left him," she blurted out.

Cliff drew in a deep breath. "You can't just leave somebody like him," he said evenly.

Kimberly spoke evenly, measuring her words. "I need a place to stay. I wanted to come to somebody I thought was a friend. Please don't force me to—"

She stopped, not quite knowing where the thought would lead her. "Look. Worse things can come from not helping someone than from helping them."

He looked at her strangely and slowly stepped aside.

"Thank you," she said, and walked into his apartment.

* * *

Within two days, Kimberly and Cliff were taking on some of the tics and habits of longtime roommates, effortlessly sliding past each other at the kitchen sink, unconsciously imitating one another's gestures. Kimberly, formerly the main attraction, realized she was falling into a little-sister, tag-along role, but she didn't fight it; there was too much comfort in it.

On the third night, Cliff took her to a crowded downtown cafe and led her into a dimly lit back room. Jeffrey was waiting there, seated at a small table. He didn't rise or smile as she and Cliff sat down. She stared at him, his dark face partially illuminated by the candle that was on the table. She recognized him from his Natnet appearances as a reporter and suddenly realized that he was the man who had helped her home after the raid.

"This isn't too smart," Jeffrey said to Cliff. "Anybody recognize you?" He looked at Kimberly.

"I don't think anybody's looking for me."

A smile played on his mouth, the candlelight shining in his dark eyes. "And I guess this is not the way your public is used to seeing you."

She self-consciously touched her hair. "I guess I'm pretty much of a mess."

"Let me put it this way," he answered. "I used to think a pretty woman could never look bad."

"You know just what to say to a girl."

Jeffrey looked at Cliff. "This lady could be trouble."

"She's a friend," he said.

Jeffrey nodded and looked sharply at Kimberly. "You want to be a part of the resistance."

She smiled softly. "Well, I think I have been, in a way."

Jeffrey snorted skeptically. "Yeah?"

"I want to be involved," she said with almost tangible determination.

"What is it you want to resist? You got something special in mind?"

"No, I don't know."

Cliff felt Kimberly struggling. "Kim hasn't really thought it out intellectually," he said protectively.

Jeffrey ignored him, staring hard at Kimberly. "You mean, you believe in capitalism instead of communism?"

"I don't know very much about it."

"As I see it, your life's pretty good," he said. "Things aren't so bad that you're desperate. Most people fight back when they can't think of anything else. Or if there's something personal. You want to get even with your boyfriend? Maybe bring him down a little, so he notices you a little more?"

She shook her head.

Jeffrey continued like a drill sergeant. "You ain't been hurt, you don't believe in anything—and you sure don't understand anything. I liked you better when you were a dilettante doing outlaw cabaret because you felt like it. Let me tell you something: the way you look here—if you get nothing for yourself, you got nothing for the resistance. You understand?"

He stood abruptly and moved for the door. Kimberly looked down, tears welling in her eyes. Cliff stared at the candlelight, embarrassed and intimidated. Jeffrey turned at the door.

"You want to be part of the resistance? You find out what you believe in, what really matters to you, not whether you're a little uncomfortable, or scared and helpless. The best thing you could do for us is get back into bed with your Russian. That's a great place for somebody who wants to help, but you'd better figure out what you really want before you start playin' in real life."

He left. Kimberly and Cliff looked at each other. "I won't go back," she said. "I can't."

Alan Drummond sometimes told himself that everything being relative, he was doing pretty well. He was thrice-protected from the reality of his position: by his profession, by his sense of irony, and most of all by his thick black skin. To be a doctor was important, because it was not only the Exiles who needed his skills, but the entire town of Milford.

Irony helped too. "A gift of laughter and a sense that the world was mad." Who said that? No matter; it described Alan's condition: he knew the world was mad and he was pretty damn sure it was getting worse every day. If it was getting better, the improvements were still a secret in Nebraska.

And finally to be black was to know in your bones that white men had an infinite capacity for greed, stupidity, and evil; to expect the worst from the white race meant you would rarely be disappointed. He knew some good whites, but as a race they were definitely to be avoided.

Still, Alan Drummond was doing okay. In Omaha, he was doing even better than he had in Milford. He'd gone to Omaha with the Milford Exiles who were wounded in the SSU raid, to oversee their treatment. No one bothered him and the hospital staff seemed oblivious to the new arrivals. He was free to go into Omaha whenever he wished. He had a small apartment on the hospital grounds, but he was rarely there, as he routinely worked sixteen- and eighteen-hour days.

When his Milford patients didn't need him, he volunteered to help with others.

He had not been at People's Acceptance long when he became intrigued by the secretiveness of the psychiatry unit. Every day he passed the door with the armed guard and the NO ADMITTANCE sign. The first couple of times he asked a fellow doctor about Psychiatry, he got only shrugs. "Experimental," one said. "Top secret—don't even ask," another advised.

Drummond had been helping out in Pathology when one night the corpse of a young man was brought in. A doctor named Mead puzzled over him for hours, shaking his head unhappily.

Alan looked over his shoulder. "What's it look like?" he asked.

"As far as I can tell—and it isn't much—it's natural death. If I were going to take a wild guess, I'd say there was some similarity to the signs we used to see in acute depression patients."

Alan stared at Mead as if he didn't understand.

"There are people who get so depressed that they literally will themselves to death," Mead explained. "Some of it shows in brain cells. Atrophy without any reason. In the nineteenth century they used to call it dying of a broken heart."

"Any drugs?"

"Yeah," Mead said, and looked back to the corpse. "Heavy traces of something I don't recognize—got properties of prochlorpherazine."

"Behavior modification."

"Where'd this one come from?"

"Here," Alan said. "The section they call psychiatric—"

Mead turned to Alan suddenly very nervous. "I

253

should've known. Look, this could be real bad news. They don't like anybody even close to that operation. It's some kind of special deal that spells big trouble for anybody who gets too close."

"Okay," Alan said, heading for the door. "I understand."

"No, I don't think you do," said the other doctor.

Drummond nodded and filed the episode away. Excessive curiosity had always been one of his vices.

Once Peter returned to Omaha, the political honeymoon was over. No more speeches to Congress, no more dinners at the White House, just plenty of hard work and uncertainty. He was governor-general of Heartland—but what did that mean? He had a big office overlooking the Missouri River, a telephone console with plenty of buttons to punch, and four secretaries bustling about his outer office. But did he have power?

Power was elusive, quicksilver. You had to find it, create it, or steal it. The reality Peter faced was that he had an impressive title but other people made things happen. Andrei had power, because ultimately he had the Soviet military might at his disposal. Marion had power, because of her status within the PPP and not incidentally because she was General Samanov's lover.

But Peter did not possess those things. Instead, he found himself talking to lawyers and administrators, trying to decide whom to trust. Dozens of people reported to him, but he had to assume that many of them gave their true loyalty to Andrei and/or Marion. Who gave a damn about Peter Bradford?

Peter had a growing sense that his power, if it was to exist, had to come from the people. If they trusted him, and cared about him, then he would have true power, of a magnitude that even Andrei and Marion would have to respect. But how did you win the trust, the love even, of millions of people over a five-state area, people who had every reason to be suspicious of you? People in Milford trusted him, but that was because they had known him all his life. He didn't have forty years to woo the good people of Heartland—he thought it might be more like forty days, before the whole thing blew up in his face.

His first day in office was a blur of names, faces, handshakes, glib compliments, and suspicious glances —a governmental gauntlet he had been required to run.

He had met with his department heads—his cabinet, as it was pretentiously called—and one man had made the biggest impression on him: General Fred "Bull" Sittman, a gruff, burly old soldier who headed the Area National Guard. Sittman was no backslapper.

"Mr. Bradford, you don't know if you can trust me and I don't know if I can trust you," Sittman said. "It'll take some time to find out and the rest is mostly bullshit. But I'll tell you this, I run a tight ship and my men do what they're told to do. If you're a front man for the Russians, then I say to hell with you, but if you care about this area and want the laws enforced and the peace maintained, then we might get along."

"I think we might get along," Peter said, and reminded himself to find out more about General Sittman.

Later that day, the red phone in Peter's office rang.

"Peter? Andrei. How was your day?"

"Confusing."

"That's to be expected. A lot of new names and faces. It takes time. I'm calling to pass on some news. Devin Milford has been arrested here in Chicago. He

255

kidnapped his older son and was attempting to seize the younger one when he was apprehended. The older boy escaped, incidentally."

"Perhaps *kidnapped* isn't the right word."

"Marion will think so. In any event, Milford was beaten, either during or after his arrest. Some overzealous PPP security person, I suspect. I have had him transferred to my control. Perhaps eventually he should be under your supervision."

"No, I wouldn't think so."

"I thought you should know, but I must request that you keep the matter confidential for the time being."

"Of course. Andrei, there is one other matter."

"Yes?"

"Someone said plans are under way for my inauguration in Chicago. But I haven't been notified."

"My God. Yes, I wanted to discuss that with you, but something of an urgent personal matter came up. I apologize."

"No harm done."

At the end of the workday, he rejoined his family at the Friendship Hotel's presidential suite, high above Omaha. A suite so large and pretentious that even Scott was impressed.

"God, you could put a basketball court in one of these rooms," he declared at dinner. "You know, we have the whole floor. Can you believe it?"

"If you think this hotel is something, you should see the house," Jackie said. "Margaret took Mom and me out there this afternoon. It's a mausoleum."

"What's that—where they bury people?" Scott asked.

"How do you feel about the governor-general picking up where the meat-packing barons of Omaha left off?" Amanda said.

"You said you didn't want the White House," Peter said.

"I take it back," Amanda said. "You know, our things are going to fill about three rooms in that house. At least the White House comes furnished."

Several waiters were moving about the big dining room now, bringing food and wine to the elegant table. There were armed guards just outside their door as well. Peter had protested that he didn't want so much security, but the party security chief, a lean, somber man named Laird, persuaded him that he had no choice, that these were violent times and the governor-general's first obligation was to keep alive.

Abruptly, Jackie said, "What's going to happen to us?"

"What do you mean, honey?" Peter asked.

"I don't know. I feel like it's not my life anymore."

"I know, darling," Amanda said.

"Hey, what's this gloom and doom?" Peter demanded.

"You went to your new dance class, didn't you? Wasn't it okay?"

Jackie nodded. "Sure, it was great. The Russian woman who teaches the class is fabulous."

"Okay, I wouldn't worry too much," Peter said. "You guys will go to school. You'll dance. Scott'll play ball. You'll make new friends. Your mom will be busy with the new house—"

"Yeah, and you'll rule the world," Scott quipped.

Peter shrugged. "A few more days and it'll all seem normal," he said.

The kids laughed, but Amanda did not. That night, when the kids finally went to bed, Peter and Amanda retired to the presidential bedroom. It was a charming old room with its four-poster bed and huge chandelier;

this was, Peter realized, the first time they had been alone together since he flew off to Washington. Much had happened; Amanda wondered if he understood just how much.

They stood for a moment at the window, watching the silver ribbon of the Missouri slide by in the moonlight.

"Remember the last time we looked down at that river?" Peter asked. "The night of the big dinner?"

"A thousand years ago," Amanda said with distance in her voice. "If I'd known all that was going to happen, I might have jumped in."

"Hey, come on."

"We were different people then."

"I'm the same."

"Are you?" she asked. "I'm not. I've seen things I'd never dreamed of. The Exiles—it was like finding yourself in a Nazi concentration camp. Then, presto, here I am surrounded by guards and servants with the entire top floor of a hotel for me to roam around in."

"Not to mention the meat-packer's mansion," he said, but his quip didn't help. She walked away from him.

"The Exiles in Milford, they're all still there, their homes destroyed. What do I mean, homes? That damned camp, that shantytown, where they were forced to live."

Peter stopped listening. It had been a long, long day, and he had problems she couldn't even begin to understand. He could see the big picture now, and she was still focused on one tiny corner of it.

"Amanda, I know how you feel . . . " he ventured.

"You *don't* know how I feel. You weren't there. It wasn't just some *incident*. It was an atrocity."

He tried to take her in his arms but she turned away.

"I don't want comfort," she said. "That's not what I need. I saw something happen that you don't have any way of understanding. In the middle of all the horror, when the camp was destroyed, our people took the Exiles in. At great danger to themselves, they did the decent, humane thing."

"That's fine," he said. "But having the Exiles in town may not be such a good idea."

Peter didn't know what else to say. Maybe the raid on the exile camp had been worse than anyone had told him; to him it remained distant and unreal, an item on an agenda.

Amanda took his silence for indifference. "I don't think I know you anymore," she said.

Peter, pained, fought back his weariness, his annoyance. He reminded himself how good she was, how decent, how much he had missed her when they were apart.

"Amanda, when I was in Washington, I needed you so much. When I went to the Lincoln Memorial, I wrote you a letter. I've gotten so used to our being together. It was hard for me not to be able to talk it all over with you. What I wrote was about visiting the memorial and thinking about what Lincoln really means, should really mean. And it was all tied up with you and all that you mean to me." He paused and looked toward her, seeing if he should go on. She said nothing; he continued, "I guess the main thing is, no matter how bad our society may seem now, it's going to be worse unless people like me make an effort to work things out. Not heroic stands, but hard work and compromise—dealing with reality as it is. I thought about Lincoln, what he would do if he were here now. Maybe the most important thing wouldn't be to preserve the Union, but to hang on to some of our principles, our dignity, just the hope that things can get better. We're more like the South, after they lost the war, just trying to survive, settling in for the long haul. Robert E. Lee was a great general, but maybe he was an even greater man after the war, when he was the president of a little college and set an example for his people of dignity and hope."

Amanda was moved by his sincerity, even if she didn't fully understand his meaning. She crossed the room and took his hand. "Milford is our home," she said. "Everything we are we learned there. We can't just turn our backs on what's happened there. What's still going on."

Peter shut his eyes wearily. "Amanda, are you here with me, or are you still back in Milford?"

"I'm your wife."

He drew her close and this time she did not resist. "Honey, we'll work this out," he whispered. "Just help me. I need you. We'll do the best we can, for as many people as we can."

She nodded and he held her for a long time, not wanting to lose the moment. He thought briefly of Devin. He had meant to tell Amanda the news of his arrest but he knew this was not the time. So he would keep that secret from her for a while. He wondered how many more secrets there would be before this was over.

"He must be killed."

Marion tried to sound dispassionate, but could not keep the fury from her voice. It was so logical to her; why couldn't Petya understand?

They were having coffee in his second-floor bedroom, overlooking the rolling Virginia countryside.

Petya, confident and serene, sipped from his cup and seemed not to have heard her.

"Petya! He took my son! And God knows what he would have done if I'd been there. It's me he hates, Petya, me he wants to destroy."

"You betrayed him," the Russian said matter-of-factly.

"That is not the issue. He has committed many crimes. He has shown that reeducation will not stop him. He has shown how dangerous he is—" She stopped, feeling as though that were more than enough.

"You loved him once," Petya said, evenly.

"For God's sake, Petya. Will you support me or not?" Petya watched a colt trotting playfully across the frosted field beside its mother. Marion stared at him furiously.

"It is a political matter," he said. "Talk to Andrei."

"Andrei sees Devin as some sort of American saint. He is entirely irrational."

"Andrei's instincts are good. Talk to him when you're back in Chicago. Then we'll talk again."

Marion stared at Petya, her face clouded.

Petya smiled. "Everything will be fine."

She shook her head slowly. "You're keeping something from me."

"No. You have as much information as I do."

"I don't mean about Devin; I mean about you, about—"

"Why do you think this, Marion?"

"You've never let me know everything," she said.

He smiled at her. "And you?"

"More than everything."

"Ultimately there are things none of us knows.

Ultimately, no matter how much we think we know, or plan, there is always the unexpected." He shrugged, opening his arms to her. She went into them, his arms encircling her tenderly. "Be well, my little American. Soon, who knows, you may be leading your own country."

Marion stepped back, smiling. "Why is it, every time we part, I feel that I will never see you again?"

"One time it will be true."

They heard the chatter of a helicopter landing in front of the mansion. He pushed her gently away. She started to move toward the door, then turned back to him. He had walked to the window.

"Petya," she said quietly. He turned from the window. "Do we love each other?"

He laughed, not at her vulnerability, but in sympathy, charmed. "Of course we do. Lovers and comrades."

"I betrayed my husband—with you," she said, reluctant to leave.

"For *you*. For the cause," he said wryly. "And we were a wonderful result."

She smiled and walked out the door. He turned back to the window and watched her climb into the helicopter. She waved. He waved back as the helicopter took flight, cutting across the cold, gray sky.

Once again, Devin heard the rattle of keys, the heavy metallic banging of a cell door. He stood and saw the SSU officer looming in the doorway.

"Mr. Milford? This way, please."

So now they were sweetness and light again. The first ones, the PPP thugs, had handcuffed and beaten him, then some sort of struggle ensued—they fought over him, like dogs over a bone—and the SSU had brought him here. They cleaned him up, fed him, and treated him like visiting royalty. They had interrogated him, yes, but routinely; they asked the questions and he answered them by rote. He was playing the game now, not fighting, determined to stall them as long as he could.

The SSU officer and two of his men led Devin down a long underground corridor and into a parking garage, where a van awaited them.

They opened the rear of the van, Devin stepped inside, and they locked the doors behind him. The truck shot up the ramp onto the rain-wet, deserted Chicago streets.

Ironically, Devin Milford himself was one of the few people in Chicago who did not know where Devin Milford was headed that morning. News of his impending trial had been widely disseminated by Natnet; in their telling, after all, the story of his "attack" on his own children made wonderful propaganda. Here was this renegade Resister—so the official version went— who was so pathetically envious of his former wife's political enlightenment and subsequent rise to prominence, that he struck back at her in the most cowardly way imaginable. . . . That Magistrate Marion Milford Andrews would herself be presiding at the trial lent a soupçon of intrigue to the proceeding that neither press nor public could resist.

Not that the entire public was seduced by the official version of events. To those who still remembered the Devin Milford of 1992, the charges against him seemed ludicrous. Among the Resisters, support for the framed man was strong, and the kangaroo court provided a welcome forum for protest. Jeffrey, Cliff, Kimberly—

who had persuaded Jeffrey to let her come along—and their comrades in the Chicago movement had been working to make sure that Devin's trial would not be a quiet affair. By the time the black van covered the six blocks from the SSU security building to the Cook County courthouse, sympathizers were lined up three-deep on the cold sidewalks.

Devin crouched in the van, tense, wondering what lay ahead. He'd broken many of their laws; he'd break more given the chance. But he was tired.

They had driven only a block when he heard the faint sound of clapping. It snuck up on him; he thought for a moment it was rain on the roof of the truck. He listened more closely and realized it was the sound of people clapping, a lot of people, as his van passed along the streets. It didn't register at first that the clapping had anything to do with him, and he idly wondered what there was out there that everybody could agree on.

Jeffrey, now in his role as the perfect citizen, had his Natnet mobile unit positioned at the courthouse steps. Riot police lined the street. Jeffrey, too, was amazed at the turnout. He had hoped for dozens but there were hundreds here and more streaming in every minute. The rhythmic applause echoed off the buildings around the courthouse square. He could see the confusion, the panic, on the faces of the police. Jeffrey's heart raced with excitement as the black van rounded the corner.

He nodded to his cameraman to start rolling; this would be one of those times when the picture would tell the real story and no one would be deceived for long by the words he was forced to say. "The van bringing the infamous Devin Milford to justice is now arriving at the courthouse," Jeffrey intoned solemnly into his micro-phone. "A large crowd has gathered, to make its feelings clear about this convicted criminal, now accused of adventurism of the worst kind."

Just then Michael Laird, the PPP security chief, raced down the steps, followed by three policemen. "What the hell do you think you're doing?" he demanded.

Jeffrey fumbled for his press card, all innocence. "Man, I'm Natnet. They sent me."

"Cut off those cameras," Laird snapped. The policemen surrounded Jeffrey's unresisting cameraman.

"Look, I just go where I'm told. The assignments come out of the advisory committee office," Jeffrey protested.

"If Magistrate Andrews wants media coverage, she'll notify the PPP information office," Laird said.

"Hey, all right. Looks like a mistake to me." He shook his head. "It's a good story for the magistrate," Jeffrey said. "Pack 'em up, boys." His coverage seemed to be over. But it wasn't. Stepping back into the crowd, Jeffrey kept his small, personal camera trained on the scene. He wondered how this tough-guy Laird would deal with those hundreds of people who wouldn't stop coming, whose caring had never ceased.

When the door of the van flew open, Devin saw the light, a split second before the rush of sound hit him. No words, no chants, just a steady hand-clapping that was at once ominous and exhilarating. He knew now that it was for him, and he stood, tall and proud, gazing out at the sea of faces. The guards took him by the arms and hurried him into the silent courthouse.

Marion watched the arrival of the van from her chambers, high above the street, but when Devin emerged, she turned away. Andrei, beside her, studied the scene intently until Devin had been taken inside. Then he turned to Marion, who was fumbling with a cigarette, clearly shaken.

"I will not be intimidated," she said firmly.

He made a little shrug. "No, but I trust you will consider all the facts."

"What facts? That he's dangerous? That's all that mob proves."

"Dangerous? Or a symbol who can be turned about, used to our advantage? Who could have imagined Abraham Lincoln as a patron of socialism?"

"How do you keep them straight?" she raged. "All your little games and deceptions? Don't you see—the man must be eliminated. He wants to destroy me, everything I've built. He wants . . ."

Andrei chose to ignore the allegations, pending further evidence. "Revenge?"

Her beautiful face hardened. It registered a dawning awareness. "You admire him, don't you? You won't help me because you want to protect him."

"I do admire him," Andrei said. "I don't want to protect him."

"You do," Marion insisted. "You want to protect your little fantasy of American guts and American goodness."

"Be rational. I am, if anything, protecting you. My work—"

"You had no right to take him out of party custody."

"Stop being a fool," he said angrily. "You seek political leadership. You need popular support. But if you blindly pursue an act of revenge, the murder of your ex-husband, the father of your children, you will be despised. Even with Petya's support, you will not survive."

She wanted to scream. If Andrei was right, her two

266

deepest passions, for Devin's death and for her own political success, were in hopeless conflict.

"Kindly leave, now," she said coldly. "I have to prepare for court."

"This way," the bailiff said, and pushed a door open.

Devin gazed into the huge, bright courtroom and was surprised to see that the chamber, except for the functionaries, was empty. He had been prepared for a show trial, but the rows of heavy benches were vacant and every sound bounced unimpeded off the paneled walls. He noticed an elegantly dressed man sitting alone in the rows of seats reserved for the public. After a moment, Devin recognized Andrei Denisov from his newspaper pictures.

The bailiff led Devin to the prisoner's dock, a small platform, enclosed on three sides, where he would stand facing the judge. He saw, to his left, two lawyers, a man and a woman, at the prosecution table. But the defense table, and the judge's bench, were vacant.

In the silence of the courtroom, Devin thought he could still hear the faint echo of the clapping outside the courthouse.

"All rise!" the bailiff called out.

Everyone stood, except for Andrei, who habitually ignored such conventions.

"The Fourth District Area Court is now in session. People's Magistrate Marion Andrews presiding."

She came in from the left in her black robes. Devin leaned forward, studying her, trying to recognize in that hieratic figure the flesh and blood he'd once loved. It was the first time he'd seen her in five years.

Marion refused to look at him. She took her chair, busied herself for a moment with papers, then glanced at the prosecutors. They rose.

"The prisoner has refused counsel?"

"Yes, your honor," the prosecutor said, though no counsel had been offered.

After a long pause, she turned her eyes to him. She felt a jolt, to see how thin, how aged he was. Then she willed herself to do what must be done.

"It is my duty to inform you of your right to counsel—if not of your own choosing, then by the court."

Devin smiled and shook his head, as if amused.

"Do you understand the seriousness of the charges against you?"

"I understand that you have the power to do what you wish to do."

"This is a court of law. You will be treated fairly."

Devin closed his eyes. Court, trial, judge, prisoner, evidence—those words had no meaning in reality. Even to abide by the protocol was a mockery.

"For five years I've imagined the ways we might meet," Devin said, heedless of the consequences. "What you'd look like, what we'd feel. Now here it is and it's not what I expected at all."

"I would expect you to try and turn this into something personal," she said evenly.

"Isn't it?"

"It is not," she snapped. "You have very serious charges against you, Mr. Milford. You should be aware that a lack of decorum may prejudice the court."

"I understand that you're afraid to talk to me," he said.

"How do you plead?"

"I don't plead, Marion. I won't be judged by you."

Her face reddened. She began to rise out of her chair. "This court has the power to judge you. And it will."

"That means you win. But of course there's no surprise in that."

Devin did not know when he had felt so good, so pure. It had nothing to do with what might await him; all that mattered was right and wrong. No matter what her "court" might say, he knew he could not be more innocent, nor she more guilty.

"I pity you. It's sad that you destroyed your life," she continued, and her voice sounded calm. "And now you come back here to destroy the lives of others?"

"I'd say I'm a little late for that," he replied. "You've done a fine job of destroying the children, of trying to twist and corrupt them—"

She slammed down her gavel. "You are in contempt of court!"

"On that we agree."

There was a long pause and gradually Marion Andrews' granite composure seemed to crack. Her face flushed, her eyes took on an expression that was almost pleading, and she seemed almost on the verge of tears. "Where's Billy?" she demanded.

"I thought we weren't going to make this personal," said Devin, smiling.

"Where is he?"

"He's free."

His words were like a slap in the face. Marion started to reply, then took a breath, trying to regain her control. Andrei leaned forward in his bench, fascinated, more than a little amazed to realize that this man—this apparently powerless man—was not afraid.

"I had hoped you would be more reasonable," said Marion, once again composed, a portrait of professionalism. "At least where the welfare of your own child is concerned."

Devin shook his head. "Do you remember when he

was born? For the longest time the kid refused to be born. Then all of a sudden he came. Pushing his way out—big, strong, yelling—nothing could stop him. He wasn't yours; he wasn't mine. He was on his own."

"I see that prison has done nothing to help you become a better citizen. You are still a dangerous subversive. You are blinded by thoughts of revenge toward me and would use innocent children to get at me."

Devin almost smiled. "You know what's funny? I don't hate you. I wish I could. But I do hate what you've done to the children. What you tried to do to Billy and what you have done to Caleb. That's why I will fight you."

"I find in you clear evidence of mental imbalance," she said, hurrying the legal jargon. "You are remanded for psychiatric evaluation to determine your competence for trial."

She struck the gavel and stood, then strode away from the bench.

"All rise," the bailiff shouted.

As the courtroom guards moved forward, Devin said loudly, "Marion, if you have the power, why are you so afraid?"

She looked at him a moment, held by the strength of his gaze, before turning and walking out the door to the safety of her chambers.

Andrei was still assimilating the confrontation between the former spouses as he entered Marion Andrews' chambers.

"You lost control, Madame Magistrate," Andrei said, sitting down across the desk from her.

She ignored the comment.

Andrei had watched the little courtroom drama closely and with some satisfaction. He thought Marion had exhibited womanly weakness and that was of interest. But more important was Milford's performance. The man knew all that could be done to him, yet he was not afraid. What a strange thing moral strength was, Andrei mused, a kind of force of nature, perhaps part of the evolutionary process. You could take away wealth, rights, freedom, even life—but you could never destroy the enduring human quality that produced heroes. It always returned. This time it had returned in Devin Milford.

Marion interrupted Andrei's thoughts. "I have two formal requests to make. I would like you to order the Special Services Unit in Milford to search the town for my son. And I want Devin hospitalized far away from here."

"I have a trade to propose."

Marion was suspicious. "What do you want?"

"I want to prevent you from doing something that will damage yourself and our overall plan."

"You're still trying to protect him."

He shrugged. "Believe me or not. Allow him to make a public statement."

"I think you're mad."

"What harm can he do us? The real message will be that you—we—are not afraid of him. Strip away the mythology and let his admirers see that he is only one powerless, meaningless man. Then I will turn him over to the governor-general's office to carry out your court order."

Marion tried to think it through, to see what tricks he could be playing. But in truth, what he said made sense. She would have Devin in her control within hours; that was all that really mattered.

"If I agree, you will have the SSU search Milford?"

"Yes."

"And you give me your word you will deliver Devin for evaluation?"

"Wherever you choose."

"Omaha. The People's Acceptance Hospital."

"Fine," he said. "Then it's agreed?"

She nodded.

They had taken Devin to a windowless holding room in the basement of the courthouse. He waited patiently, still savoring his exchange with Marion, not letting himself think about what might come next.

The door opened and the man he recognized as Andrei Denisov entered. Devin did not rise, nor did the Russian sit down.

"I trust you know who I am," Andrei began.

It was not a question and Devin gave no answer.

"I really don't understand you, Milford. What was your intention after obtaining your children? Go live in caves? Or take them back to your hometown? Certainly you know that Marion would tear down that town, house by house, brick by brick, to get her children back. And to destroy you."

Devin returned the Russian's gaze but still did not reply.

"Such a brave man, and such a fool. To let a woman betray you."

"What do you want?" Devin demanded. "Why are you here?"

"Perhaps to help you," Andrei told him. "Would you trade your freedom for the return of your son?"

"You should know the answer to that."

"Do you understand what can happen to you?"

"Yes."

"And you're not afraid?"

"I'd be a fool not to be."

"I hope to save your life."

"Why?" Devin asked.

"Because I see no purpose served by your death."

"I don't trust you, Denisov. You're very clever, but you're still trying to destroy my country."

"I am responsible for things being much better than they might have been in your country. I am searching for a solution that leaves your country with some honor, some hope for the future."

"Yes, I've seen your hope for the future," Devin said bitterly. "I see it in my son Caleb."

Now Andrei's eyes blazed. "There will never be another America, as you knew it, that's a fact," he said. "The only issue that remains is the nature of what is to come."

Devin shook his head and turned away.

"You could help your countrymen," Andrei continued. "Your friend Peter Bradford—do you believe he is a good man?"

Devin faced him again, trying to understand the game Denisov was playing and the role Peter might have in it. "He has decent instincts, if he's allowed to exercise them."

"I have put him in office because I believe his dedication to his country is compatible with the interests of the Soviet Union."

Devin waited, skeptical but curious.

"He needs support if he is to survive. Not least of all against the ambitions of your former wife."

Devin began to understand. "Are you saying I can somehow help Peter against Marion?"

Andrei was leaning against the door now, his hands in the pockets of his flannel pants, his shoulders hunched forward. "Perhaps you noticed the people outside when you arrived. Quite an impressive turnout. It seems you still have influence."

"And you want me to express support for Peter?"

"Only if you mean it. Perhaps, if you think of it yourself, make some comparison between him and his second-in-command, your former wife."

The outlines of it were coming clear. Denisov was asking for a testimonial. Devin waited, trying to make up his mind.

Andrei turned to leave, then paused to add, "There is also the matter of your eventual freedom. Perhaps even your reunion with your son."

He went out, confident that he had found the key to Devin Milford.

The tall bronze doors of the courthouse swung open. A dozen police and security men ran out, forming a kind of beachhead at the top of the courthouse steps. Other police made a line across the bottom step. The crown surged forward—to look, to cheer, maybe even to do battle. Devin Milford was about to emerge.

Cries rang out as he stepped forward into the cold, swirling Chicago air. He seemed oblivious to the security men who encircled him. His eyes searched the crowd, as if he were looking for some lost friend. A current of electricity passed between him and his listeners—the same galvanic spark that had made him such an unforgettable orator in his days as a congressman and as a presidential candidate. That gift of inspiring others flooded back into him now, coming from a place in him he hadn't felt for a long time.

Finally, from the top step, Devin held up his hand for silence.

He spoke softly, yet his voice seemed to carry undiminished through the humming canyons that were the streets of the captive city: "I pledge allegiance to the flag . . . of the United States of America." Devin turned toward the crowd. They began to join with him in his pledge, and the sound of the forbidden words, spoken solemnly, with great feeling, reverberated through the streets. "And to the republic for which it stands, one nation, under God, indivisible, with liberty and justice for all."

Devin paused for a moment, and felt the expectant crowd, that sea of faces turned up to him. Then he began to repeat the words again. The crowd gained strength: all tension drained from their bodies and they stood proud, their voices resolute.

When he had finished, Devin was silent for a long moment. It was as if he were summoning something from even deeper within his experience, within his past, within his soul. Instinctively, he wanted to compress all his wisdom and struggle and patriotism into one simple word or gesture. He raised his arms above his head—straight up—reaching.

"America!"

He said it simply and powerfully. Andrei was mesmerized.

"America!" Devin said again, this time almost yelling.

His arms were still raised and when he said it a third time, their arms were raised too, their voices joined with his.

"America! America! America!"

The words thundered through the square; it seemed that the buildings might shake and the walls tumble.

"America! America! America!" The words exploded

even louder than before, and then Andrei gave the signal to the security men. They surrounded Devin and hustled him into the van.

For an instant Andrei feared the crowd might riot—they could not have been stopped without a massacre—but they only continued their mighty chant of "America! America!" And that, Andrei knew, was more dangerous than any riot.

Inside the van the sound reverberated. Devin sat forward, intense, suddenly crying. He heard the chant for what seemed like miles, as the van sped through the city. He no longer cared where he was going; all that mattered was that pure, perfect place he had been.

Chapter 11

THE NEXT MORNING Petya summoned Andrei to Washington.

"I have just talked to Moscow, Andrei," he told him, "and now I must talk to you. Face-to-face."

But there were matters that Andrei had to see to before departing. Mikel had rushed into his office first thing that day and announced with smug satisfaction that Kimberly had been located. With malicious triumph, Mikel revealed that she'd been cohabitating with a male actor in a south-side slum.

"Have her picked up," Andrei had said. "Have her brought to my apartment. Don't hurt her."

When he went to his apartment—their apartment—a few hours later, she was waiting. She did not look up when he entered; she was sitting at the far end of the living room, rigid with anger. At first he did not understand.

"Are you all right?" he asked.

"I was until your bullies broke into my friend's apartment, beat him up, and took me prisoner."

"Oh God," he sighed. "There was not to be any violence."

"Somehow the message didn't get through," she said bitterly.

"Kimberly, I'm sorry, but we must talk and I don't have much time."

"Well, that's surprising," she said. "When did you ever have time to talk to me? When did you ever think about me except when you wanted sex?"

He opened his mouth to object, but found he could not.

"When you were away, had us raided, did you worry about me? Did you even know what happened?"

"You were under my protection."

"Well, while I was under your protection, you lost me."

He sat beside her on the sofa, close but not too close. She wore jeans and flannel now, and no makeup, yet she had never been more desirable. "What do you want?" he asked gently.

"I don't know," she admitted, sadly, candidly. "But I know you're Russian. I just need to be something other than somebody's mistress."

He leaned toward her, speaking with rare intensity. "We are special people; people like us live in our work, live at the edge, defining ourselves by the challenges we confront and triumph over. The qualities that unite us go beyond politics or nationality; we share a state of mind that is universal."

She wouldn't look at him. "Being with you is destroying me."

Andrei's eyes flashed with anger. "I'm not destroying

you. You are frightened because you are weak. You need things outside yourself to flatter you, to make you think you're desirable or talented. You never think what someone else might need."

She looked at him tentatively. "What do you need, Andrei?"

"You, perhaps." He leaned toward her and touched her face gently with his hand.

She sat rigid. "Don't touch me, please. It isn't fair."

"Come with me to Washington. Today. Maybe we'll stay there. My work here is almost finished. We can start a new life."

"No," she whispered.

"Why not?"

After a silence, she said, "Something has happened to me."

"A new romance? The actor?"

She smiled. "No, not the actor. Not romance."

"Then what?"

She threw her head back, gazing at the ceiling. "After you left, after the raid on the club, I needed you. I tried to call, I begged, but nobody would help. I didn't know what to do. I left here. Ran away. Not sure what I was running from or to. But I was lucky. I discovered something—something bigger than myself."

She broke off. He laughed grimly. "Don't tell me you joined the resistance."

"I don't expect you to take anything I do seriously. But I found something and it doesn't matter whether you respect it or not. This is for me."

"All right, Kimberly, I will take you seriously, really. What is your discovery?"

She looked him in the eyes, an odd smile on her face. "I realized I'm an American."

He frowned, not understanding, thinking he had missed something. "Yes?" he ventured.

"I never understood what it meant before. I always thought it was me against the world. I never thought that all those other people . . . that we were all Americans, all part of the same thing. I never thought I could be disloyal to anything because I'd never been loyal to anything. Some people called me a traitor, because of you, and I thought they were silly. I understand it now. And I don't think I can be with you anymore."

"Do you love me?"

"Don't ask that. It doesn't matter."

"Of course it matters. I have given it a great deal of thought. In the end, we live for ourselves."

"I'm not as smart as you, Andrei. I just know I've changed; I can't go live with you in Washington."

He stood up. Andrei understood the art of strategic retreat. "I want you to think it over," he said. "Stay here; I'll be in Washington the next day or two."

She nodded slowly.

"Good. In the guest room, if you prefer. I put no pressures on you. Except the inconvenient fact that I love you. Perhaps I'd forgotten. Perhaps I needed reminding."

She smiled at him. "You are very kind, Andrei, sometimes."

"I will have the charges against your colleagues dropped."

She stood. For a moment she felt herself surrendering to the old passion. Then she pulled back. "Goodbye, Andrei."

Her kiss had given him hope, yet he knew not to push. "Goodbye, my little actress."

* * *

From his limousine on the way to the military airstrip, Andrei put a call through to Peter Bradford at the Palmer House hotel in Chicago. "How goes the Heartland speech?" he asked.

"The rhetoric still throws me," said the new governor-general with a modest laugh, "but I'm getting there."

"The rhetoric is the easy part," said Andrei. "Glory. Prosperity. A brighter tomorrow. After the secession, Heartland will truly be independent, standing on its—"

"Whoa, my friend," Peter interrupted, "you seem to forget that the word *secession* has rather negative connotations in this country."

"*Used* to have," corrected Andrei. "But then, so did words like *socialism* and *collective*. You seem to underestimate the plasticity of your beloved English language. But listen, I have another matter to discuss with you. Are you alone?"

"My wife is with me."

"I urge you, for your own sake, to keep this to yourself. Marion has ordered that your friend Milford be transferred to a hospital in Omaha for psychiatric evaluation. There is, I believe, a special program there."

"What sort of program?" Peter asked, and Amanda started at the queasy fear in his voice.

"Let's not turn squeamish at this point in the game," said Andrei, an unaccustomed steeliness coming into his voice. "Behavior modification. Brainwashing, in your crude parlance."

"Andrei, please . . ." Peter's tone was suddenly imploring. To Amanda it sounded almost like a whimper.

"Don't confuse small issues with great ones, Peter. I'm on my way to Washington."

"What was that about?" Amanda insisted when Peter had hung up the phone.

"Please don't ask, my dear."

But she did ask, and Peter Bradford needed her comfort too badly not to tell her.

"What if he tries to bite me?"

"Good God, it's stupid to be afraid of a dumb animal."

"For you, maybe . . . actually, I'm the best example of why it was such a bad idea to send people like me to the country."

"Dammit to hell. Let's take a break. The damn tractor's no good anyway. I just hate to give up on it."

They leaned against the side of the barn, breathing hard. "Gerta was like that," Dieter said. "Never threw anything away. She said the things you accumulated in your life could tell you how you were going. Or what it was you were doing. I forget."

Will nodded. "Mary called it leaving a trail. She used to say your kids never appreciated you until it got to be too late to do anything about it. If you left them an attic full of junk to root around in, then maybe they'd appreciate you."

"We never had children. I often wish we had."

"Yeah, well, they're not all they're cracked up to be."

"You've been blessed. Your Devin, such a courageous man."

Will drew a red bandanna from his pocket and blew his nose noisily. "Well, it seemed to me he was always fighting somebody—me, the government. To me it just seemed that nobody else's life, what they did, what they were, stood for much unless it fit into his way of thinking. I guess the first time I thought I understood that boy was a few weeks back, at that parade thing, when they wanted him to apologize, or whatever it was. I looked at him and damned if I didn't see the face of my own father. The look he got when he walked out on a field of wheat that'd been beat to the ground by hail. He'd just look at it, not say anything, but you knew from the look on his face that he wouldn't let it beat him. I saw that in Devin; it was like looking at my dad up there."

Will looked away, into the distance, embarrassed by his emotions. He noticed a man and a boy walking up the drive to the house.

Will took a step forward and squinted, watching intently as they drew near. He didn't recognize either of them—a big, bulky man in his thirties and a slender, dark-haired boy in his early teens. Yet something about them gripped his attention.

"What can I do for you?" he asked, not unkindly, when they were a dozen feet away.

Will did not recognize his grandson and namesake, who had changed so much in the seven years since they had been together. But Billy recognized his grandfather; the old man had hardly changed at all. Yet Billy held back, with the uncertain dignity of adolescence. The four of them stared in awkward silence, until the boy finally said, "Grandpa . . ."

Will reacted slowly, as if this was too much to hope for or believe. "What the hell?" he said. "It's not . . ."

"It's me, Billy."

"I know, boy," the old man said stiffly. "I know . . ."

Billy stepped forward cautiously. When they were three feet apart he extended his hand. They shook hands solemnly.

Will said, "Don'cha think I recognize my handsomest, ugliest grandson from Chicago?"

"Well, I knew my old coot of a grandpa," Billy said, and their arms went out and they embraced.

Dieter and Clayton watched from a distance as the old man and the boy hugged, laughing and crying at the same time.

"Damn if you haven't grown up," Will said, holding the boy at arm's length.

"You look great, Grandpa."

The grandfather shrugged. "Still kicking." He looked around at the others and remembered his dignity. "Now, William, tell me who this fellow is, and what the blazes you're doin' here."

"That's Clayton. He's a friend of my dad's. We came here on the underground railroad."

"The what?"

"It was neat. We've been in trucks, ridden the rails—you know, on trains. All these people helped us."

Will laughed with amazement. "Okay, you two runaway slaves, let's go up to the house. Meet my friend Dieter here. Dieter, this is my most handsomest, ugliest grandson, William, and his fugitive friend Clayton."

Clayton shook both the men's hands. Then he took Will aside. "Mr. Milford," he said. "I brought Billy here at your son's specific request. It was what they both wanted. But the authorities are looking for the boy. I'm sure they'll come here. I want to warn you, there could be trouble."

Will pondered the younger man's warning, then unaccountably laughed. "Mister, us Milfords are close kin to trouble. I reckon we'll handle it, whenever it comes."

He threw his arm around Billy and led them into his home.

As they left Soldiers Field, Peter told his driver to drop him at his office in the Federal Building and then take Amanda back to the hotel. Peter wanted some time to polish the inaugural speech he would give the following day, but once he was settled at his desk with pages of manuscript scattered around him, he found it impossible to concentrate. There was just too damn much on his mind. For openers, Andrei had been summoned to Washington, and that almost always meant trouble.

His problems with Marion gnawed at him, too, compounded now by the news of Devin's arrest. And complicating everything was Amanda's demand that she be allowed to visit Devin. She was changing so much, worrying about the Exiles and politics and other things she'd never worried about before; he wasn't sure he knew her anymore.

And there were the kids, too. He was so busy with his work, and they with their passions—Jackie's dancing, Scott's basketball—that they barely had time to speak. Jackie loved her new Russian ballet teacher, and she'd thrown herself into her studies, but she worried constantly about Justin. Amanda had made inquiries, but it was as if he'd vanished from the face of the earth. The one time Peter had tried to discuss it with her, she'd turned away, as if he were somehow to blame for the boy's disappearance.

Peter was startled by a knock at his door. He looked up to see General Fred Sittman's ruddy, pockmarked face in the doorway.

"Burning the midnight oil, chief?"

"Just working on this damn speech," Peter said.

"The rehearsal looked sharp," the general said.

"Your men looked sharp," Peter said. "But of course they always do."

"Never bullshit a bullshitter, chief. See you in the morning."

Peter grinned. Fred Sittman was turning out to be one hell of an interesting character. At first glance he looked like your basic short-haired, thick-necked, gung-ho marine officer. And it was true that as a young man, he'd proved his courage in Korea, and he'd gone on to be one of the most decorated officers in Vietnam. Sittman had them all: the Purple Heart, the Congressional Medal of Honor, and a list of wartime commendations as long as his arm.

But that wasn't all; Peter had done some checking into Fred Sittman's record. After the war, when a *New York Times* reporter interviewed him at the Pentagon, the general declared that the Vietnam War had been a colossal mistake, a blunder that pigheaded civilians had forced on military men who knew better. "It was the wrong war in the wrong place at the wrong time for the wrong reasons," Sittman had declared. It had been the *Times'* Quote of the Day.

There had been a flurry of protests from the Pentagon and Congress, and some talk that Sittman would be reprimanded, but his record was too outstanding for that. He continued as one of the marine corps' top generals, and just in case anyone missed the point, he proceeded to write a book about what went wrong in Vietnam.

The irony was that all this "radical" behavior had made him one of the highest-ranking American military men in the country. The Transition had not been an easy one for the U.S. military. The Soviets were willing to deal with American lawyers, politicians, journalists, and corporate executives, but they hated and feared the American military. Peter had heard rumors that dozens of senior Pentagon generals were assassinated during the first months of the Transition, and that hundreds of others were sent into exile, or to prison for "reeducation." And if you believed the rumors, many others were somewhere in the mountains, leading an armed resistance.

Fred Sittman was a dramatic exception. Because of his opposition to the Vietnam War, the Soviets had decided to use him as an example of a "good" general; they needed "good" generals to lead and maintain order among the national guard. They had asked Sittman to serve as a national guard commander during the Transition, and he replied, "I'm a soldier, and I serve my government, whatever it may be."

There were those who called him an opportunist, or worse, but the fact remained that he was the national guard commander for Heartland, and thus the most important American military man in the new, demilitarized America.

Peter's door flew open again, this time without anyone knocking, and Marion stormed in, head high, eyes flashing.

"What is this about your wife going to see Devin?" she demanded.

Peter was taken aback. It had been only a few hours since Amanda had spoken to Andrei—how had word reached Marion so fast? Someone standing nearby must have told her—unless Andrei himself had. As always, it was impossible to know who was playing what game. Still, it amused him to see Marion so agitated. She liked to keep others guessing; let her have a turn.

"I sure wish I knew what was going on as well as you do." He smiled.

"That's why I'm invaluable as your deputy," she said coldly.

"I thought it would be a good way to try to find out where your son is."

Marion looked at him with less suspicion and more respect. "Really?"

"And possibly work out a way for Devin not to be killed."

"What makes you think his life needs saving?"

"Just an educated guess, Marion. But I'm saying that if you get Billy back, no purpose would be served by Devin's death, except to make you look bloodthirsty, which won't help either one of us."

Marion studied him thoughtfully. He had a knack, she had to admit, for seeing all sides of a solution. "If he cooperates in finding my son, I might agree to a program of behavior modification. Or prison."

Peter thought about his choices. The recollection of Devin's behavior at the interrogation office gave him a shiver. "Prison," Peter said. "A short term."

"If he cooperates."

Peter nodded, sealing the deal.

"Perhaps we can work together, Peter," she said, with a cool smile.

"You're tough. You don't give much for nothing," he said, not without respect. This woman made him very uneasy. He wondered what had attracted Devin to her in the first place. Or had she changed? Did all wives change? Did any man at forty know the woman he had loved at twenty?

"No, I don't," she said. "Not for love or money." She smiled again. "Or old time's sake."

* * *

Devin did fifty pushups, rested three minutes, then did fifty more. Before the night was out he would do five hundred, and an equal number of situps. He'd let his exercises lapse while he was free, but a prisoner could not afford such sloth. He had to be diamond-hard again, in mind and body, to survive what lay ahead. He was refusing the food they brought him, except for a cup of water and a piece of bread each day, and he would not sleep more than two hours at a time. They could kill him, but short of that there was little they could do to him that was more harsh than what he would do to himself.

When he was not exercising, he spent most of his time thinking of Billy. He remembered how casual and easy they'd talked on the shores of Lake Michigan a few days before. Now, with time, miles, and bars between them, he knew Billy was thinking of him. Devin knew his son was in Nebraska now, that Clayton had helped him through to be reunited with his grandfather and the rest of the Milfords. Devin could feel that; it was a truth. It was the most real thing in the world to him.

Enjoy your family, son, he thought to himself. They're a little crazy, like most families, but they're your flesh and blood, and they'll give you more love than anyone else in the world.

Chapter 12

WHEN ANDREI ARRIVED at Petya's Virginia mansion, Petya's chief of staff, a plump young major named Josef, announced that the general was at the Pentagon.

"At the communications center," the young officer said. "He's been there all day, on the secure line to the Kremlin. I don't know when he'll return."

Andrei smiled to hide his annoyance. "Shall I join him there, Josef? He may want my assistance."

"No," Josef said. "He left word he was not to be disturbed."

"I have flown a long way," Andrei said. "He sent for me. Will you tell him I'm here, please?"

Josef, normally a ruddy, robust fellow, was pale and grim. "He is upset, Andrei. It is something very serious. If he summons me, I will tell him, but you may simply have to wait."

Josef left, and Andrei settled in by the fire. After

downing two brandies but receiving still no word from Petya, he went up to his room and tried to sleep. Outside, a cold March wind howled over the dark fields where presidents once laughed and rode.

Amanda went early, just after dawn. Everyone at the jail was very polite, but it seemed almost surreal to be walking down those long corridors, past locked bars and guards, not twenty minutes after she had left the presidential suite of Chicago's finest hotel.

Then someone turned a key and she was standing in the doorway, looking at him, and she thought her heart would break. She had desperately wanted to be there, but suddenly it was too painful, like seeing a bird in a cage, its wings broken but its eyes still blazing. The strange thing was, he didn't seem to mind; he rose slowly, an odd smile on his face, and waved her into his cell. She guessed he took a certain perverse pride in being here, but it did her no good to see him like this.

He gestured for her to be seated in a straight-backed chair, and perched on the edge of his bunk.

"How are you?" she asked.

"I've had nicer vacations."

It was the wrong beginning, but what did you say when you had said so very little for so very long?

"Really," she said. "How do you feel?"

He shrugged. "Sad for my sons, but not for myself."

She remembered the day they'd met in the refugee camp and talked at his little tent beside the stream. He'd seem dazed, withdrawn. Now, even here, he seemed more sure of himself, more at peace.

"What will happen to you?"

"Probably prison again. Only I don't think I'll make it so easy for them. Actually, I'm a little surprised,

291

given what Marion's become, that they haven't just executed me, gotten it over with."

"How can you talk that way?"

He shrugged. "Because, it's a reality that has to be faced."

She looked at him and the years tumbled away; the memories of so long ago seemed almost tangible, hanging in the air like the very dankness of the cell. "I don't want to lose you," she said.

The words jumped out by themselves. She lowered her eyes. "But I have no right to say that, do I?"

He touched her face. In that moment he had remembered their young love, yet he felt no sorrow for what might have been. He thought his life had been inevitable, from Vietnam to Marion to Congress to this prison cell, and he could not regret what could not be changed. He only felt a certain bittersweet sadness, for this was the sweetest, kindest woman he had ever known. She simply had not been his destiny.

"You have the right if you want it," he said.

Now she made another leap. The words popped out too quickly here, in this frightening place. "If you'd let them have Billy . . ."

"Is that what you came to tell me?" he asked, not unkindly.

"Peter wants to help you. But he thinks you've got to give her Billy. For God's sake, Devin, don't you think it's better to think about helping your children after you're free?"

He shook his head emphatically. "No, the time has come to resist. My life isn't what's important. We need a deeper kind of resistance, something with roots. It's got to stand *for* something, not just against the Russians."

His words meant nothing to her. It was like when Peter spoke of compromise and lesser evils—political talk, abstractions. She was talking about flesh and blood, life and death. "You've given enough," she said. "Five years in prison camp. Why should you have to be the one who takes the stand? Look at what you have to lose."

"Most people have their lives to live," he said. "It's been hard for them, just to survive, to draw each breath, eat, make sure their children don't starve, have enough clothes to keep warm. But they haven't given up. They aren't broken. I saw them, heard them, on the courthouse steps yesterday. Their spirit is still alive. They just need someone to remind them, encourage them. It's not me, it's all of us, in this together. I'm not what matters."

She looked at him for a long time. It was as if they were speaking two different languages. He was saying that life and freedom didn't matter and she believed they were all that mattered. Perhaps he was right, perhaps he glimpsed some greater reality, but she could not accept that.

"You matter to me, because I love you," she said.

Those words popped out too. She stood up, wondering if she should leave, and he stood too.

"There. How do you like that?" she asked, more to herself than to him. "I always have. I guess we just never had the chance to destroy it. When I saw you at the exile camp, I knew in an instant, it was all still there."

"Amanda," he said, and took a step toward her.

"No, don't touch me," she cried. "I'm so damn mad at you. That you would risk your life when you don't have to."

He smiled at her. He couldn't help it.

"And don't laugh at me," she said. "I thought of you so much, for so long. You were always there. My God, do I sound like I'm sixteen?"

He put his arms around her and she entered his embrace gladly. She didn't know whether to laugh or cry, and she found herself doing a little of both.

"You really thought about me? All those years?"

"I tried to shove you down, out of the way, but you were there. Peter knew. We didn't deal with it. I said it was absurd. But he knew. He lived with it."

"And he wants me out of here?"

"He's your friend. In some crazy way I loved you both. His reality and your memory. I guess I always knew you'd come back. That's why I can't bear to lose you again."

"But . . . if I get out of here, you'll stay with Peter."

"Of course. I love Peter. He needs me."

Devin smiled. "So after all this you're going to stay with your husband."

She laughed. "Yes."

He lifted her and swung her around and gently set her back down. "You're much stranger than I remembered," he said.

It was far past midnight when Andrei fell asleep in the big canopied bed in Petya's guest room, and it was dawn when the squeak of the door awoke him.

Andrei leaped to his feet—KGB officers sleep lightly —only to see that the intruder was his host.

Petya put a hand on his arm. "Sit down, Andrei," he said. "I am sorry to disturb your rest."

Not until Petya had eased himself into a Louis XIV armchair did Andrei pull on his robe and settle nervously on the edge of the bed. He had never seen Petya looking like this—pale, distracted, unfocused, his uniform disheveled.

"What is wrong?"

Petya sighed, staring into space. "Much is wrong. There have been several major reverses worldwide. Eastern Europe is a powder keg and more sparks are being ignited. Shipments through the Panama Canal have been halted because of terrorism—due to the destruction of one of the locks. I'm afraid we miscalculated there, too. Premier Castro acts as though he's still the revolutionary. The Afghans have taken one of our generals hostage. And the Kremlin, despite all my assurances, continues to fear the Americans and to think that all of the disturbances worldwide exist because of a belief that somehow America will rise again."

"It isn't America," Andrei cried. "It's an idea, one that is universal."

Petya shook his head wearily; he had not slept in thirty hours. "Our colleagues in the Kremlin see the world through reports and monitors. They are not very good at running the world. They are unworthy of the power you and I gave them, Andrei. How much easier it is to conquer than to rule."

"We are making progress," Andrei said. He was almost pleading now. "Today Peter Bradford will be sworn in as governor-general of Heartland—a major ceremony to be televised nationally, and the beginning of our new policy. Within weeks Heartland will form a separate nation. Soon other nations will be formed. The United States will cease to be; we will have Balkanized it. In one or two decades it will be only a memory. My God, what more do they want?"

"Much more, Andrei. The hotheads have gained control of the politburo. I spent the night arguing against their plan to explode low-yield nuclear weapons over three American cities, as an example to America, and the rest of the world, of our resolve."

"My God, are they mad?"

"Worse. They are frightened."

Andrei walked to the window and stared out like an imprisoned man. Sunlight glistened like gold on the frost-crusted fields outside, and its beauty made Andrei all the more depressed. For years he had felt in control of his world; now he sensed his certitude, his power, slipping away.

"What was decided?" he said.

"A compromise of sorts. Not the nuclear explosions. Instead, I will give them . . . a symbolic victory. One that will convince them that America is finally dead. It will not be pretty, but neither will it kill innocent millions."

"For God's sake, Petya, tell me . . ."

"No. This is my responsibility. I must begin immediately."

"But what . . .?"

"You will know when the deed is done. Meanwhile, wait here. Begin making plans. The other areas must secede within two weeks."

"They're not ready. They—"

"They must. The alternative is worse. As soon as possible, the new regions must form the North American Alliance. You must see that this is done. You will receive credit. Then they cannot keep you off the central committee. But you must do your job, Andrei, as I must do mine, however repugnant it may be."

He rose heavily to his feet. Andrei rose, too, and stepped toward him. For an instant he thought Petya might fall. "What can I do?" he asked.

Petya lifted his head and gazed into Andrei's eyes. The proud, tough soldier Andrei had admired for a dozen years now seemed a broken old man. "You have done so much for me already," he said. "Now you must carry on this difficult task we have undertaken. Remember always that we are a noble people, whatever evil the extremists may force upon us."

He awkwardly reached out and touched Andrei's face. They embraced. Samanov stepped back and held him at arm's length. "You are a son to me."

They embraced again.

"And you a father."

Petya released Andrei and started slowly to the door. "I will be in Washington," he said.

"Petya, is there anything at all I can do?"

"Await developments," the old general said, and he was gone.

A little after eight o'clock that morning, Michael Laird pulled up in an old sedan outside an abandoned warehouse in Chicago's deteriorating north side. Despite his status as the PPP's chief of security, Laird did not mind moving about the city alone. He was armed, and could protect himself, as his was a solitary profession. Laird had been an FBI agent before the Transition, and he had watched the bitter split among his old colleagues. Some, militant anticommunists, had resisted the new regime. As a result, many had been arrested and imprisoned; others had gone underground, joined the resistance. The most hard core had formed a secret society called the Hoover League, which carried out assassinations against Russian officials and American collaborators.

Others, like Mike Laird, had invoked the legacy of J.

Edgar Hoover in another way. Hoover had been an absolute dictator who guided the bureau with an iron hand—you loved it or left it. The new regime was like that, too, enabling Laird and others to move from the old regime to the new with a minimum of trauma. They were, after all, only carrying out the orders of duly constituted authority. The ideology at the top might in theory be different, but in practice one dictator was like another.

Mike Laird was alone on a deserted slum street to carry out a task some might have called illegal. But it was at the urgent and personal request of Marion Andrews, a party leader and now the deputy governor-general, so how could her wishes be illegal?

A pale young man in jeans, sneakers, and a windbreaker stepped out of the warehouse and approached the sedan. As the young man reached the car, Laird cracked open his window.

"We're ready," the man said.

Laird handed him a sheet of paper. "Here's the route."

The man glanced at the paper with quick brown eyes. "All right," he said.

"Be thorough," Laird said. The young man spit on the street and walked back to the warehouse. Laird cursed and drove away. He hated trusting other people, but this time he had no choice.

A few miles away, in his cell at the SSU Security Center, Devin Milford faced a difficult decision. A guard had brought him a breakfast of eggs, bacon, toast, and real coffee. "Same as our officers get," the guard declared. After a moment's hesitation, Devin decided to eat the breakfast. He was still fasting, but he rationalized that it might be a long time before he saw fresh eggs and real coffee again.

Soon after he finished, an SSU officer, a handsome soldier named Ramirez, entered his cell. "Your breakfast was satisfactory, Mr. Milford?" he asked.

"Fine, thank you," Devin said.

"And you have been well treated while you were with us?"

"Yes."

"Good. Those were Colonel Denisov's instructions. You will be leaving now, if you are ready."

"I'm ready," he said, gathering up his few belongings. "Where am I going?"

"To Omaha, I understand."

Devin frowned. "What's in Omaha?"

"I really don't know, Mr. Milford," the guard said, and they started down the corridor toward the elevators.

The Bradford family spent the night in the Palmer House Hotel, and that morning they hosted a ceremonial breakfast there for Marion and Caleb as well as various political leaders and PPP officials. Marion wore a dramatic pink wool suit, but Peter thought Amanda was more beautiful in the simple elegance of her blue outfit. Following breakfast, the party of more than two dozen hurried out to the limousines that would take them to Soldiers' Field.

A cheering crowd greeted them as they emerged onto the sidewalk outside the hotel. They chanted "Brad-ford!" and "Heart-land!" and waved hand-lettered signs. Peter waved back—it was an automatic gesture now—and wondered if they were for real. He knew the live coverage had already begun, and it would not have been beyond Andrei, or Marion, to have arranged this "spontaneous" show of affection.

He turned to Amanda and winked.

Amanda smiled but her heart was not in it.

They emerged from the elevators into a big shadowy garage packed with SSU vehicles. Captain Ramirez led Devin toward two black vans parked side by side. The driver of one of the vans produced papers for Ramirez to sign.

Glancing around, Devin imagined that he glimpsed General Sittman far across the room, but he wasn't sure. The lines of authority here were tangled beyond his understanding—the PPP, the SSU, the national guard. All he knew was that Marion hated him and Andrei Denisov wanted to protect him, and that he wasn't likely to receive the same royal treatment in Omaha that he'd enjoyed here.

Ramirez nodded as Devin stepped into the back of one of the vans. "Good luck, Mr. Milford," he said, and the door shut.

The crowd cheered as the limos pulled away from the hotel, the sirens of their motorcycle escort howling. Peter, waving to the people on the street, glanced back and saw Marion sitting expressionless in her limo, clutching Caleb to her side. He had come to realize that she resented her number-two position, and he wondered how long she would settle for it.

His two children, dressed for the occasion, were sitting on jump seats. Jackie hadn't looked so happy in weeks; she waved enthusiastically, even as the crowds began to thin out. Scott, seeming somehow grown up in a dark suit, gazed out at the city in wonder. Peter guessed it had been a big jump for the boy from Milford to Omaha and now to the hugeness of Chicago. He knew he should spend more time with Scott but didn't have any time to call his own anymore.

Amanda leaned close to Peter and whispered. "I saw Devin this morning, early."

"How was he?"

"He seemed very at peace with himself."

He studied her face, trying to glean understanding from her expression. "Is he willing to give up Billy?"

"I don't know."

"I can't help him if he won't."

"I told him that," she said, almost sullenly, and turned to the window.

Scott turned from the window and said, "Can't they go any faster?"

"They're going fast enough," Peter said, and got out his speech for some final polishing.

The iron doors to the SSU's underground garage slid slowly to one side, and the convoy moved out. First came two motorcycles, then a jeep with a mounted machine gun, a light attack vehicle, then the black transport van that held the prisoner. Behind the transport vehicle were more attack vehicles and motorcycles. The convoy picked up speed, and when pedestrians saw them coming, they slipped into doorways.

A few moments later, Andrei's limousine slid out of the garage and drove off in the opposite direction. In the distance the sirens from Peter Bradford's motorcade could be heard, but it was going in the opposite direction and soon the sound died out.

The convoy moved south on Lakeshore Drive at fifty

miles an hour. There was little traffic and the few cars they saw pulled over to the side when they heard the sirens.

It was a routine run until they reached a corner where a delivery van was parked. The pale young man in the windbreaker was at the wheel of the delivery van and when the SSU convoy came round the corner he shot forward, heading straight for the black transport van. The SSU van swerved to avoid a collision, skidding onto the sidewalk and crashing into a utility pole. An antitank gun fired a rocket from a nearby building and the transport van exploded in flames. As the delivery van sped away, there was shooting from all directions. Soldiers leaped from the jeeps and were pinned down by machine-gun fire. The SSU officer in charge, at the risk of his life, ran to the burning transport van and tried to open its door, but he was beaten back by the flames.

Suddenly it stopped. The attackers abandoned the van and disappeared into an alley, leaving only the sound of the utterly shredded and burning vehicles. The SSU officer, cursing in Spanish, ran down the street looking for a telephone.

The limousines stopped on the infield and the guests of honor climbed out. Twenty bands blared the Heartland anthem, yet the roar of the crowd still drowned it out. Peter gazed up in awe; he was not prepared for this. A hundred thousand people packed Soldiers' Field and thousands more ringed the stadium, just to have the music and the speeches piped out to them. Peter, stunned by the spectacle but remembering that the cameras were on him, waved with both arms.

There was an awkward pause as all the officials and their families got in line to proceed to the speakers' platform. Peter waved to General Sittman, who with a group of national guard officers would form an escort platoon. Peter squeezed Amanda's hand.

Amanda was too awed by the mass of people to speak.

Peter paid no attention as a dark-suited man, vaguely familiar to him, hurried up to Marion and drew her aside.

"It's done," Mike Laird whispered.

She looked at him sharply. "You're sure?"

"The convoy was hit by what appeared to be a resister group."

Marion sagged, took his arm. Laird tried to look solemn, as if this was urgent party business. In a moment she composed herself. "Thank you. That will be all."

Laird nodded and walked away.

Peter walked over to Marion. "Are you all right?"

"Yes, of course. Just butterflies," she said with a smile.

"It's nice to know you're at least a little like the rest of us," he said.

She smiled. "Are we supposed to walk separately or can I take your arm—as though we were getting married?"

Peter smiled, offering his arm. "You can take my arm until we get outside, but under no circumstances are you to say, 'I do.'"

The bands began "Hail to the Chief" as they marched to the platform to begin the festivities. Upon seeing them, the crowd began to chant "Heartland . . . Heartland."

Alethea and Ward were having coffee when the patrol car came roaring up the driveway. They had the television on, with pictures of the Heartland rally, but Alethea had decided to keep the sound down until either Peter or Marion spoke. "We ought to show some respect," she said. "I mean, they gave us a holiday."

Ward rose to his feet as the deputy, Cy Spraggins, leaped out of the patrol car and ran toward the house.

"Something's up," Ward muttered. "Cy hasn't moved that fast in twenty years."

The deputy burst in the door. He was a lanky, jug-eared man, and his face was red with excitement. "They're coming," he yelled. "The SSU. Out of the barracks, full strength!"

Ward held up his hand. "Hold on, Cy. Maybe it's just maneuvers."

"They were headed for town. Right behind me. It didn't look like no maneuvers."

Will Milford, his friend Dieter, his grandson Billy, and Clayton Kullen emerged from the barn, saw the patrol car, and hurried to the house. "What the hell's going on?" Will demanded.

"The SSU's headed for town, Dad," Ward said. "They may be coming here, looking for Billy."

The old man nodded grimly. "Ward, you and Cy get on out of here. The less you know, the better. Stall 'em if you can."

Ward scowled—he hated to run from a fight—but he knew his father's plan made sense. He and Cy drove away, leaving Will, Alethea, Dieter, Clayton, and Billy. There was a moment's awkward silence.

"Maybe the exile camp?" Dieter suggested.

"No, they'll look there," Alethea said. "They'll tear it apart. They always do the obvious, so we've got to be smarter than them."

"The root cellar," Will said.

"Too easy to find," Alethea protested.

She looked at Billy and saw the uncertainty on his face. "Hey, handsome, it's gonna be okay. We've just got to formulate the plan, as the deep thinkers say."

Billy did not return her smile. "Maybe . . . I ought to go back," he said. "They just want to take me back to my mom. I don't want to get anybody hurt."

Will put his hand on the boy's shoulder. "I appreciate the thought, but do you want to go back?"

Billy seemed near tears; he silently shook his head.

"Devin indicate to you it was okay to give up the boy?" Will asked Clayton.

"The word from Devin was to take care of him. He thought that was pretty darn important."

"Well then, by God, that's what we'll do," Will declared, and Billy hugged him with relief.

At the House of Representatives, some members were drifting into the chamber, and others lagged behind in the cloakroom, watching the Heartland ceremony on TV. Marion Andrews was making her speech, and several of the members watched attentively as she proclaimed her dedication to freedom, justice, and progress.

Other members of Congress, indifferent to the Heartland spectacular, milled about, exchanging rumors about this emergency session that Petya Samanov had called. But the fact was that no one knew why they were there.

Finally, bells began to ring, summoning them to the chamber. They began to file inside. On the unwatched TV, a hundred thousand voices were chanting "Bradford, Brad-ford," as Peter got up to speak.

Back at the Virginia mansion, Andrei gazed indifferently at the ceremony on TV. It was clearly the culmination of months of scheming and planning, but now it held no interest for him. All that mattered was what was happening in Washington, the "symbolic act" too dark for Petya to describe.

Andrei paced about the guest room. It was just down the hall from Petya's big bedroom and, on impulse, he marched to the bedroom.

Petya's bed had not been slept in. The uniform he had worn home at dawn was still on the floor, where he had thrown it. Andrei realized that Petya had come all that way just to tell him what little he had told him. He remembered their final embrace, like father and son. There had been something final to their farewell.

His eyes fell upon the tape cartridge half buried under Petya's discarded jacket. Andrei grabbed it, examined the date scribbled on it—the night before—and knew at once what it was. It was Petya's habit to tape-record all communications with the Kremlin—as the officials on the other end were also doing—as a means of self-protection. In his haste and fatigue, Petya had neglected to file this tape before returning to Washington.

Andrei ran back to the guest room, inserted the tape into a player, slipped on headphones, and began to listen. What he heard chilled him to the core.

This is not the Stalin era, Petya was protesting, in Russian.

The choice between alternatives is yours, another man said. Andrei recognized the voice as that of Nicolai Malkiev, the first deputy, a powerful, stubborn, and formidable man.

And if I refuse?

Many of us still prefer the detonations, Petya Petrovich. You know that. We have accepted your compromise and now you resist even that. If you do not act, someone else will, and your brilliant career will end in disgrace. Of what value is that? All we ask is that you do your duty.

This act may have the opposite effect. Upheavals . . .

It is your proposal, Comrade. The logic is quite convincing.

That was ten years ago. An alternative that never became necessary. Can't you see? The Congress is without power, a mere symbol of former America.

Precisely. A potent symbol, one that can still rally people, can still be used against us. Do your duty, Petya, and return to Moscow to accept the honors you deserve.

Andrei grimaced in shock and horror. He remembered that ten-year-old contingency plan. They had joked about it, called it their Doomsday Plan. But this was no joke.

After a long silence, Petya said, *If I carry out the plan, then I have your word that Colonel Denisov will be permitted to function here, in my absence, with no further interference?*

Must I say it again? Yes, you have my word. Barring some terrible disaster, Denisov will be given a free hand. You will have guaranteed his success.

All right, Comrade Malkiev. I will proceed. But I say again, this action is antithetical to the generosity and greatness of the Russian people.

And I say again that this Committee differs with you on that point.

I may not be able to return to Moscow immediately.

Don't be foolish, Petya. End your affairs, romantic and otherwise, and return to Moscow. That is an order.

The tape ended. Andrei hesitated only an instant, then leaped to his feet and raced out of the gracious old mansion, toward the nearby field where his helicopter waited. With luck, he could reach the Capitol in fifteen minutes.

Just as Will decided on a hiding place for Billy, they heard the ominous clatter of helicopters. "You stay here, Dieter," Will yelled, and the rest of them ran pell-mell toward the treeline. Sheltered by the trees, they ran and walked about a mile before reaching their destination, a hillside overlooking a pond, deep in the woods. Will knelt and tore at the earth with his hands until a wooden trapdoor was exposed.

"Thank God," Alethea said. She kept looking around, half expecting SSU troops to appear.

"What is it?" Billy asked.

"A dugout," Will told him. "We haven't got much time for history right now, but when your great-great-grandmother and grandfather arrived in these parts, the snows had already started and there wasn't time to build a cabin. So they dug this and survived their first winter in it. I reckon you can manage there a day or two—your dad and your uncle Ward used to play here all the time. Alethea brought you some food and water and we'll bring more when we can. We'll cover the top over with sticks and leaves but make sure there's air getting through."

"Dad, hurry!" Alethea pleaded.

Will lifted the trapdoor and shone his flashlight down into the darkness. "Okay, old hoss, climb in and don't be afraid."

Billy peered in uncertainly. "Might as well see what it was like a hundred and thirty years ago," Clayton said.

"It ain't the Waldorf Astoria," Will said, "but it'll have to do."

Billy nodded solemnly and took the flashlight from his grandfather. Alethea hugged him, then Will, and the boy lowered himself into his hiding place. Clayton followed, asking Billy, "You don't think they're still in there, do you?"

Petya Samanov was greeted with polite applause as he rose to address the joint session. He wore the brown uniform of a general in the Soviet army, complete with his medals, battle ribbons, and Order of Lenin medallion. He also carried a revolver in a holster on his hip, as Russian officers often did in America. Those members who knew him personally could see how drawn, how haggard, he looked. He spoke from a few scribbled notes, gazing out at his audience through dark-rimmed reading glasses.

"Thank you for your indulgence," he began. "You have been patient and cooperative in what we have all hoped would be as peaceful and easy a transition as possible." Samanov hesitated, as though intending to add something to that thought, and then looked up. "My friends," he continued, "I have learned much during my time with you, to appreciate much of who and what you are and have been. At one point in my life, I thought of America as an implacable enemy." He paused. "I no longer feel that. Not because we happened to succeed and you happened to fail—but because I know you better, understand you better. Understanding is a long and difficult road. It requires closeness, a closeness which our two countries were never able to achieve."

Samanov let his gaze ramble across the crowded room before he continued. "Our two systems are so different and in many ways possibly incompatible. But we are all of us human beings, after all not so different." He moved his reading glasses further down his nose and pushed his notes to the side.

"But there are those who have not had a chance for the closeness—the understanding. When events are seen at a great distance—and seen only as extensions of policy—there can be no understanding. I beg you to cooperate, so that the opportunity for such understanding will be able to develop—somehow.

"I beg of you—in your own best interests, in the interest of peace, of your people—please accept the inevitable. However great the idea of your country, however noble those original purposes, this body no longer serves them. Please take this opportunity to disband this . . ."

A few cries of "No!" rose up from the chamber.

". . . and relinquish its power to the several administrative areas."

Many Members of Congress were on their feet now, shouting their protests.

"And I must ask for an immediate vote," Samanov declared, his voice rising.

"Vote, vote!" demanded the PPP delegation, but they were shouted down by cries of "No!" and "Never!"

Samanov gazed out sadly at the chaos, the long-quiescent remnant of democracy, and when he was sure there would be no vote, that a majority of Congress would not voluntarily disband, he turned and left the chamber. He was torn by conflicting emotions: admiration for their courage and sorrow for the price they would soon pay.

As Petya made his exit, an armed guard bolted the door behind him. Inside the chamber, various members attempted to leave, only to find all doors circling the room locked. The congressmen looked at one another in annoyance, then dread, as they realized that they were prisoners.

Petya stepped into an elegant hideaway office, once the domain of the speaker of the house, that boasted a priceless chandelier, Oriental rugs, a wood-burning fireplace with an ornate marble mantelpiece, and a massive oak desk that had once belonged to President Madison. He slumped at the desk. A Soviet army officer stared at him from the doorway.

"Sir, we are ready," the officer said.

"Proceed," Petya said, the word caught in his throat.

Peter had agonized over his speech for days, but once he reached the podium it all seemed natural. He hardly looked at his text; the words flowed easily before this vast multitude that filled the stadium and the millions more he knew were watching on TV. He felt wonderful, ten feet tall, and his conviction gave strength to the words he spoke. Andrei's plan for the division of America could have found no more eloquent spokesman.

"Heartland is larger than most of the nations of Europe," he declared. "Our productive capacity is unmatched, our potential unlimited. Our need is to break with the past, to assert our independence and resume our greatness."

"What the hell's he trying to say?" Will Milford demanded. He and Alethea had hiked back to the farmhouse and were watching the ceremony on TV in their kitchen.

"Regional pride, I think," Alethea said. She was worried about Billy; his hiding place might be secure, but it was also monumentally depressing. Would he climb out of there and get himself caught?

"He ought to get to the damn point," Will muttered.

"As in the past we were proud to be Americans," Peter continued, "let us now be proud to be Heartlanders."

"What is this Heartland shit?" Will grumbled. "We live in goddamn Nebraska."

On the screen, Peter lifted his arms to the heavens. "I ask you, all of you, to join me in proclaiming our new identity, our future . . . Heartland! Heartland! Heartland!"

The throng in the stadium picked up the chant. The camera panned around, showing tens of thousands of midwesterners on their feet, their fists raised, chanting "Heartland! Heartland!"

As Alethea shouted her anger at the screen, a line of black SSU vehicles was racing up the road. A moment later Helmut stepped from one of them and marched toward the house, his narrow face a cold mask.

The regular Capitol police had been sent home that morning when General Samanov's crack Soviet troops arrived. Now they controlled the building. Explosives experts moved about its corridors setting their charges. Heavily armed troops dressed not in SSU uniforms but in guerrilla garb waited outside the doors to the house chamber where more than five hundred Members of Congress were captive. At a nod from their commanding officer, they threw open the doors to the chamber and stormed in, firing as they went.

Members of Congress fell to the floor, dead or dying. Others raced about, shouting for mercy, hiding beneath their desks, seeking refuge—but there was none. Soon the chamber was awash with blood, and still the carnage continued. Only PPP members were spared—herded out a side door—and a few others, women and old men for whose lives Samanov had been forced to negotiate. The massacre had not yet ended when subterranean explosions began, deep in the bowels of the Capitol, rocking the monumental old building that had stood like Gibraltar for almost two centuries.

Petya Samanov, alone in the elegant office, heard the explosions and the crackle of gunfire. The chandelier trembled as the blasts drew nearer. This was the darkest moment of his life. He had devoted thirty years to the study of America, and the past ten years to achieving a responsible Soviet occupation of its once-great rival. He had dreamed that the Soviet actions there would live in history as a monument to the wisdom and decency of the Russian people. Now all his dreams were shattered by hotheads in Moscow who understood only hate and power and inevitable destruction. They would have their victory, their conquest, their symbolic rape of a great nation, but generations yet unborn would curse the Russian leaders, would equate them with Attila and Hitler and other of history's most despised monsters.

Petya Samanov buried his face in his hands. Amid the disaster he had won one small victory: in the years ahead, if all went well, Andrei would be able to build a better America out of the ashes of this tragedy. But that was little consolation. He wondered now, listening to the sounds of destruction and death from below, how he could ever have agreed to come here and carry out these orders. Why had he not had the courage to refuse?

Another blast broke the windows of his office. The

officer in charge rushed in. "General, it is time to go. The building may collapse at any moment."

"It's done?" Petya said, as if in a trance.

"Yessir. The helicopter is ready. We only have a few minutes."

Petya nodded slowly, as if he did not understand. "Give me a moment," he said. "Wait for me outside."

When the officer was gone, Petya crossed the hallway to the now-silent house chamber. The scene there chilled his heart. Bodies were tossed about like rag dolls. Men of honor, men who had served their people as best they could, were killed; some were still sitting at their places, and now, in death, seemed oddly normal. The walls of the chamber had started to burn.

Samanov walked slowly to the chair in which he had sat. He was devastated—his eyes beyond tears—his spirit killed by what he had caused. He felt the walls tremble as another charge of dynamite racked the building.

Yes, Petya thought, it is time to go. Time to go with honor, with dignity, with a final gesture that perhaps a few would understand, would even respect.

He unsnapped the holster at his side and drew out the small revolver. The building trembled as he did what his honor demanded. He looked out upon the carnage one last time, shook his head slightly, and pulled the trigger.

The SSU troops jabbed them with rifles and forced them to sit on the ground—Will, Alethea, Ward, Betty, and Dieter—while six troopers searched the house and outbuildings. Helmut personally supervised the search, and when it proved fruitless, he marched up to them, seething.

"I will ask one last time. Where is the boy?"

Huddled together on the hard ground, they did not answer, did not even look at him.

"We have searched the town and the exile camp. We have information that he is here with you. Produce him or suffer the consequences."

Still the Milfords would not reply. Helmut drew his pistol and pressed its muzzle against Will's forehead. "Where?" he demanded.

The old man looked straight ahead.

Helmut stepped back. He would gladly have shot them all, but he had specific orders against bloodshed. He turned away in frustration, then fixed his gaze upon the hundred-year-old farmhouse that stood tall and proud in the midday sun.

His orders had said nothing about farmhouses. The thought brought a smile to his thin lips.

"Burn it," he called to his men. "Burn it to the ground."

Long before he crossed the Potomac, Andrei saw the smoke rising from the Capitol. He landed there on the grounds and rushed up to the officer in charge. He could see the shattered windows, fallen columns, the dust and debris rising, the smoke and flames, as new explosions tore at the building.

"The general never came out," the officer said grimly. "He told me to go ahead, that he would come, but he did not follow. I attempted to reenter the building, but . . ." He gestured to indicate the futility of such an action.

"I am in command until he is located," Andrei said. "I want this entire city cordoned off. The roads, railroads, airports—no one is to enter or leave without my personal approval."

"Yes sir," said the officer, who watched in amazement as Andrei raced into the burning remains of the Capitol.

Peter's speech was a glorious success. He knew that from the cheers that swept over him like a great wave, lifting him up, giving him strength, and he knew too from the way the other politicians flocked to him as he left the platform. PPP officials, governors of the states, generals, reporters—they all gazed at him with new respect now, they all wanted a word, a handshake, a moment of his time.

The Bradfords rode back to the hotel in silence. Peter was lost in his own thoughts, savoring his triumph. The children were exhausted by the day's events, and Amanda stared out the limo's bulletproof window in moody silence.

She didn't speak until, back in their suite, he started talking about the evening's reception for the governors.

"I'm not going," Amanda announced.

"You have to go. It's important."

"I'm an American, Peter. I'm sure you don't want too many of those around."

Peter was immediately on guard. "Come on, Amanda. I don't have time for this."

"Was that the plan all along? You just neglected to tell me that you and the Russians were starting another country."

His face darkened. He had changed into his tuxedo pants and shirt and, as usual, had reached an impasse when it came to tying his black tie.

"You heard that crowd today," he declared. "They know we need a change. They know this is our best chance of having any freedom again. Look, we're midwesterners. Do you know anybody in California? In South Carolina? When we finally get the North American Alliance set up, we'll still be Americans, but more in the sense that Frenchmen or Germans are Europeans."

"But, Peter, at least France still gets to be France. What they're saying . . . what you're saying is that America doesn't get to be America."

He turned away from her, his voice choked with emotion. "Amanda, there is no America anymore. The Russians could destroy us—some of them would like to—but instead they say we'll call these five states Heartland, and then we'll have more autonomy. That's the reality I face. The rest is sentiment and emotionalism and history."

She sank onto the edge of the bed and began to sob. "We're Americans, Peter. It's worth fighting for."

He might have comforted her but he did not. He thought they might as well have this out now. He was sick of her, and some others, treating him like some sort of traitor.

"You know, Amanda, I get awfully tired of people giving me this 'I'm an American' bull. Where was all that patriotism when it counted? There hasn't been any real American spirit, any willingness to sacrifice, since the Second World War, and that was before we were born. Who wanted to serve in the army? Who gave a damn about us poor bastards in Vietnam? How many people wanted to perform any public service? How many of our best people went into politics, except for personal advancement? How many people even bothered to vote? You're a fine woman, but your interest in public affairs, as best I can figure, started just a few weeks ago, when you saw an exile kid digging in our garbage—or was it when Devin came home?"

"Peter, that's not fair."

"Just let me finish. I may not be the smartest guy in

the world, but I've thought this through, and I think I'm doing the right thing. I'm trying to help my fellow Americans—yes, Americans, whatever we're called—as best I can. Maybe I'm not a sensitive soul like some people, but I'm trying to look to the future, the world our kids will live in, and not wallow in the past and what might have been. That's why I'm here today, that's why I'm going to this damn reception, and that's why I wish you'd go with me."

She looked at him for a long time. She felt more angry than anything else. She realized that their lives had changed, that Peter was a different man now, and yet she still loved him, as much, perhaps more, than when they were married.

"I'll go with you tonight, Peter. Not because what you've just said is anything more than half truth, but because I still believe that you're trying to do the best thing. That you're not like the Russians or Marion and the party people. You really do want to do some good. And there are a lot of forces ready to drive you away from that good part of you, so I guess it's my job to stick by you."

Peter smiled. "Like a thorn in my side."

She walked over to where he stood. "Something like that." She studied his undone tie. "Do you want me to tie your tie?"

He smiled again, a boyish grin, and held out his hands to her. "If you don't, I'm darned if I know who will," he said.

She smiled, allowing herself to be taken in his embrace.

Chapter 13

ANDREI ENTERED THROUGH the Rotunda. Shafts of light fell through gaping holes in walls and ceilings, the flames glittering off the cluttered broken glass and chunks of marble strewn across the floor. He moved through the debris, past smoldering images from America's past. The enormous paintings of the revolution, of Columbus discovering America, the embarkation of the Pilgrims, all the priceless artifacts of the beginning of the American dream, were ripped and burned. The majestic statue of Thomas Jefferson lay broken across the floor. Glass showcases filled with replicas of the Declaration of Independence, the Articles of Confederation, the Constitution, and the remnants of other cornerstones of American society were smashed.

He raced along the smoke-filled corridor until he came to the house chamber. All that he knew had not prepared him for the gore and devastation he found.

He grew dizzy and grabbed for support against an unburned railing. As he leaned forward, he recognized the upturned face of a senator, a Californian with whom he had once played tennis. The senator's face was a mask of anguish, staring up at him. He leaned against the wall and sobbed, trapped in the reality of the massacre. The room was only partially damaged by the fire, scorched but almost too preserved amid the rest of the carnage. Andrei stood there, unaware of his own tears until an involuntary sob wracked his body.

He looked across the room and finally saw Samanov, awkwardly sprawled on the floor, next to his chair. Andrei walked numbly over and gently rolled over the body of his closest friend. He removed the gun that had remained tightly clutched in Petya's grip, and slipped it into his pocket. In a gesture of respect to the man who had been almost a father, he struggled with the body, finally lifting Petya into a semisitting position; no great man should have to die looking like that. He gently closed Petya's eyes. It was all too much to comprehend.

Darkness was falling as Andrei emerged from the building alone. Captain Selovich of the SSU stood with the fire and police chiefs, a national guard colonel, and an officer from the old army, as well as a couple of men in civilian clothes from the Committee on Information. Selovich stepped forward as Andrei approached.

"May the rescue crew proceed with the removal of bodies?" he asked.

Andrei nodded. "Have our men help. The . . . general is to be removed immediately. I will accompany the body to headquarters."

An SSU security official stepped forward. "Sir, a resistance group called the Fourth of July Brigade has called the media and claimed responsibility for the attack."

A man from the Committee on Information said, "Colonel Denisov, with your permission, we need to issue a statement, to head off rumors and misinformation."

Andrei nodded thoughtfully. "Yes," he said. "You may announce that the Fourth of July Brigade, representing militarist and reactionary elements of the former government, has committed this outrage, and that General Samanov died a hero's death while fighting to save the lives of the members of Congress whom he so admired and had served so well."

"Excellent," said the information official.

"But hold the statement until tomorrow," Andrei added. "I must notify certain officials first, personally."

"As you wish, Colonel."

Only the charred and smoldering shell of the Milford farmhouse was still standing at dusk when the SSU troops finally drove away. Will approached what remained of the kitchen door, but a gust of wind sent it crashing to the ground, and embers shot up, minifireworks spiraling into the shadows. Alethea came up behind her father and put her arms around his waist.

"Oh Daddy," she whispered.

His face was set in a resolute look she remembered—the unyielding expression he had seen on his father's face, years before, and on Devin's face just a few weeks back.

"We'll salvage what we can," he said. "I reckon we can make the root cellar livable."

"We'd all be welcome at the exile camp," Dieter said.

"No, this is home, and we'll stay here," Will told him. "Houses come and go, but us Milfords keep hanging on to this land."

"I've got some blankets in the car," Ward said.

"You take charge here, son," Will told him. "I'm gonna walk out to the dugout and check on Billy. Night's coming on, and we don't want the boy being lonely."

They all moved into action, with a sense of determination that left no room for anything resembling self-pity.

Marion Andrews sat bolt upright, awakened by a shrill ring. Her head was pounding, her heart raced wildly as she stared straight ahead into the darkness that enveloped her bedroom. After a second or two the bell sounded again. She settled back into the pillows, no longer disoriented. She looked at the phone, allowing it to ring yet a third and fourth time before picking it up.

"Hello."

A voice on the other end spoke, and the message in the words had just as dramatic an effect on her as the first ring. "What?" The panic in her voice sliced through the quiet of her room.

Mike Laird was on the other end of the phone, sitting in his office, a bright light from a desk lamp illuminating his drawn, tightened face. "He arrived at the hospital tonight. Denisov must have used the escort as a screen."

Marion sat back against her headboard and closed her eyes for a moment. "My God, will this ever end?" She opened her eyes, resolute. "They've got to kill him—right away."

Laird sat forward in his chair. "Ma'am, I told them that. They—Dr. Collins—said they were researchers, not executioners."

"How dare she—" Marion stammered, struggling for control. "Where is he now?"

"At the hospital," Laird informed her. "Under sedation; the first stage of the program. Dr. Collins assures me he's quite secure."

Marion shook her head slowly, lost in thought. Laird's voice brought her back to reality. "Marion, are you there?"

She sighed heavily. "I'm here."

Laird stood up, pacing in front of his desk. "I'll go myself, if necessary."

"All right," she answered resignedly. She hung up the phone and sat, lifeless, on the edge of her bed.

Peter and Amanda danced the first dance at the inaugural ball amid many cheers. After that, they retired to their table beside the dance floor, where a seemingly endless line of politicians stopped by to pay their respects. Peter was enjoying the attention, feeling very much like an overnight sensation, but Amanda felt as if she were under siege. In the background the band played sweet ballads from the forties and fifties, and yet all these men wanted to do was talk politics. In exasperation—even desperation—she called upon Scott to dance, and Peter turned to a reticent Jackie and did the same.

Jackie felt instantly at ease on the dance floor with her father, following his lead effortlessly.

"I couldn't believe it," Peter said, looking down into his daughter's eyes. "The most beautiful girl in the room talking basketball with her brother."

She smiled up at him. "You wouldn't think a guy who just started his own country would have time for a mercy dance."

"I'll always have time for my baby girl. What I don't understand is why she isn't dancing with any one of the hundred very good-looking young men who would give almost anything imaginable to be where I am."

"Dorks."

Peter raised his eyebrows. "Dorks?"

"Believe me, Daddy. Dorks."

"Jackie, can I say something?"

"No."

"Honey, you've got to forget Justin Milford. You can't stop your life. You should be going out with people your own age."

Jackie was silent. The music stopped and they started toward the side.

Peter smiled at her. "'Shut up, Daddy.' Right?"

She smiled and nodded. An aide walked up to Peter. "Sir. Colonel Denisov would like to speak with you and Mrs. Bradford."

"Thank you." Peter turned to Jackie. "Go find a dork." They walked over to the table where Amanda and Scott sat laughing.

"Dance with your sister," Amanda told Scott as Jackie arrived.

"Jesus, Mom, that's no fun."

"Andrei is on the phone," Peter said after the younger Bradfords had gone. "He wants to talk to both of us."

"I haven't had any better offers," she said, and followed him back to the suite.

Andrei was calling from Petya's Virginia mansion. The general's body lay in state in the drawing room, and the top Soviet advisers in the United States had gathered to discuss what they must do next.

Andrei, for his part, contributed little to their deliberations. In his anger and grief he had already decided what he must do next, and it would be a one-man action, not a group effort. But first he had to make this phone call.

"Peter, how are you?"

"Fine, Colonel. It's been a long day."

"Your speech was a great success. I have heard only praise."

"Good. People here seemed to like it."

"Peter, there is some news I must give you. Is your wife there?"

"She stopped off at the ladies' room. She'll be here in a moment."

"You may not want to share this news with her immediately. It will be announced to the public in the morning. You might want to spare her until then."

"My God, what is it?"

"This afternoon, a resistance group attacked the U.S. Congress. The Capitol building was bombed and severely damaged. Even worse, many members of Congress were killed or wounded."

"My God!"

"And General Samanov, who was addressing the Congress, was himself slain. It was a great tragedy for all of us."

Peter slumped on the edge of his bed, unable to comprehend this terrible news. Instinctively, he looked to Andrei for guidance. "What . . . what should I do?"

"Peter, listen carefully. It is imperative that Heartland be perceived as a success and that the other regions quickly form independent nations. You must work for stability in these dangerous times."

"Yes, of course," Peter said numbly.

"One other thing, Peter. An attempt was made on Devin Milford's life as he was being transported to Omaha. Several of my men were killed in saving him."

"Who—" Peter started to ask.

"We suspect the party intelligence agency."

"Marion? We had a deal—" Peter protested.

"I think you should consider the advantage of releasing him. There is no purpose served by his death, and that is what will happen if he remains in custody."

Peter didn't know what to say. Too much was happening too quickly. All he could think was that if he tried to save Devin he might have one hell of a fight with Marion, and he was too stunned to face that dilemma now.

"Of course, it's up to you," Andrei added smoothly. "Now, perhaps I should pay my respects to the first lady of Heartland."

Amanda was standing across the room, studying her husband's pale, pained face with concern. Peter handed her the phone, then stumbled into the bathroom, where he started to sob, hoping no one could hear him. It all suddenly seemed so hopeless; he felt as if he was a general, trying to fight a war without weapons, not even sure who the enemy was.

Behold the governor-general, he thought bitterly.

Andrei was all charm when Amanda came on the line. "I saw you on television," he told her. "You were lovely."

"Thank you."

"Please listen to me and try not to react. Devin Milford is in the hospital in Omaha. He is in great danger. I have warned Peter, but—you must find a way to influence him."

"Thank you, Colonel," she said, and it was the first

time she had truly liked Denisov. Perhaps he was only playing games, but she thought he was genuinely kind.

"Mrs. Bradford—I've been thinking a lot about what you said the other day—about the consequences of our actions. Even if we try to do the best thing, we can't always control the outcome, can we? Something may come along and upset even the best of intentions."

"Is that happening?"

"I'm afraid it's always happening. Goodbye, Amanda. And good luck."

"Goodbye," she said softly. As she hung up the phone, Peter came back into the bedroom. She looked steadily at him, his face still pale and shaken. "He said that Devin is in danger," she finally said.

Peter sighed. "Devin has always been there, hasn't he?"

"I've always loved you for you—separately, not through Devin."

Peter shook his head slowly. "It doesn't matter. He's still with us."

"He's a part of us," she said gently.

He threw himself into an armchair, staring at the floor. "You know, today in the stadium, in front of that crowd, I felt comfortable. I didn't feel afraid, or in second place. I didn't wonder what would Devin say, what am I doing here. I knew. And it felt right."

"Yes, I know."

He stood up abruptly, smiling lightly. "If you don't mind leaving this shindig, maybe we'd just better get back to Omaha."

Amanda, relieved by Peter's good qualities winning, went into his arms. "Thank you," she said.

"For Devin?"

She stood back at arms distance. "For you."

* * *

The Milfords were huddled together in the old root cellar, beneath the remains of their kitchen. Alethea could not sleep, so she climbed the ladder to the burned-out shell of their home. Ward was standing in the yard, smoking a cigarette, his thatch of white hair bright in the moonlight.

"Couldn't sleep," she announced.

He put his arm around her. "How you holding up?"

"Not bad, I guess. Know what bothers me most?"

"What's that?"

"Not losing the house. Not even them having Dev again; I figure he did what he wanted to do. No, what gets to me is I haven't *done* a damn thing. Devin did his thing. Even Peter Bradford is doing what he thinks is right. Jesus, if only I'd killed Helmut when I had the chance. That might at least have justified a misspent life."

"You couldn't kill anybody, Ali."

They grew quiet, the sounds of night enveloping them. Finally Alethea spoke, thinking aloud. "I wonder what's happening in town."

"The report I got said the SSU locked up a lot of people, when they couldn't find Billy. Herb Lister was out with Gurtman, fingering anybody he had a grudge against. The jail's probably full by now. They've even got the sheriff's office doing their dirty work for 'em."

Alethea stared at what remained of the house. "It's not right, Ward," she said softly.

"I know."

"They push people and push people—don't they know people will finally push back?"

They fell silent again. Ward followed her gaze to the house where they both had been born. Now it was just a charred memory.

"Before we went to bed," Alethea stammered. "I probably shouldn't have done it—but I was looking for blankets in the back of your patrol car. You know what I found?"

Ward was quiet for a long moment. "Yeah," he said finally. "A riot gun that nobody thought to take away from me."

She nodded and turned to her brother. "Why don't we take a little ride into town?" she asked.

He extended his arm to her.

"Madam, your carriage awaits."

Amanda decided not to return to the reception after her discussion with Colonel Denisov, but Peter had one more official appearance to make. One that he had said little about, but one that he looked forward to most of all. Peter thought back to the day when his father gave him his first shotgun, the pride that came when entrusted with an instrument that could kill. Tonight Peter would be trusted again, this time with far greater power.

The auditorium was packed with Area National Guard commanders—captains, majors, and colonels. General Sittman addressed the group, as Peter listened from his seat of honor on the stage.

"You have been selected from your Area National Guard units to become part of the new Heartland Defense Force. You will be responsible for selecting the best men from your units. They must be willing to follow any command against the enemies of Heartland, from within or without. The remainder of the national guard units will be disbanded." Sittman paused, looking the assemblage over carefully, as though checking for flaws of character or courage.

"Are you with me?" he boomed. The officers roared in response. "Are you with me?" the general demanded again, provoking an even louder response.

Slowly, Sittman nodded his satisfaction.

"And now let me give you the man who is ending this occupation. The man who is liberating us from Soviet domination. The man who stands between us and the domination of our land by the Communist party. Your commander-in-chief, governor-general of Heartland, Peter Bradford."

The men jumped to their feet in a roar of applause. Peter responded with a ceremonious salute.

"Governor-General Bradford, you have your army," announced Sittman, with husky pride.

Earlier that evening, soon after Andrei reached the mansion in Virginia, he called Kimberly at his apartment in Chicago. In his despair over Petya Samanov's death, he reached out to her, as an embodiment of life and sanity in a world gone mad.

Kimberly had made her decision. She was throwing some additional things into a suitcase when the phone rang. She was not going to answer it, but then realized it might be Cliff or one of the others calling with some last-minute change in their plans.

She lifted the receiver cautiously.

"I needed to talk to you," Andrei implored.

He sounded lifeless. "Are you all right?"

The question amused him. *"No,"* he said.

"What's wrong? Are you in trouble?"

He did not answer. Kimberly became uncomfortable with the silence.

"Andrei . . ."

Andrei took a deep breath. In that moment, he wanted to reach out for the simplest thing—love—the

love he felt for Kimberly; that spirit and insolence she
represented to him.

"What do you think of me, Kimberly?"

"What a funny question."

"I need your love," he said evenly.

"You've never needed me. Really." She laughed
suddenly, and it seemed inappropriate. "Bored with
running the world already?"

"I have never had time for love. Maybe that's why
you mean so much to me. I've always needed your
insolence, your unconcern for things the rest of us
thought were so important."

Kimberly was quiet, not quite sure of what Andrei
was trying to say. "I'm . . . I'm leaving Chicago."

"Where are you going?"

"I won't tell you. I don't want you to find me."

"If I asked you again to come to Washington?"

Kimberly sighed. "I can't."

"I can't let you disappear—"

"You said you wouldn't stop me."

"No. I won't." Andrei searched desperately for a
way to keep their contact alive, even for a moment.

"Do you remember that little song—from the musi-
cal you did in that church?"

"*The Fantasticks?*"

"Yes."

"The one you said was silly and sentimental."

"Yes. Could you sing a little of that song to me?"

"Now? Over the phone?"

"Please."

Kimberly laughed. "There must be—"

"Please, Kimberly."

"Okay . . . 'Deep in December, it's nice to remember the fire of September that made us mellow. Deep in
December, our hearts should remember, and follow,

follow.'" Kimberly caught herself longing for Andrei again, but then fought it off.

"Goodbye, Andrei." She hung up the phone.

Kimberly sat for a moment, crying softly. Then she gathered her belongings and hurried out to meet her newfound friends.

In the next few busy hours, she all but forgot Andrei. Miller, their man inside the police force, had somehow arranged for Cliff, Kimberly, and himself to fly to Omaha aboard a transport jet.

In Omaha, at the air freight terminal, no one questioned their documents and they caught a cab into town. They got out on a dark, deserted street, in what had once been Omaha's stockyards. It was a blustery night, and they walked along, heads bowed against the wind, for more than a mile before a dented, rusty old delivery van pulled alongside them. The driver was a young black man in workclothes. Beside him was a fleshy, white-haired man in his sixties, who, when he spoke, sounded drunk.

"Hey, this the Chicago shipment?" he called. "Or are you people lost?"

"Eric?" Miller yelled. "Dammit, get us out of here."

Eric lumbered out of the cab and opened the door of the van. After he and the newcomers climbed in, the young black, who never spoke, slammed the door on them.

Kimberly looked around in the dim light and saw that the van was filled with old broadcasting equipment.

Miller said, "Eric, Jeffrey said he needs you back at Natnet."

Eric pulled a bottle of homebrew from his pocket and took a swig. "That'll be the day," he said. "He and I won an Emmy together before the Bolshies took over.

He was a young hotshot on the rise, and I was an old-timer on the skids."

"You're Eric Plummer?" Kimberly asked. "I remember you from the 'Nightly News,' like when I was in high school."

"The very one, madam," Eric said with a bow. "Behold how the mighty have fallen. Welcome to Radio Free Omaha."

"You broadcast from here?" Cliff asked. He was shocked.

"I do indeed. Usually one step ahead of the law. My driver is a very talented young man; we've dodged their patrols and electronic gear for three months now. Drives 'em crazy."

"And there are people listening?" Miller asked.

"I daresay I have the highest ratings in Omaha. People twist their dials all night long, hoping for a few words of news, satire, or truth. And do I understand that this charming lady is to be my guest performer tonight? That we have a special message for my listeners?"

"That's right," Miller said. "We took some serious chances to get her here. And I think we'd better get started."

Eric took another long pull of rotgut whiskey. "Say no more," he declared, and started twisting the dials on his radio equipment. Lights began to flash and transmitters to hum. The truck was headed uphill now, toward higher ground. Kimberly began to feel nervous. Before she left Chicago, even when she talked to Andrei, the idea of "danger" had been an abstraction, but now, closed up in this old van, banging around the streets of Omaha, knowing that police cars would be searching for them, the danger seemed very real indeed. And yet, when she thought of Devin Milford, and the courage he had shown, and the love of America that he had stirred within her, she knew she could not turn back.

The van rattled to a halt. "Okay, kids, this is it," the old newsman said. "Do your stuff, then we'll move to another location for an encore."

He handed Kimberly a microphone. She smiled at him, at all of her fellow conspirators, and began to speak in a sweet, passionate voice.

"Hello, fellow Americans, we have important news. Devin Milford, the founder of the American party, has been arrested and brought to Omaha. He's in the psychiatric unit of the People's Acceptance Hospital. He's been fighting for us and now he needs our help. Please help any way you can: give him your prayers, show him your support. Now I want to play you a remarkable tape, of Devin speaking to the people of Chicago from the courthouse steps last week. Please listen; his message touches us all. I know it touched me."

Kimberly set back, emotionally exhausted, as Eric punched a button and the tape began to play.

Over the airwaves of Omaha, the voice of Devin Milford began to proclaim "America, America!" and the people of Chicago chanted back "America, America!"

The tape played on for three minutes. Then, lest the police patrols pin them down, they stopped broadcasting and lurched off to their next stop. Kimberly was grinning, glowing, looking ahead to an encore of her greatest performance.

General Sittman arranged for a national guard plane to fly the Bradfords back from Chicago to Omaha. At

Peter's invitation, he joined the flight. They had not been aloft long before Amanda and the children were asleep. Peter and the general sat at the rear of the plane talking in whispers.

"You don't want a head-on collision with Marion Andrews and the party, not yet," Sittman insisted.

"No, but I'm not going to let her walk over me, either," Peter insisted.

"You've got to pick your issues carefully," the general said.

Peter was still in his tuxedo. "My issue has been picked for me," he said. "It's Devin Milford. Marion and I had a deal and she broke it. Now he's in the hospital and I have to assume she'll try it again. I can't tolerate that."

"You can't take him out of there," Sittman said. "All you can do is make his treatment as humane as possible, which depends on whether the doctors are taking their orders from you or from her."

Peter stretched out and pulled loose the black tie Amanda had tied for him that afternoon. "It's bigger than that, Fred," he said. "I found out something today. I'm a popular figure and that translates into power. I've run some checks on that hospital they've taken Devin to. It's a perfectly okay hospital, except for one sealed-off wing where they use human beings— mostly political prisoners—for guinea pigs. I think people would be outraged if they knew what's happening."

"Just what do you propose?" Sittman asked.

"I have to assume that's where they're taking Devin," Peter continued. "Like you say, I can't send in tanks and bust him out. But suppose the new first lady of Heartland was making a routine inspection tour of the hospital. And suppose the commander of the national guard was with her, to add a little muscle to the operation. Naturally there'd be television coverage, and suppose they stumbled onto an ugly, really inhuman brainwashing experiment, and the cameras shot it, and it was shown on Natnet's regional news show that night. How would people react?"

"They might be shocked," Sittman said cautiously.

"I think they'd be mad as hell. I think that if the popular new governor-general protested, they'd support him, and the PPP would have to get rid of their nasty little program. I don't think even Marion would want to defend that kind of treatment of her ex-husband."

"It's risky," Sittman cautioned.

"What isn't?" Peter demanded. "The way I figure it, if you and Amanda go to the hospital, and anything goes wrong, I don't get blamed."

Sittman was about to object.

"What I mean is I wouldn't be directly involved," Peter said.

"No, but if everything worked out perfectly, you could step in and take the credit, right? Hell, that sounds like just another goddamn scheming politician, Bradford!"

Peter took the accusation with a smile. "Well . . ."

Earlier that evening, Alan Drummond had watched from a distance as Devin was brought into the hospital in handcuffs and whisked into the psychiatric unit. Alan was still unsure how he could help Devin there. He had gotten inside that house of horrors only once, by impersonating a visiting African doctor, and had very nearly gotten caught for that. He heard later that the hospital's administrator had been asking questions about the visiting doctors, but by then the visitors were halfway around the world and nothing could be proved. Alan gave thanks each day for the relentless confusion of the hospital bureaucracy.

Alan had come to People's Acceptance to minister to the people wounded in the raid on the exile camp. In truth most of them were well now but he was stalling their departure. In the first place, the Exiles were better off in the hospital than back at the shattered remains of the camp outside Milford. And in the second place, ever since that one heartbreaking look at the psychiatric unit's behavior modification program, Alan had vowed not to leave that hospital until he had found a way to free whatever remained of Justin.

Thus far, he had made little progress. Security around the unit had been tightened. He had tried to cultivate a friendship with a nurse named Helen Quint, who supervised the unit's day to day activities. She had been flattered by his interest—she seemed to find a black exile doctor from Philadelphia, by way of Milford, an exotic creature—but he had never been able to persuade her to give him a tour of the hospital's most secret, sinister wing.

Then, this night, as he watched Devin Milford led into the psychiatric unit in handcuffs, Alan had a feeling that his "treatment" would start immediately. Alan could not permit that. He had been too late to truly save Justin, but with Devin, he stood a chance.

Alan walked across the hospital grounds to his little bungalow and turned on the radio. Several nights he had caught some sort of outlaw, underground radio broadcast, that ridiculed the authorities, challenged the official "news" broadcasts, and hinted at resistance and rebellion around the country. This night he listened for a while to a dispiriting medley of Kenny Rogers' greatest hits, then, suddenly, a young woman's voice broke in. She was speaking of Devin Milford. Her words startled him and, Devin's own voice, following hers, filled him with pride and hope. He was not alone, none of them was: that was the truth they must always remember.

Alan grabbed his black bag and started running through the night, across the frozen grass, back toward the hospital. He still didn't know what he would do, but he knew he must do something.

Chapter 14

ALTHOUGH WARD HAD been fired from the sheriff's office for not finding his nephew Billy, no one had bothered to take back his patrol car, his riot gun, or his keys. Thus it was a simple matter to admit Alethea and himself into the jail during the predawn stillness.

Their friend Cy Spraggins was asleep on a cot in the front office. To the rear, the cells were packed with Exiles and the townspeople who had befriended them. Ward gazed at the gently snoring deputy.

"He's too decent to be involved with the likes of us," he whispered to Alethea. He took out his blackjack and carefully, even lovingly, whacked Cy on the side of the head. The sleeping deputy went limp, whereupon Ward handcuffed him. "I think we just got ourselves our first prisoner of war," he muttered.

"Gimme those keys," Alethea cried, and raced to the jail. She began to free her friends, Exiles and townspeople, and they were surrounding her, embracing her, with tears in their eyes. Alethea didn't know what might lie ahead, but she knew she'd never felt more worthwhile, more loved and needed in her life.

They packed the front office, thirty or forty of them, where Ward had unlocked the storage room. Soon he was handing out riot guns, tear gas, even a brace of M-16s, to every one who wanted a weapon.

"I don't know what's coming, folks," he said, "but these things can be helpful sometimes when you have to deal with the wrong sort. Which we've been having to, lately."

"Ward, get the deputy to tell you what's happening in Omaha," one of the Exiles urged.

"Omaha? What about Omaha?" Alethea demanded.

"I don't know, except he got a phone call, something about Devin being on the radio."

"Hell, I put him out, now I got to wake him up," Ward grumbled. Alethea soaked a washcloth and brought it to him, and he gently stroked the deputy's brow until he began to mumble incoherently.

"Take it easy, pal," Ward whispered. He was sitting on the edge of the cot, cradling the deputy's head on his lap. "You've fallen into the hands of dangerous revolutionaries. You resisted bravely but you're our prisoner now and we need some information."

"Won't tell you nothing," the deputy declared.

"Hell, I ain't asked you nothing yet," Ward said. "Listen, all I want to know is what was the call about Devin tonight. If you don't tell us, I reckon we'll have to blow your head off."

"Aw shit, Ward," the deputy protested.

"Spill it fast, pal. We're bad hombres."

"Heck, all it was was some actress on the radio, saying he was at that big Omaha hospital, and everybody should help him," the deputy said.

"Thanks, Cy; go back to sleep," Ward said. Then he looked at Alethea. "What do you think, sis?"

"Omaha," she said.

When Alan reached the door that led to the psychiatric unit, he paused to compose himself. If he lacked much of a plan, he was nonetheless well fortified with determination, rage, and an abiding faith in the stupidity of bureaucracies.

He glanced for a moment out the window, at the front gate, bathed in iridescent lights. What he saw confused him. At this hour, in the stillness before dawn, the gate should be deserted, except for a few guards and deliverymen, but Alan saw perhaps a dozen people gathered there, standing, waiting.

He turned from the window, poised for his own solitary action. He strode down the hallway and confronted the young national guardsman on duty outside the heavy door marked PSYCHIATRIC—KEEP OUT!

The soldier was talking in a monotone on the phone. He looked up in annoyance.

"I'm Dr. Drummond," he said loudly. "They called me."

The soldier, a gawky, rawboned youth, whispered into the phone and cupped it in his hand. "They didn't tell me nothin' 'bout it, doc."

"I can't help that, young man," Alan declared.

The soldier sighed and punched the hold button on the phone. "I'll call the nurse on duty," he announced.

"Helen Quint," Alan said casually.

"Naw, she's off. It's Nurse Tate."

He dialed a number and got a busy signal. He redialed, but the line was still busy. "Shit, probably talkin' to her old man." He thought for a moment, taking a leap of faith. "Just go on down there, doc."

The soldier pushed the button that unlocked the door. "Thank you," Alan said, and walked confidently through the doors.

Outside, thirty or forty people were gathered at the front gate. The guards threatened them, but the people remained. And their numbers grew. New arrivals, moving like ghosts through the predawn mists, were fanning out along the fence that surrounded the hospital. There was barbed wire atop the chain-link fence, but it was old and broken, easily surmounted by determined men and women.

The nurses' station was a blazing island of fluorescent light in the dark corridor. A young nurse was perched on a stool, chewing gum and talking animatedly on the phone. Alan charged up to her.

"Nurse Tate, get off the phone!" he demanded. "I have been told there is a man whose condition is critical here."

Linda Tate dropped the phone and stood up, shaken by his wrath. She was a shy woman who hated this assignment—the zombie ward—but it paid extra money and she needed it to be married. "Who?" she stammered. "What?"

"I'm Dr. Alan Drummond. They called and told me that the Milford patient was dying. Where is he?"

"Who called . . ."

"Nurse Quint. Dr. Page. An emergency. Didn't they tell you?" He looked from her to the phone that lay haphazardly on the desk where she dropped it. "Perhaps they couldn't get through to you."

She followed his gaze to the phone and looked up at him ashamedly. "Follow me," she said, and started anxiously down the corridor.

Alan was stunned when he saw Devin. He was in a private room, strapped unconscious to the bed, with IVs in both arms and electrodes fastened to his temples and chest. He was pale and sweaty, and his heartbeat was slow and irregular.

"That will be all, nurse," he said beginning to examine Devin.

"But—"

He looked at her incredulously. "Nurse Tate, I am a patient man, but I've just about reached the end of my rope with what I've witnessed tonight. So, if you'll leave me to do my work . . ."

He turned back to Devin and heard the door open and close quietly. Alan kept one eye on the soldier at the door and leaned down to Devin, who seemed to be out. "Hang in there." He rushed to the door where the guard stood. "Get me the nurse!"

After a moment Nurse Tate entered the room with a burly attendant in a dirty T-shirt.

"This man is dying," Alan announced.

"Oh no sir," she said. "It's the normal procedure—"

"Don't argue with me, nurse!" he yelled. "We've got to get him to ICU."

"We can't let him out of the unit, doc," the attendant said adamantly.

"Have you got a medical station? Respirator—I'm going to need a respirator."

"Yes," Linda stammered. "But it's not an intensive-care setup."

"It'll have to do," Alan proclaimed. "Let's go. Unhook him."

Linda quickly began to remove the IV lines and the electrodes. The attendant scowled but went off to fetch a gurney.

Alan leaned over the silent Devin and said, "Hang on, hang on!"

Alan knew he had gotten this far because hospital workers, like these, had been taught to regard doctors as gods whose decrees must never be challenged. But there might be tougher characters on guard elsewhere in the hospital, standing between him, his patient, and freedom.

Alan still didn't know where this drama was leading, but they were moving and that was half the battle.

Outside against the predawn darkness, people were slipping over the fence, onto the grounds, and into the hospital. They mingled there with Alan's exile band, moving up and down the corridors, embracing, whispering, seeming to have a plan, a destination, that no one else could fathom. The nurses, the attendants and the guards watched nervously but could not imagine what was happening.

They took him on a gurney to the psych unit's small, cramped treatment room and hooked up the respirator. By now Alan had convinced Nurse Tate that Devin was at death's door. "We don't have the equipment here for a medical emergency," she protested.

"Dammit, this is a hospital," Alan roared. "We'll go where the equipment is." He was caught up in the drama he had created. It had momentum now, a reality all its own. "You push the respirator," Alan told the surly attendant. "She and I will take the gurney."

"We've got *orders*," the attendant protested.

"Don't you understand? This is one of the most important men in America. If he dies . . . would you like to explain his death to the PPP Discipline Committee?"

Alan began to push the gurney, and after a moment the attendant did the same. Soon they reached the door that led out of the psych unit. The young national guardsman was there, still on the phone. "Get that door open!" Alan demanded. The young soldier reacted to the urgency of the scene and unlocked the door without a word.

They moved quickly through the corridors, toward the distant ICU, and people were surrounding them, ghosts appearing from out of the shadows. Alan recognized his fellow Exiles; he didn't know the others but he remembered the young woman, broadcasting on the radio, and how her words had emboldened him, and then it seemed natural that these good people should be here, and become part of the procession.

They jammed aboard an elevator, more than twenty of them, to travel down a floor. "Unhook the respirator," Alan told Nurse Tate, who by then was wide-eyed and trembling, terrified by this mysterious journey and the multitude of people surrounding her. "It's slowing us down; we'll be all right without it for a while."

The elevator doors opened as Alan and one of the newcomers steered the gurney. Four of the most able-bodied Exiles now engulfed the unhappy attendant, and somehow in the confusion he did not get off the elevator at their floor but was last seen heading for the basement.

"Down that way," Alan called, guiding his little army toward the back door.

"This isn't the way to ICU," Nurse Tate protested.

"Trust me," Alan muttered.

"Are you . . . is this an escape?" she asked. She was having a hard time keeping up as the newcomers formed a tight circle around the gurney.

"Weren't they great." Alan gestured to the Exiles.

"That's about the best work a bunch of bedridden folks have done in a long time."

"I don't want to be part of this," Nurse Tate protested. "I'm getting married." She saw another nurse coming toward them, an elderly woman with a kind but puzzled face. "What's happening?" she cried. "Where are all the guards?"

"Something's going on outside," the older nurse said. "A lot of people. It's all very queer. These aren't visiting hours at all."

"I'm going to find a guard!" Nurse Tate cried, and fled wildly down the corridor.

Alan saw Devin's eyes flutter open. He was fighting to come up from the drugs. "Devin, you with us?" Alan whispered. Devin tried to speak but only mumbled. "You're doing fine, boy, just fight to stay awake," Alan told him, hoping he could understand.

They emerged onto the loading dock. An ambulance waited there, with an Exile, Rick, dressed in an orderly's white uniform at the wheel. Some other vehicles had been commandeered, too, to carry the Exiles and anyone else who wanted to join them. When they saw this waiting convoy as they emerged from the hospital, the Exiles and townspeople sent up a great cheer. Alan and two Exiles quickly got Devin off the gurney and into the ambulance. Rick was about to shut the rear door.

"Hop in, doctor," Rick said.

Alan smiled. "I can't go," he announced.

"You're crazy," Rick said. "When they get this unraveled, they're gonna fry your brain in that place."

"I have to try to do something for the others. Justin Milford's in there," Alan said, reaching across Rick and closing the ambulance door. "Get going," he said, and clapped the young man on his shoulder. "Thanks. I'll see you in Milford."

Rick ran to the driver's side of the ambulance, put the van in gear, and pulled away. Alan watched it a moment, smiling, then turned back to the hospital, his smile faded, his face darkened.

There were now a couple hundred people on the grounds of the hospital, forming a human chain around the building. The ambulance, siren blaring, approached the line. It stopped.

"Excuse me," Rick said urgently, leaning his head out the window.

The chain accommodatingly parted, and the ambulance continued on toward the main gate. Along the way, Rick noticed the people, many sitting down with makeshift signs that read FREE DEVIN MILFORD. As the ambulance approached the gate, the guards automatically opened them. Even the protesters assumed that the ambulance had some official purpose and gave it room to pass, not missing a beat in their chants for Devin's freedom.

Andrei was awakened by Captain Selovich, an aide he had "inherited" from Samanov.

"Sorry to disturb you, Colonel. An urgent call from Chicago."

Andrei feared calls in the middle of the night, especially if they came from Moscow. From Chicago, and his aide Mikel, the news would probably be no more than an annoyance.

"Yes, Mikel, what is it?"

"Sir, in Milford, a group of Exiles and townspeople have taken over the sheriff's office. They have armed themselves, and are in control of the town."

"What has the local SSU done?"

"Commander Gurtman is on the phone now, requesting permission to put down the rebellion with maximum force. As an example to any others who might be so inclined."

"Tell Gurtman that it is my personal order that he and his men remain at the barracks," Andrei said firmly.

"But sir . . ."

"Mikel, I will hold you personally responsible if those troops leave the barracks before I give specific orders allowing them to do so."

"Will the colonel explain?" Mikel stammered.

"No, the colonel cannot explain!" Andrei snapped. Then he calmed a bit. "Mikel, I do not need a massacre in Milford at this particular moment. We have already had one of those, as you will recall. The SSU force is confined to barracks until you hear otherwise from me."

"Yes, sir!" Mikel said smartly.

Andrei hung up the phone, returning to bed, and perhaps to his dreams of Kimberly.

The riot police arrived only minutes after the Resisters roared away with Devin Milford.

Helen Quint, the head nurse of the psychiatric unit, was soon on the scene, as was the hospital administrator, a nervous man named Rose. They had confronted Alan Drummond, but their efforts to get at the truth were frustrated by the stunning news that, on top of everything else, the new governor-general's wife was on her way for an unannounced tour of the hospital, complete with television coverage.

"They cannot enter my unit," Helen Quint declared. "Just stonewall it."

"How am I going to do that?" Rose was incensed. "What if they want to see it?"

"We don't know they're even interested in the unit," Quint said.

"Don't be naive, Helen. You've been around as long as I have. This Milford man arrives and the next thing you know we're having an impromptu tour." Rose fidgeted nervously. "This smells like a power play to me and I don't want to be caught in the middle of it."

"I'll take the responsibility. I'm sure Deputy Andrews will back me up," Helen insisted.

Rose walked toward the door. "You do that, Helen."

Alan Drummond stood at the doorway watching. He felt only scorn as their panic mounted. "I know Peter Bradford," he said. "He's a decent man. When he finds out what's going on here . . ."

Rose walked up to Alan. "I have nothing to do with that unit. I've never even been inside it. Nobody can blame me—"

A secretary interrupted him and spoke to Alan. "Doctor, they're coming up the driveway."

"There's really no need for me to be here," Rose said, and walked out the door.

Helen tried to fight the panic inside her head. She wasn't sure what she should do.

Alan watched her closely. "You're not going to win this one, Helen. Not now, not here," he said quietly. The truth of his words fed his confidence. "It's turning," he continued. "Do you realize this is the first time I've seen someone like you lose in ten years . . . the first time . . ."

Helen walked to the door and stood in front of Alan. "It's not over. We've done breakthrough work here. Breakthrough!"

Alan smiled slowly. "We'll see."

She ran out the door; Alan remained in the doorway. A huge sigh of relief escaped from him, then he laughed, permitting himself the luxury of his victory.

Amanda was both frightened and determined. Ever since she had heard that Devin was here, perhaps being drugged and brainwashed, she had known she must come. And yet, as she approached the steps to the hospital, she knew she was afraid of what she might find.

General Fred Sittman was at her side, and two armed guardsmen flanked them: people of their importance could not move without protection. Amanda wasn't sure if she was relieved or frightened by her armed guards.

They were flanked too by Jeffrey and his camera crew, burly men carrying bulky cameras, restless, relentless men who barged in wherever they pleased. Even in the New America, the spirit of "Sixty Minutes" still lived.

Amanda saw the little white-coated knot of officialdom that loomed ahead: a nervous man in bifocals, a tough-looking woman, and a couple of unhappy security guards.

And off to the side, a black man, a familiar face, smiling, but one that stumped her for a moment, in this unexpected setting.

She stopped and stared at him, and watched his smile widen with delight. "The first lady of Heartland, I presume," he said.

"Alan? Alan Drummond? Is it really you?"

He held out his arms and she flew to him. They embraced—as the hospital staff grew nervous—and she whispered, "I've come to get Devin."

"We got him out early this morning; he's okay."

Amanda felt dizzy with relief; she held on to Alan for support. "Thank God," she said. After a moment, she began to smile. "Well, I guess that ends the tour," she said.

"Amanda," Alan said quietly. "There's more."

They had stepped a few feet aside. General Sittman and the others were watching this encounter with curiosity and, in some cases, anger. Jeffrey was scribbling notes and his crew was filming silently.

"What do you mean, more?" she asked.

"The psychiatric unit, where Devin was. I . . . think you'll need to prepare yourself for what's here."

He didn't tell her about Justin. He wanted her to go into that evil place because it was right, not because she knew one of the victims. Besides, he feared that if she knew what lay ahead, she might turn back.

Amanda summoned her courage a second time. "All right, Alan, if you say so." She turned to the administrator. "You're Mr. Rose?"

"Yes, Mrs. Bradford, and I want to welcome you to People's Acceptance. We believe we're one of the—"

"Mr. Rose, I want to tour that unit," she said, and pointed to the door that said PSYCHIATRIC UNIT—KEEP OUT!

"No, you can't go there," declared Nurse Quint. "It's classified—off limits."

Amanda turned to Fred Sittman. "General?"

"Folks, the lady can go where she pleases," he said.

Quint turned to the security guards. "Stop them!"

Fred Sittman's two guardsmen put their hands on their holsters, and three more guardsmen, armed with rifles, fanned out across the corridor.

The hospital security men stepped back. "I believe they have clearance," one of them said.

With the national guard leading the way, and Jeffrey's camera crew close behind, Amanda, Sittman, and Alan Drummond marched toward the forbidden unit. Rose, the hospital administrator, walked unhappily in their wake.

Alan led them into a dimly lit ward with a double row of beds packed close together. It took a few moments for Amanda's eyes to adjust. She started uncertainly up the aisle, clutching Alan's arm, then she cried out in horror as she saw the unconscious man on the bed nearest her, then the man next to him, and realized she was looking at two dozen men, with IV tubes in their arms, pale, shrunken creatures who seemed more dead than alive.

"My God!" she cried. "Alan, what . . . what is it?"

The camera crew switched on its lights; the glare illumined the gaunt faces of the patients but did not stir them from their trances.

Alan put his arm around Amanda. "This is where they start them off. When they first get here, they put them on various drugs, which prepare parts of the brain for conditioning: the films, the tapes, the individual therapy."

The cameras were on Alan now as he softly explained the chamber of horrors.

Amanda walked over and looked into the subjects' faces. They stared without focusing. She shrank suddenly from the horror of it. "We've got to stop this!" she cried. "How do you stop it?"

She ran to the nearest IV machine and twisted its knobs. "How does this work?" she demanded.

Rose, the administrator, suddenly confronted with lights and a camera, blinked back like an insect flushed from under a rock. "I don't know," he stammered. "I've never even been here before."

"I'll show you how to cut them off!" Fred Sittman was consumed in righteous anger. He ripped the lines from the nearest machine and sent it crashing to the floor. Then he crisscrossed the ward, tearing out lines, breaking bottles, knocking over IV machines. The cameras kept rolling and Amanda began to quietly sob, her head against Alan's shoulder.

He led her to the door. "There's more," he said. "I'm sorry but there's more you have to see."

She dried her eyes and followed.

They walked along a narrow corridor with several small doors opening off it. Alan nodded to an attendant, who unlocked one of the doors. It, too, was dimly lit; at first they saw only a small, padded cell, then they saw the figure crouched in the corner.

"No, no, no," she whispered, before she even recognized the ravaged creature huddled in the shadows.

It was Justin, what remained of him. The tall, confident boy she remembered astride his motorcycle now weighed barely a hundred pounds. His skin was ashen, his blond hair and ragged beard were streaked with gray. He was clad only in shorts, he looked tiny and withered. His eyes were open but empty as he huddled in the corner, his face to the wall, holding himself.

"Justin!" Amanda cried. She was frozen with fear and disgust for an instant, then she crossed the cell with quick, determined steps and knelt at the boy's side. Slowly, she put out her arms, but it was like embracing a statue. He showed no sign of life or recognition. "My God, my God," she whispered. She sat on the floor beside the boy, trying to get his attention, trying to embrace his stiff, ravaged body.

Alan knelt beside her, touched her shoulder, but she

saw only Justin now, the broken body, the empty, fearful eyes. Gently but firmly she pulled him to her until his head was cradled against her breast.

"Ah, Justin," she whispered. "I'm sorry."

A people's militia controlled Milford that day. More than fifty men and women occupied the jail and the courthouse square and guarded the roads into town. They were armed with the weapons seized at the jail, and with others that had miraculously appeared from a hundred hiding places. Even some dynamite had turned up, and been buried in strategic points around the square for possible use against an SSU invasion.

It was during the morning that Herb Lister burst onto the scene. "What are you people doing?" he demanded. "This is treason. This is insurrection; you can all be shot!"

Ward and Alethea Milford had returned to their farm, and Ward's fellow deputy, Cy Spraggins, commanded the irregulars. "I'll kiss a pig if we ain't got space in the jail," he drawled.

"Well, then arrest that little prick," another of the militiamen declared.

"You can't arrest me," Herb shrieked. "I'm the chairman of the Community Advisory Committee. I represent the PPP. I—"

As Cy advanced upon him, Herb turned tail and fled across the square, but Cy pursued, tackled him, and dragged him screaming off to jail.

The arrest of Herb Lister raised morale for a time, but the insurrectionists still waited anxiously, wondering what the SSU would do. They were well armed but how long could they hold out against its might? They expected at any moment to hear the clatter of helicopters or the rumble of armored cars.

Ward, Alethea, and various other exiles were collecting weapons that had lain hidden in various caches all over the town: some beneath the crushed structures of their former camp, some in old basements and attics. They had handguns, a couple of hunting rifles, and a small case of dynamite.

Over the hill a ways, Billy, Clayton, and Will stood outside the dugout, watching the activity.

"Don't get too far from that trapdoor," Will told Billy. "Don't know whether they gave up or are just givin' it a rest. With them helicopters, they suddenly appear and surprise hell out of you." He patted the boy's head and started back toward the farmhouse.

Billy watched him for a moment, then took off after him. "I'm sorry they burned the house, Grandpa," he said, catching up with the old man.

Will stopped walking. "Wasn't you. Guess it was more they didn't like our attitude. Us Milfords have always had an attitude problem." He put an arm around the boy's shoulder and smiled into the familiar eyes. "You stayin' safe is what's important."

"You too," Billy said.

Will winked at his grandson and walked away. Billy watched a moment, then headed back to the dugout.

"I have to tell you, young man." Clayton smiled. "I am out of stories, and if I have to go back there too many more times, you're on your own."

"Oh, don't be such a crybaby."

Clayton laughed, and soon Billy joined him as they started back down the dugout.

Will joined Dieter, Alethea, Betty, Ward, and a handful of Exiles as they sifted through the ruins of the farmhouse. Each one found different little treasures partially burned. Will was collecting the pictures of the

355

family from the dining room. They were all damaged, but some were still worth keeping.

Everyone looked toward the sound of the ambulance pulling up the driveway. Nobody moved toward this strange, out-of-place vehicle. Two Exiles got out of the cab of the ambulance. Dieter recognized one of them as Rick. Rick saw Dieter and walked toward him, his hand extended.

"Dieter, what the hell happened?"

Dieter shook Rick's hand. "You can guess. What are you doing?"

Rick smiled and looked at the Milfords, who by this time had moved toward the ambulance. He walked to the back of the vehicle, where the other Exile, Enos, had already opened one of the doors. Rick opened the other, and they reached inside the ambulance.

Devin pushed himself up on his elbow. "Let me try to . . . sit up," he said refusing the assistance. "Don't take me out on the stretcher."

Enos hopped inside the ambulance and helped Devin sit up.

There was anxiety on all the Milfords' faces. So much tragedy had left them wary of something like this. Alethea first caught sight of Devin bending out of the back of the ambulance, being helped by Enos to sit there.

She rushed to him. "Devin! My God . . ."

Devin grinned weakly as she rushed into his arms. "Hi, Ali."

The others rushed around him, helping him to stand. Will stood back, watching. Devin was not certain what kind of reception his father might have for him.

"Hi, Dad . . ."

Will looked at his son and smiled. "Welcome home, son."

He walked up to Devin and embraced him. The others stood close by watching this touching moment, one which had been so long awaited.

"Let's get you inside." Will held on to Devin's right arm. As they moved slowly, Devin noticed the shell of the burned house.

"My God . . . the house."

"I guess now's as good a time as any to tell you," Alethea quipped. "Your old room isn't quite ready."

Devin felt incredibly weak and dizzy as he leaned into his father for support. "We'll take you down to the cellar. It's better than you'd expect." He smiled at Devin and gave him a quick hug around his shoulders. "We'll be rebuildin' soon."

The Milford meat-packing plant was a large two-story building, corrugated metal from top to bottom. The factory-window glass was webbed with wire, giving it the look of a state penitentiary. The walls were straight, the corners of the building sharp; it possessed an overall boxlike shape without character or architectural style. The loading docks were falling apart; it was almost impossible to think that they had ever been used. The place was like a deserted tree house, beaten, weathered, and uncared for.

Inside the packing plant, the residue of its past could be seen in the empty and rusted hooks and the conveyer belts, long since split and broken.

Several people sat around a circle listening to the tinny sound of a small transistor radio. Kimberly sat next to Jeffrey, who held the receiver. The group listened intently.

It was a Natnet announcement of the bombing of the Capitol the day before and the murder of more than a hundred members of Congress. The official report announced that American Resisters were guilty of the attack.

Everyone in the group was horrified, their faces twisted with despair.

"Why, how could anybody do such a thing?" It was one of the camera crew that had been in the psychiatric ward earlier.

"Like a wounded animal biting itself," Ken said quietly. He was another member of the camera crew.

"We're going insane, all of us—Resisters, collaborators . . ." said a woman from the group.

"Sure gonna make people think twice," Ken said, shaking his head.

"Think twice?" Jeffrey shouted.

"About supporting any kind of resistance," Ken continued.

"I think people might just line up behind this new Heartland deal pretty fast."

"Andrei used to say that American resistance was like the outlaw theater we did." Kimberly spoke quietly. "Fun and just a little daring, but ultimately safe."

Jeffrey stood, his body rigid, his face angry. "I'm going to Milford. I don't believe all this crap. I don't believe it about me, about a lot of folks I know, and a lot I don't know. And I don't believe Devin Milford'll want to roll it up." He searched the faces of the group intently. "I don't, that's for sure," he added dramatically.

Kimberly stood beside him. "Can I come?"

Jeffrey smiled and looked at Ken, who shrugged and stood.

"Sure can. You and any of the rest of you who want to give it a longer ride."

Everyone in the group stood except for one man.

"There ain't nothin' I can do in Milford I can't do in Omaha," he said, shaking his head.

The group started to walk toward the front of the warehouse. Ken turned to the man and yelled, "Stay tuned." His words reverberated off the tin walls for several seconds as Jeffrey and his cohorts hopped into their cars and sped away.

Chapter 15

MARION WAS GLAD to receive the morning telephone call from Andrei.

"Andrei, I've been trying to reach Petya. I can't get through."

Andrei hesitated a moment. "Yes. How are you, Marion?"

"I hope you are not part of this conspiracy . . ."

"What do you mean?"

"Devin has escaped. And the experimental conditioning unit has been compromised. Somehow Amanda Bradford was taking a public relations tour or something—the whole thing was photographed by a crew."

"Well, simply censor it, I don't see what harm is done," Andrei said with studied nonchalance.

Marion struggled to maintain control. "It's an obvious attempt by Peter Bradford to damage me. Well, he's going to find things are a little more difficult than that. I've called a general strike. And we're moving to take control of as many facilities throughout the area as we can."

Andrei's voice grew sterner. "You're overreacting again."

"We'll see. I demand that you allow me to be put through to Petya. I want the SSU forces throughout the area on alert—and prepared to support the party—and you know that Petya will do it. And don't try something to prevent me."

"Marion," Andrei said evenly. "Samanov is dead."

Marion sat back, stunned. Her face was ashen. "You're lying."

"I wish I were," he said hoarsely.

The tone of Andrei's voice told Marion that he was not lying. But the terrible fact of her lover's loss was momentarily subsumed by her compulsion to solve the immediate problem. "He can't be dead."

"There will be an announcement later in the day. Not just about Petya. I'm sorry." Andrei's tone softened. "I know you . . . that there were strong feelings between you."

Marion nodded absently, as though he had just reminded her of that fact. "We loved each other," she said quietly.

"I'm sorry."

"And the SSU?" In an instant she was back to business, unable to let go of the immediate situation.

"I will retain exclusive control of the units," he announced. "I will need them—all of them in America. You'll soon understand why."

Marion sat at her desk, listening to his words impassively.

361

"Marion," he continued. "Find a way to reconcile with Peter Bradford. Believe me, it is best for both of you."

She did not reply.

"Marion, did you hear me? Find a way to reconcile with Bradford. You must believe me, it would be best for both of you."

She did not reply but stared straight ahead, as if she had already disconnected the phone in her mind.

"Goodbye, Marion. You cannot win. You can only bring chaos."

She heard Andrei disconnect and slowly, numbly, hung up the phone.

The small farm jeep bumped across the Milford land. Will drove as Devin held on; watching the familiar land filled his eyes with joy. He appeared weak, but more rested since the ambulance journey. Finally Will stopped the jeep abruptly and walked over to the trapdoor. Devin climbed out of his seat gingerly.

"Got a visitor," Will said, banging on the trapdoor.

The door slid back; a musty, earthen smell escaped.

"We're goin' crazy in there. Can we come out? Especially Clayton; he can't take it at all—" Billy abruptly stopped talking. He saw Devin standing by the jeep and yelped. "Dad!"

He pulled himself out of the ground and ran full-tilt to Devin. The force knocked him down and Billy was instantly concerned. "Oh, jeez, I'm sorry. Did I . . .?"

Devin started laughing and grabbed the boy back to him in a huge bear hug. Meanwhile, Clayton had climbed out and walked over to the father and son.

"What took you so long?" Clayton asked, grabbing Devin's hand.

Will walked over to the trio. "Let up on him. He's a sick man."

Clayton looked at Devin. "Well, is it over?"

Devin, still hanging on to Billy for dear life, looked up to him. "It's just beginning."

Calyton helped Devin and Billy up and followed Will to the jeep. They headed back to the farmhouse, where three more carloads of townspeople had arrived. When they saw the Milford men reunited, three generations of them, they let out a great cheer. Devin waved to them proudly, and then his father and his son helped him into the root cellar that was now their new home.

Amanda thought she would never trust a hospital again. She wanted Peter to see Justin too, to see what the wonderful "new regime" had done to this proud, brave, beautiful boy. She feared that Peter was so entranced by the charming Andrei Denisov and by the speeches and ovations that he forgot the ugly realities behind the scenes.

But was that fair? After all, Peter had sent her there, with General Sittman, to do precisely what she had done. And the Natnet crew had rushed off, vowing to get their film on the air if Peter would stand behind them. It was all too confusing. All she really knew as she sat in the back of the ambulance, holding the broken boy's limp hand, was that she felt profoundly sad and alone. Even with Alan there, she felt agonizingly alone. She thought of a scrap of poetry, half remembered: "man's inhumanity to man." It just kept getting worse. She dated her awakening from the morning she'd seen the exile girl in her yard, digging in her garbage, but that was nothing compared to this, this psychiatric unit, this inhuman destruction of the human body and soul.

What more could there be? Tanks in the streets? Nuclear war? Death for millions? She was so weary she wasn't sure she cared. She only wanted to be home.

Home was not the white-columned mansion on a bluff outside Omaha, built by a meat-packing czar who had fallen into disfavor, but her true home, in Milford, where she and her family had true friends, and real lives, before they put on the borrowed masks and costumes of politics. But she couldn't return, not yet, and so that afternoon the ambulance, and its national guard escort, stopped on the graceful, graveled drive in front of her "official residence." She gasped to see her daughter running out to greet her and leaped out to intercept the girl.

"Jackie—wait a minute!"

"Justin—you found Justin. What's the matter with him?"

The ambulance drivers were coming around to open the back doors. Amanda realized suddenly that her daughter had been shielded from the world's ugliness all her life, that the worst she had seen was the wounds in the movies, where heroes wore a bandage around one arm, or over one eye, and said jauntily, "Just a flesh wound."

She held Jackie close. "Darling, he's . . . he's very sick."

Jackie didn't understand what all the fuss was about. She was impatient to see Justin after all this time, and she was surprised, and a little annoyed, when Alan Drummond leaped out of the ambulance.

He stepped before her, blocking her way, and she strained to see over his shoulder as the attendants lifted a stretcher from the ambulance.

"Jacqueline," Alan said cautiously. "You've got to prepare yourself for a shock."

"What shock?" she whispered, for she was frightened now. What could be so terrible about Justin?

She broke away and peered at the figure on the stretcher. Suddenly nothing made any sense: she did not know this gaunt, hollow-eyed old man.

"It's not Justin!" she said, turning to her mother and Alan, seeing their anguished faces. Then, slowly, she began to understand.

She looked again at the unconscious figure; she followed alongside the stretcher as they carried him up the steps, and then she cried out, "No, no, no, I don't believe it!" and ran into the house.

"Take him to the guest room," Amanda said to Alan. "Top of the stairs." Then she raced after Jackie.

Jackie crashed blindly through the house, until the back door blocked her flight. As she fumbled with the lock, blinded by tears, her mother seized her. Jackie was sobbing.

"It's not him," Jackie cried.

"Listen to me. That *is* Justin. And he's been brainwashed. We don't know how bad it is or if he'll ever recover. Dr. Drummond will stay here and treat him. And we must help."

"It's not Justin," the girl said, suddenly calm. "Justin's dead."

Amanda was angry now. "He's not dead. He's hurt. He needs us. He needs you."

"What for?" Jackie said.

Amanda was chilled by the coldness, the toughness of her daughter's question. Would she, to protect her own feelings, turn her back on the boy she loved?

"My God, Jacqueline. He's all broken up. He needs our love . . . your love . . . something to make him whole, to make him come back."

"Come back?" Jackie asked numbly.

"In his mind. From wherever they've sent him."

Jackie looked away, at the floor, at nothing. Amanda wondered if her daughter had reached her limit. Was she only capable of Hollywood love, make-believe love, and not of the pain and toughness and compassion that were the real thing?

"Jackie, you're going to help him. This is the most important thing that's ever happened in your life; someday you'll understand that. You're going to love him no matter how much it hurts, no matter how bad he looks, no matter if it all seems lost and wasted. Because love is never wasted. No matter how hard it is, you're going to do it. Because, if you don't, you'll never forgive yourself."

Jackie looked blankly at her mother for a moment, then nodded slowly.

Peter knew that Natnet would announce the news of the Capitol bombing at noon. At twenty minutes before the hour he had his driver take him home. He gathered Amanda and the kids before the TV console in the formal living room of their borrowed mansion, and he beat down Scott's protests that he didn't care about the news, except sports. "You will watch this with us," Peter ordered, and his children obeyed.

Scott slouched before the TV, looking bored. Jackie sank on the sofa wearily; she had slept little, as she and her mother took turns nursing Justin. So far there had been no signs of improvement but Peter was glad to see Jackie's concern and her commitment: she was giving Justin the sort of dedication she had once reserved for her dancing. He never thought he'd live to see the day, but Peter was proud of his daughter's devotion to that boy.

Amanda was apprehensive—should he have told her

earlier?—as the grim face of the Natnet anchorman filled the screen.

". . . terrorist bombing of the U.S. Capitol . . . a suicide attack . . . charges strapped to their bodies . . . more than a hundred dead . . . Fourth of July Brigade . . ."

"Jeez, a suicide attack," Scott muttered. "They must have been crazy."

Soon Peter switched off the news: there really wasn't much to report, beyond those initial, scanty "facts."

"It's a terrible thing for our country," he said.

"You knew," Amanda said reproachfully.

He nodded. "Andrei told me part of it last night."

"You could have told us then," she protested. "Instead of leaving it to television."

"God, Am, what's the point?" he demanded.

She was angry, and tried to fight back her tears. "Look at our children, Peter. They don't even understand what they've lost."

"Hey, Mom, I understand," Scott protested. "But I guess I don't see the big deal. I mean, it's too bad a bunch of creeps blew it up and all, and I'm sorry somebody was killed, but we're not a part of that anymore, are we?"

"It was part of our heritage, son," Peter said. "It'll always be a part of us."

"Yeah, well, I don't know why Mom's always getting on my case lately," Scott said heavily.

Amanda stood. "I—Peter, it's too much for me. I want to go home. Be in my own house. I want to walk down a street and know where to watch out because the elm roots are pushing up the sidewalk. I need to do that for a while. Maybe I can never be what you want—I could be your wife, but I'm not sure I can be your first lady. I'm sorry." She was quiet for a moment, staring at the husband she loved very much. "Can you have someone drive me?" she asked. "I think I'll take Justin back to his folks. Alan says the more he's around people who love him . . ." She was suddenly aware that everyone had been watching her talk nonstop. She caught herself and shrugged. "Anybody can come. Scotty, Jac, Peter?"

Peter leaned against the doorway, shaking his head in wonder. Andrei was unreachable, Marion had her stormtroopers in the streets, his new "nation" was on the brink of anarchy, and now his wife was leaving him. He shrugged his shoulders a little.

"Maybe it's a good idea," he said. "For a while. This Capitol business is going to create some trouble; maybe Milford's the safest place right now."

She moved to where he stood. "You'll come?"

"You know I can't, Am. But I'll come and get you as soon as this has settled down a little."

"That won't be too late?"

He smiled sadly. "It's never too late. You know that. That's what we've always said."

Jackie stood. "I'll go with you, Mom."

Amanda was a little surprised. "Your dancing?"

"It can wait awhile." Jackie smiled.

"I think I'll hang around here," Scott said, avoiding his mother's look, staring down at his size-12 basketball shoes.

"Sure, honey. Whatever you want."

Peter walked over to Scott. "He'll be fine. We'll batch it."

Amanda threw her hands open in a small gesture of uncertainty. Now that she had done it, she wasn't sure she should have. And yet, someone had to decide where their home was, and did it matter?

"Well," she sighed. "We'd better get packed."

"The house is pretty empty, isn't it?"

"Not entirely," she said. "We stored a lot of things in the basement. We'll camp out, so to speak."

She smiled at her husband and walked out of the room quickly, before she could change her mind.

Jackie looked at her brother, not quite sure of how to deal with her emotions toward him. Peter watched them a moment, then threw his arms open. Jackie ran into them.

"Daddy, you'll be all right?"

"I'll be fine."

"You could come, you know. Mom really wants you to."

Peter closed his eyes, taking in the scent of his daughter.

"I know, baby. I know."

General Sittman and three truckloads of well-armed troops from the Heartland Defense Force pulled up to Peter's home. As they sped away with her husband, Amanda idly wondered if they would ever give him back. Oddly, her speculation was more out of curiosity than concern.

The convoy sped toward Natnet's Omaha studio. As they approached, Peter tried unsuccessfully to suppress a hope that this mission might somehow help him get back his wife. When they arrived, the soldiers moved out smartly, strategically surrounding the building.

Inside, Peter confronted the station manager, Reg Holly, a plump, balding man, who was soon sweating profusely. Jeffrey joined them in the office, clutching the film he and his crew had shot at the psychiatric unit of People's Acceptance Hospital.

"I don't see how we can possibly run that report," the station manager protested.

"Why not, Mr. Holly?"

"In the first place, it's sickening. Those patients are like . . . *zombies.*"

"It's strong," Peter agreed. "Tough, dynamic TV—great for your ratings."

"To hell with my ratings," Holly said. "In the second place, the PPP would never approve it."

"Mr. Holly, you don't seem to understand the situation," Peter said. "I'm the governor-general of this region. I don't give a damn about the PPP censors; I'm ordering you to run that film, or I'll take over this studio and run it without you. Do I make myself clear?"

The station manager wiped his sweaty brow. Peter could appreciate his distress. Nothing like this had ever happened before. Except for Peter, the top political officials had always been loyal PPP members, so there had been no reason for conflict.

"When do you want to go on the air?" Holly asked.

The footage was powerful, brutal. The camera missed nothing: the drugged, deathly figures with tubes in their arms, Amanda's anguish, Justin's pitiful condition, even the hospital administrator's protestations of innocence. Jeffrey's commentary was cool and understated: as he well knew, the pictures said it all.

When the twenty-minute report was finished, Jeffrey appeared on the screen live. "That is our report, from the psychiatric unit of the People's Acceptance Hospital," he intoned. "Now we have here in the studio, for his comments, the governor-general of Heartland, Mr. Peter Bradford."

Peter sat at a desk, with some law books and the new Heartland flag behind him. He wore a dark blue suit, a light blue shirt, and a red-and-blue regimental-striped tie—the politician's basic TV outfit. As county administrator in Milford, Peter had made a point of dressing like everyone else—jeans, plaid shirts, windbreakers, an old tweed coat on the most formal occasions—but he'd changed that now that he was governor-general.

Peter felt supremely confident as he began to speak. He'd been thinking about this ever since he heard of the Capitol bombings and the trouble that Marion's thugs were causing. He knew that he would have a large and responsive audience. In the wake of the massacre at the Capitol, people were anxiously watching TV, wanting more news. And he would give them more: he'd give them one hell of a show.

"My fellow Heartlanders," he began. "Some terrible things have been happening. We just saw a dramatic report on the cruelty and inhumanity that can result when people stop caring about their fellow human beings. I say to you that this sort of inhumanity has no place in Heartland, and I will put an end to it, once and for all!

"We saw another instance of inhumanity at the U.S. Capitol, when invaders bombed it and slaughtered scores of our elected representatives. It isn't clear yet who was guilty of that attack, but this much is certain: they represent an alien philosophy, whether it's home-grown or foreign.

"Now, in the streets of many of our cities, we face demonstrations, riots, vandalism, hooliganism. Why? Because of real grievances? Or because certain political zealots are trying to twist national concern to serve their own ends?

"I say the troublemakers are politically inspired, and they must be stopped. It is time for the decent, hardworking, law-abiding Heartlanders to say no to anarchy and opportunism. If the extremists call a

strike, then go to work early that day. If they demonstrate, then get your friends and neighbors to form a
bigger and better demonstration. If they start fights or
break windows or otherwise break the law, then see
that they're arrested—if you have to do it yourself.
Speaking as commander-in-chief of the Heartland Defense Force, I promise you that my full authority will be
used to support the law-abiding majority of Heartland.

"But I need your support. I intend to tour all the
major cities of Heartland in the days ahead, to meet
with local officials and ordinary citizens. Please come
meet me; give me your ideas, your support, and your
prayers. Thank you and God bless you."

Marion Andrews and Mike Laird watched the news-
cast in her library. "Why didn't we stop him?" she
asked, keeping her anger in check.

"As I told you, he had the national guard surrounding the studio. I can't send my men to fight a war with
them."

"Call all our people—get them into the streets. I
want a general strike! We've got to topple Bradford
before it's too late."

"It may already be too late," Laird said. "He's going
to have his own people in the streets, the way it looks."

She looked at him, her eyes burning with a fierce
determination. "You can give up," she said. "But I
won't; the people are counting on me."

The Milfords listened to the broadcast on the radio,
huddled around the fire in the root cellar. "What do
you think?" Alethea asked all of them as Peter Bradford finished.

"Just another slick damn politician in a three-
hundred-dollar suit, if you ask me," Will declared.

Dieter Heinlander's face was sad. "That part about going into the streets, it frightens me. That is the way it all started back in Germany."

"What do you think, Devin?" Alethea asked.

Devin was wrapped in blankets, eating some potato soup. He considered the question for so long that she thought he wasn't going to answer. "Peter's become quite a politician," he said finally. "I know he means well, but sometimes meaning well just isn't good enough."

Peter's office called later that afternoon to alert Amanda of the fact that the film of her dramatic visit to the psychiatric unit would be shown that evening, followed by comments from Peter. Amanda took the portable TV upstairs so she and Jackie and Justin could watch the show together. She thought that perhaps seeing that hospital on the TV screen might rouse Justin from his apathy. Ever since they'd been home, Justin would sit up and sip milk or soup, but he did not speak or give any sign that he could recognize anyone.

It wasn't easy. You talked to him, you fed and bathed him, you read to him, but nothing came back. Amanda knew how tired and discouraged she was, but Jackie's blind faith filled her with pride and the will to continue. About the only consolation they had was the improvement in his appearance. They had shaved him and trimmed his hair, and he was gaining back some weight and color: his body was improving but apparently not his mind.

So Amanda decided to risk the TV program; perhaps seeing pictures of the unit, indeed of himself there, would shock or frighten him—by now Amanda was ready to settle for any response at all, even fear. But despite the horrific images that appeared on the screen, she didn't even get that response: Justin might have been staring at the wall.

After Peter's speech, Jackie switched off the set and said, "I'll read to him; you get some rest," and picked up the copy of *Lonesome Dove* that they'd been reading, at Amanda's suggestion. Amanda loved the novel, because the story was so exciting, and because its portrait of America in the 1880s meant so much more to her now. Those people in the west had lives filled with incredible danger and, at the same time, lives of almost total freedom. Perhaps danger went hand in hand with freedom, and somehow in modern times their mistake was in thinking there could ever be real freedom without great risk.

Amanda went down to the kitchen to straighten up and have some time to herself. The house seemed awfully big and quiet without Peter and Scott stomping around. She poured a cup of coffee and sat at the kitchen table, looking out at the fields. The sun was out, slowly melting the snow, leaving the yard a muddy quagmire. Soon she'd have to think about planting her garden. Sometimes she thought that human beings were intended to live on farms and raise their own food, and somehow "civilization" had turned them away from that—and brought with it the Nuclear Age. She needed the garden, not for the tomatoes, potatoes, beans, and lettuce, but because she needed to feel some contact with a simpler, better past.

Amanda couldn't keep the images of the psychiatric unit from her mind. When they had come on the screen, she had turned away: she had lived that nightmare once and had no wish to experience it again, even on film. But she couldn't force those images of deathly pale men and boys from her mind. They were far more real to her than the speech Peter had made on TV just a few minutes before. In truth, when Peter appeared, she barely paid attention to his words. Her real attention was on Justin. Since she had returned to Milford, Peter's political battles had become quite unreal to her. They were like a movie, playing in some distant theater, one she chose not to patronize. Peter was trying to save America, or Heartland, and she was only trying to save that pathetic speechless boy upstairs in her guest room.

Amanda put away some dishes and hoped no more of her neighbors would drop by that day. People had been nice, they had brought food and offered to help with Justin, and they tentatively asked questions about Chicago and Omaha or Peter's job. No one seemed quite sure why Amanda was back in Milford when Peter was still in Omaha. She had to laugh at herself. She knew how people gossiped in small towns. She just hadn't often been someone who people gossiped about.

My turn at last, she thought.

And the truth was, she welcomed the gossip, in one way. She wanted to hear about Devin. She knew he was back, that they'd rescued him from People's Acceptance, and she guessed he was in pretty good shape. Ward and Betty had been by that morning, to visit Justin, and they'd spoken of taking him home, but the truth was that they had no home now, and Amanda convinced them it was best to leave their son with her. Ward feared for the safety of the farmland, with Devin there, and Billy still hiding nearby. No one trusted the fact or understood the reason why the SSU had stayed in its barracks, and Ward constantly wondered when its tanks and helicopters might come charging forth.

Amanda promised to speak to Peter about the dangers, but Ward didn't seem to think Peter mattered anymore. He and his friends were armed, he said, and they were prepared to deal with the SSU on their own terms.

Amanda wanted to see Devin, to talk to him; she thought that he could make sense of what was happening, if anyone could. She knew that Devin and Peter embodied profoundly different philosophies of how Americans should deal with the Russian takeover, and she wanted to hear Devin's side of it. She'd heard Peter's side often enough.

He was out at the remains of the Milford house—they were already starting to build a new cabin, Ward said—but she couldn't go there. She felt an allegiance to Peter, their home and their marriage. She felt too vulnerable to go to Devin.

"Mama! Mama! Come quick!" Jackie called from the head of the stairs, snapping her out of her reverie.

Amanda dashed up the stairs. Jackie's face was flushed—alive and animated, filled with hope. "What is it, darling?"

"It's Justin. He . . . he sort of smiled at me. Come see!"

Justin was in his wheelchair, facing the window, his unblinking eyes fixed on the rolling countryside where he had spent so many carefree years. Jackie put her face close to his, and Amanda knelt beside him.

"Justin, it's me, Jackie, my mom and I are here with you. Can you see us? Are you okay?"

Amanda's eyes were fixed on the boy's thin, pale face, but she saw nothing; he might have been a Greek statue, of the purest white marble.

"See, Mama? See?"

Amanda searched his face, almost pore by pore,

looking for the miracle, but she saw only the same, agonizing immobility.

"Don't you see? His mouth? He's smiling; he's trying to talk."

Amanda looked even closer. Was that a twitch at the corner of his mouth? Had those lips seemed to move, to tremble? Or was it only her—their—imagination?

"Can't you see . . . he's trying to talk to us!" Jackie declared.

"Yes, I see," Amanda said. "You're right, he is trying to talk. And he will, Jackie, any day now. You just keep giving him your love."

Jackie threw her arms around her mother and began to sob, her tears wet and hot against Amanda's old U of N sweatshirt. "Mama, I can't stand it if he doesn't talk to us soon," she cried.

Amanda stroked her daughter's soft, chestnut hair. "Yes, you can, darling," she said. "Yes, you can."

The next day broke windy and bright, the sky a deep, cloudless blue, the sun hot on their faces, a sweet foretaste of spring.

"What day is it?" Devin asked.

"Friday," Ward told him. They were out by the barn, savoring the morning's gentle paradox: the warmth of the sun and the chill of the breeze.

"Friday," Devin repeated. "Then I declare a holiday. And on this Good Friday we'll all take a walk."

"Gonna be muddy out there," Ward cautioned.

"You don't know how I've missed mud," Devin said. "I've been places where mud was against the law. Let's go slogging around. Show Billy the sights."

Alethea joined them. "Dev, you sure you're up to this?"

Devin grinned. "It's all that soup you been feeding me," he said. "I'm full of piss and vinegar. Ready for a ten-mile hike, anyway, if you civilians can keep up."

"A couple of miles is my limit," Ward said. "Us law-enforcement types aren't much for forced marches."

"I'll see what food we've got," Alethea said. "And I'll break the news to Dad: he's not one of the world's great hikers, either."

She turned back to their root-cellar home. They had a canvas roof over it now, and a wooden floor in it. Mostly, they just slept there, because they spent their waking hours hunting food, working on the new cabin, or planning for their defense when the expected SSU attack came.

Before Alethea could descend the ladder, a car came roaring up the poplar-lined drive.

"Who's that?" Alethea demanded.

Ward squinted at the oncoming car. "Well, it's not the SSU, unless they've taken to driving banged-up old Pontiacs."

The car stopped and three men and a young woman climbed out, looking around uncertainly. One of the men sported a modified Afro and a wide grin on his broad, black face. Clayton ran up to Jeffrey, embracing him.

"Well, I guess we can start some trouble now that the press is here."

"I want you to meet my friends," Jeffrey said, pointing to the three others. "That big lummox is Ken, my cameraman. Those two beautiful people beside him are Kimberly and Cliff, a couple of actors who've joined up with what we laughingly call the resistance. You may have heard we did a little broadcast over in Omaha the other night."

"Good to see you again, Jeffrey," said Devin.

Devin looked at the three newcomers, then greeted them warmly. "You turned out the people who took over the hospital and got me out of that hellhole. Thank you."

Kimberly clung to his hand, her face glowing with affection and awe. Looking around, at the burned-out house, the cellar with its canvas roof, the gun that the big, white-haired man carried on his hip, all she could think was that these people looked like the survivors of a war. "It's an honor to meet you, Mr. Milford," she said. "We . . . when we heard what happened at the Capitol, we felt like we had to come here, to see what you'd say."

"The first thing I say is you damn well better call me Devin," he told her. Kimberly was wearing jeans and a parka, but her head was uncovered and the sunlight sparkled on her blond hair.

"I want you to meet my family," Devin continued. "Then all of you can join our picnic celebration!"

Thus began one of the best days any of them ever knew, a day for memories and magic. With the bright sun melting the snow, with the breeze playing on their faces, they trudged through the trees, over the hills, across the land that had once been the Milfords' domain, past many of the milestones of their family members' lives.

Alethea could not recall a better day. Not in her whole life had she ever seen her family together like this, happy and laughing and affectionate. She had grown up knowing her father to be an angry, embittered man, most often barely speaking to his two sons, or to her either. But on this sun-bright day, all three of his children, and his grandson too, walked gladly across the fields arm in arm with Will. It was as if losing his land, even the burning of his home, didn't matter, because he had been reborn with the love of his family.

Devin led them to the dugout where Billy and Clayton had been hiding, and Will explained its history to the visitors. They picnicked there, and Devin and Billy and Kimberly went down to the pond to skip rocks on the water. Jeffrey, Cliff, and Clayton napped after they ate, and Will went and sat by himself at the top of the hill. Alethea was moved to see him up there, alone, gazing down at them with all the wisdom and courage of a long, hard life. She saw his mortality then, as if he were already dead and he had come back to watch over them. The thought did not depress her or seem improper. Will would die, just as they all would; the tragedy would have been for him to die before enjoying this one magnificent day with his family.

For a time, Jeffrey took Devin aside and talked to him—interviewed him—while Ken filmed them with his portable camera. The others stayed a respectful distance away, granting them their privacy, except for Billy, who delighted in making faces at his father, poking gentle fun at the solemn tone of the interview. When the interview stopped, Devin chased the boy around a tree, pretending great ire at his disrespect. In truth, Alethea thought she had never seen a sweeter love flow between two people.

In midafternoon, they set out walking again. People moved about, talking first to this person, then to another, but Alethea would have been blind not to see that Devin and Kimberly were often drawn together—he boyish and grinning, she blushing and nervous, in the first flush of their attraction. Alethea felt a sister's unease at this flirtation, and something more than unease when Ken, the cameraman, let it drop that

Kimberly had until recently been the mistress of Andrei Denisov. Ken went on to tell her how Kimberly had left the Russian and joined the underground and that her broadcast in Omaha had paved the way for Devin's escape.

A few minutes later, when they stopped by a stream for a drink of water, Alethea walked up to Kimberly and hugged her. When she backed away, Kimberly smiled uncertainly.

"That's because I like you," Alethea told her. "And because maybe we've got more in common than you know."

They rested by the stream and, at Jeffrey's insistence, Kimberly sang to them, a sad, haunting song from *The Fantasticks*. Everyone was touched by the song and applauded when she finished, even Will.

Kimberly buried her face in her hands. "Please," she whispered, "it's nothing really."

On the way back, in the late afternoon, they stopped at the Milford family graveyard. An old iron fence surrounded the plot, where nearly a hundred headstones stood, many of them worn with age, their inscriptions almost unreadable. Will knelt beside his wife's grave, absently brushing away snow and leaves. Devin knelt beside him, and dropped an arm across the old man's shoulders. The old man tousled Devin's hair, a gesture Devin often did with Billy. Standing a few feet away, Billy watched the rekindling of love between father and son. He ran over to them to be a part of it.

Alethea watched all this, feeling somehow detached, knowing only that life was fragile and these moments precious. As they returned to the camp, huge thunderheads were blowing in from the west. No one else seemed to share her mood—they bustled about, busy with this chore or that—but to Alethea the huge dark clouds seemed to dwarf them, to mock their human concerns; their little band, each with his or her loves and sorrows, courage and hope, seemed tiny and helpless, silhouetted against the great brooding sky.

In the face of infinity, Alethea thought, all we have is our love.

Chapter 16

ANDREI, IN FULL uniform, paced his Virginian communications center impatiently while technicians prepared
for his broadcast. He had much on his mind that
afternoon. His intelligence reports showed continuing
unrest across Heartland. Party loyalists in several cities
had clashed with pro-Bradford partisans. The general
strike had faltered but there had been outbreaks of
sabotage—the public bus service in Cincinnati had
been disrupted by slashed tires, power outages were
caused by bombings in southern Illinois towns. A police
station in St. Louis captured by the PPP had been
retaken peacefully, but there were reports that Marion
Andrews planned a new appeal to the party cadres.
And since his dramatic television appearance, Peter
Bradford had not returned Andrei's phone calls.

The need was for Peter to use the Heartland Defense
Force to restore civic peace with minimal force rather

than for Andrei to unleash the SSU. Of course, the next question was whether Andrei could then control Peter and his troops, but that was the risk inherent in his new policy.

"Ready, sir," the director called.

Andrei straightened his coat and stepped before the cameras. Across America, a dozen SSU commanders awaited his instructions.

"Gentlemen," he said crisply, "your role in America is entering a new stage. Effective immediately, you will no longer be responsible to PPP officials. You will take no action that does not have the specific approval of this Command. As of this moment, you are on full readiness alert, but restricted to your barracks. You may defend yourselves, but you will not otherwise involve yourself in local conflicts. Any deviation from this order will result in immediate termination of command."

The cameras switched off and Andrei turned to Captain Selovich, who stood in the shadows. "Get me Major Gurtman on the telephone," he ordered.

The call was quickly placed. Andrei remembered Gurtman from their one meeting: a very tall, thin East German, cold and capable.

"Major, I trust you saw my broadcast," Andrei began.

"Of course, sir."

"Good. I wished to speak with you directly because of the special conditions in your area. What is the situation now?"

"The situation is serious, sir. The people of Milford are armed. They are protecting the two fugitives, Devin Milford and his son. I urgently request permission to retake the town and capture the fugitives."

"Permission denied."

Helmut Gurtman struggled to hold back his anger. "May I ask why, Colonel?"

"The townspeople may be armed, but at the moment they have no one to shoot, except perhaps each other. As for the Milford boy, it is not the role of the SSU to pursue missing children, no matter how impassioned their mothers may be. As for Milford himself, I will ask Peter Bradford to see to his recapture, using the defense force if necessary."

Helmut Gurtman was beside himself. To be confined to his base while the occupied townspeople ran rampant was an outrage to everything he believed as a military man. And to have his former mistress's family leading this rebellion added insult to injury; it was almost more than he could bear.

"Sir, one further question," he said stiffly.

"Yes?"

"We may defend ourselves—fire back if fired upon?"

Andrei nodded wearily. "Yes, Major, I thought I made that clear: you may fire back if fired upon."

"I thank the colonel," Gurtman said coldly.

When the Milfords and their visitors returned from their walk, Dieter Heinlander invited everyone to the exile camp for dinner.

"We should go," Devin told Jeffrey. "These are people you should know. They're the ones who've really suffered and yet hung on to their dignity."

"Can we film?" Jeffrey said.

Devin shook his head. "Don't ask me, ask them," he said.

At dusk, they crossed over the hill to the exile camp, where they were greeted with hugs and cheers. Dinner was a huge, savory stew—"Don't ask what the meat is," Dieter warned—and after dinner they all gathered in the barn. They sang for a while—"You Are My Sunshine" and "This Land Is Your Land" and "On Top of Old Smokey" and "Blowin' in the Wind" and "We Shall Overcome," a grab bag of gospel songs and love songs and protest songs from better days—and in time the singing gave way to political talk.

One man said he'd buried his guns ten years before but now he was ready to use them.

Another man protested that violence only begat more violence.

A woman defended Peter Bradford and his support for Heartland, but others denounced Peter as a puppet and a traitor.

The talk flowed back and forth like that; some wanted to take up arms, others to turn the other cheek, and there seemed to be nothing on which everyone could agree.

There were cheers when Ward Milford declared, "The trouble is we've been spineless for ten years. I stood there and did nothing while those bastards stole our land, even burned our house. I took it. But I'm not going to take it anymore."

Then another man quickly defended Peter Bradford. "I've got no love for the Russians," he declared, "but maybe Bradford's right, maybe this new country, this Heartland business, is the fastest way to be rid of 'em."

"Dammit, we're Americans!" one man cried.

Another demanded, "What the hell difference does it make, anyway?"

Devin was seated quietly on the floor, against a bale of hay. Amid the general clamor, his voice was gentle. "I think I know the difference it makes," he said.

The people around him raised their hands for silence.

"I think deep inside, we all know," Devin continued. "We don't want to be afraid anymore. Fear is driving us away from being Americans. Fear of pain, fear of suffering, fear of death. When I ran for president, I was afraid if no one followed my lead, it would prove I was wrong. When they sent me to prison camp, I was afraid I'd lose my . . . my understanding, my clarity. When I was released and came back here, I was afraid that someone would notice me, ask me to participate—to live."

He was speaking so softly that people began to inch forward, so they could hear. Ken was quietly filming the scene.

"Thank God for this town," Devin continued. "Thank God for an Exile from this camp, a black doctor who saved my life. Thank God for an Episcopal minister who lost his faith in the church, but not the people. Thank God for my father and my sister, who reminded me about our ancestors. They showed me that tragedy and nobility are the same thing, that the human condition demands that we endure the pain and simply live our lives.

"My son. The miracle is that my son spent the last two days in that dugout, just like his great-great-grandmother and great-great-grandfather did. My son's survival is worth any price I have to pay. My son taught me the most important lesson, and I'm not afraid anymore."

People leaned forward intently; they nodded but did not speak.

"Our ancestors fought for an idea, sacrificed for it, died for it, and we are the result. The idea of America lives in us, and how can we give it up? I know I can't. Because ultimately I have to be true to my forefathers, just as I have to be true to my son. He's here, free, and no price is too great to keep him just as he is."

Devin raised his hand and Billy ran and nestled in his

arms. He tousled the boy's hair, and Billy contentedly leaned his head on his shoulder. The barn was silent and soon the Exiles began moving out into the night, nodding and whispering to one another.

Devin spent most of the next day working with his father, brother, and son, digging the foundation of the new cabin. In the late afternoon, Ward insisted they call it a day, and Devin took Billy for a walk, down by the stream. When they returned, Ward was waiting for him, along with Jeffrey, his cameraman Ken, and Alan Drummond.

"Could we talk to you?" Ward asked solemnly.

Devin nodded and sent Billy off to help Alethea with dinner.

The men gathered under an oak tree. Devin looked from one face to another, waiting.

It was Alan Drummond who spoke first. "The thing is, Devin, everyone felt strongly about what you said last night, about not being afraid anymore, about being willing to pay the price of freedom."

Devin nodded.

"But it's not enough to tell fifty people here," Jeffrey injected. "We want the whole country to hear what you're saying, millions of people. Then it could make a difference."

Devin had to smile. "Well, then we'll just have to reserve me a half hour on Natnet and I'll make the greatest speech you ever heard."

None of them returned his grin.

"Actually, we've got something sort of like that in mind," Ward said.

Jeffrey broke in. "See, Ken here isn't just a cameraman, he's kind of an electronics genius. We've filmed on a couple of SSU bases, and they've got some real fancy communications equipment. Ken figures that if we can get onto the base and find the satellite frequencies, he could use their transmitter to intersect the Natnet satellite. Then you *would* be on Natnet, for five or ten minutes, before they caught on and jammed you out."

Devin leaned against the tree, his face grim, as he felt the weight of what they were saying.

"These satellite frequencies, where would they be?"

"Most likely in the commander's safe," Ward said. "But, Alethea, she's been out there, and knows where the safe is."

"To get onto that base, to get into the safe, to make the broadcast—it'd be like robbing Fort Knox." Devin shook his head.

Ward ran his fingers through his thick white hair. "Thing is, Devin, we've got us a plan," he explained.

As the delegation was leaving, Devin took his brother aside. "Would you drive me over to Peter Bradford's house?" he asked. They had an agreement that, for safety's sake, none of them would leave their property without a partner.

"Peter's not there," Ward said.

"I know. It's Justin I want to see."

Ward winced. "Devin, I went by there this morning and it's not easy—"

"I know," Devin said. "But I still want to see him."

"Sure," Ward said. "I think it was seeing Justin that made me understand what you meant, about not being afraid anymore. After I saw what they'd done to my son, I knew there wasn't any more room for compromise."

They drove to the Bradford house in silence. Ward spoke to the defense force lieutenant in charge of the unit there, and after a few minutes Devin was admitted; Ward waited in the car.

Jackie opened the door. "I'll take you up," she said. "I've been reading to him."

He remembered her as a child and he was startled by her grace and beauty. "You remind me of your mother when she was your age," he told her as they climbed the stairs. "You don't look so much like her, but you've got that same . . . I guess you'd call it determination."

Jackie smiled but didn't respond. She led him into the guest room, where Justin was sitting in his wheelchair. "He's put on weight," Jackie said. "He looks real good. He just doesn't . . . speak." Her lips trembled but she kept control of herself. "Do you want me to leave?"

"No," he said. "No, not at all."

He knelt beside Justin and held his hand and began to speak softly, but there was no response, nothing at all. The boy's eyes were open, he blinked sometimes, his heart was beating, but his mind, his soul, were somewhere far away. Devin had seen men in shock in Vietnam, but never anything like this.

He continued to talk to Justin, just as if he were perfectly conscious, until he realized that Jackie had fallen asleep and he shouldn't stay too late. They all had a big day ahead tomorrow.

"Sure could use you, Justin. If you can hear me—you know I need you for this. We all need you," he said.

"You know nobody's accepting this. We're just going to pound away until you come back. You're a Milford, one of the best of 'em, and we need your heart and your head—America's got some big battles ahead. We can't afford for you to miss 'em."

He stood and touched the boy's silky blond hair, then hurried out of the bedroom, leaving the two young people there, Justin staring into the darkness, Jackie asleep.

Amanda was waiting at the foot of the stairs. She wore a simple pink cotton dress, sleeveless and with a high neck, and her hair was bound up with a scarf. He thought she looked strong, yet so delicate too—the wonderful paradox of femininity.

"Alan says he's improving," she said.

"It must be subtle."

She nodded. They stopped at her front door. She had her back to the door and he made no move to leave.

"What are you doing?" she asked.

He shrugged. "Starting the revolution."

"Are you serious?"

"I'm afraid so."

"The revolution against Peter," she said flatly.

"It doesn't have to be."

"Except you want to be an American," she said bitterly.

"You do, too."

She turned away, then faced him again, her eyes glistening. "It's been hard," she said. "Hard to know what's right and what's wrong. Hard to know what to do when you love somebody but you hate what he's doing. Or even love two people and hate what both of them are doing."

He had to smile. "Can we both be wrong?"

"Maybe you're both right, I don't know," she cried. "All I know is that I'm afraid . . ."

"Don't be," he said. "Please don't be."

Her laugh was pained and harsh. "How the hell could I not be?" she asked in anguish.

He took her hands and her arms reached out to embrace him. They kissed, tentatively at first, then greedily. It was he who was cautious, and she who wanted to keep him, to become part of him, to have as much of this stolen and delayed moment as possible. But he knew that there could be no more, not here, not now. His hands loosened on her arms; she understood the signal and stepped back, as if she had been the one to break away.

"Raincheck?" he said.

"You bet." She nodded, doubting the future, fighting back her tears.

The town square was silent and empty when Puncher set out on his mission, with the first hint of morning light. He rode his old Harley, much like Justin's but even more battered, gliding serenely along the road out of town, beneath branches just starting to bud. He wore his black leather jacket and a cocky, lopsided smile, as if he weren't worried at all. His assignment was not too difficult: he could get shot but, besides that, not much could go wrong.

When he came in sight of the SSU base's front gate he muttered, "This one's for you, Jus," and gave the Harley full throttle.

The guards in the watchtower, all four of them, watched openmouthed as Puncher drove full throttle toward the gate.

The tallest guard hoisted his rifle instinctively, although they were in no danger—it was the kid who was in danger of killing himself; the iron gate was built to stop cars.

"Be cool," one of the others muttered. He was young and slim, and had recently made sergeant. "We got our orders, you know?"

Puncher hit the brakes at the last instant and skidded to a halt beneath the tower.

"Hey, you cocksuckers, wanna fight?" he yelled. "Come on down, I'll blow your asses away!"

As he shouted at them, Puncher was gunning the Harley, spinning in mad circles—to shoot him they'd have to hit a moving target.

The young sergeant frowned in annoyance. "Go away, kid," he yelled, and waved at Puncher to leave.

Puncher waved back, mimicking him. "Screw you, Pancho," he shouted. *"Chinga su madre—you dig?"*

The guard stiffened. The tall one laughed, but sighted his rifle on the cyclist. "No!" the other snapped. "We have orders not to shoot. We'll send someone out."

Some other soldiers had gathered near the gate. Puncher saw them and knew the fun and games were over. Smooth as silk, he lit his Zippo, reached inside his leather jacket, touched flame to wick, and tossed the homemade bomb with precise nonchalance at the watchtower's base. The explosion rocked the tower, set it leaning precariously, but did not quite topple it.

All four guards, knocked to their knees, came up cursing and firing, but by then the crazy kid was rocketing away.

"Go after him!" the young sergeant cried, opening the gate, but when the first troops stepped outside they were raked with gunfire from a distant treeline.

The tall guard scrambled down the ladder. "Wait. We are under attack," he yelled.

Alarm sirens bit into the morning calm. Helmut was already strapping on his gunbelt, running toward the sounds of battle. The tall guard quickly explained what had happened. "It was a plan to draw us out, but the plan was bungled in execution. We have only one wounded. Shall we pursue them now?"

Helmut smiled a cold, reptilian smile. "Wait, sergeant. We have been fired upon, attacked, and we must now defend ourselves with the utmost deliberation."

He turned and marched back to his command post. Within minutes the base was fully mobilized for attack.

Devin was saying goodbye to his father when they heard the distant rattle of gunfire.

"It's started," Ward said, and he and Jeffrey ran to the car.

"I'll be right there," Devin said. He embraced his father a final time and then put his arm around Billy and led him aside.

"You're going to fight," Billy said. Not protesting, just stating a hard fact.

"Sometimes you have to," Devin said. "But I still believe the best kind of resistance is nonviolent. It's sort of funny actually, we've got to fight to get on the air so that I can tell people not to fight."

"What do you want people to do?" the boy asked.

"Don't go along. America will only be divided if we let it. We can ignore their boundaries. We can refuse to participate. We can own ourselves. That's the best thing of all."

Billy bit his lip. "Why does it have to be you?"

Devin held him close, feeling his hair soft on his cheek. "I just happen to be somebody they'll listen to," he said. "This has been a long time coming. Maybe it'll be the start of something. They'll know what to do. I'm just going to remind them."

Billy turned his head away. "People will be killed. Maybe you."

Devin nodded slowly. "Freedom has a price, like everything else. Some people will die, but at least they'll have died for something. I guess you can't live

394

for something unless you think it's important enough to die for."

The boy was blinking back tears. "I want to go."

"Next time."

"Then don't you go, not without me."

"I won't be without you, Billy. I'll never be without you, or you without me. You stay here and help your grandfather. He needs someone strong like you. This is a good little town. If things work out, maybe we could settle down here."

"Wherever you want is okay with me," his son said. "Just don't leave me. Please, Dad. I love you."

Billy's tears flowed freely now. Devin saw Ward and Jeffrey, waiting in the car, ready for battle; his time was up, for this morning, maybe forever.

"I love you too, Billy, more than you can know. I love your brother, too, and wish he was here. Try to remember one thing. It may not make sense now, but it will someday. I couldn't love you this much if I didn't love freedom more."

He kissed the boy, held him close, kissed him again, then turned and hurried to the car. As they drove away, he allowed himself to look back and saw his father and son, arm in arm, waving goodbye.

The heavy iron gate lurched open and the first motorcycles shot out, followed by rumbling tanks and glistening armored personnel carriers. The SSU's jet-black helicopters rose gracefully into the morning sun and hovered, like bumblebees buzzing near a flower, while the unit's awesome ground force uncoiled like a huge snake along the road to Milford.

Helmut Gurtman smiled as he watched from his command helicopter, for he saw beauty in the power of his machines and the precision of his men. He had waited a long time for this; as he had destroyed the squalid exile camp, now he would smash the smug little town that had bedeviled him for too many months. He had left behind only a token force to guard the base, for he wanted the full iron fist of his might to pound down the people of Milford. They had almost escaped him, but this morning's attack by the boy on the motorcycle had provided the excuse he needed: he had been fired upon and now he would fire back, with a fury these people would never forget.

Gurtman had only contempt for Andrei Denisov's "new policy." As a soldier in the field he knew there was only one policy, as old as war itself: the power of the conqueror that forced the submission of the conquered. Men won wars in order to enslave their enemies, not to quibble with them.

He watched contentedly as his first units entered the town. The tanks and attack vehicles unleashed a deadly barrage of machine-gun fire, shattering windows and immobilizing any would-be defenders. Within minutes his forces occupied the town square. It was here where Helmut expected serious resistance. As the merciless machine-gun fire continued, his men leaped from their vehicles and began to kick down doors, firing as they went.

Helmut watched with pride; it was a textbook attack, perfectly executed.

Except his troops found no one to vanquish; there was no one around.

He saw his men pull back from the stores, confused and huddled in the street. He soon received radio confirmation of what he had guessed: "No resistance, sir. Nobody is here."

"They're in the houses," Helmut shouted. "Search the houses!"

As his men fanned out along the tree-lined residential streets that opened off Milford's town square, Helmut ordered his pilot to land. His anger was rising; his desire to hover god-like above the attack was not so keen as his lust to plunge headlong into the heat and joy of battle.

His helicopter had barely touched down when he leaped out and ran to the nearest house. He found his men inside, puzzled, clumsily knocking over antique furniture as they searched for victims who were not there.

"Search the cellar!" Helmut commanded. One of his men opened a door to a dark basement, and tossed a grenade down the stairs. The house reverberated, windows shattered, and when the debris settled, one of the soldiers ventured into the cellar and returned to report, "Nothing but stored things down there. Canned tomatoes, peaches, all kinds of stuff, blown to smithereens."

Helmut went out to the street. Up and down its length, the story was the same: his men could find no one.

A lieutenant rushed up to him. "They're hiding, sir," he reported nervously. "What shall we do?"

"Find them," Helmut said coldly. Then, after a moment's thought, he added, "Burn one house on each street."

He watched with little satisfaction as his men rushed to obey his order. Within minutes, four houses were ablaze and smoke rose high above the town.

Helmut received a radio message from one of his patrol helicopters.

"Major? Are you there?" The sound of heavy static and machine-gun fire almost overpowered the radio operator.

"Yes, what is it?"

"We've found them. They've fired on us."

"Where?"

"In the grain silos, south of the town."

"Let's go," Helmut shouted, and leaped into his helicopter to lead the attack.

Amanda became aware of the gunfire at the same moment that Jackie left Justin's room and ran downstairs to ask what was happening.

"I don't know," Amanda admitted.

"Don't you care?" her daughter asked.

Amanda shut her eyes. "Maybe I'd rather not know," she said. It was true. She knew that Devin was out there, starting his revolution, risking his life, pursuing his mad or noble destiny, and she did not want to imagine what his fate might be.

Someone knocked on the door. After a moment, Amanda opened it, and found two members of their defense force detail there, with a young woman whose face was somehow familiar. "She says she's supposed to be here, Mrs. Bradford," one of the soldiers said.

Amanda stared at the woman in confusion. "I'm Kimberly Ballard," the newcomer said. "Devin sent me."

"Let her in," Amanda said, and Kimberly stepped inside, looking terribly weary.

"How is he?" Amanda asked. "Devin?"

"I don't know," Kimberly said. "We were up all night, getting ready for the . . . the attack. He wouldn't let me go with them. He told me to come here. I almost got caught; it's terrible in town."

"You must be tired," Amanda said. "You can have my room."

Then Jackie, who had silently watched this exchange, pointed toward the window. "What's that?" she cried.

They looked out the window and saw the smoke rising above the town, less than a mile away. "My God, Mom, it's like a war," Jackie cried. "What if they come here?"

The three of them went onto the porch for a better view, and the young defense force lieutenant who was in charge of their protection rushed up to them. "Please, ladies, stay inside," he said.

"What's happening?" Amanda asked.

"It looks like the SSU is attacking the town," the soldier said.

"That can't be," Amanda said. "I talked to my husband last night. Colonel Denisov gave orders for the SSU to stay on its base."

The lieutenant gazed again at the four pillars of smoke rising over the town. "Ma'am, it looks like those orders have been disobeyed," he said.

"They won't bother us, will they?" Jackie demanded.

The lieutenant looked at Jackie with a quiet resolve on his face. "I hope not, miss. Now, if you'll all please come inside."

When the women had returned indoors, the lieutenant ran to the communications truck parked in the driveway. Soon he had the force's Chicago headquarters on the line. "We're under attack," he shouted. "Repeat, under attack. SSU forces are in full assault on the town of Milford. We need help!"

As Gurtman's finely honed troops raced toward the silos south of Milford, a ragtag band of nearly a hundred townspeople and Exiles finally began its attack on the SSU base to the north of town.

Two ancient Caterpillar bulldozers, borrowed from a nearby construction site, emerged from a ravine and went rumbling toward the fence surrounding the base, drawing heavy fire from the twenty-odd soldiers who had been left behind to guard the barracks. As the defenders fired furiously at the bulldozers, a hundred men, townspeople and Exiles, scattered around the perimeter of the barracks, attacking the fence with explosives. By the time the first bulldozer crashed through the fence, a dozen explosions had shattered its perimeter and the invaders were pouring into the compound, firing as they came.

The outnumbered SSU troops fought back with their superior firepower. Devin, Jeffrey, Clayton, and Alan were soon pinned down behind a burning truck. Devin and Jeffrey fired back with M-16s; Alan carried only a doctor's black bag.

"Haven't got a grenade in there, do you?" Devin yelled.

"Scalpel, just in case things really get tough."

"Where the hell did Alethea say the damn communications center was?" Clayton asked.

"We got separated from her," Jeffrey said. "I think she said it's in that middle barracks, across from Gurtman's apartment."

Devin stuck his head up, then hit the dirt as another burst of automatic-weapons fire raked the truck. "It's times like these that make me wonder whether it would've been easier to put a message in a bottle and float it down the Missouri," Devin said, deadpan.

The towering grain silos stood like sentinels on the outskirts of Milford, monuments to the county's more prosperous past. The concrete loading pads, grain cars, and storage silos that surrounded them formed a natural fortress.

Helmut, high above them, nodded with approval. It was a good place for the townspeople to make their stand; resistance always made the game more interesting, the victory more sweet. He nodded for one of his attack helicopters to go in for a closer look. It dropped within a hundred feet of the nearest silo, when suddenly a barrage of small-arms fire blazed from one of the grain cars. The helicopter shuddered, struggled for an instant, then crashed and exploded into a mighty ball of flame.

"Pull back," Helmut commanded. "Wait for our ground forces."

Ten minutes passed before his tanks and attack vehicles could traverse the narrow road that led from the town south to the silos, but Helmut waited patiently, savoring the battle to come.

His tranquillity, however, was shattered by another radio message, an emergency broadcast from his base.

"We are under attack," it said. "Outnumbered . . ."

Helmut gasped, then bellowed out the order for everyone to return to the barracks.

Chapter 17

As soon as Peter got the call from Fred Sittman he raced up the stairs to the helicopter pad atop the Federal Building. Within minutes, Sittman himself arrived, piloting an old U.S. Army chopper, and Peter scrambled aboard. Four old transport helicopters hovered nearby, packed with armed guardsmen.

"Our equipment's no match for theirs—but I bet our boys are," Sittman declared.

"Dammit, Fred, what the hell's that madman Gurtman up to?"

"I dunno. He's not answering our messages. But according to my boys at your house, he's flat-out declared war on the town of Milford."

Peter slumped in the co-pilot's seat. "My God," he moaned. "Amanda and Jackie and Justin are there . . ."

"They're not alone," Sittman assured him. "Five of

my boys are with 'em. They say there's a lot of shooting going on, but so far nobody's bothered them."

Peter looked down as the outskirts of Omaha fell away beneath them. He knew it was at least a thirty-minute flight to Milford.

"Hurry," he pleaded. "Please hurry!"

As the SSU began its sudden retreat from the silos, its force was some three miles south of Milford and had to pass through the town and go another four miles north to reach its base. Under normal conditions the tanks and attack vehicles might have made the journey in twelve to fifteen minutes but the conditions they encountered were far from normal.

A hundred Exiles and townspeople had attacked the SSU base, a dozen more had formed a decoy unit in the silos, and still a hundred more were posted at strategic points along the road to town. The SSU force encountered not only gunfire from the woods that lined the road, but an obstacle course of trees, broken glass, and burning automobiles. They had to fight their way, stopping to remove the barricades, and took heavy casualties as they did.

Finally the first of the vehicles reached the deserted town square and Helmut felt relieved. The road north was wider and free of trees—his men would arrive in minutes now.

Suddenly a mighty explosion rocked the Milford square. Helmut saw two of his armored personnel carriers blown to pieces, with men's bodies flung high into the air. He burned with the knowledge that he had been lured into a trap. It was obvious that the towns-people had buried explosives under the street, and he had lost at least two dozen men. He had little feeling for his men, but great hate for the enemy that had humiliated him.

"All units," he commanded into his radio. "Break off. Avoid the square. Return to barracks by side roads. Immediately!"

When the defense force helicopters circled Milford, they could see the smoke rising from burning houses and cars and the dead and dying soldiers in the town square.

"My God," Peter whispered.

"Where the hell is everybody?" General Sittman asked, looking out both sides of the chopper.

Devin, Jeffrey, Puncher, Alethea, Clayton, and Alan had fought their way into the main SSU barracks. A band of Exiles ringed the building, exchanging fire with the remnants of the SSU defenders.

"The communications center is upstairs," Alethea cried.

"I'm staying here with the wounded," Alan said as the rest of them hurried up the stairs.

A sniper fired at them from the hallway. Puncher exchanged shots with him and soon the sniper fled out a window. Outside, as they watched, a battered old van drove through the now-open SSU gates and stopped before the barracks. Ken, the cameraman, was driving, and with him was Eric Plummer, the hard-drinking old newsman who operated Radio Free Omaha.

"Who the hell is that?" Devin demanded.

"Another communications genius," Jeffrey explained. "Come to the rescue."

"He looks like he needs help," Devin grumbled, watching the two men run for cover. Within moments

Eric and Ken joined them in the communications room.

"And now for the moment you've all been waiting for," Jeffrey announced as Eric carefully scrutinized the transmission setup.

"I need to have the combinations. They change satellite frequency every so often. They use the Natnet satellite in emergencies. They'll have the frequency codes."

"There's a safe in his room," Alethea said. "I think I might be able to open it."

"I'll go with you," Ken told her.

There was a moment's pause. Sporadic gunfire continued outside while Eric fiddled with the radio transmitters.

"You're about to have one hell of an audience," Jeffrey said. "You know what you're going to say?"

Devin smiled. "I was just wondering if it mattered. If any of us have much influence on others."

"Hell of a time to wonder about that!" Jeffrey retorted.

"I guess what I want to talk about is America, our national unity. People ask, 'What's so bad about forming a new country?'—call it Heartland or Crabgrass, whatever. Maybe that's the easy way to get rid of the Russians. We can't fight them, so why not give up?

"If it's too hard to be one people, maybe we should give that up too. Look, someone destroyed our Capitol. Who was it? Resisters? The Russians? I say we did it ourselves. We did it when we stopped building that Capitol in our hearts and minds. We saw the marble and the columns but forgot the meaning of it, the spirit. I say let's rebuild the Capitol—the building and the spirit."

"Amen. Tell them that," Jeffrey said.

"They can stop ten of us," Devin said, "but they can't stop ten thousand or ten million: that's why we have to unite. But whatever happens, as one man, I won't accept the breakup of America. I'll resist, with my spirit, with my life. I can resist because I've found the love of my children; their lives are more important than my own. Whatever happens, I'll live through them, through whatever values and truths I have taught them."

"For God's sake, Devin, just tell them that!" Jeffrey exclaimed.

Helmut leaped out of the helicopter and raced toward his barracks. An Exile challenged him and he shot the man dead without breaking stride. Inside the barracks, he confronted Alan Drummond, bandaging a wounded SSU sergeant. "Wait, stop!" Alan cried, and tried to wrestle Helmut to the floor.

Helmut didn't want to fire and alert the people upstairs. Instead, he crashed the barrel of his Swiss pistol against Alan's temple, knocking him unconscious, and charged up the stairs, three at a time. At the landing, he saw that the door to his apartment was open.

Alethea was on her knees, fiddling with the safe; Ken crouched behind her. "Dammit, he always said it was easy to open, no better than a post office box."

"Keep trying," Ken said.

"Perhaps you'd like the combination," Helmut said from the doorway.

They spun around. His Sig Sauer pistol was pointed at Ken. Before either could react, Helmut fired at the cameraman. Ken's body hurtled forward on impact with the bullet, knocking Alethea down and pinning her beneath him.

Helmut smiled wickedly, savoring Alethea's fear, entranced by her struggle to free herself from the weight of the dead, bleeding man that lay on top of her. The beauty of the moment demanded that he not shoot until her hand finally reached Ken's gun. To shoot any sooner would be to dishonor himself, to forfeit his ideal of perfection. As Alethea writhed and inched across the floor, Helmut realized that he had always known more about the drama of life than most people, had always understood the inevitability of fate. But whence came that groan? The loud, twisting rasp—from the dead man? Helmut swung his pistol at the figure of Ken, and shot into the body, knocking it back from Alethea. Then quickly, deftly, she grabbed the gun on the floor, and finished the drama. Helmut's head snapped back, his expression unchanged. The gun in his hand discharged into the floor, and he crumpled to his feet.

Several days later, when Alethea described her grotesque ordeal, she would recall no groan, no sound, no reason at all, in fact, for Helmut to have shot into the dead man that lay on top of her.

Devin ran into the room with Alan close behind. The doctor, his face caked with blood, knelt beside Ken, while Devin lifted his sister to her feet. Alethea sobbed and struggled in her brother's arms, but once again he held her tight.

"It's over, Ali, it's over," he told her. "Remember when you were nine, little sister. Shut your eyes tight and wish for the last star in the galaxy."

Jeffrey burst into the room. "We'd better get going— the marines are here, only they're the wrong marines.

The Heartland defense force has just come to rescue us."

Alan looked up suspiciously. "Is that good?"

"It's doubtful they'll appreciate our purpose here," Jeffrey said. "Come on, Devin, it's got to be now!"

Devin nodded to Alan, who came and put his arms around Alethea. "Take care of her, doc. Please," he said. He tore through the safe until he had the papers he wanted. "Okay," he said, "we're in business."

In the communications center, Eric Plummer took the paper with the Natnet frequencies, then began spinning knobs madly. Finally he slumped back in his chair. "Ready when you are," he said. "Certainly a lively studio they've got here."

"I'll keep a watch outside," Jeffrey said.

Eric smiled, pointing a gnarly finger toward a switch. "See that switch, Mr. Milford? Whenever you're ready, push it forward and start talking. You're about to give Natnet a big surprise—and provide a dramatic climax to an old newsman's long and checkered career." Then he added, "Be pleasant. No matter what you have to say, people like a nice smile."

Devin took a deep breath, groping for an opening line, his greeting to America—and then the door burst open.

Peter Bradford rushed in, with Fred Sittman close behind.

"Don't do it, Devin," Peter yelled. He was out of breath, disheveled, shaken by the bloodshed he had seen. "Listen to me."

Devin turned to face them but kept his hand on the switch.

"You, get out of here," Sittman growled at Eric.

The old newsman stood up, and moved quickly out the door. "Hell of a rowdy place," he muttered.

Devin spoke cautiously. "You have a chance to do the right thing, Peter: we can do it together."

Peter stood stiffly in the center of the room, his dark hair falling over his eyes. "Your way is over. You can't stop what's already in motion. Please, don't try to broadcast."

Devin kept smiling, as if he had all the time in the world. "Are you offering me a deal, Peter? No prison? No brainwashing? A nice peaceful exile in Milford—doing some farming and getting by . . ."

"There are worse things," Peter said coldly.

"Thanks for the offer," Devin said, and turned back to the microphone.

"Damn you," Peter's voice broke with frustration and anguish. "Devin, why is it always the hard way with you?" Peter raged. He walked out the door.

Devin looked back at Sittman, a menacing presence in the small room.

"Do you think it's possible to kill an idea, General?" he asked.

"People have died here today," Sittman said. "Somebody has to pay. If you go on the air, it'll damn well be you. I can get you out of here, to your boy."

Devin rubbed his beard. He knew he didn't have much time. "Some of those people died so I could make this broadcast. They thought it was important. I can't let them down."

Devin looked at the old soldier for a long moment, then drew a breath. "I've waited ten years. What I've found is there's always somebody who says, 'Do it later.' It's time to say, 'Do it now.'"

"Get up. Now. Leave this room." Sittman's broad,

pitted face was dark with anger. "I say do it now," he challenged.

"I can't," Devin said, sighing. "I could never forgive myself."

He turned back to the console and pushed the broadcasting switch.

Outside the transmitter room, Peter heard the shot. Even though he didn't move, it was as though the bullet had struck him. People ran past him to the broadcasting room, drawn by the sound of the shot and by the instinct that great tragedy had occurred. Peter did not even try to brush away the tears. He walked slowly, pushed past people in his way and headed down the stairs. For the car and driver that awaited him, for the loyal troops who would obey, for the world he could understand and control.

The air was crisp, the sky perfect: bright blue and cloudless. The simple unadorned wooden coffin rested on two sawhorses beside an empty grave in a corner of the family cemetery.

The Milfords were banded together. Billy, tall and solemn in a dark suit, stood between Will and Alethea, with Ward and Betty next to them. Jackie stood next to Betty, holding the hand of Justin next to her in a wheelchair.

Amanda stood behind the wheelchair, holding herself apart in her own private tragedy. In her heart she thought she had lost both the men she loved. Peter was not there, nor was Marion.

Kimberly, Alan, Dieter, Clayton, and some other Exiles were gathered to one side. Will's sad eyes sought out Kimberly, who gently led the mourners in "Rock of Ages." Even as they sang a dark sedan stopped on the road and Andrei Denisov, alone and in civilian clothes, got out and took a place just inside the gate, discreetly removed.

Andrei hoped he would not be unwelcome; he took that chance because he felt he had to be here. He believed he had seen something begin in those past months, an American saga perhaps, and he believed this funeral was a milestone in that saga, a milestone but not an ending.

As the Milford family and friends sang, Andrei studied them, their faces, their strength, and he noticed too the people who were arriving. The funeral had not been publicized—the family had insisted on that—but these people were coming, over the hills, from all directions. Some were Exiles, others were well-dressed people who might have been from anywhere. They ringed the grave, staying a respectful distance, saying nothing. The Milford family seemed not to notice, or simply to accept the swelling crowd.

Their voices rose, soared, echoed through the little valley, and when they finished singing the hymn, Will stepped forward, clutching an American flag. With the help of Jeffrey and Dieter, he unfolded the flag and draped it over the casket. That done, the old man faced his family and friends. He walked silently over to Billy and tousled the boy's hair.

The military barracks had been abandoned by the SSU troops, on orders from Colonel Denisov. Everyone assumed that the Heartland Defense Force would eventually move in, but, perhaps out of deference to the residents of Milford, General Sittman had not yet sent in his troops. So the fortress lay intact but deserted. Except for Eric's van.

Upstairs, in the communications room, Billy sat in front of the microphone. Sometimes the words caught in his throat, but mostly there flowed a clear, light voice.

"My father . . ." Billy began, and then his voice broke. He squared his shoulders and started again.

"My father died because he believed that what he stood for was more important than his life. My father gave me life. He gave me my physical life, and then he gave me a reason to live the rest of my life. I didn't have much time with him, in these last few weeks, but that time was more precious to me than all the rest of my days.

"I remember he said to me, 'These are hard times, but each of us will find the best or worst in ourselves, and that will be our immortality.'" The boy's voice broke, but then he continued. "I think my dad found his immortality, in what he taught me and others. He said that everybody has to die, so dying isn't what's bad. What's bad is having lived for nothing.

"My dad lived for something. He lived for himself. He lived for his ideals, for the America he loved. He lived for me—and for you."

Devin Milford achieved his goals. He had left a legacy that his son and his son's children would inherit. A legacy of American spirit that was priceless.